THE LUNCH CLUB

DOM PELLETIER

THE MUTANT MOUSE FROM OUTER SPACE

FOR MIKAELA

Scholastic Canada Ltd.
604 King Street West, Toronto, Ontario M5V 1E1, Canada

Scholastic Inc.
557 Broadway, New York, NY 10012, USA

Scholastic Australia Pty Limited
PO Box 579, Gosford, NSW 2250, Australia

Scholastic New Zealand Limited
Private Bag 94407, Botany, Manukau 2163, New Zealand

Scholastic Children's Books
Euston House, 24 Eversholt Street, London NW1 1DB, UK

www.scholastic.ca

Library and Archives Canada Cataloguing in Publication

Title: The mutant mouse from outer space / Dom Pelletier;
English text by Dina Ginzburg
Other titles: Cadeau mutant. English
Names: Pelletier, Dominique, author, artist. | Ginzburg, Dina, translator.
Description: Series statement: The lunch club; 3 | Translation of:
Le cadeau mutant.
Identifiers: Canadiana 20210154071 | ISBN 9781443182737 (softcover)
Subjects: LCGFT: Graphic novels.
Classification: LCC PN6733.P45 C3313 2021 | DDC j741.5/971—dc23

6 5 4 3 2 1   Printed in China   62   21 22 23 24 25

MIX
Paper from
responsible sources
FSC® C020056
FSC
www.fsc.org

THE LUNCH CLUB

DOM PELLETIER

THE MUTANT MOUSE FROM OUTER SPACE

ENGLISH TEXT BY DINA GINZBURG

Scholastic Canada Ltd.

Toronto New York London Auckland Sydney
Mexico City New Delhi Hong Kong Buenos Aires

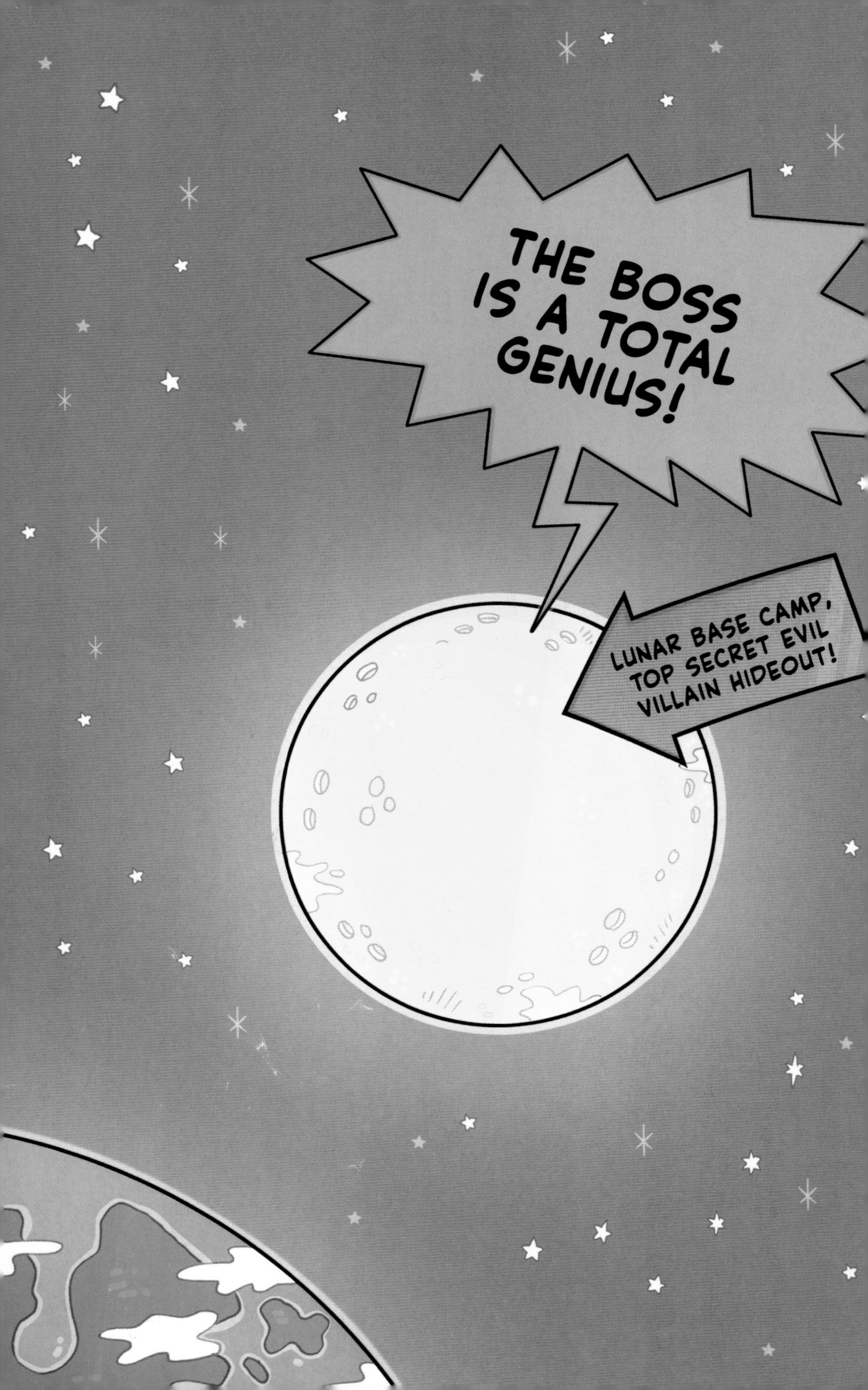
THE BOSS IS A TOTAL GENIUS!
LUNAR BASE CAMP, TOP SECRET EVIL VILLAIN HIDEOUT!

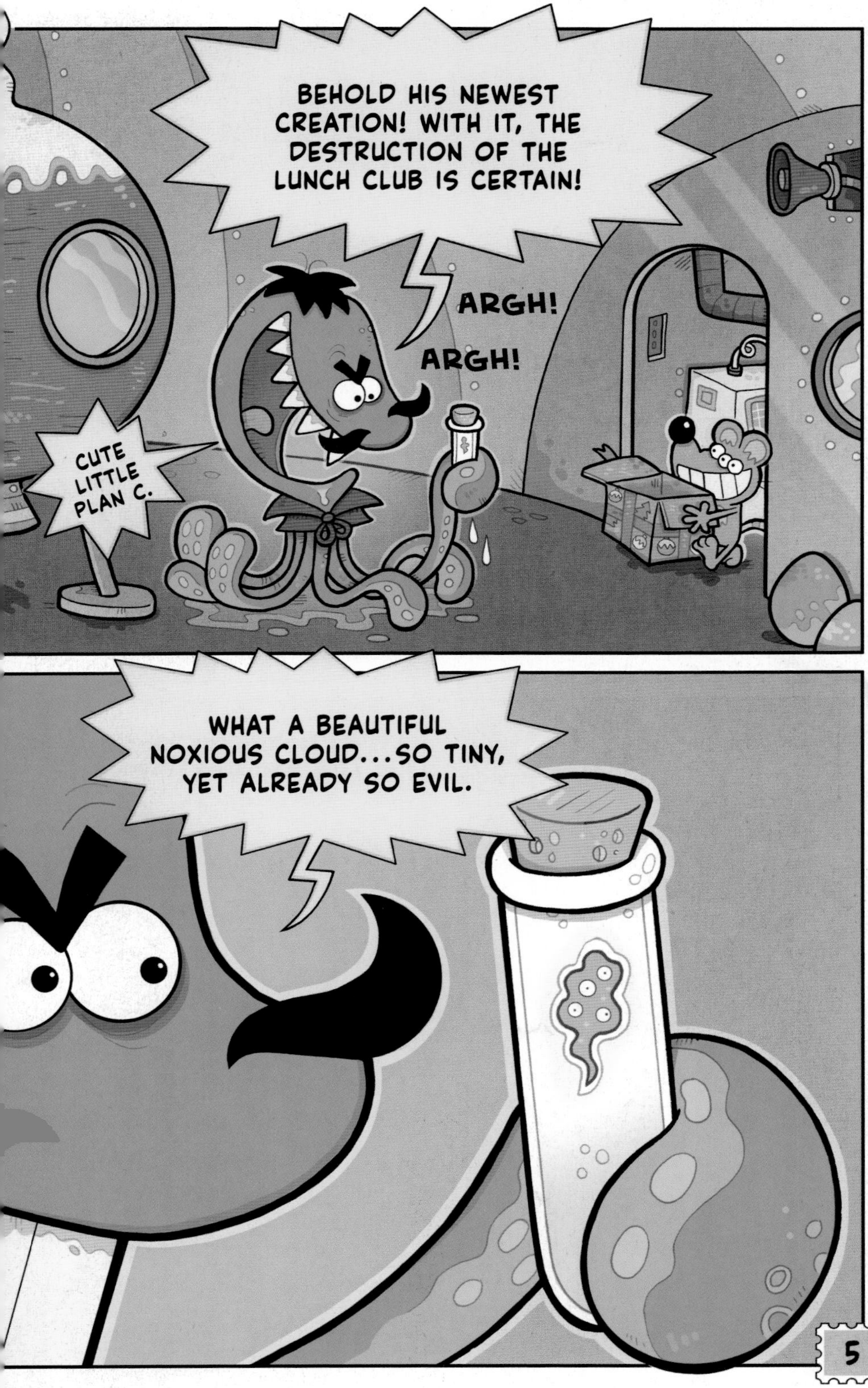
BEHOLD HIS NEWEST CREATION! WITH IT, THE DESTRUCTION OF THE LUNCH CLUB IS CERTAIN!
ARGH!
ARGH!
CUTE LITTLE PLAN C.
WHAT A BEAUTIFUL NOXIOUS CLOUD...SO TINY, YET ALREADY SO EVIL.

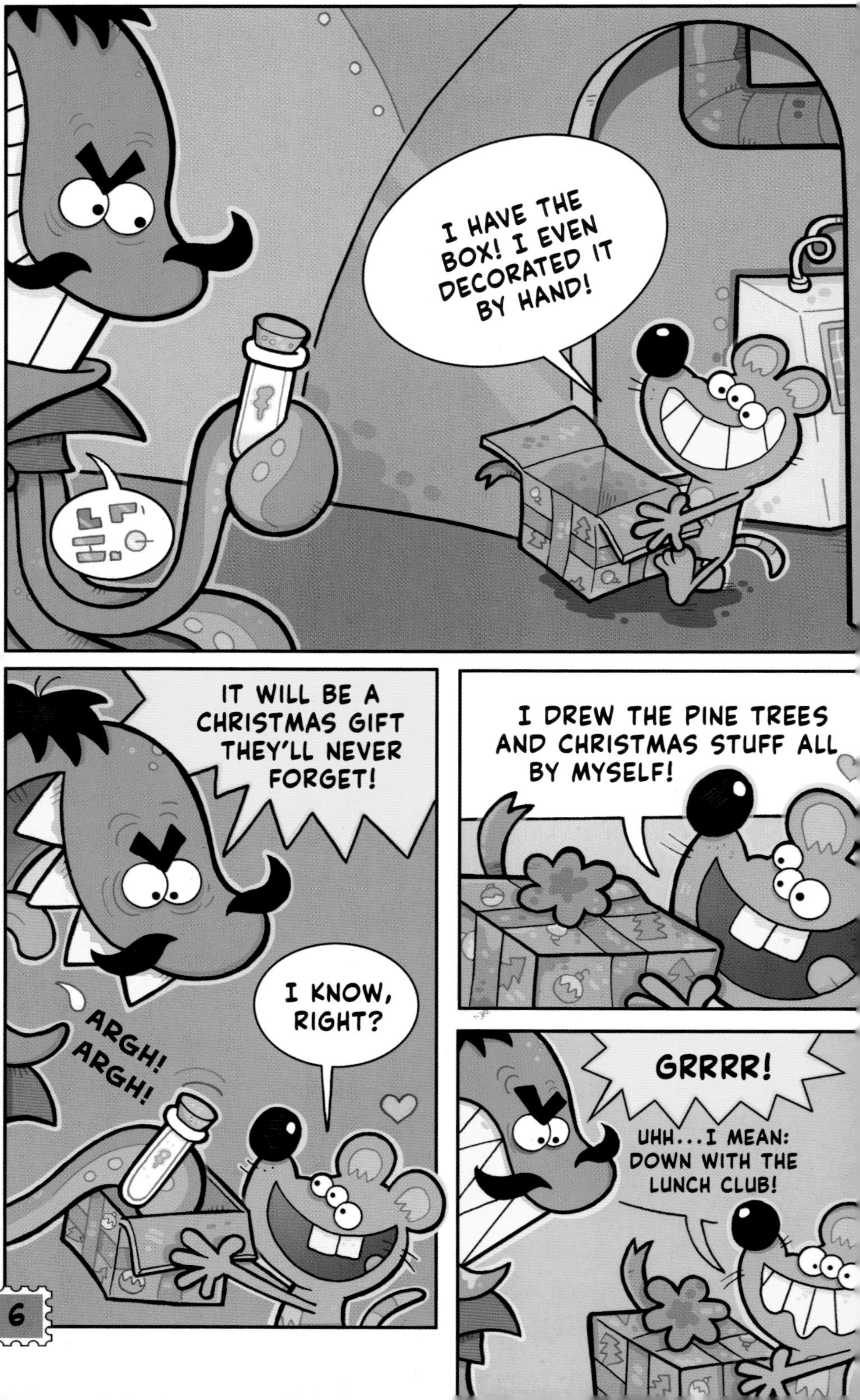
I HAVE THE BOX! I EVEN DECORATED IT BY HAND!
IT WILL BE A CHRISTMAS GIFT THEY'LL NEVER FORGET!
ARGH! ARGH!
I KNOW, RIGHT?
I DREW THE PINE TREES AND CHRISTMAS STUFF ALL BY MYSELF!
GRRRR!
UHH...I MEAN: DOWN WITH THE LUNCH CLUB!

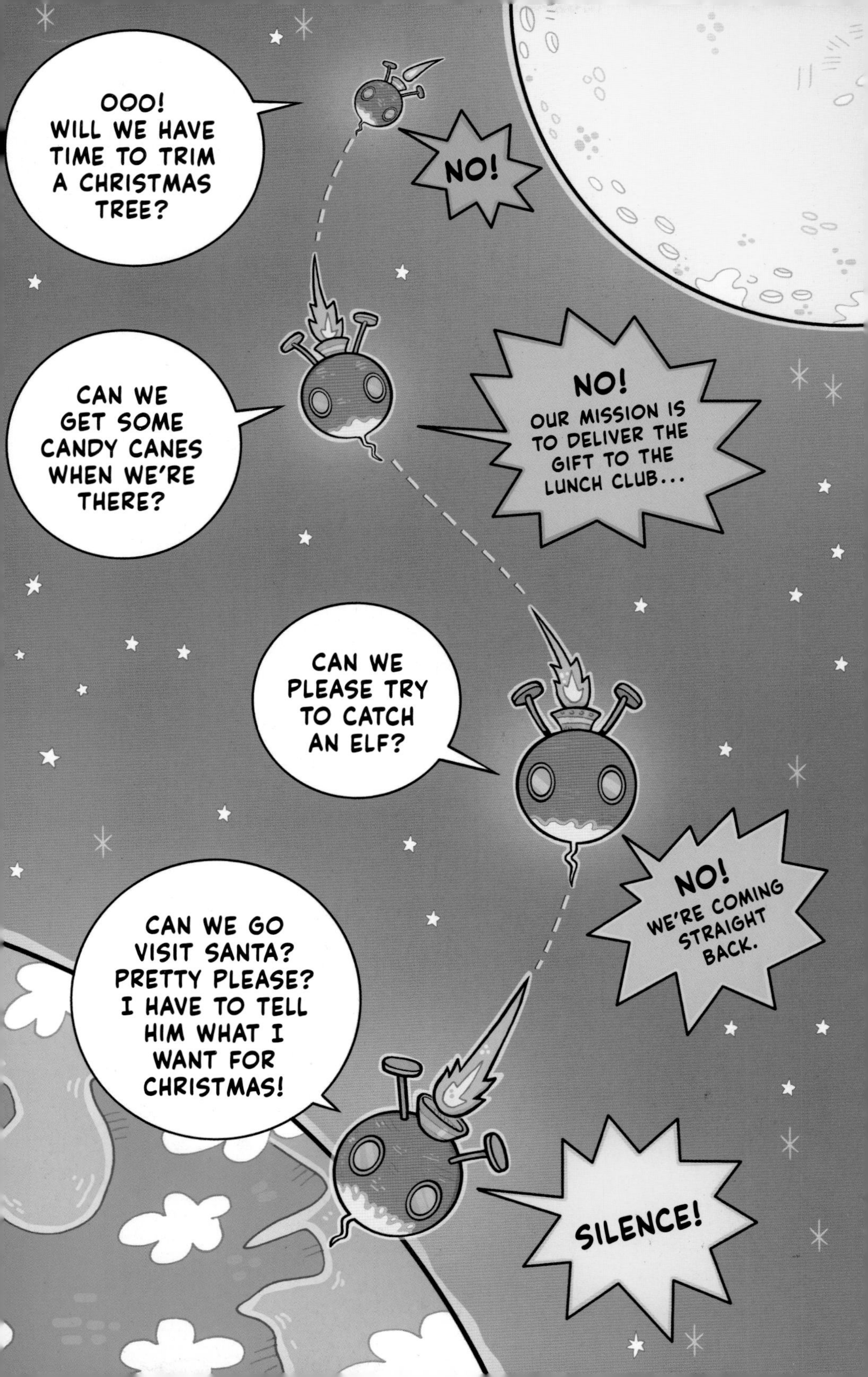
OOO! WILL WE HAVE TIME TO TRIM A CHRISTMAS TREE?
NO!
CAN WE GET SOME CANDY CANES WHEN WE'RE THERE?
NO! OUR MISSION IS TO DELIVER THE GIFT TO THE LUNCH CLUB...
CAN WE PLEASE TRY TO CATCH AN ELF?
NO! WE'RE COMING STRAIGHT BACK.
CAN WE GO VISIT SANTA? PRETTY PLEASE? I HAVE TO TELL HIM WHAT I WANT FOR CHRISTMAS!
SILENCE!

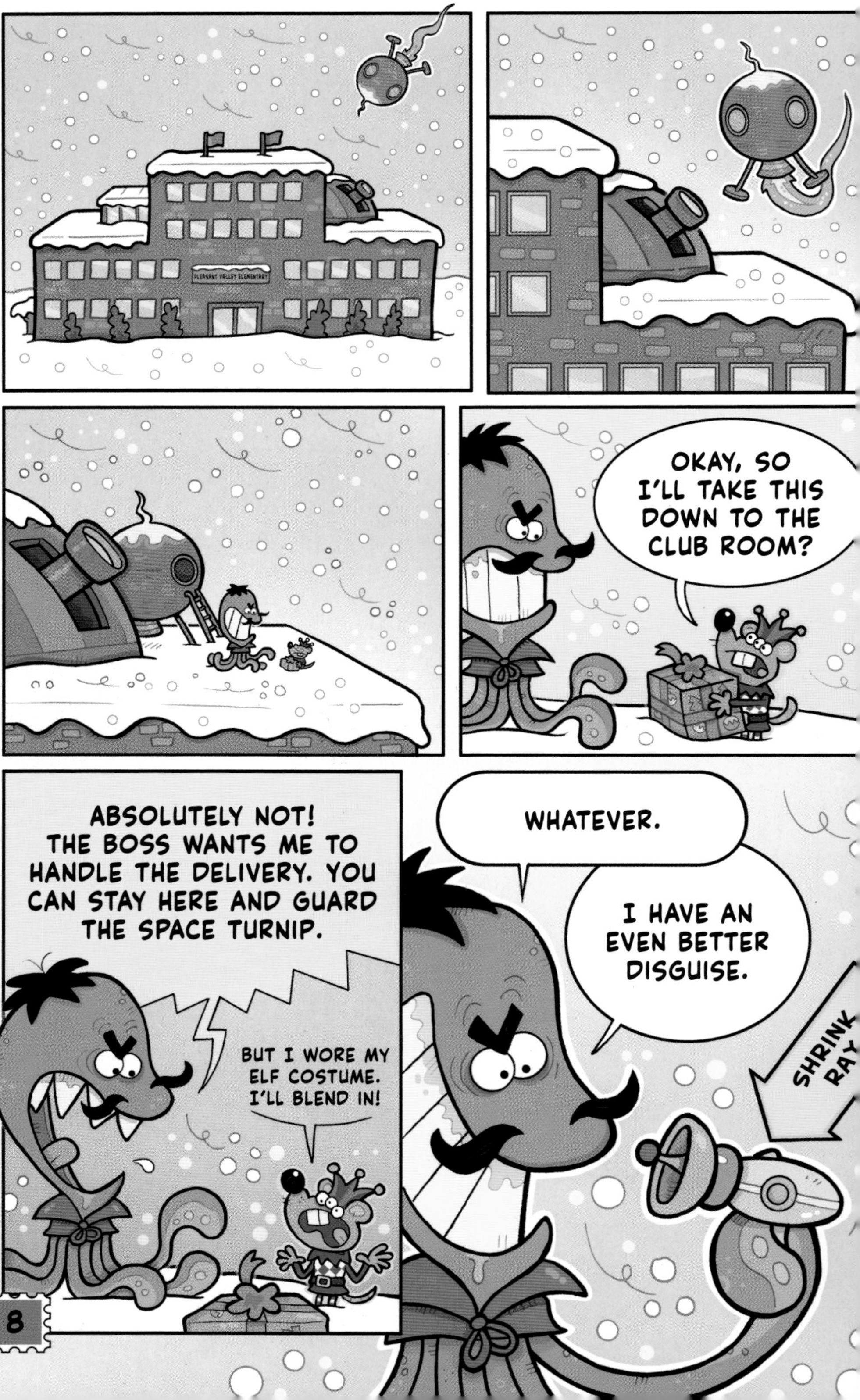
PLEASANT VALLEY ELEMENTARY
OKAY, SO I'LL TAKE THIS DOWN TO THE CLUB ROOM?
ABSOLUTELY NOT! THE BOSS WANTS ME TO HANDLE THE DELIVERY. YOU CAN STAY HERE AND GUARD THE SPACE TURNIP.
BUT I WORE MY ELF COSTUME. I'LL BLEND IN!
WHATEVER.
I HAVE AN EVEN BETTER DISGUISE.
SHRINK RAY

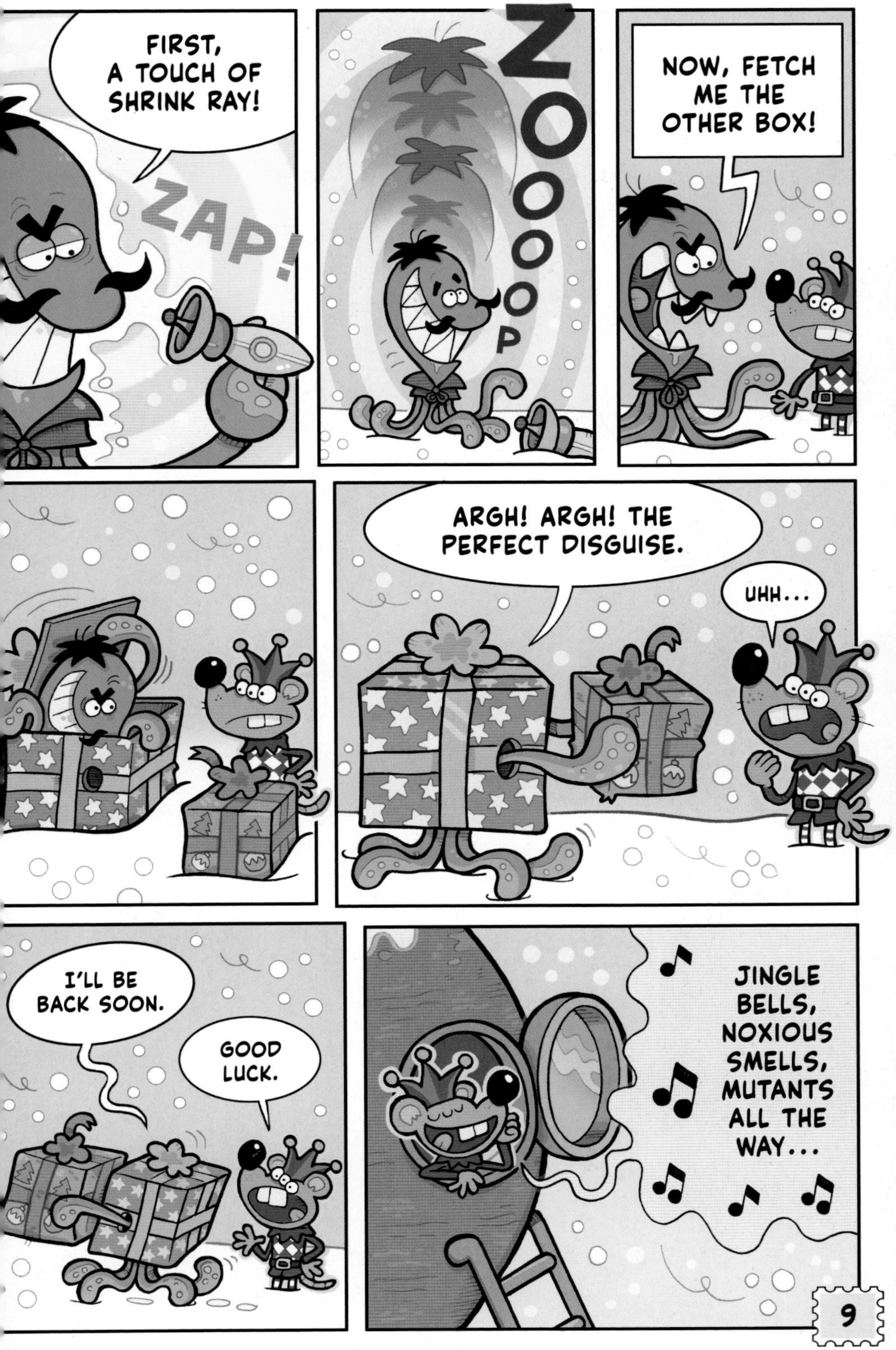
FIRST, A TOUCH OF SHRINK RAY!
ZAP!
ZOOOOOP
NOW, FETCH ME THE OTHER BOX!
ARGH! ARGH! THE PERFECT DISGUISE.
UHH...
I'LL BE BACK SOON.
GOOD LUCK.
JINGLE BELLS, NOXIOUS SMELLS, MUTANTS ALL THE WAY...

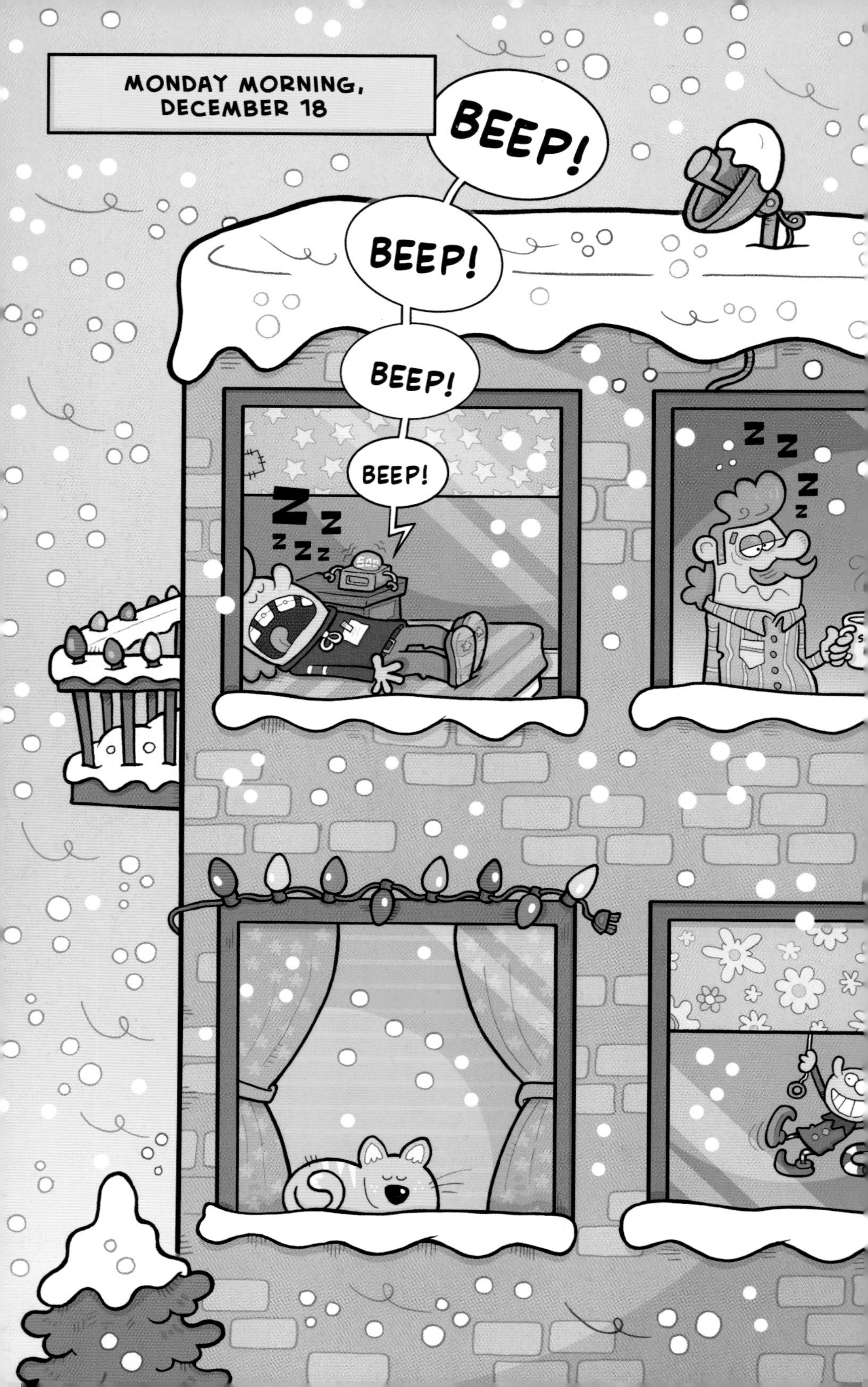
MONDAY MORNING,
DECEMBER 18
BEEP!
BEEP!
BEEP!
BEEP!

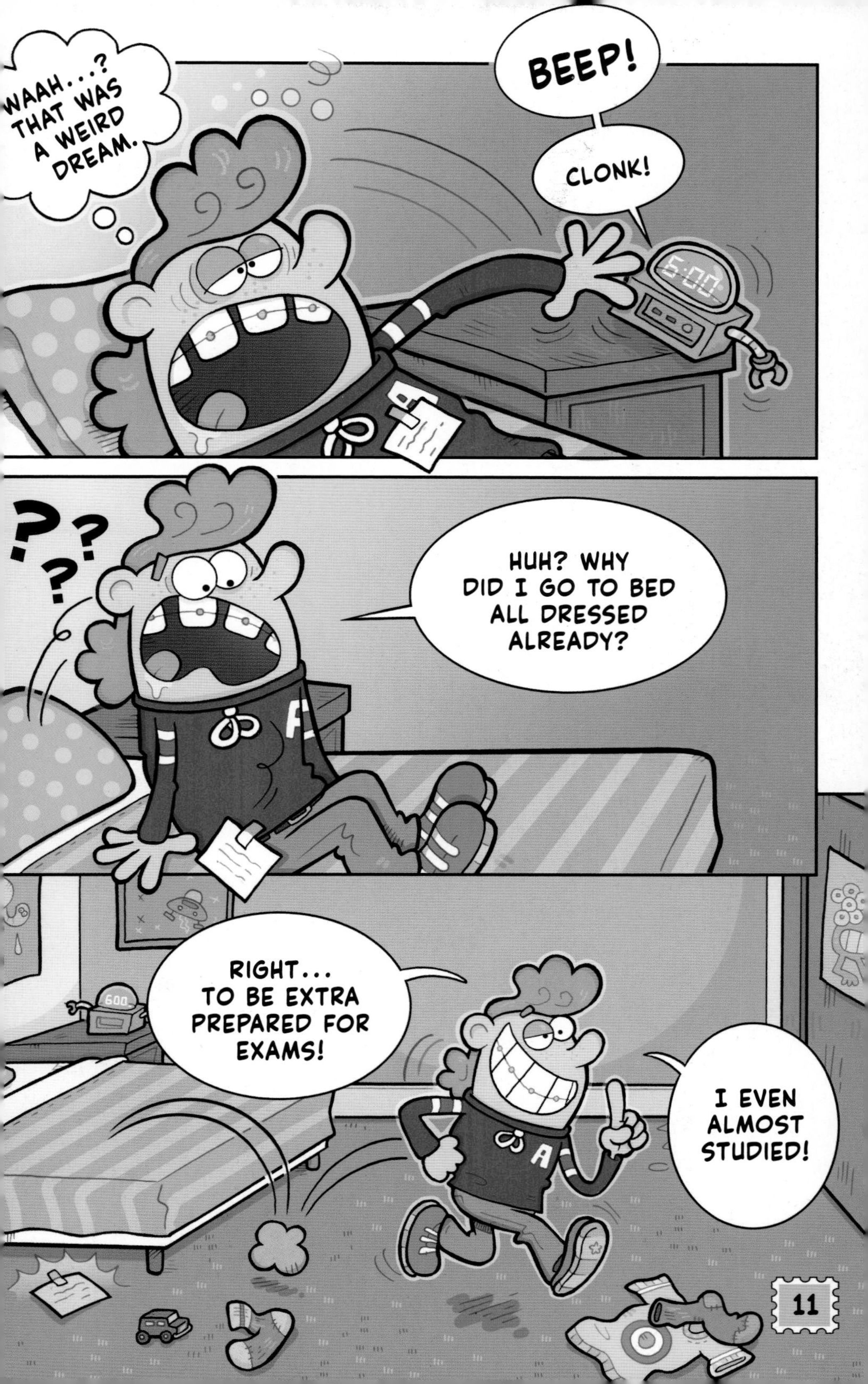
WAAH...? THAT WAS A WEIRD DREAM.
BEEP!
CLONK!
6:00
??
?
HUH? WHY DID I GO TO BED ALL DRESSED ALREADY?
RIGHT... TO BE EXTRA PREPARED FOR EXAMS!
I EVEN ALMOST STUDIED!

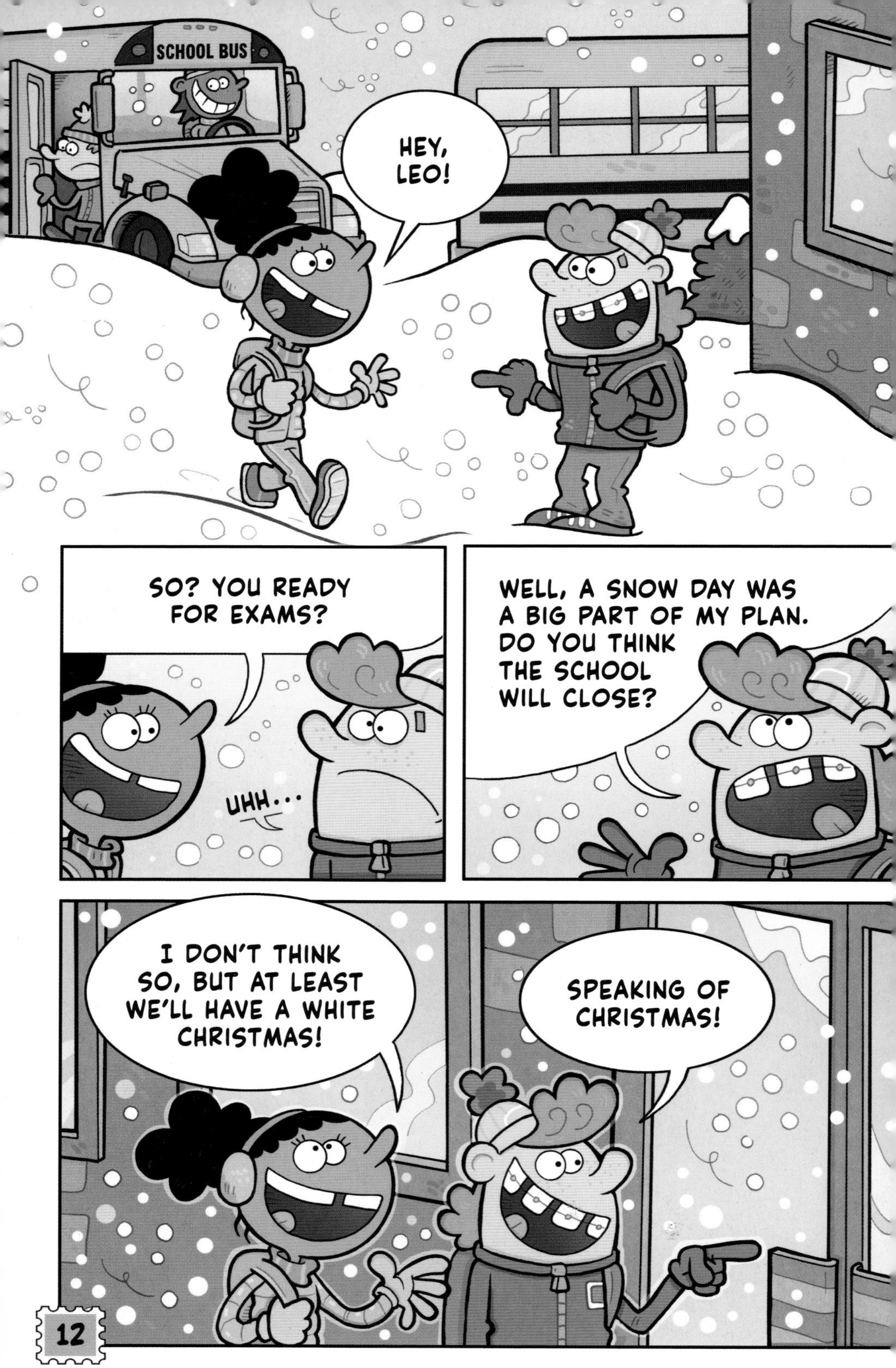
SCHOOL BUS
HEY, LEO!
SO? YOU READY FOR EXAMS?
UHH...
WELL, A SNOW DAY WAS A BIG PART OF MY PLAN. DO YOU THINK THE SCHOOL WILL CLOSE?
I DON'T THINK SO, BUT AT LEAST WE'LL HAVE A WHITE CHRISTMAS!
SPEAKING OF CHRISTMAS!

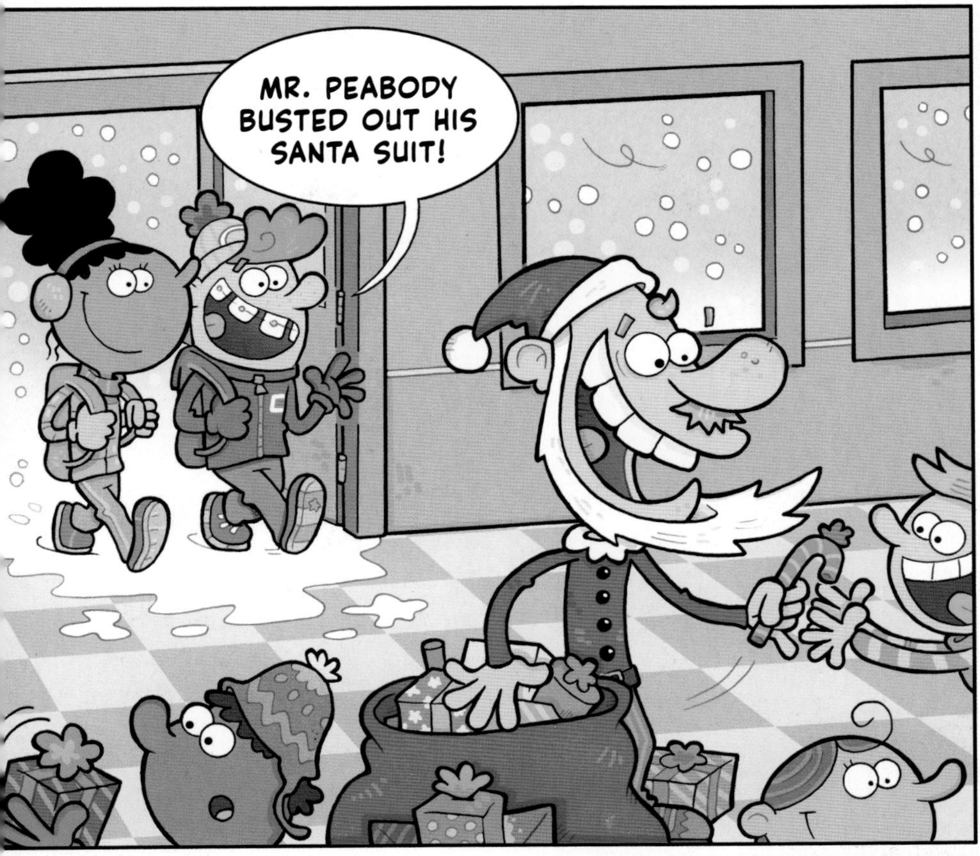
MR. PEABODY BUSTED OUT HIS SANTA SUIT!

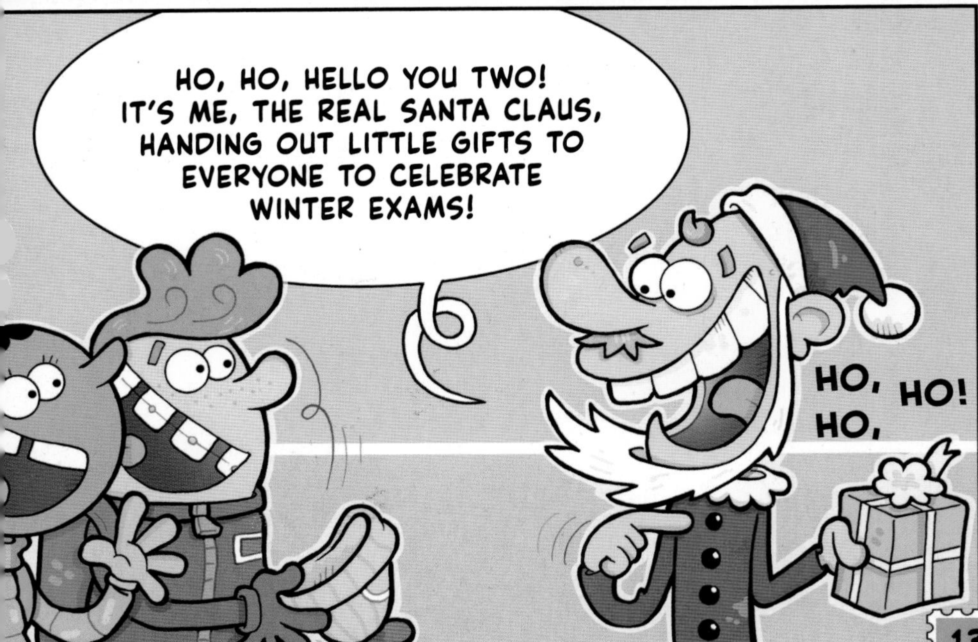
HO, HO, HELLO YOU TWO! IT'S ME, THE REAL SANTA CLAUS, HANDING OUT LITTLE GIFTS TO EVERYONE TO CELEBRATE WINTER EXAMS!
HO, HO, HO!

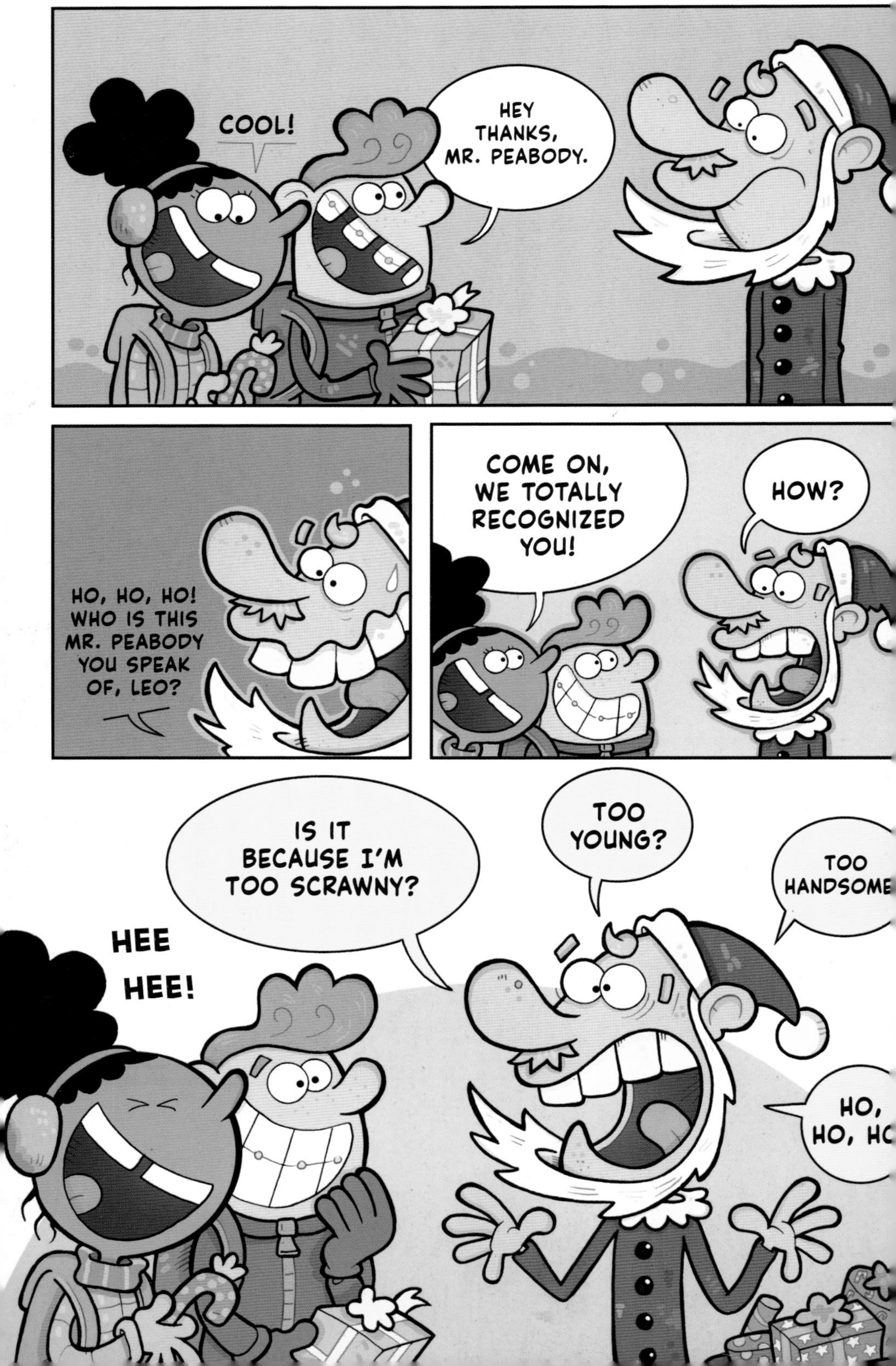
COOL!
HEY THANKS, MR. PEABODY.
HO, HO, HO! WHO IS THIS MR. PEABODY YOU SPEAK OF, LEO?
COME ON, WE TOTALLY RECOGNIZED YOU!
HOW?
IS IT BECAUSE I'M TOO SCRAWNY?
TOO YOUNG?
TOO HANDSOME
HEE HEE!
HO, HO, HO

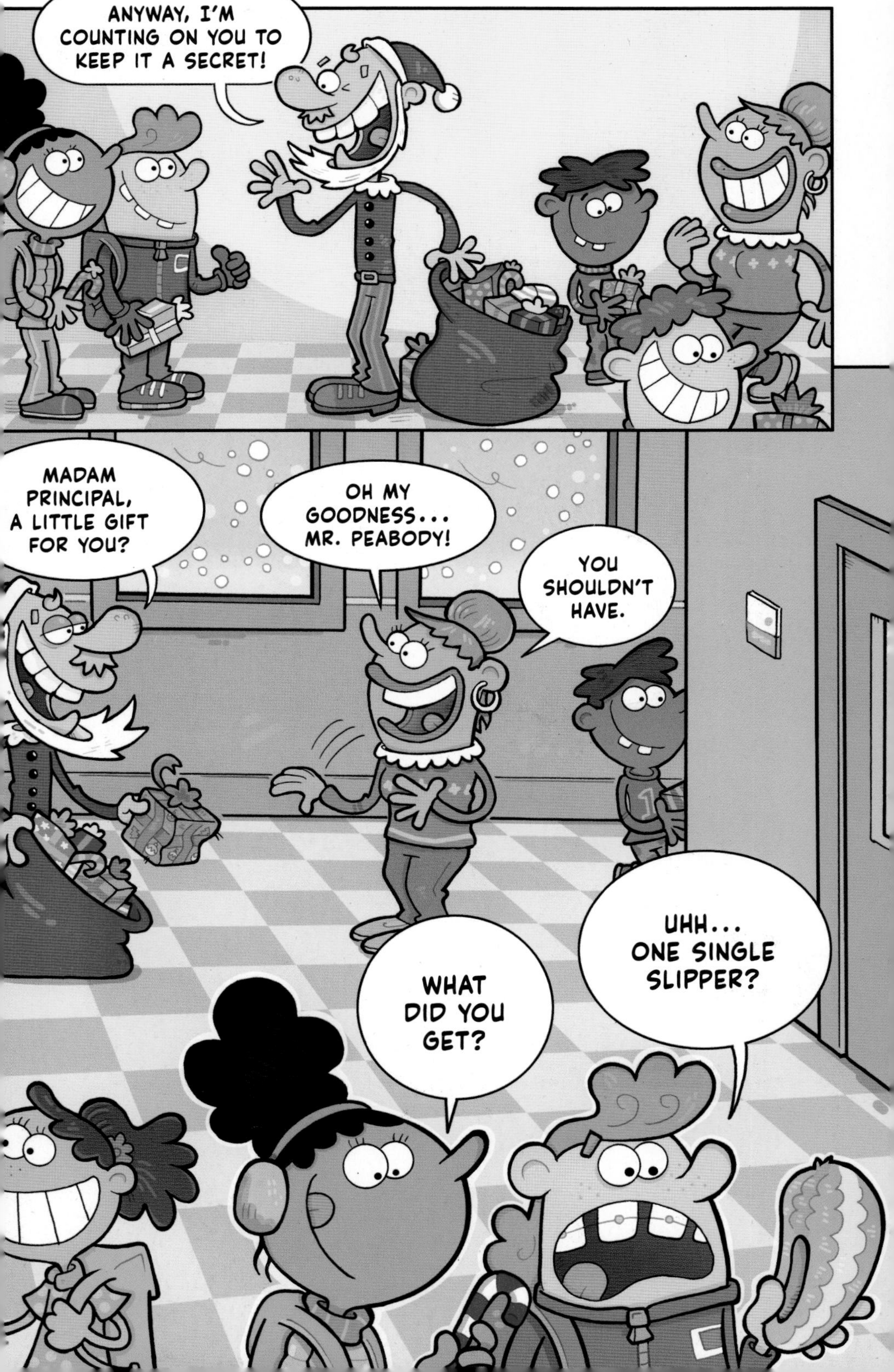
ANYWAY, I'M COUNTING ON YOU TO KEEP IT A SECRET!
MADAM PRINCIPAL, A LITTLE GIFT FOR YOU?
OH MY GOODNESS... MR. PEABODY!
YOU SHOULDN'T HAVE.
WHAT DID YOU GET?
UHH... ONE SINGLE SLIPPER?

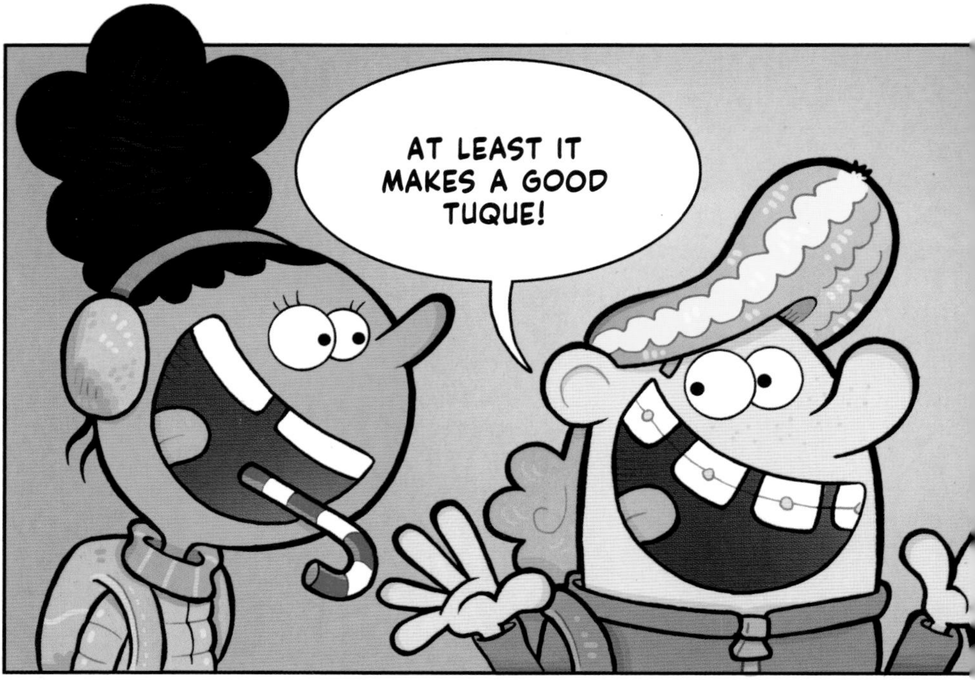
AT LEAST IT MAKES A GOOD TUQUE!

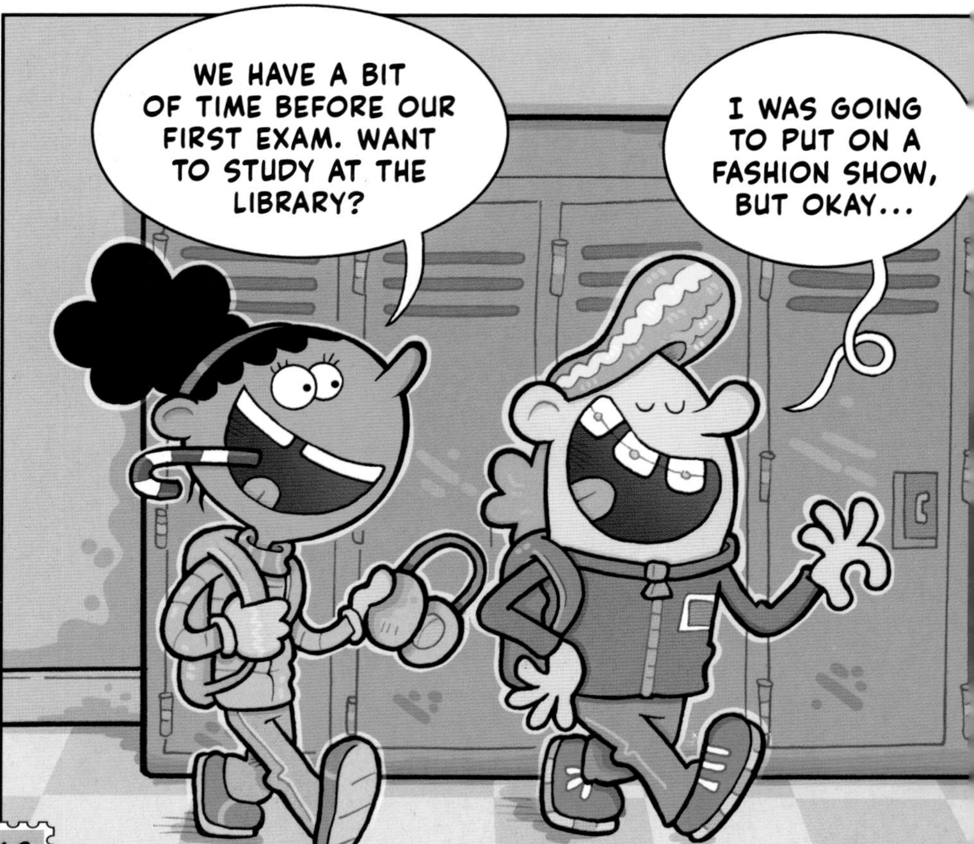
WE HAVE A BIT OF TIME BEFORE OUR FIRST EXAM. WANT TO STUDY AT THE LIBRARY?
I WAS GOING TO PUT ON A FASHION SHOW, BUT OKAY...

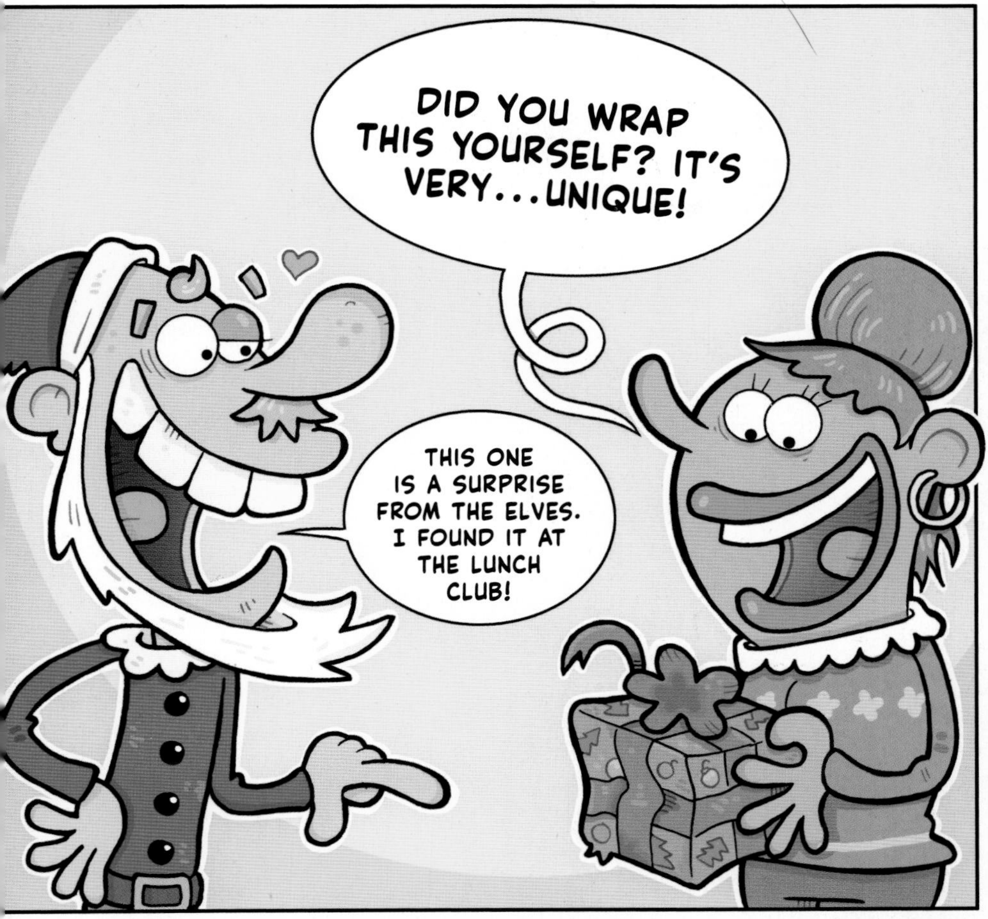
DID YOU WRAP THIS YOURSELF? IT'S VERY...UNIQUE!
THIS ONE IS A SURPRISE FROM THE ELVES. I FOUND IT AT THE LUNCH CLUB!

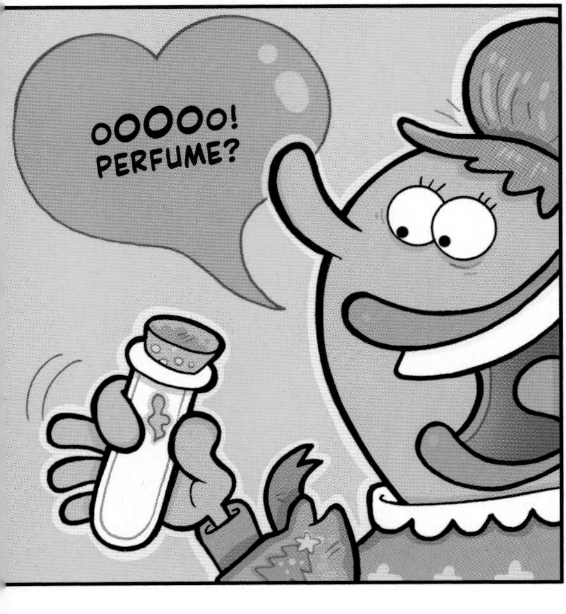
oOOOo! PERFUME?

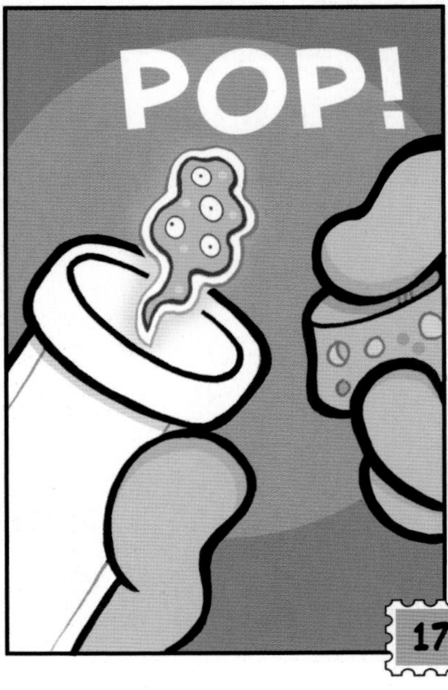
POP!

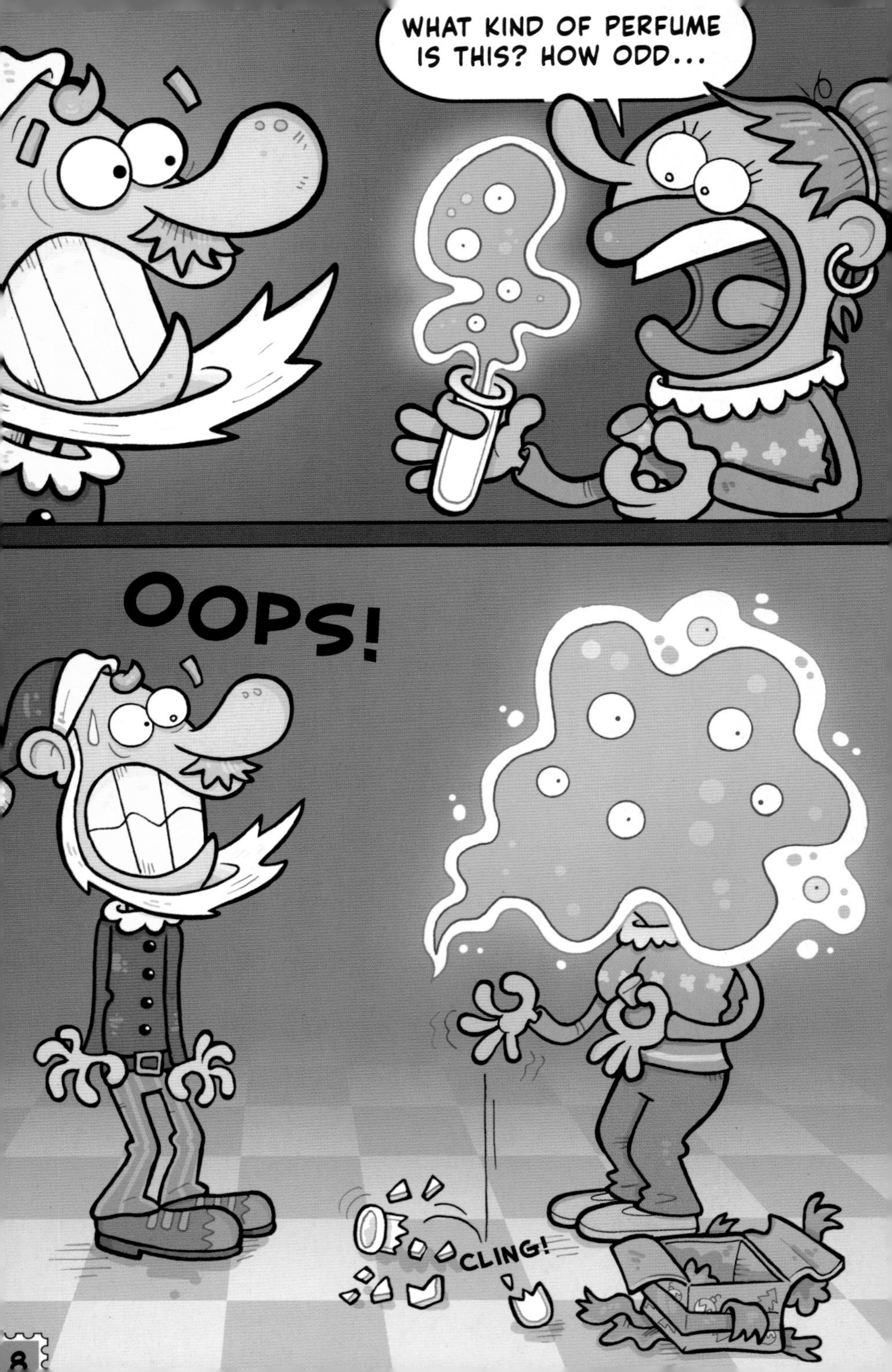
WHAT KIND OF PERFUME IS THIS? HOW ODD...
OOPS!
CLING!

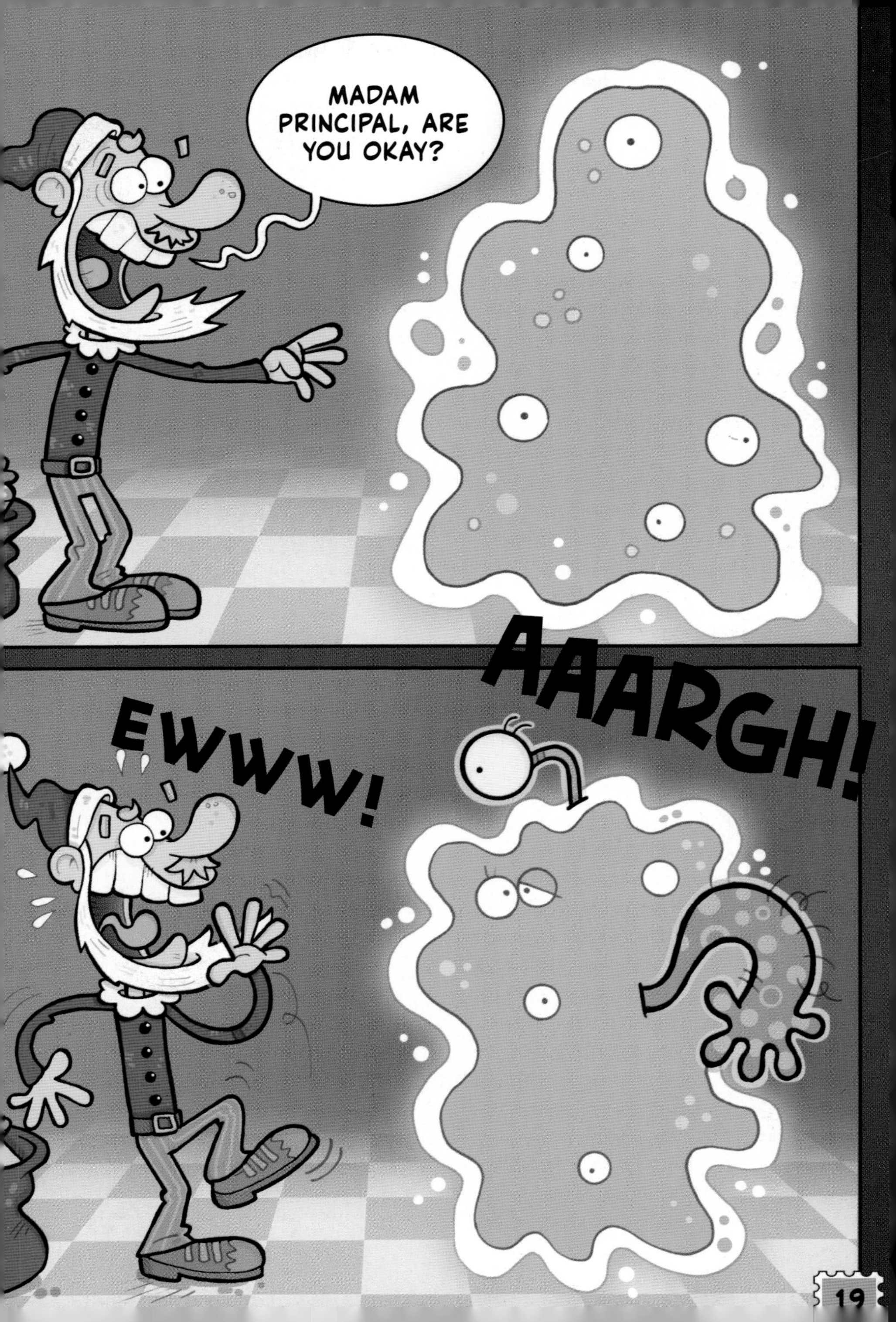
MADAM PRINCIPAL, ARE YOU OKAY?
EWWWW!
AAARGH!

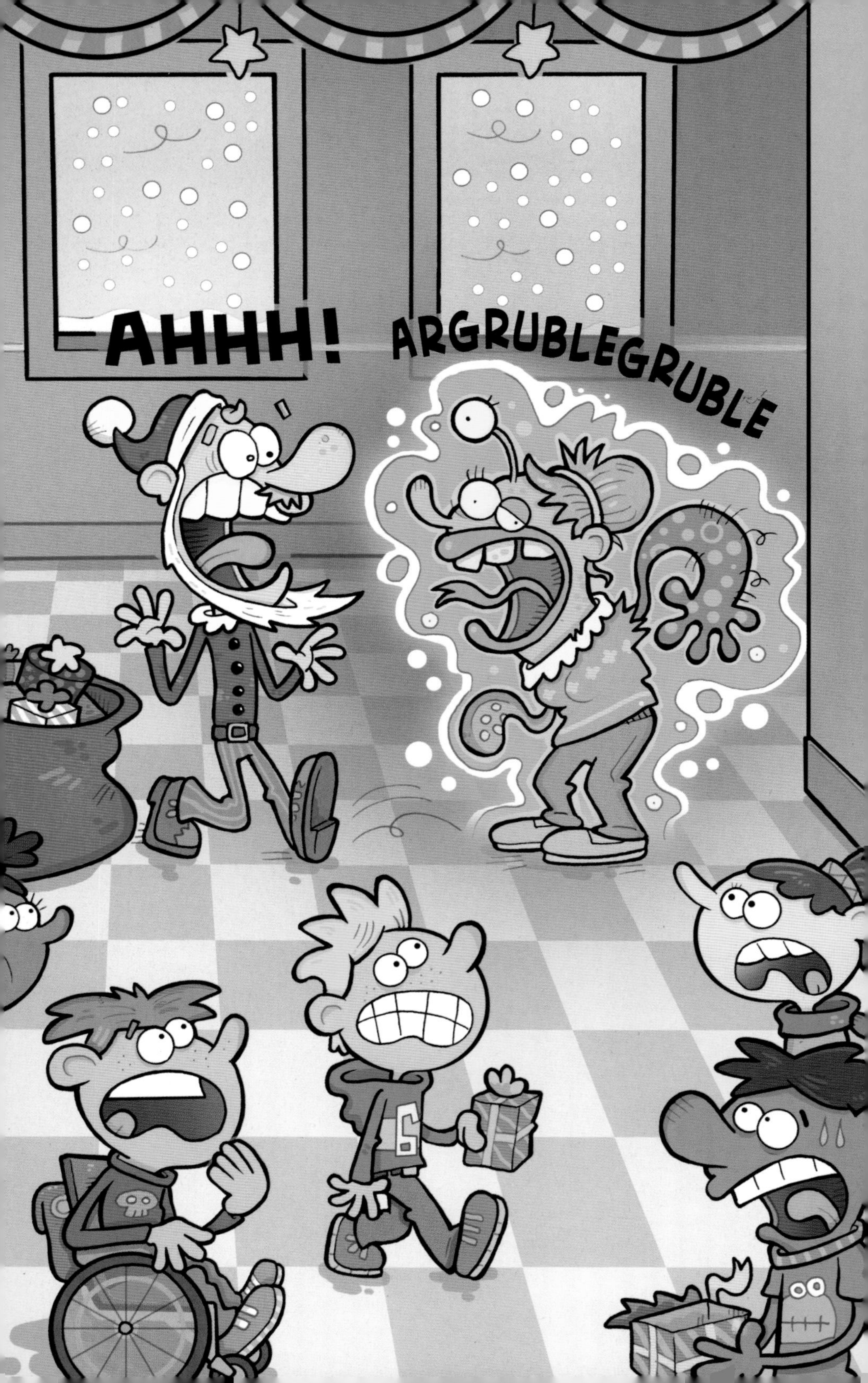
AHHHH!
ARGRUBLEGRUBLE

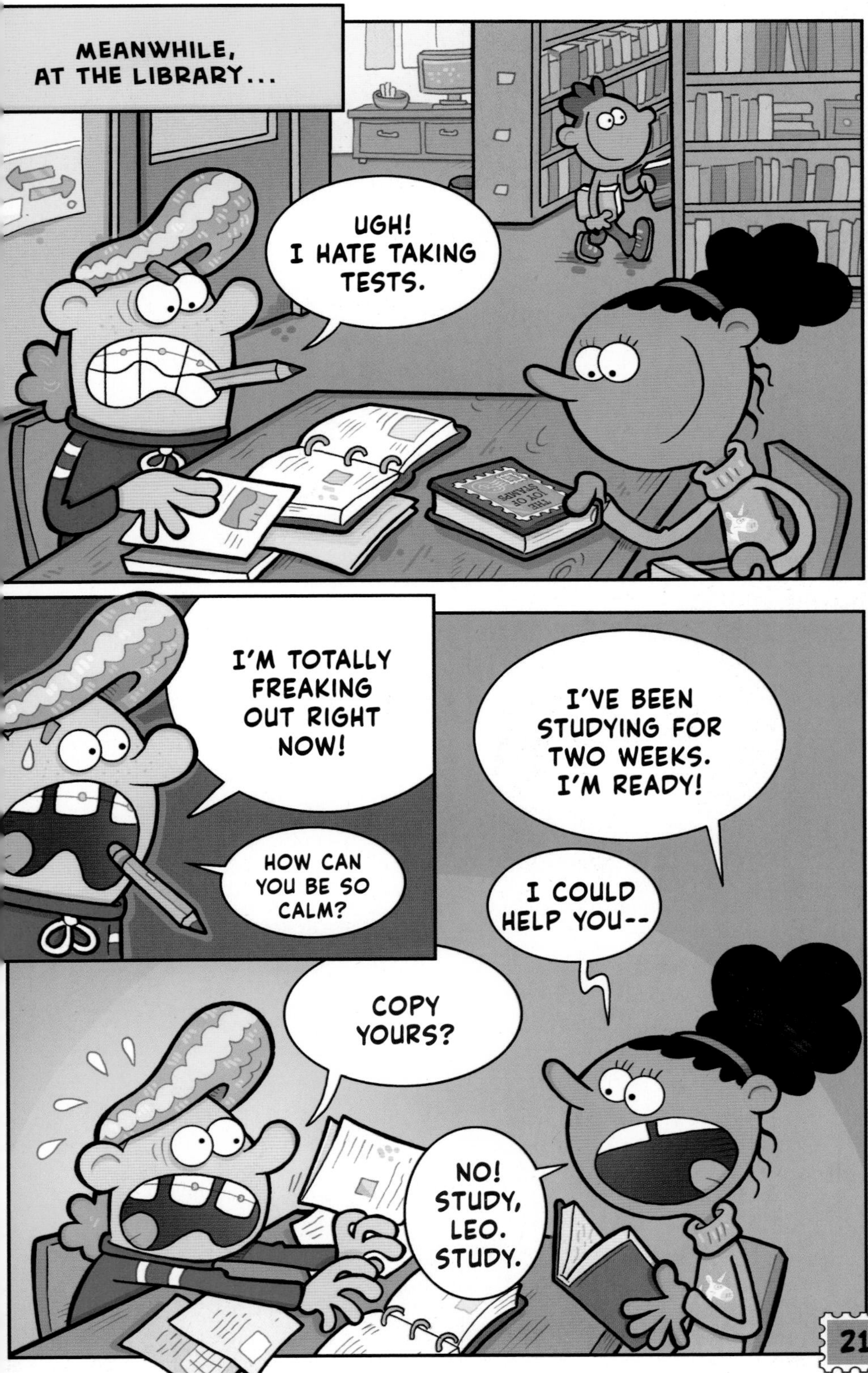
MEANWHILE, AT THE LIBRARY...
UGH! I HATE TAKING TESTS.
THE JOY OF STAMPS
I'M TOTALLY FREAKING OUT RIGHT NOW!
HOW CAN YOU BE SO CALM?
I'VE BEEN STUDYING FOR TWO WEEKS. I'M READY!
I COULD HELP YOU--
COPY YOURS?
NO! STUDY, LEO. STUDY.

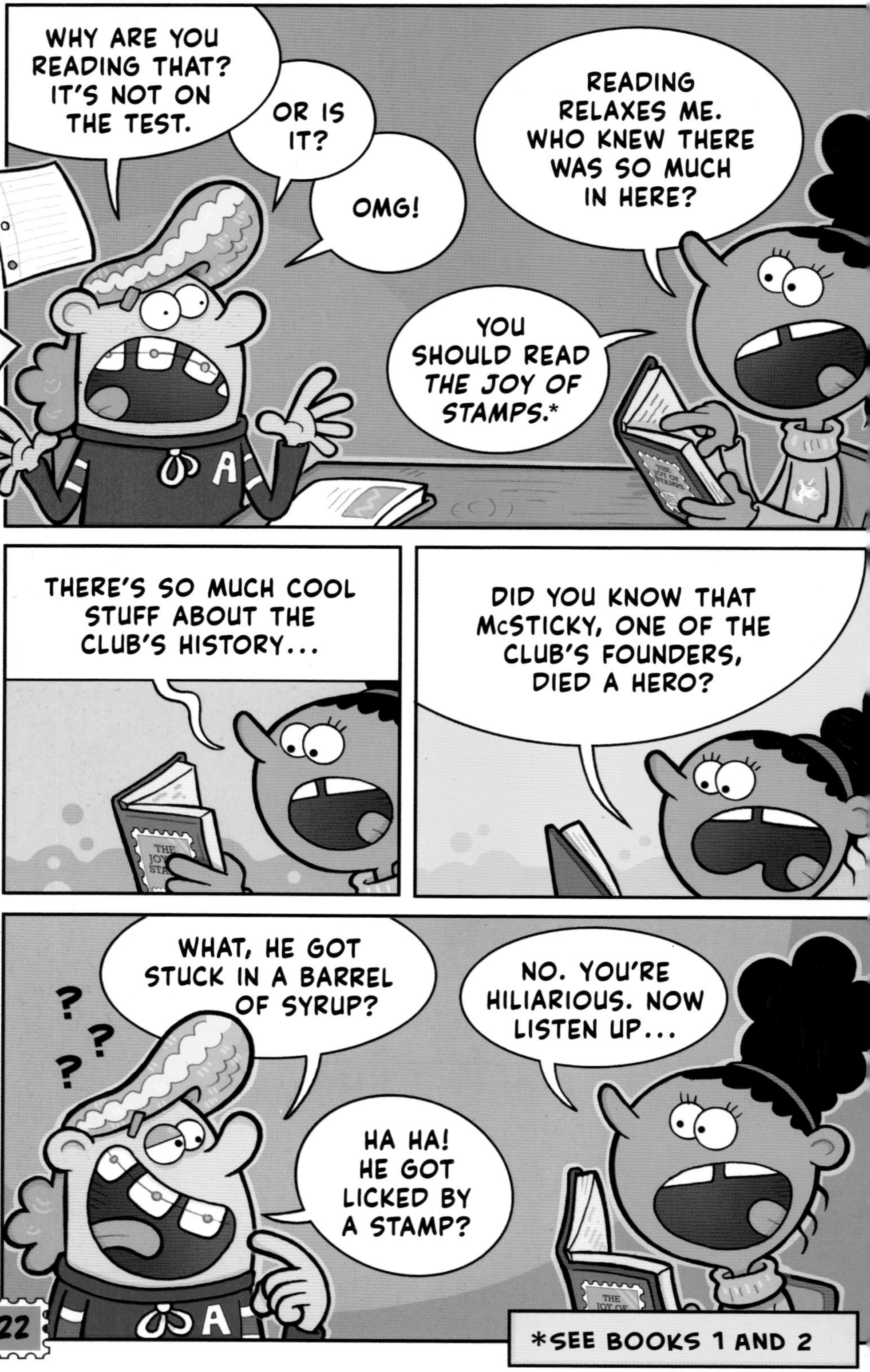
WHY ARE YOU READING THAT? IT'S NOT ON THE TEST.
OR IS IT?
OMG!
READING RELAXES ME. WHO KNEW THERE WAS SO MUCH IN HERE?
YOU SHOULD READ THE JOY OF STAMPS.*
THERE'S SO MUCH COOL STUFF ABOUT THE CLUB'S HISTORY...
DID YOU KNOW THAT McSTICKY, ONE OF THE CLUB'S FOUNDERS, DIED A HERO?
WHAT, HE GOT STUCK IN A BARREL OF SYRUP?
? ? ?
HA HA! HE GOT LICKED BY A STAMP?
NO. YOU'RE HILIARIOUS. NOW LISTEN UP...
*SEE BOOKS 1 AND 2

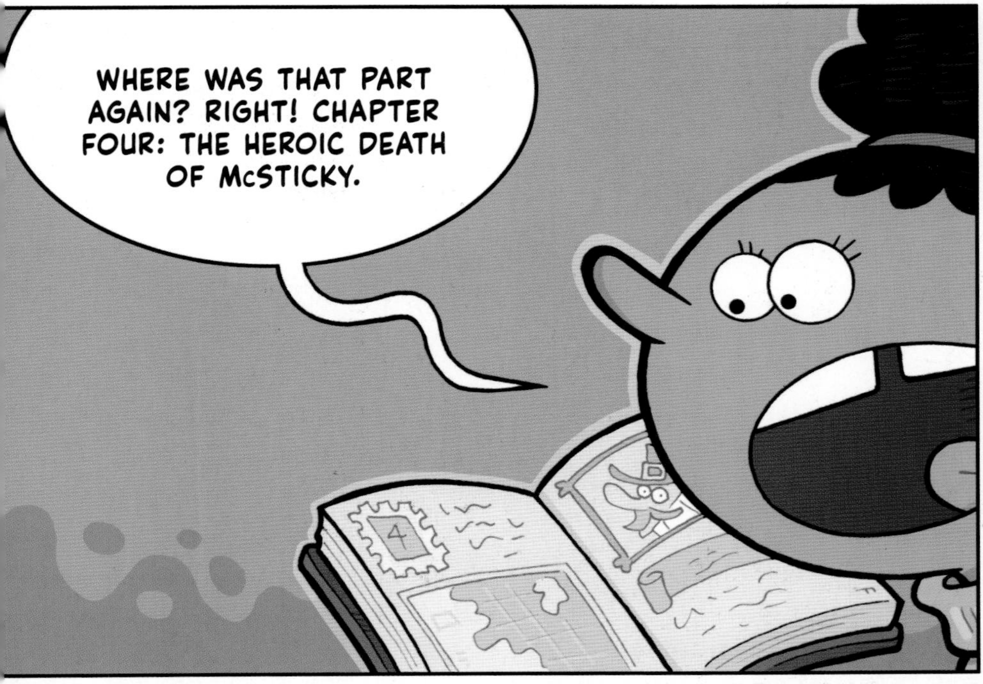
WHERE WAS THAT PART AGAIN? RIGHT! CHAPTER FOUR: THE HEROIC DEATH OF McSTICKY.
4

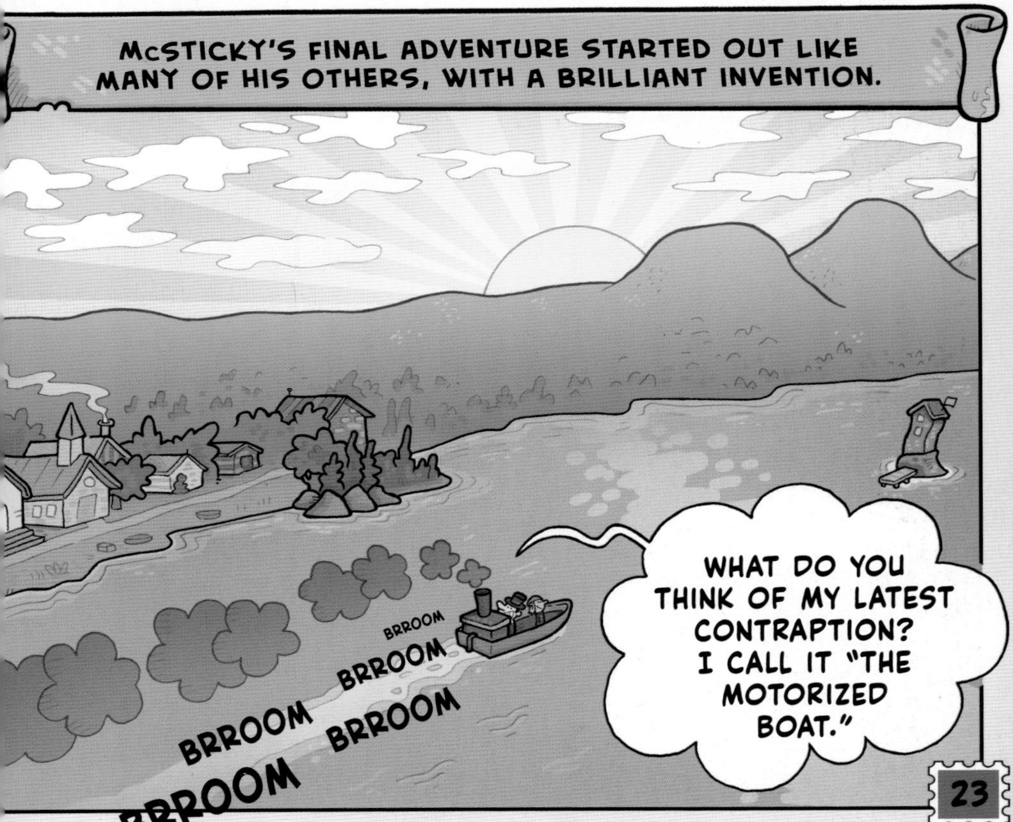
McSTICKY'S FINAL ADVENTURE STARTED OUT LIKE MANY OF HIS OTHERS, WITH A BRILLIANT INVENTION.
BRROOM
BRROOM
BRROOM
BRROOM
BRROOM
WHAT DO YOU THINK OF MY LATEST CONTRAPTION? I CALL IT "THE MOTORIZED BOAT."

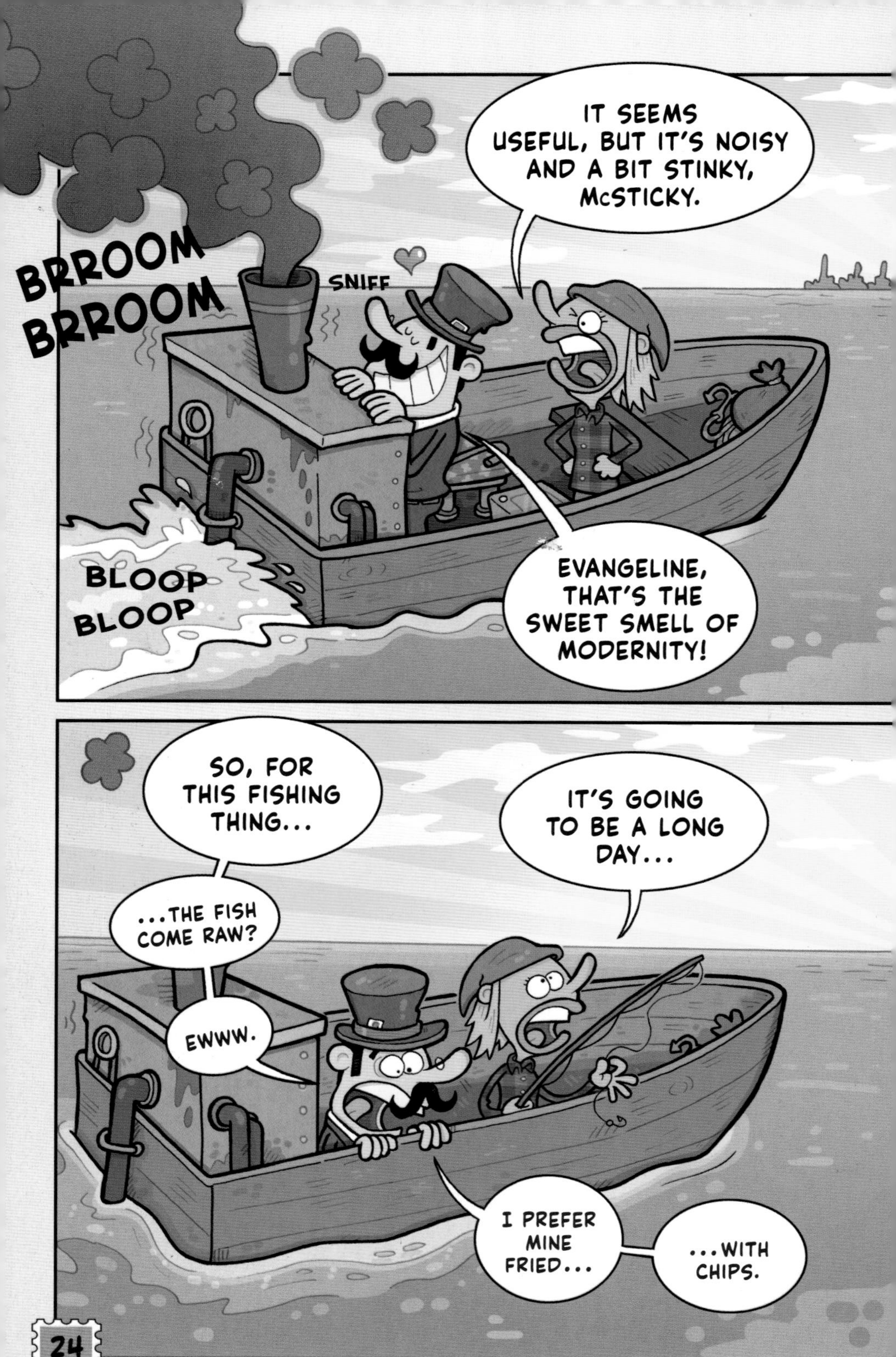
BRROOM BRROOM
SNIFF
IT SEEMS USEFUL, BUT IT'S NOISY AND A BIT STINKY, McSTICKY.
EVANGELINE, THAT'S THE SWEET SMELL OF MODERNITY!
BLOOP BLOOP
SO, FOR THIS FISHING THING...
...THE FISH COME RAW?
EWWW.
IT'S GOING TO BE A LONG DAY...
I PREFER MINE FRIED...
...WITH CHIPS.

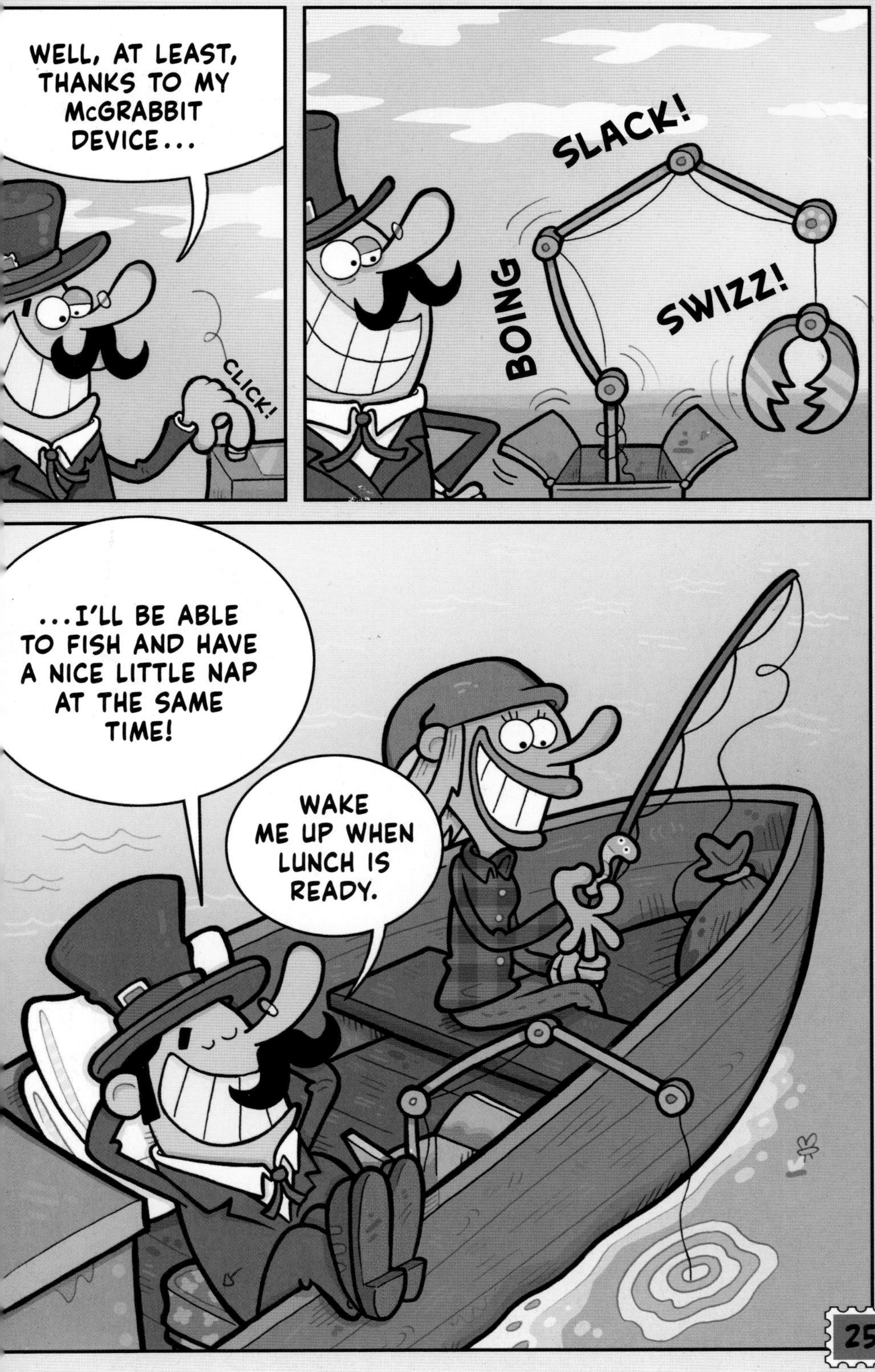

WELL, AT LEAST, THANKS TO MY McGRABBIT DEVICE...
CLICK!
SLACK!
BOING
SWIZZ!
...I'LL BE ABLE TO FISH AND HAVE A NICE LITTLE NAP AT THE SAME TIME!
WAKE ME UP WHEN LUNCH IS READY.

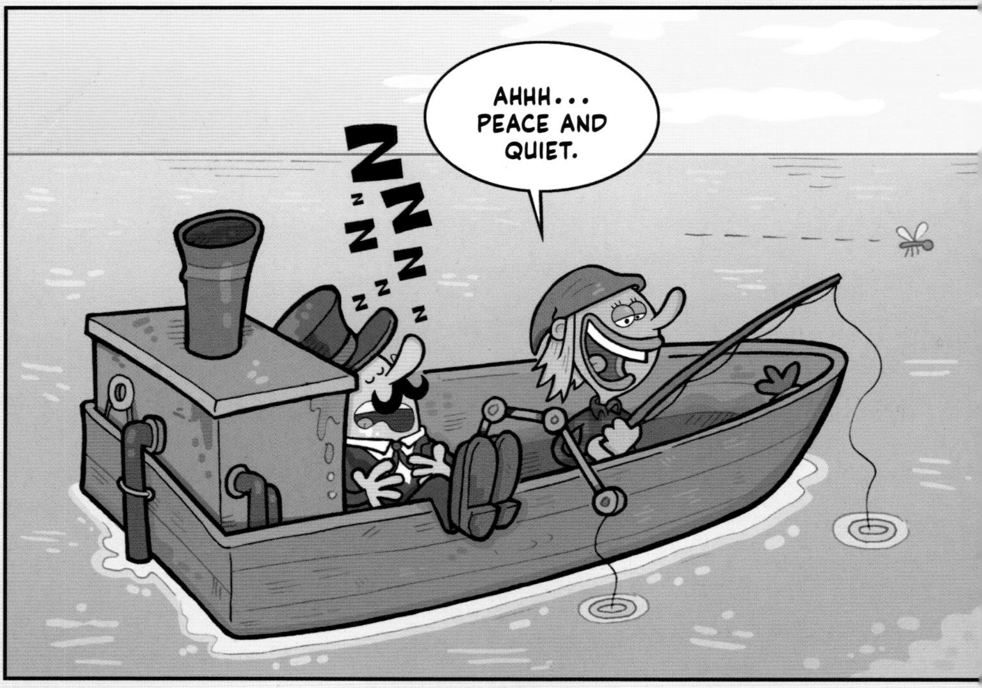
AHHH...
PEACE AND
QUIET.
Z Z Z Z Z Z Z Z

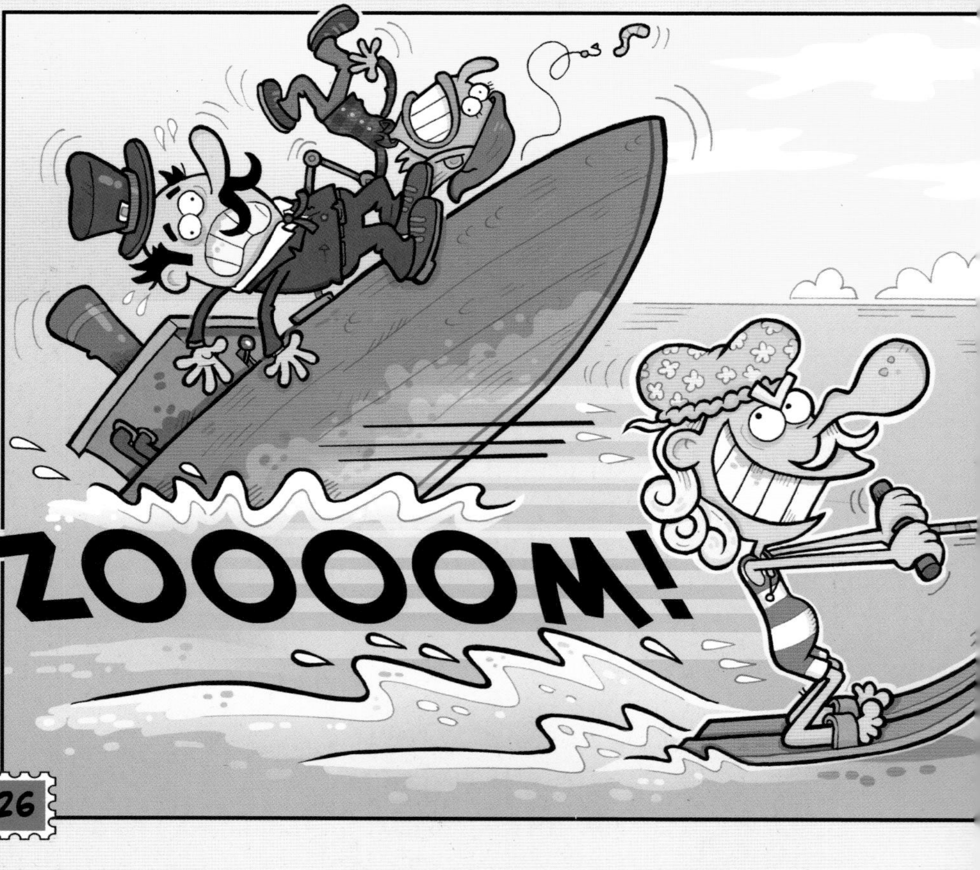
ZOOOOM!

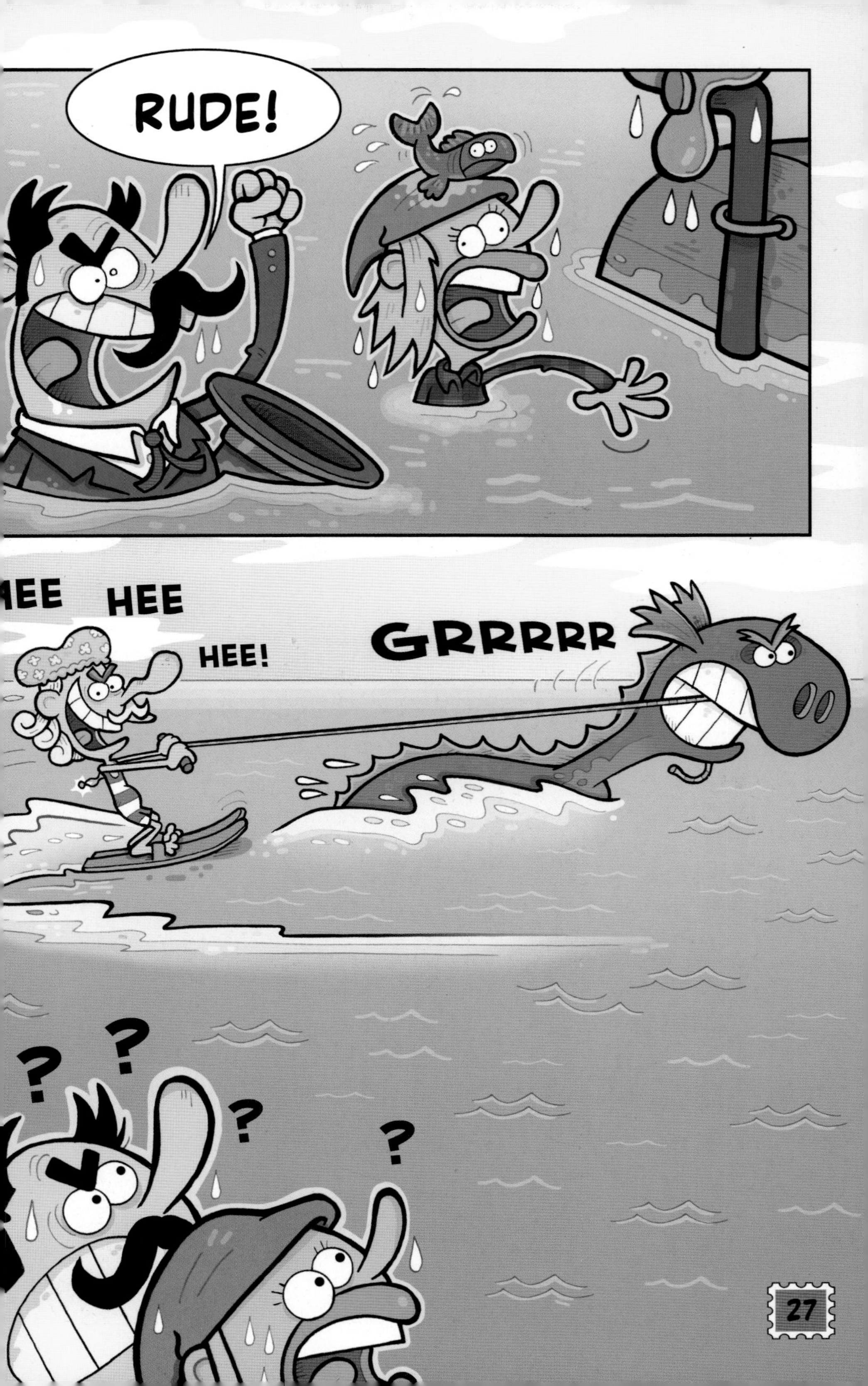
RUDE!
HEE
HEE!
GRRRRR
?
?
?
?

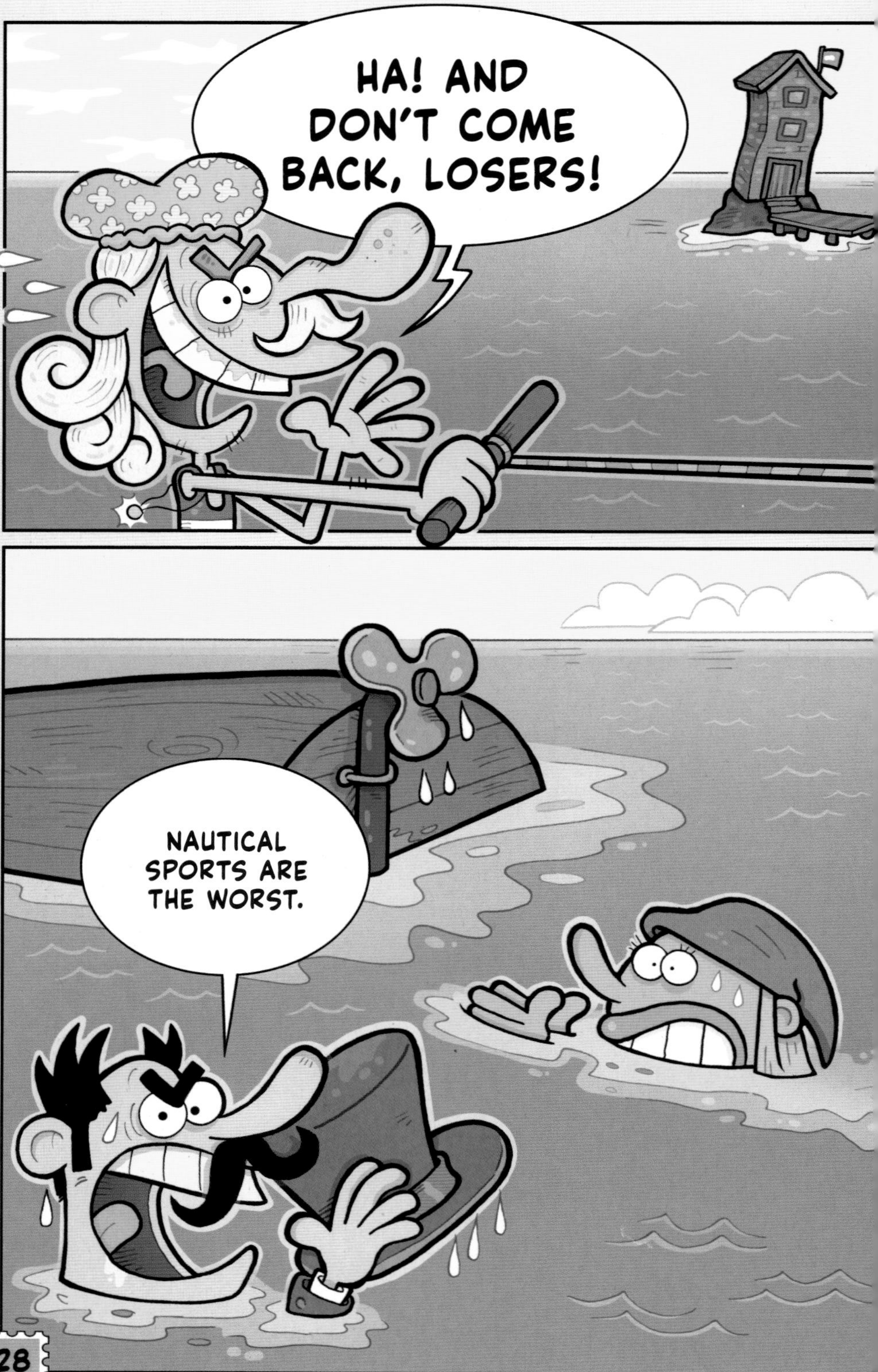
HA! AND DON'T COME BACK, LOSERS!
NAUTICAL SPORTS ARE THE WORST.

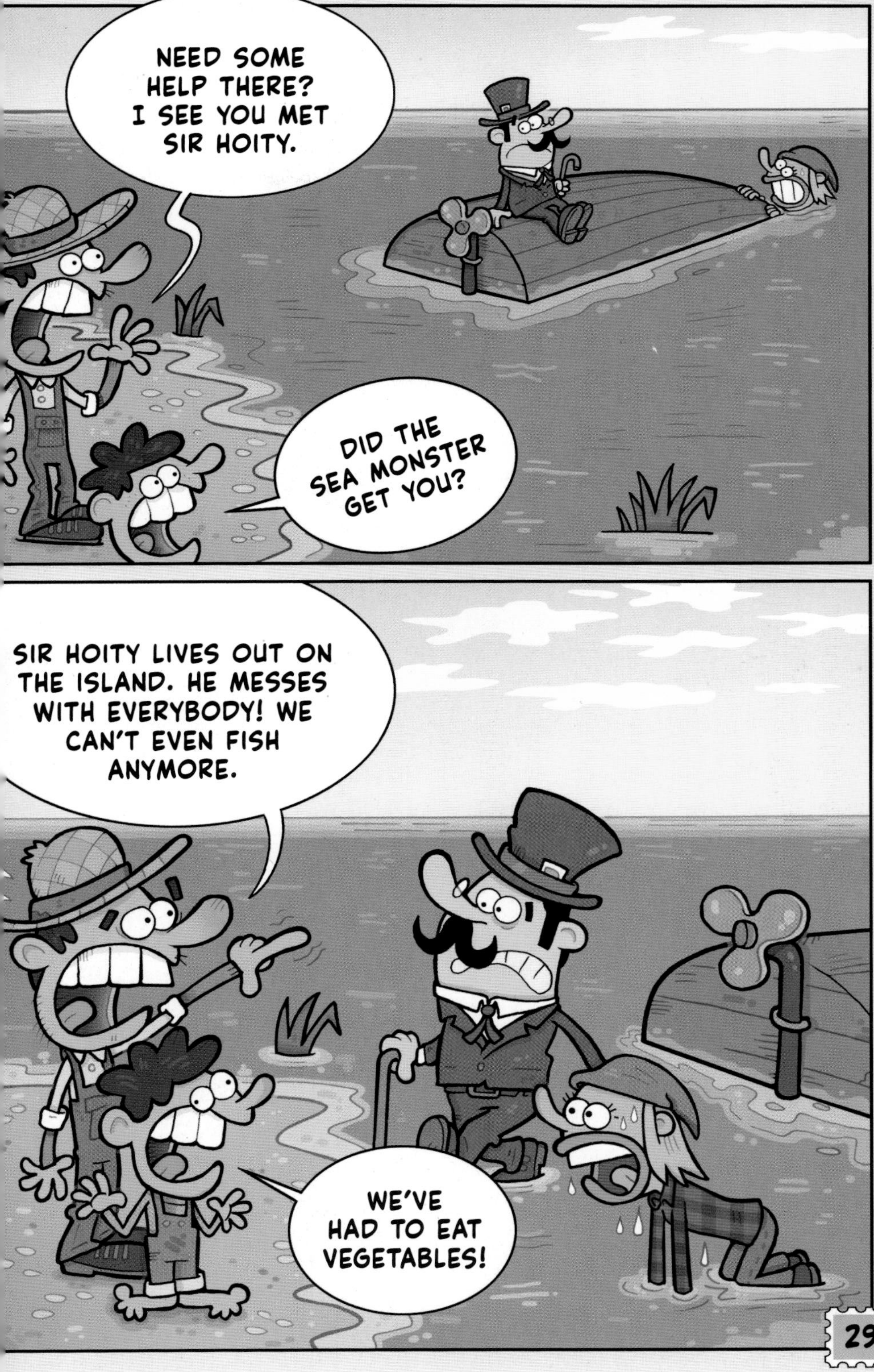
NEED SOME HELP THERE? I SEE YOU MET SIR HOITY.
DID THE SEA MONSTER GET YOU?
SIR HOITY LIVES OUT ON THE ISLAND. HE MESSES WITH EVERYBODY! WE CAN'T EVEN FISH ANYMORE.
WE'VE HAD TO EAT VEGETABLES!

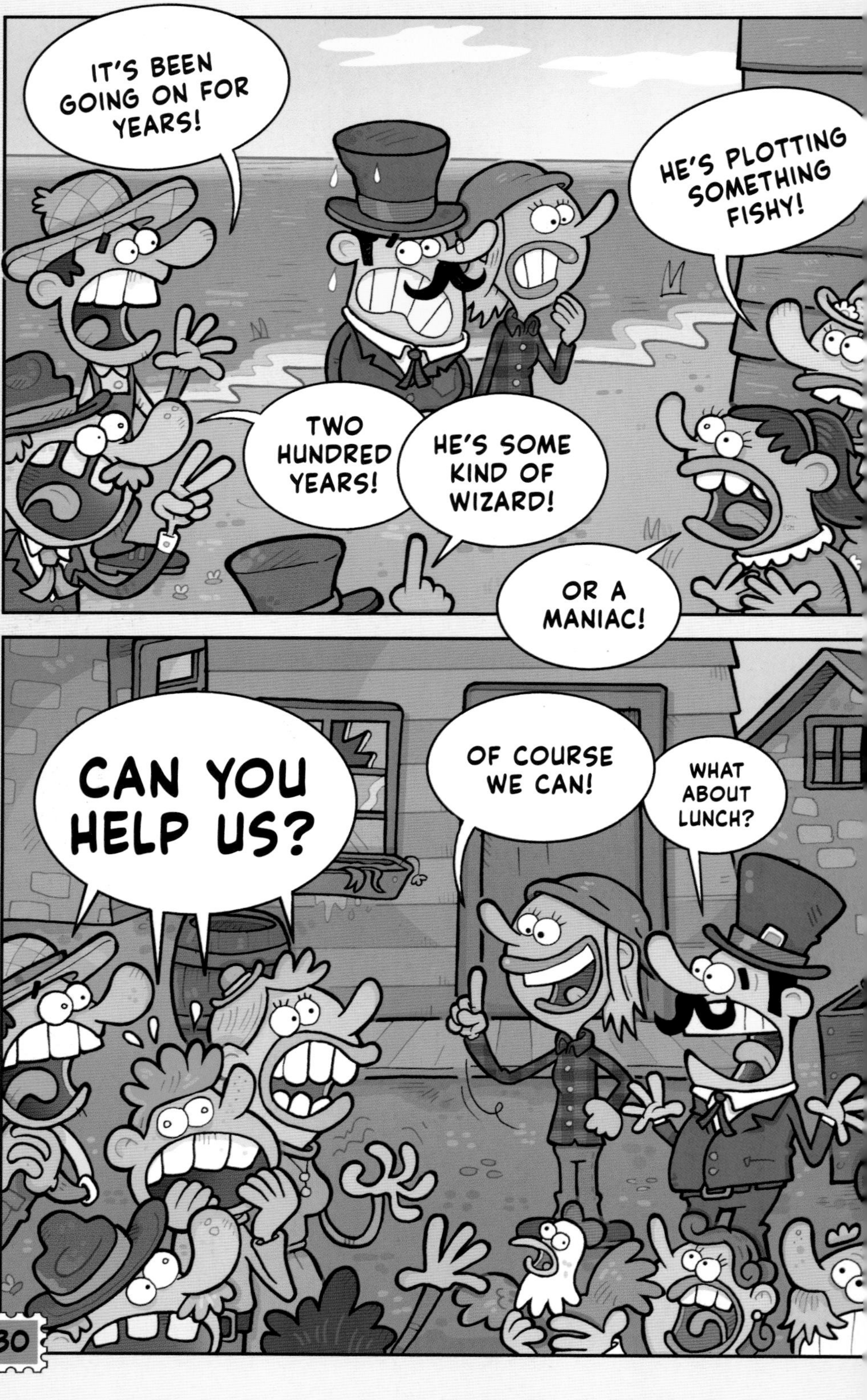
IT'S BEEN GOING ON FOR YEARS!
HE'S PLOTTING SOMETHING FISHY!
TWO HUNDRED YEARS!
HE'S SOME KIND OF WIZARD!
OR A MANIAC!
CAN YOU HELP US?
OF COURSE WE CAN!
WHAT ABOUT LUNCH?

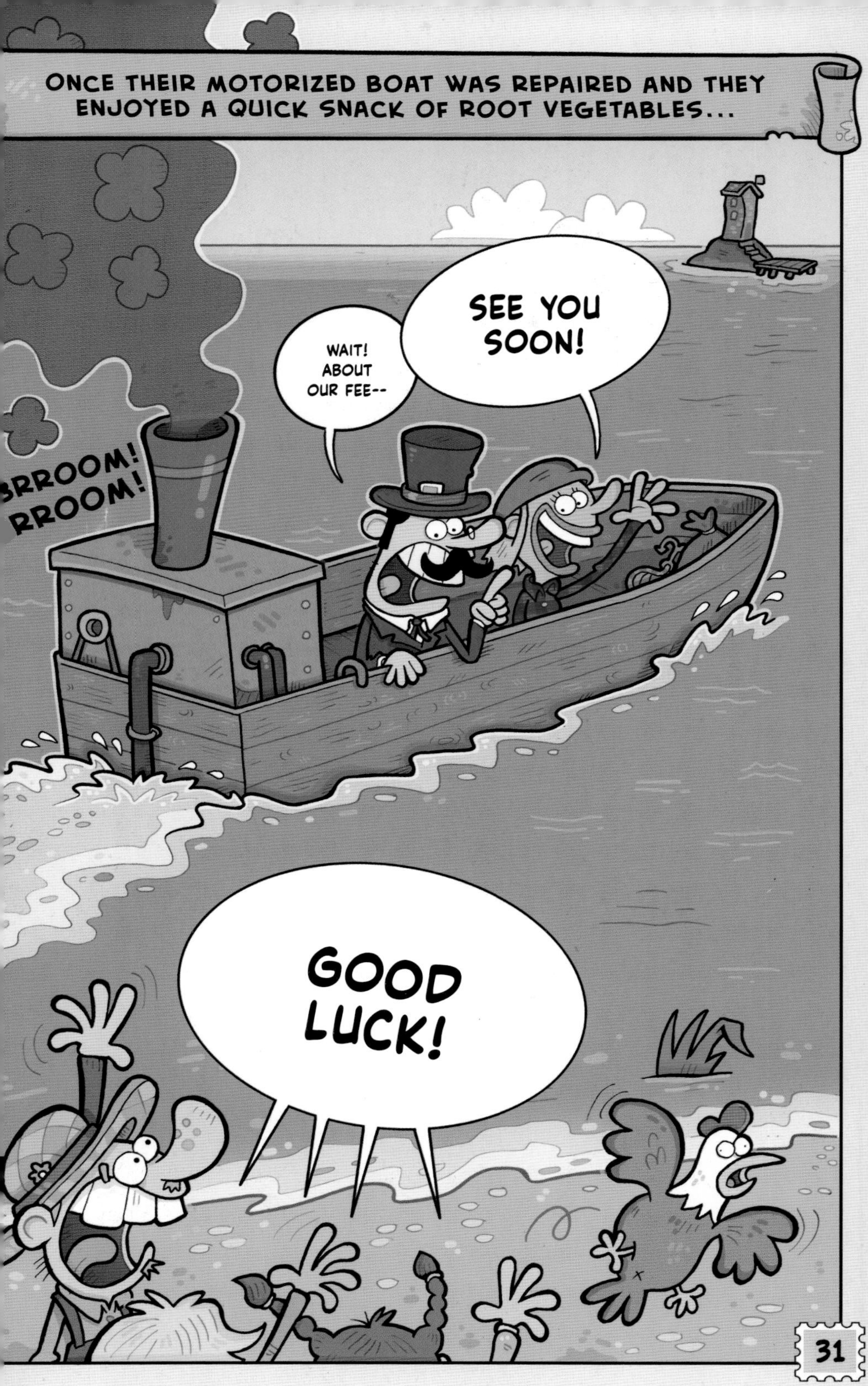
ONCE THEIR MOTORIZED BOAT WAS REPAIRED AND THEY ENJOYED A QUICK SNACK OF ROOT VEGETABLES...
BRROOM! RROOM!
WAIT! ABOUT OUR FEE--
SEE YOU SOON!
GOOD LUCK!

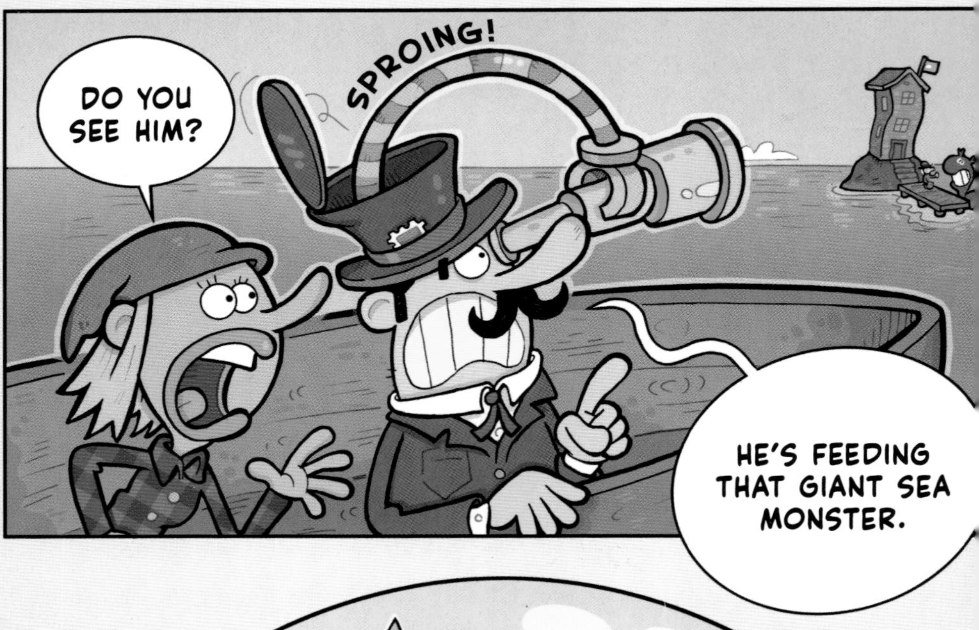
DO YOU SEE HIM?
SPROING!
HE'S FEEDING THAT GIANT SEA MONSTER.

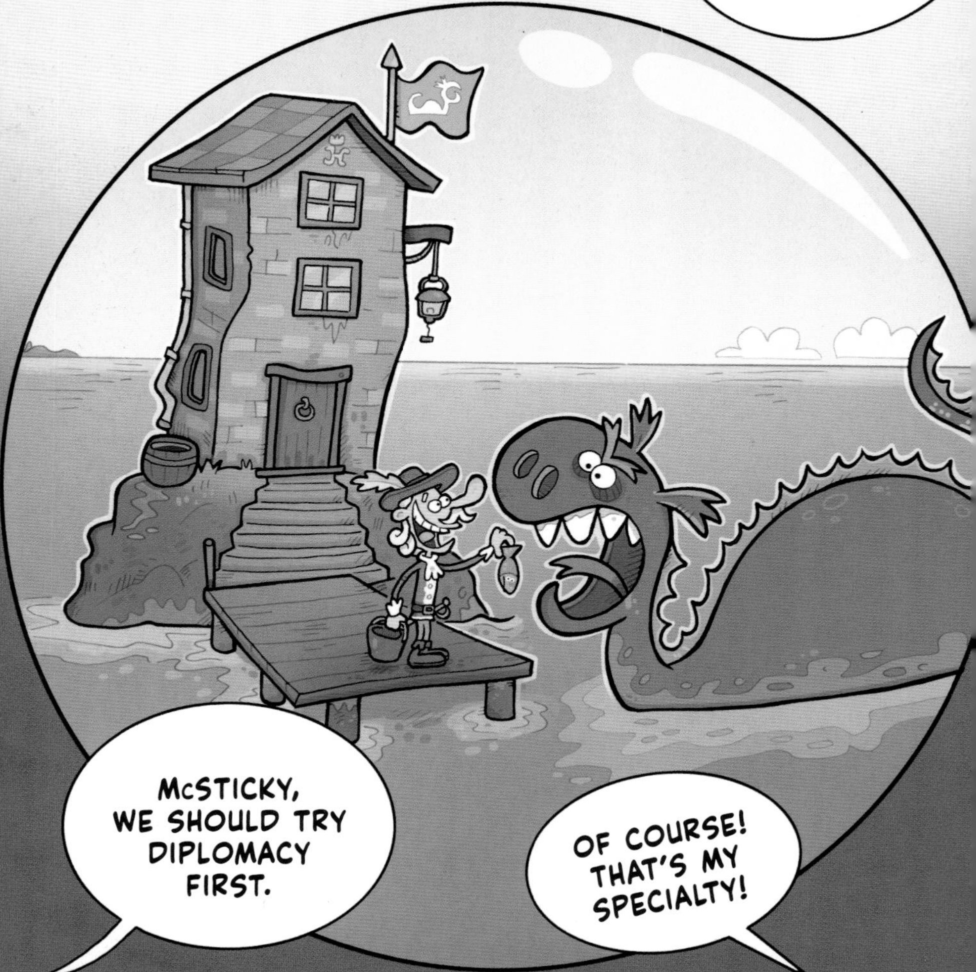
McSTICKY, WE SHOULD TRY DIPLOMACY FIRST.
OF COURSE! THAT'S MY SPECIALTY!

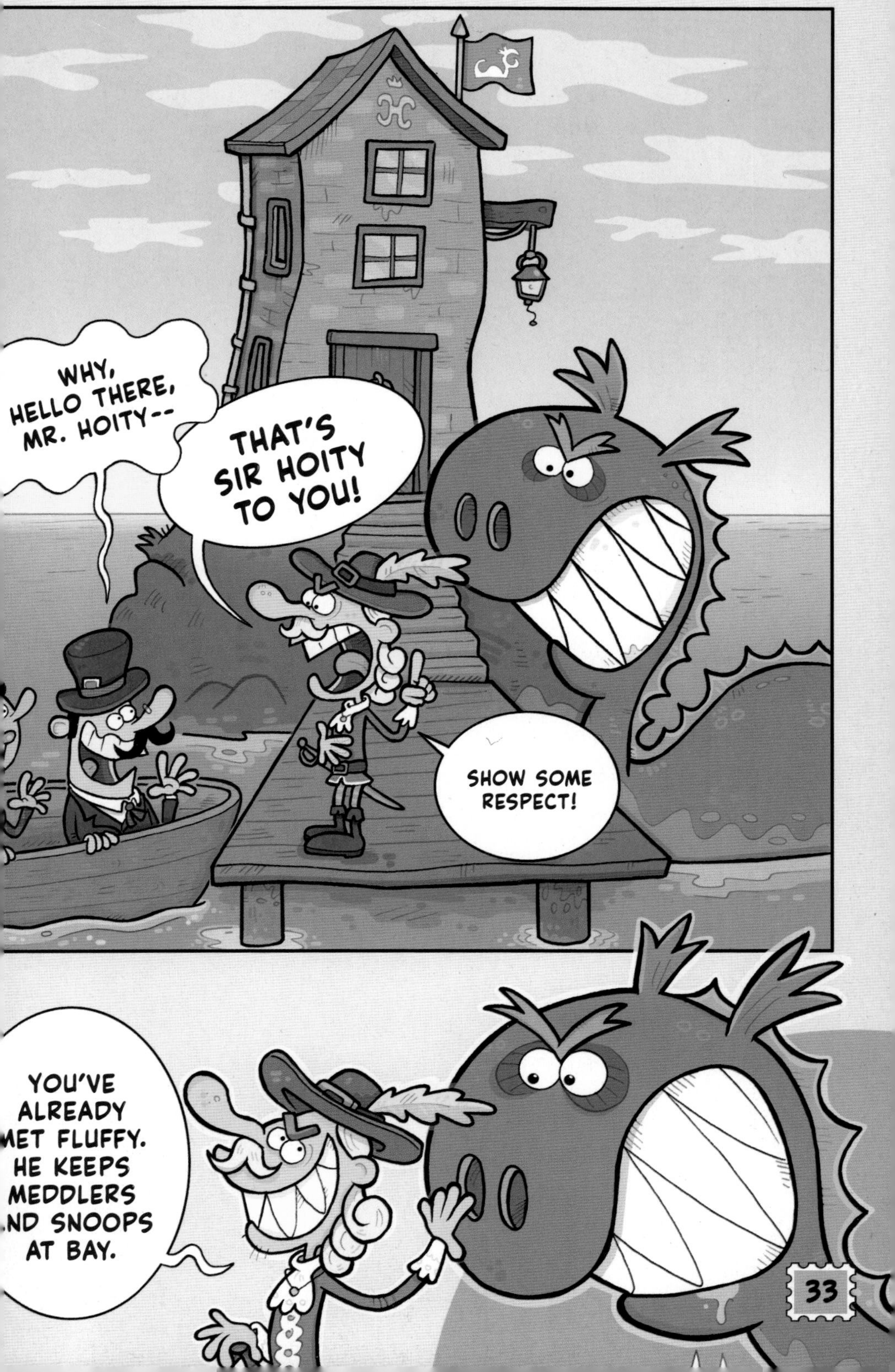
WHY, HELLO THERE, MR. HOITY--
THAT'S SIR HOITY TO YOU!
SHOW SOME RESPECT!
YOU'VE ALREADY MET FLUFFY. HE KEEPS MEDDLERS ND SNOOPS AT BAY.

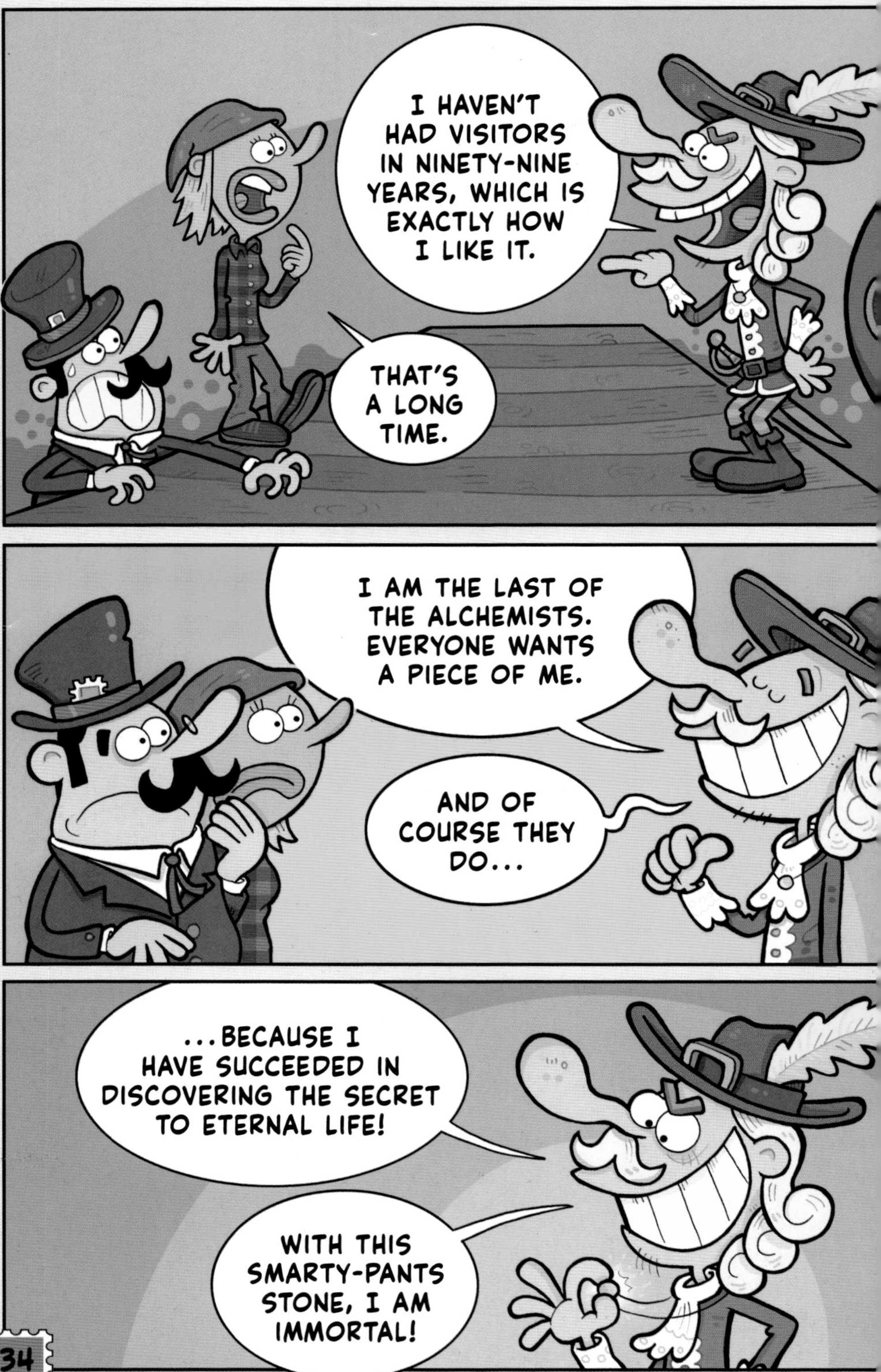
I HAVEN'T HAD VISITORS IN NINETY-NINE YEARS, WHICH IS EXACTLY HOW I LIKE IT.
THAT'S A LONG TIME.
I AM THE LAST OF THE ALCHEMISTS. EVERYONE WANTS A PIECE OF ME.
AND OF COURSE THEY DO...
...BECAUSE I HAVE SUCCEEDED IN DISCOVERING THE SECRET TO ETERNAL LIFE!
WITH THIS SMARTY-PANTS STONE, I AM IMMORTAL!

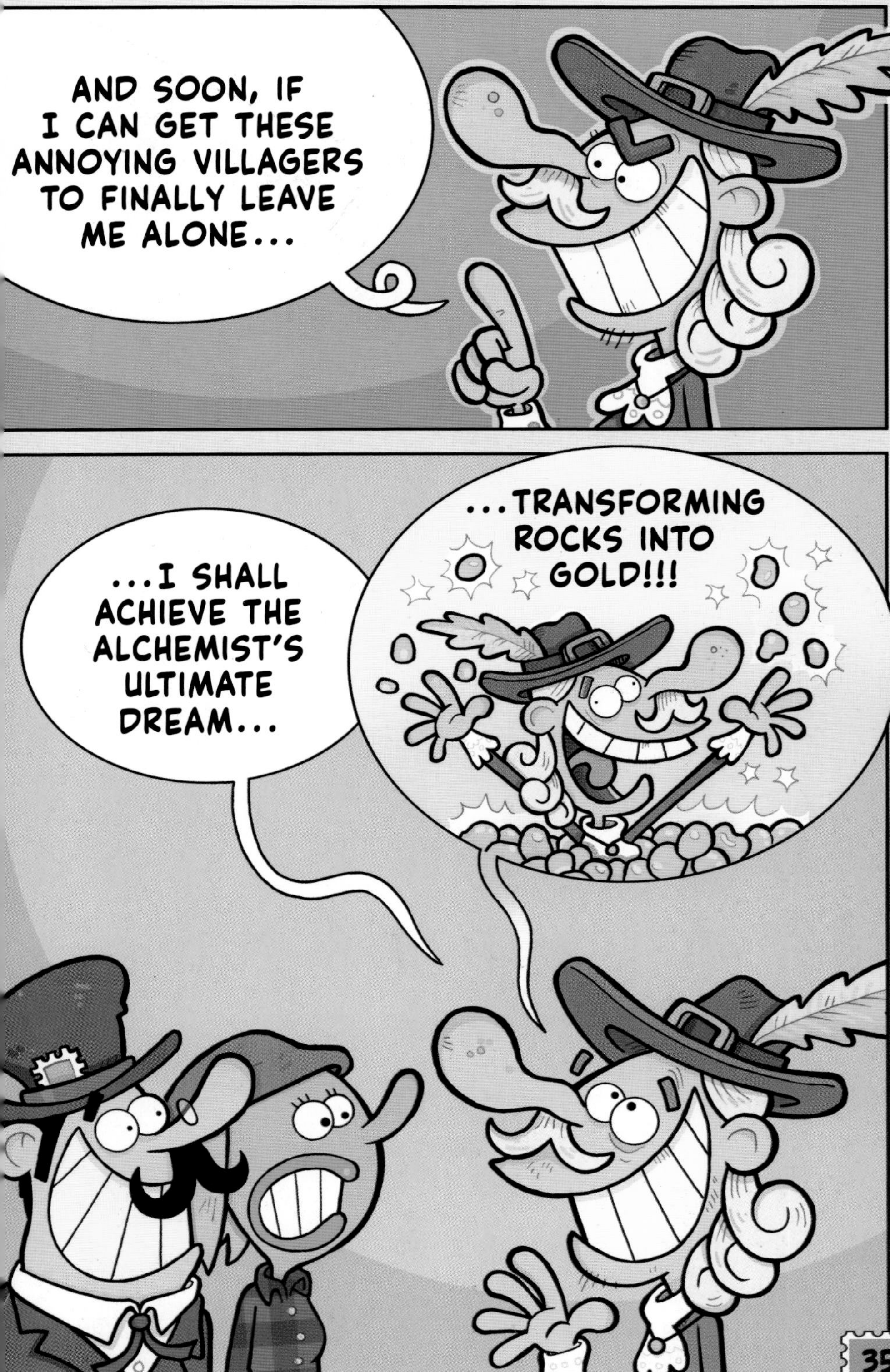
AND SOON, IF I CAN GET THESE ANNOYING VILLAGERS TO FINALLY LEAVE ME ALONE...
...I SHALL ACHIEVE THE ALCHEMIST'S ULTIMATE DREAM...
...TRANSFORMING ROCKS INTO GOLD!!!

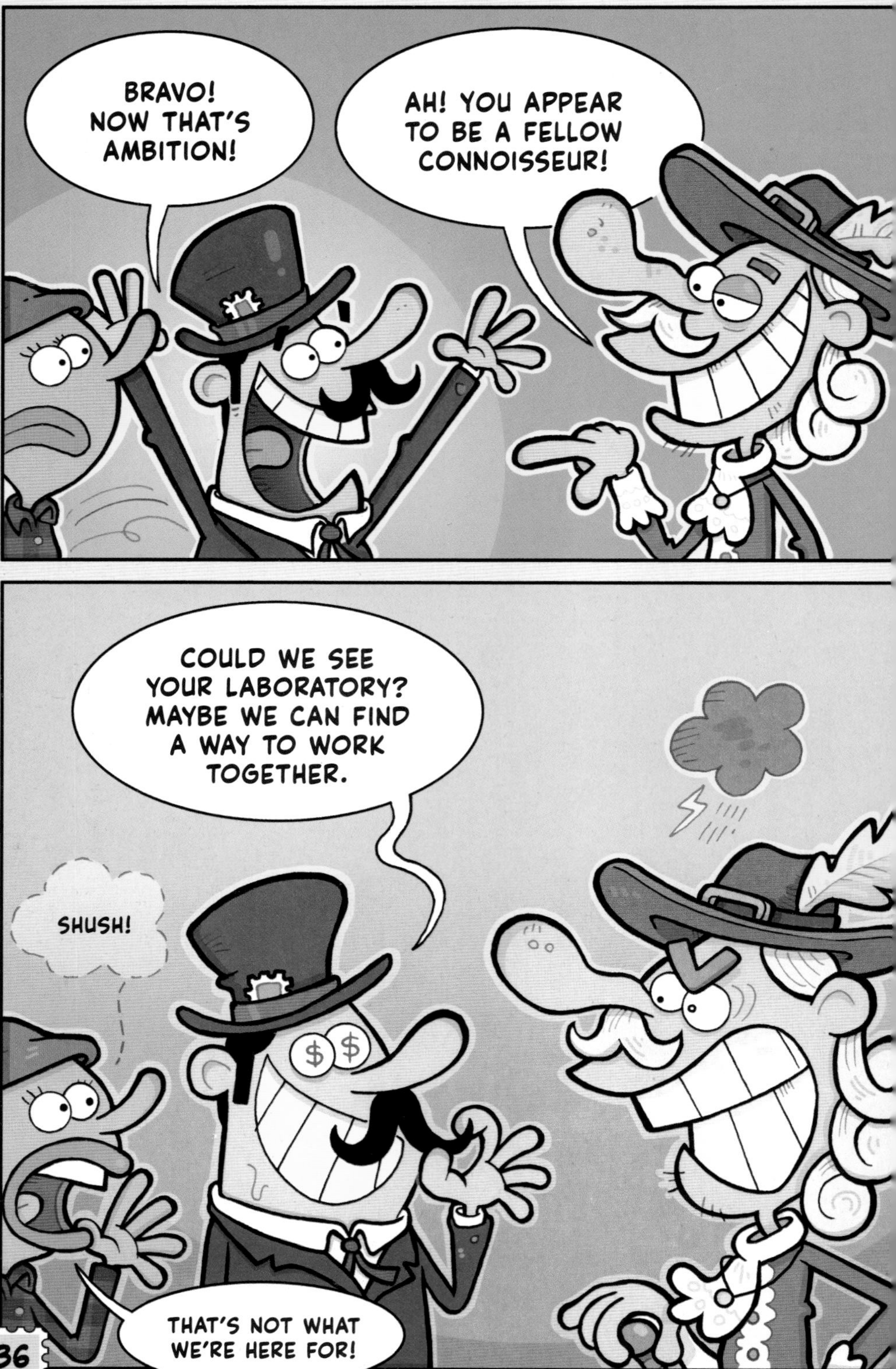
BRAVO! NOW THAT'S AMBITION!
AH! YOU APPEAR TO BE A FELLOW CONNOISSEUR!
COULD WE SEE YOUR LABORATORY? MAYBE WE CAN FIND A WAY TO WORK TOGETHER.
SHUSH!
THAT'S NOT WHAT WE'RE HERE FOR!

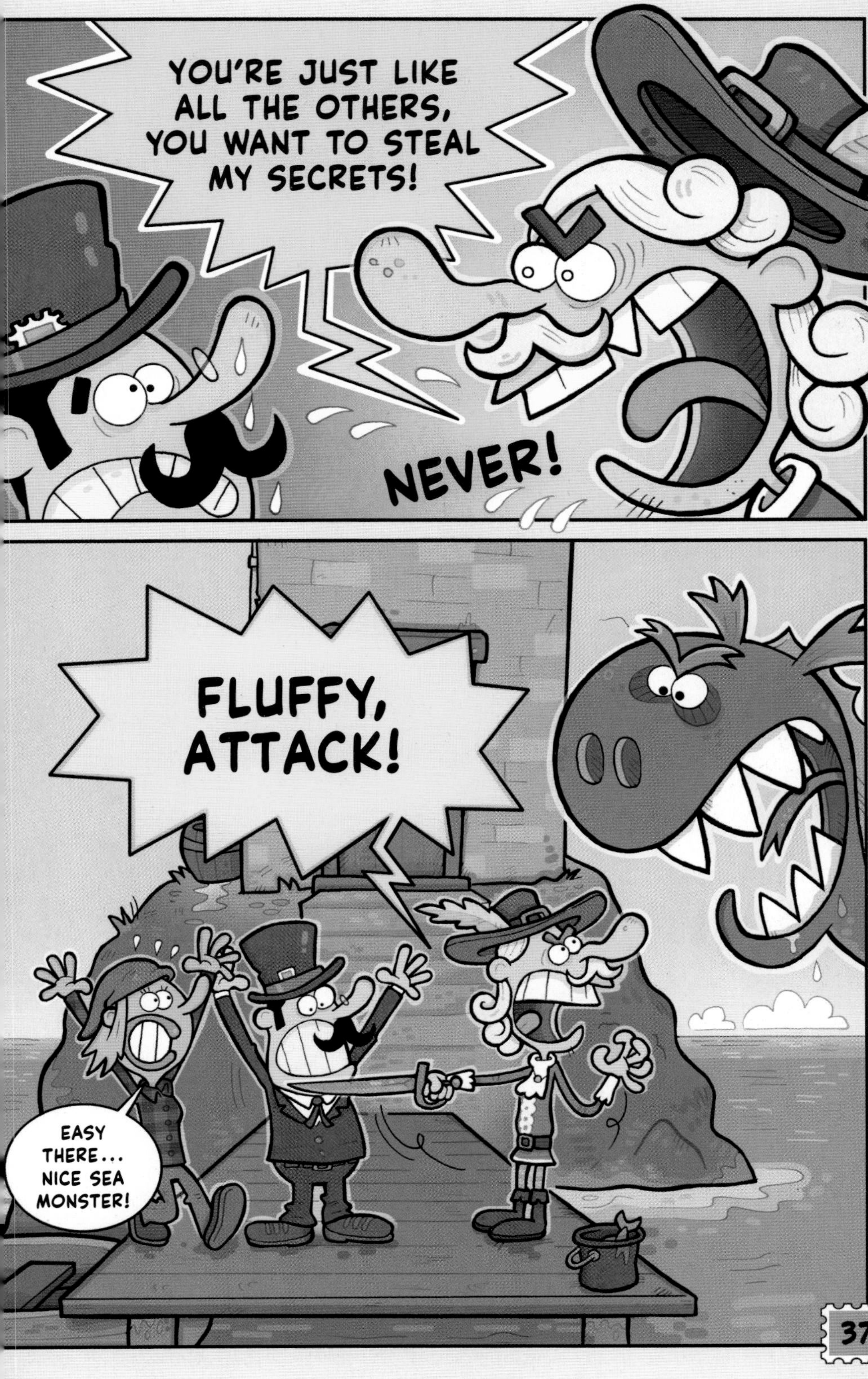
YOU'RE JUST LIKE ALL THE OTHERS, YOU WANT TO STEAL MY SECRETS!
NEVER!
FLUFFY, ATTACK!
EASY THERE... NICE SEA MONSTER!

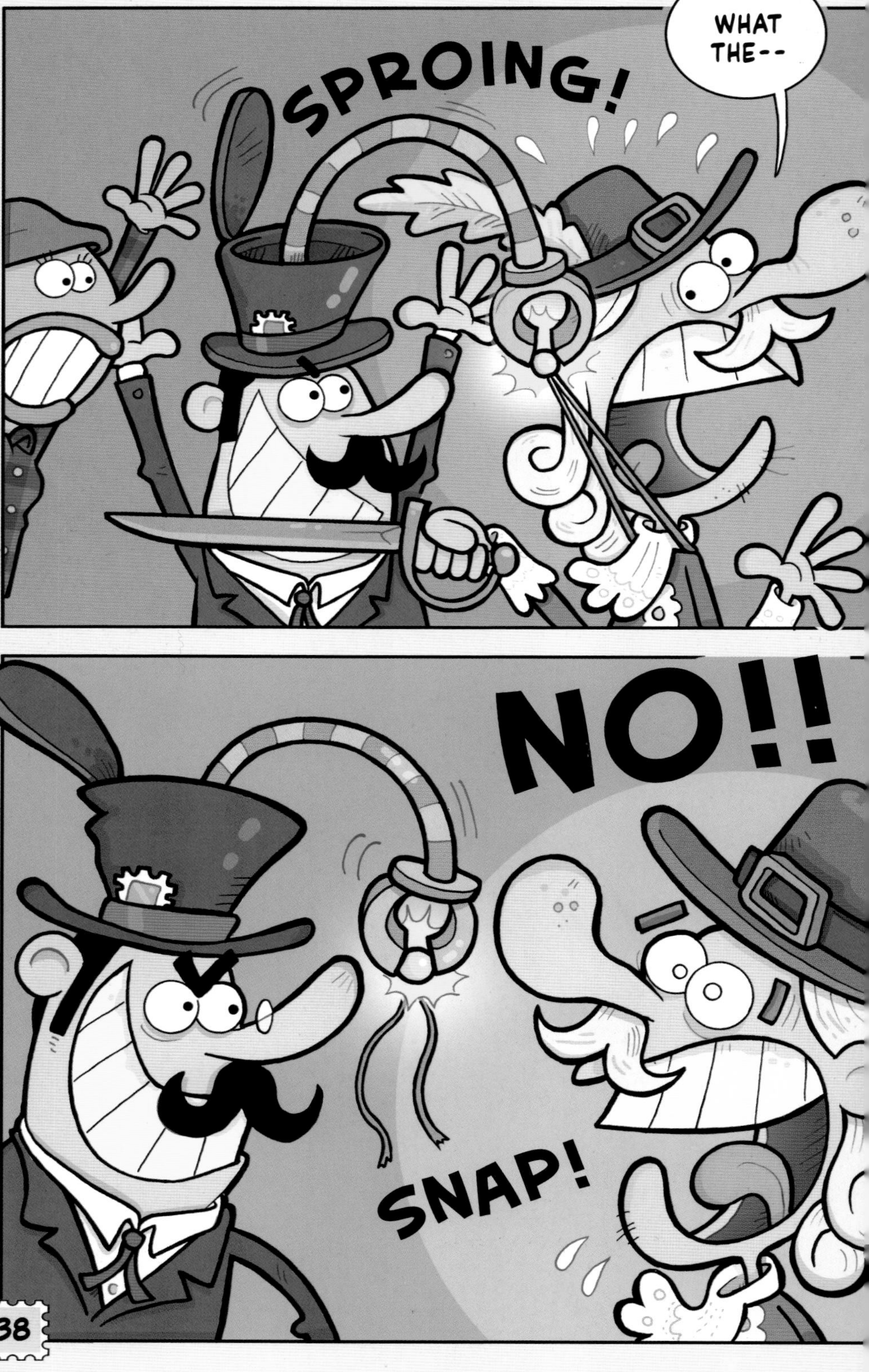
SPROING!
WHAT THE--
NO!!
SNAP!

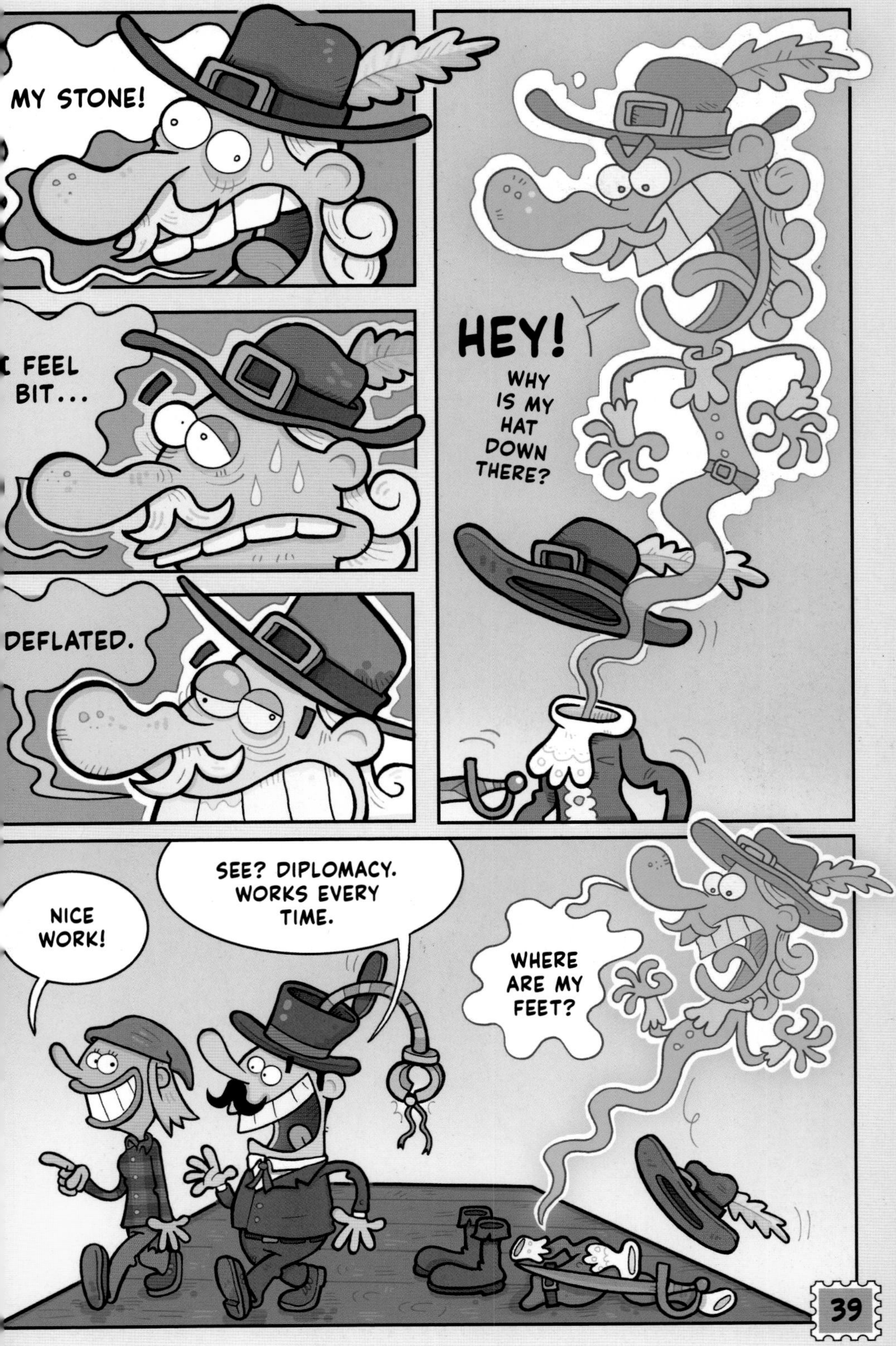
MY STONE!
I FEEL BIT...
DEFLATED.
HEY!
WHY IS MY HAT DOWN THERE?
NICE WORK!
SEE? DIPLOMACY. WORKS EVERY TIME.
WHERE ARE MY FEET?

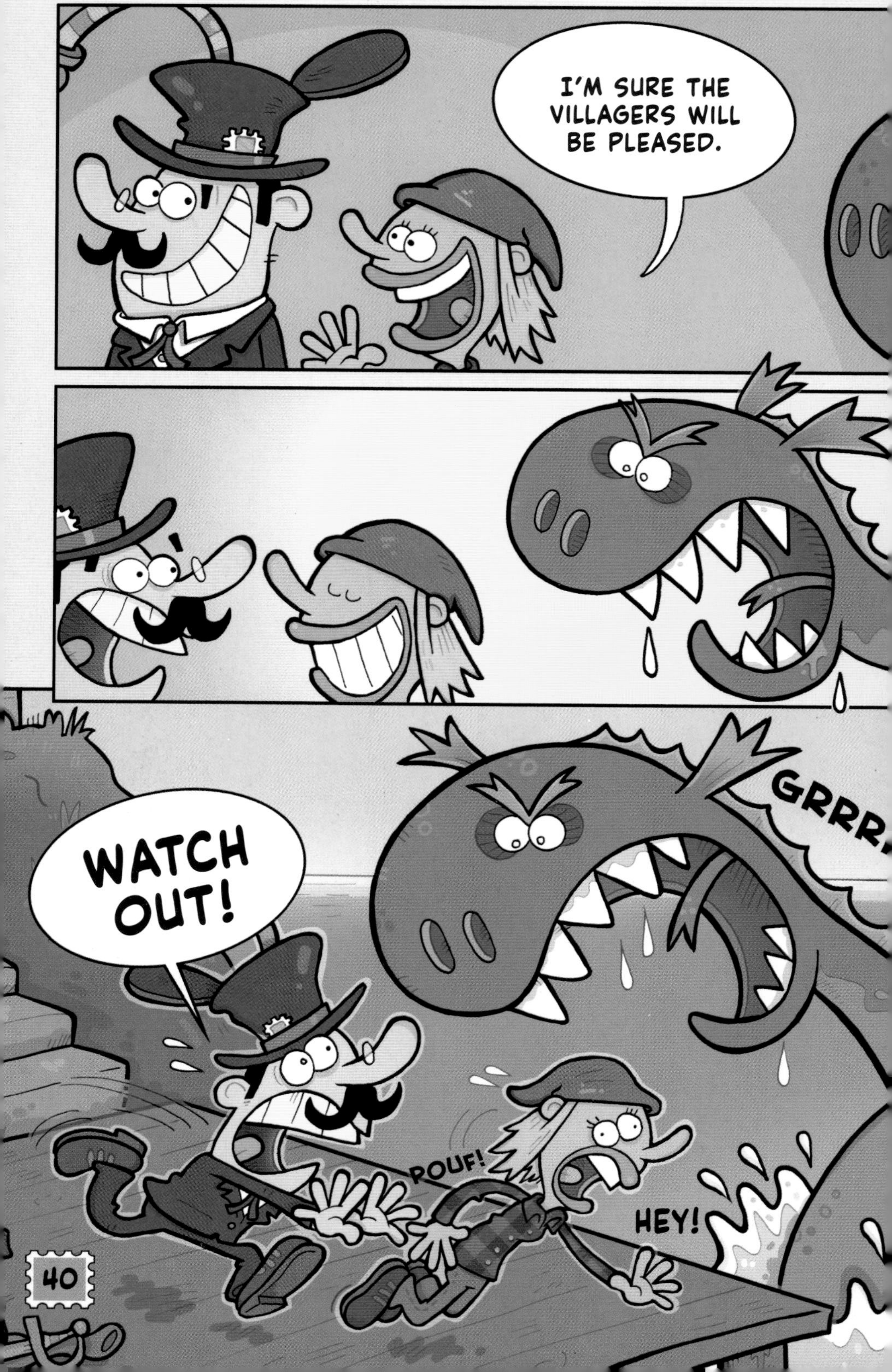
I'M SURE THE VILLAGERS WILL BE PLEASED.
WATCH OUT!
GRRR
POUF!
HEY!

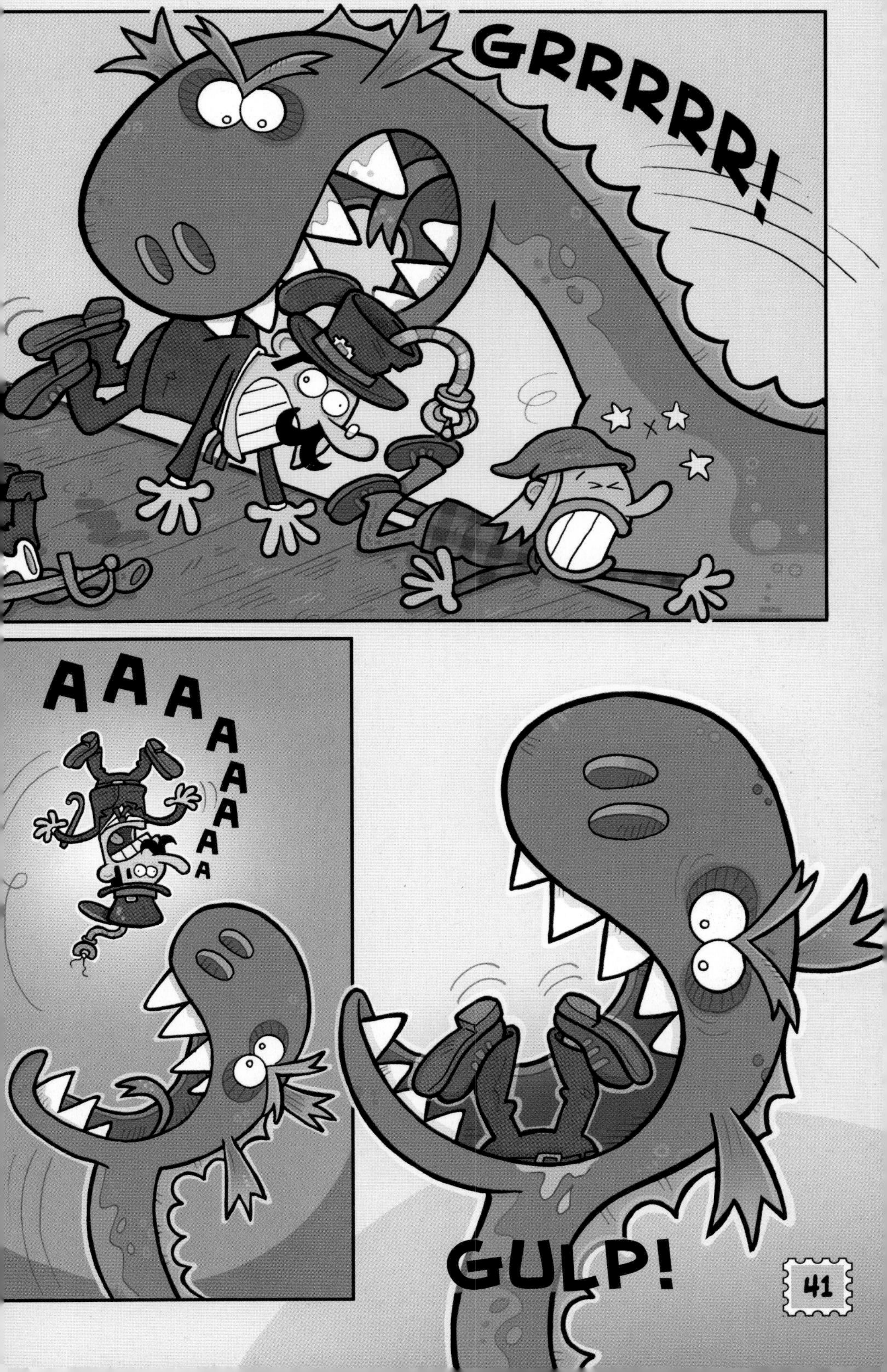
GRRRRRR!
AAAAAAAAA
GULP!

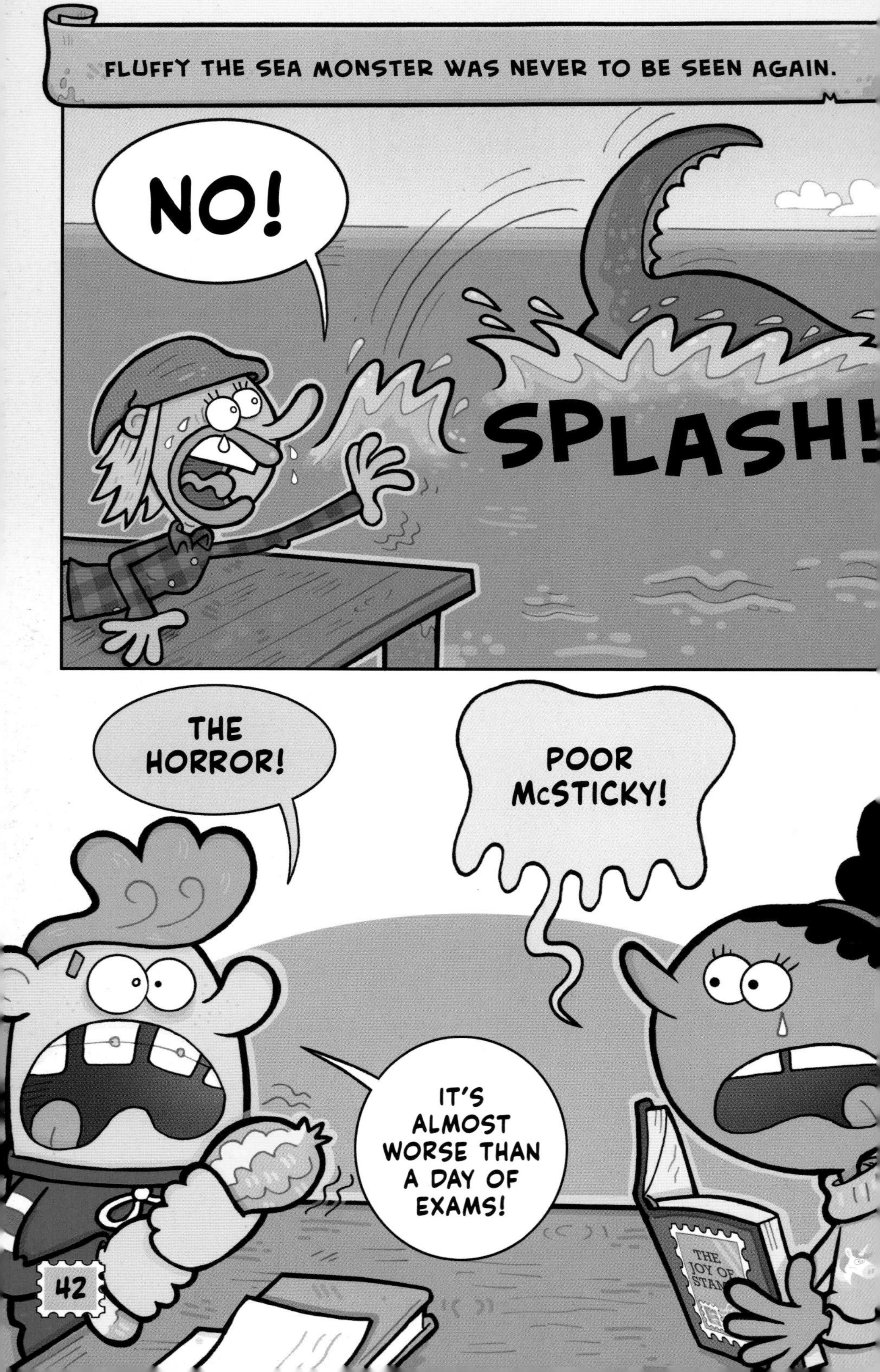
FLUFFY THE SEA MONSTER WAS NEVER TO BE SEEN AGAIN.
NO!
SPLASH!
THE HORROR!
POOR McSTICKY!
IT'S ALMOST WORSE THAN A DAY OF EXAMS!
THE JOY OF STAM

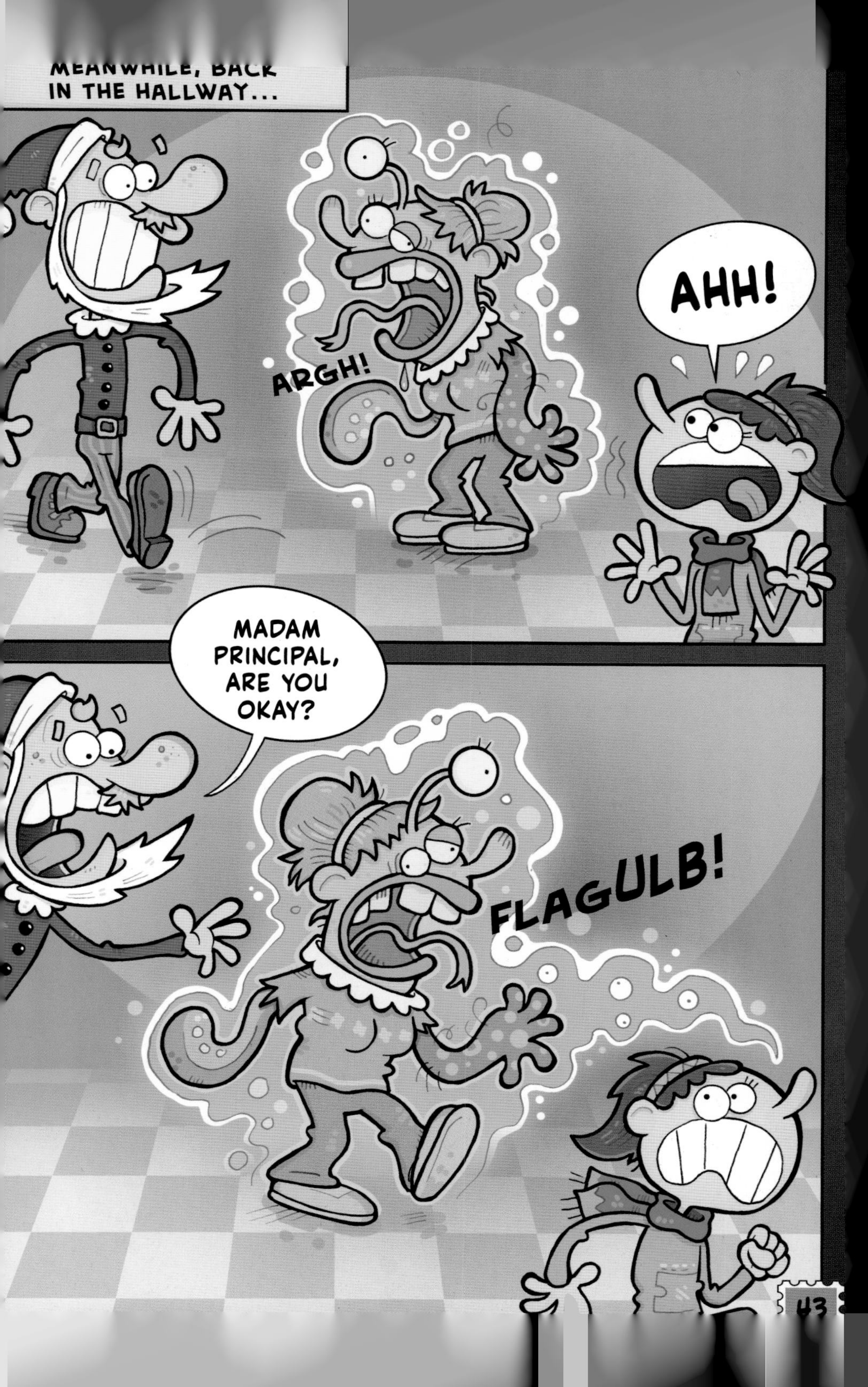
MEANWHILE, BACK IN THE HALLWAY...
ARGH!
AHH!
MADAM PRINCIPAL, ARE YOU OKAY?
FLAGULB!

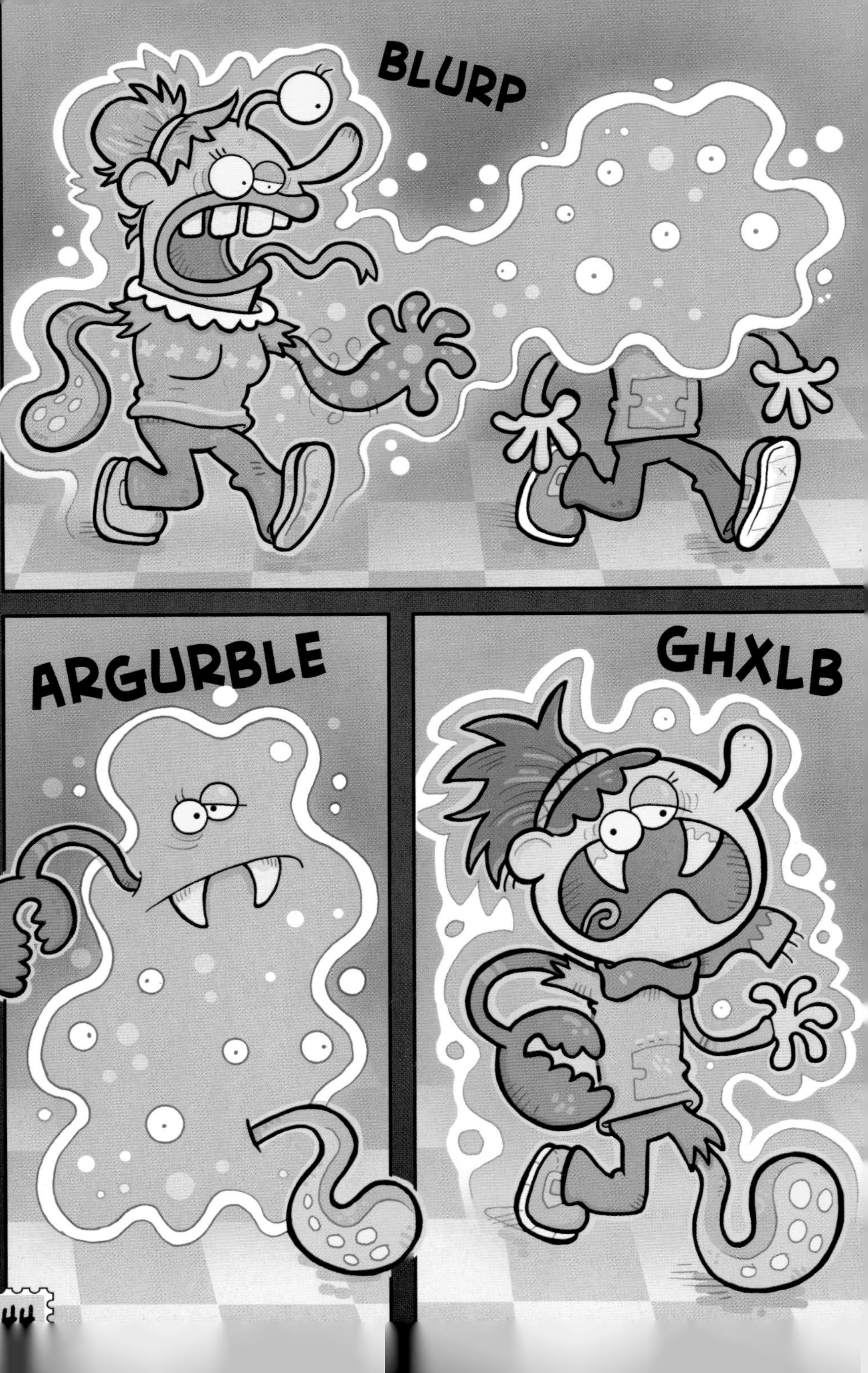
BLURP
ARGURBLE
GHXLB

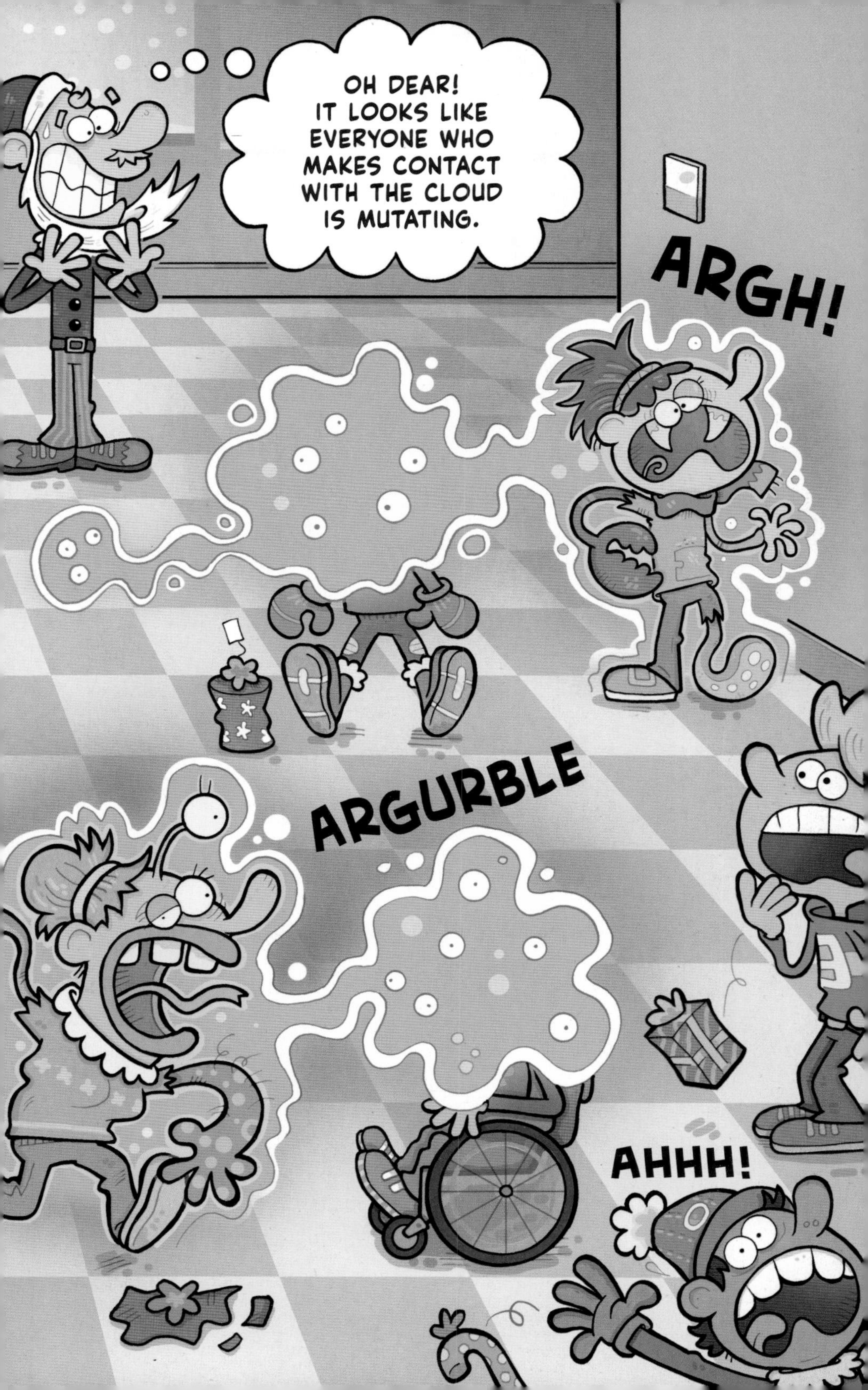
OH DEAR! IT LOOKS LIKE EVERYONE WHO MAKES CONTACT WITH THE CLOUD IS MUTATING.
ARGH!
ARGURBLE
AHHH!

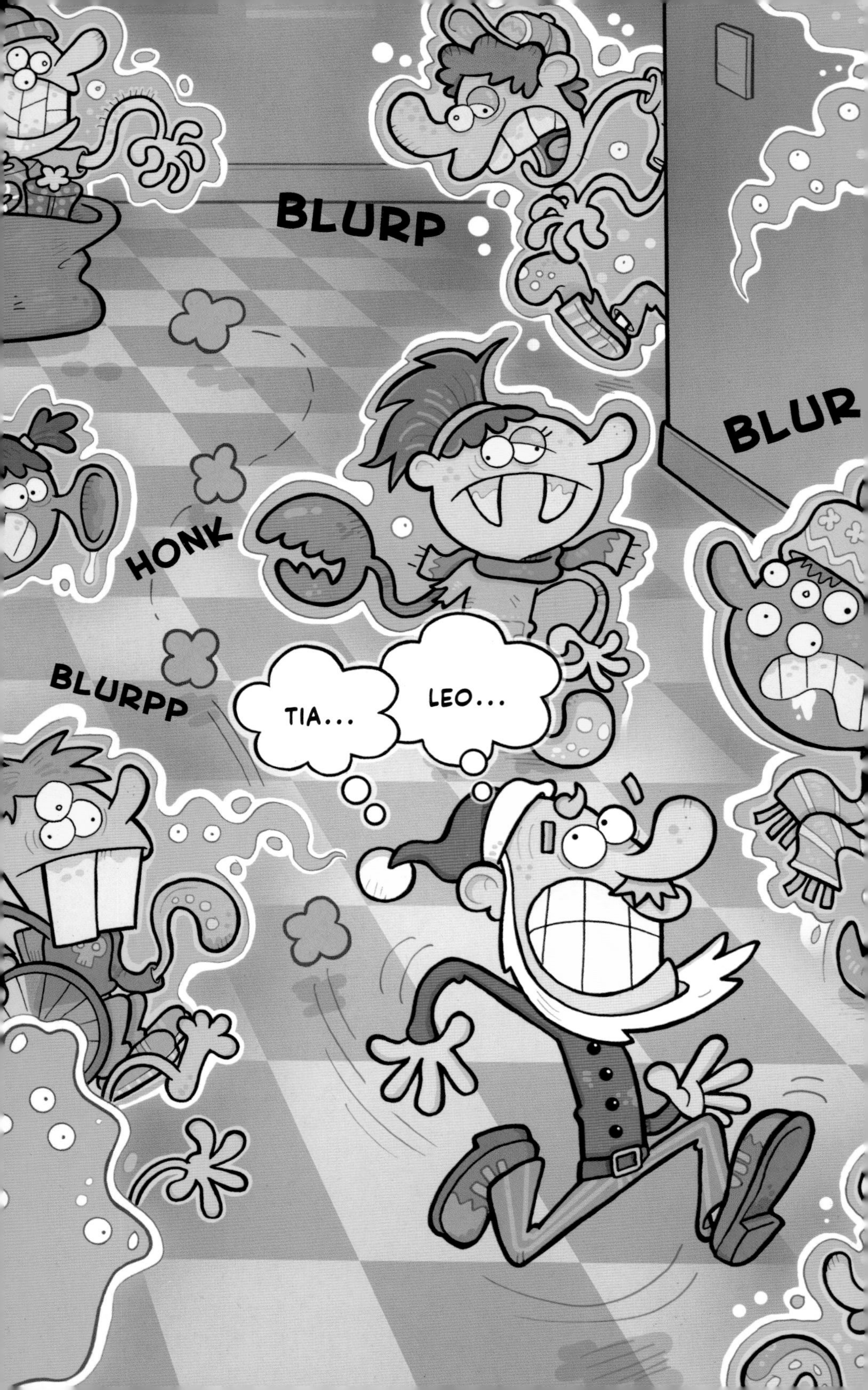
BLURP
BLUR
HONK
BLURPP
TIA...
LEO...

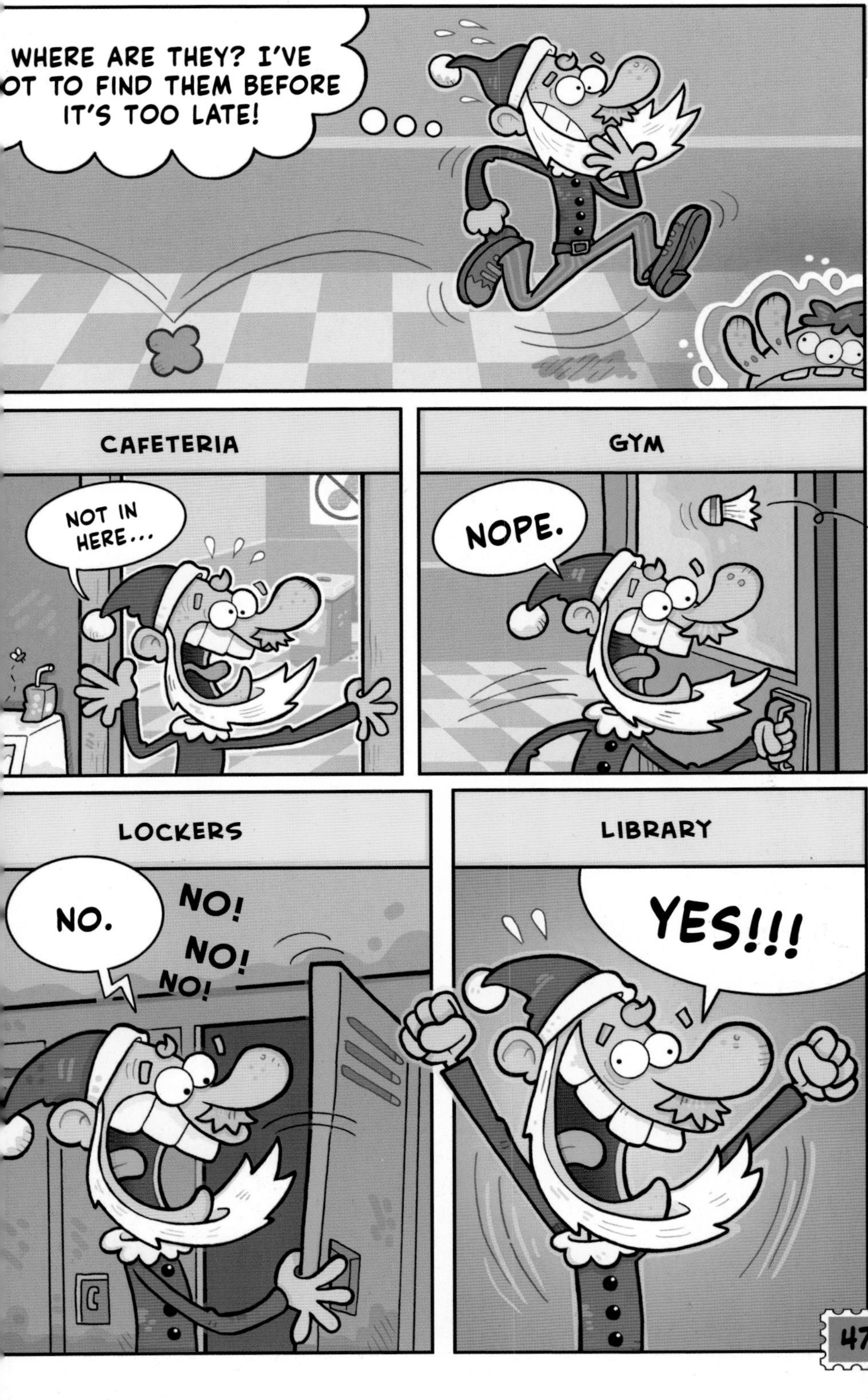
WHERE ARE THEY? I'VE
OT TO FIND THEM BEFORE
IT'S TOO LATE!
CAFETERIA
NOT IN HERE...
GYM
NOPE.
LOCKERS
NO.
NO!
NO!
NO!
LIBRARY
YES!!!

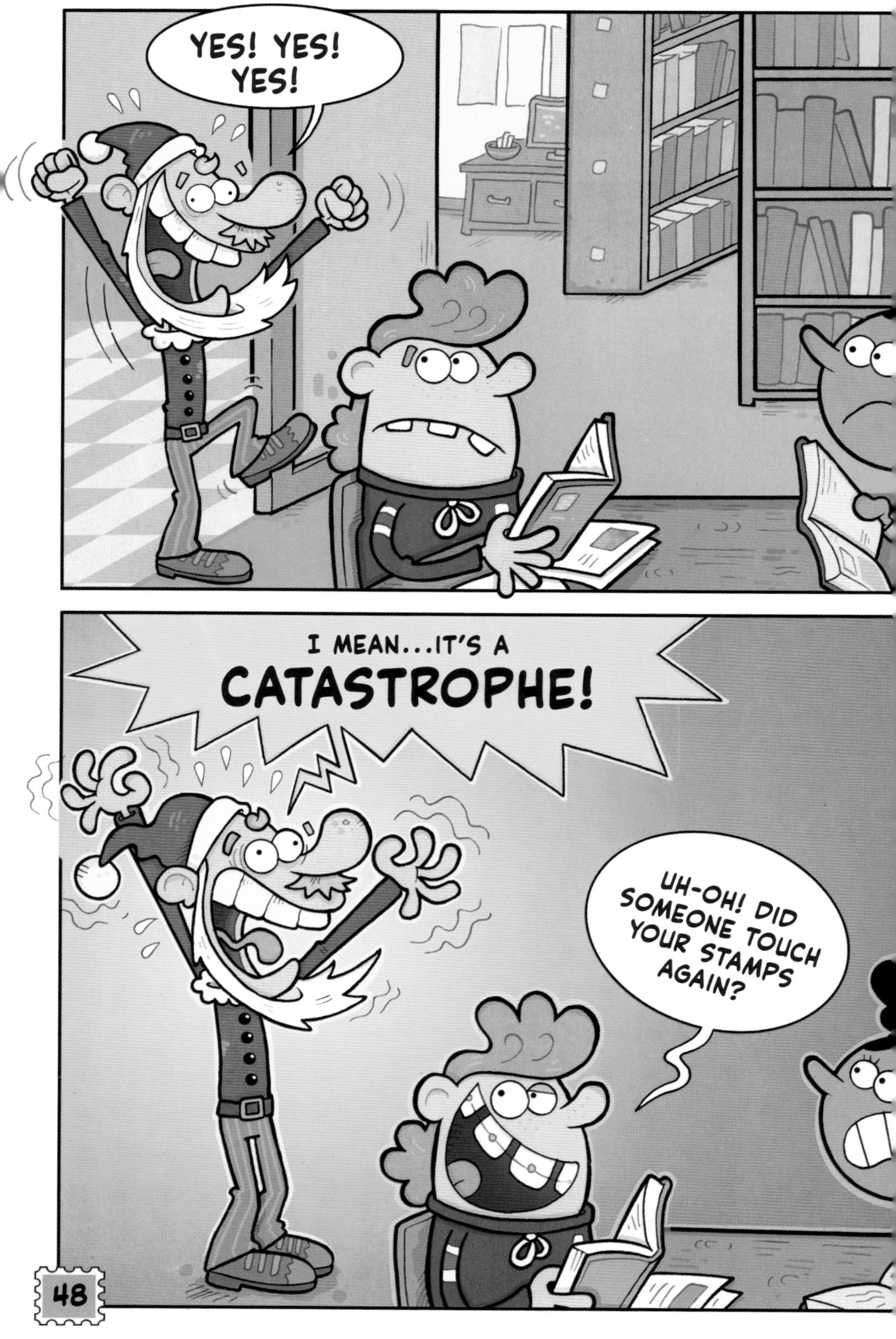
YES! YES! YES!
I MEAN...IT'S A CATASTROPHE!
UH-OH! DID SOMEONE TOUCH YOUR STAMPS AGAIN?

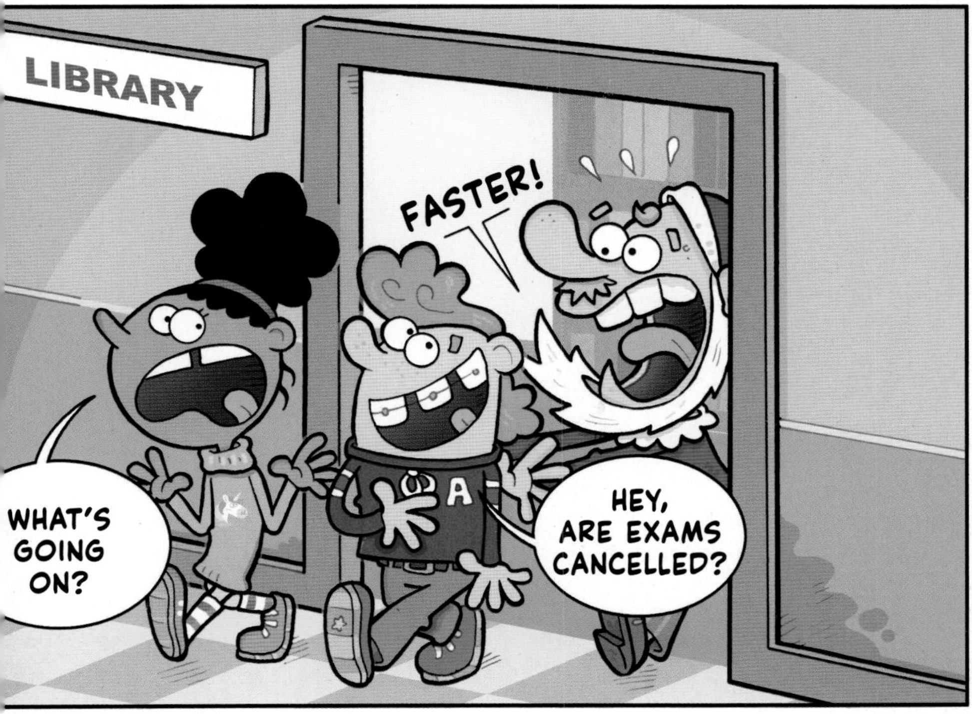
LIBRARY
FASTER!
WHAT'S GOING ON?
HEY, ARE EXAMS CANCELLED?

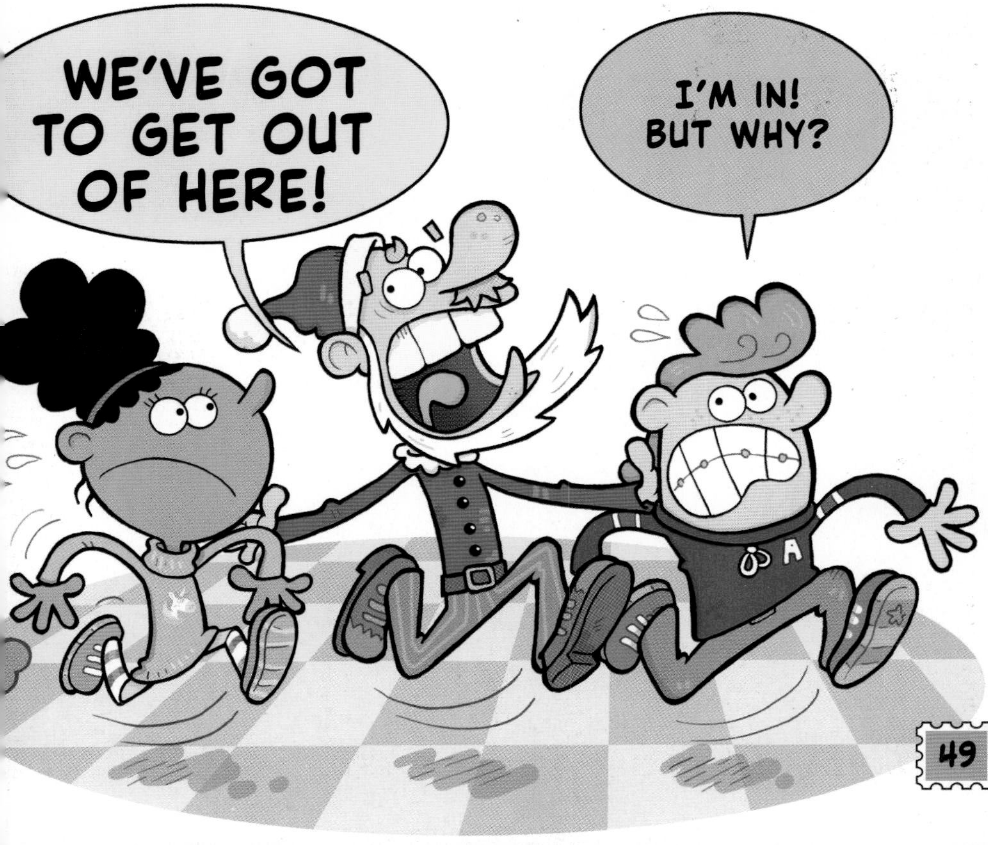
WE'VE GOT TO GET OUT OF HERE!
I'M IN! BUT WHY?

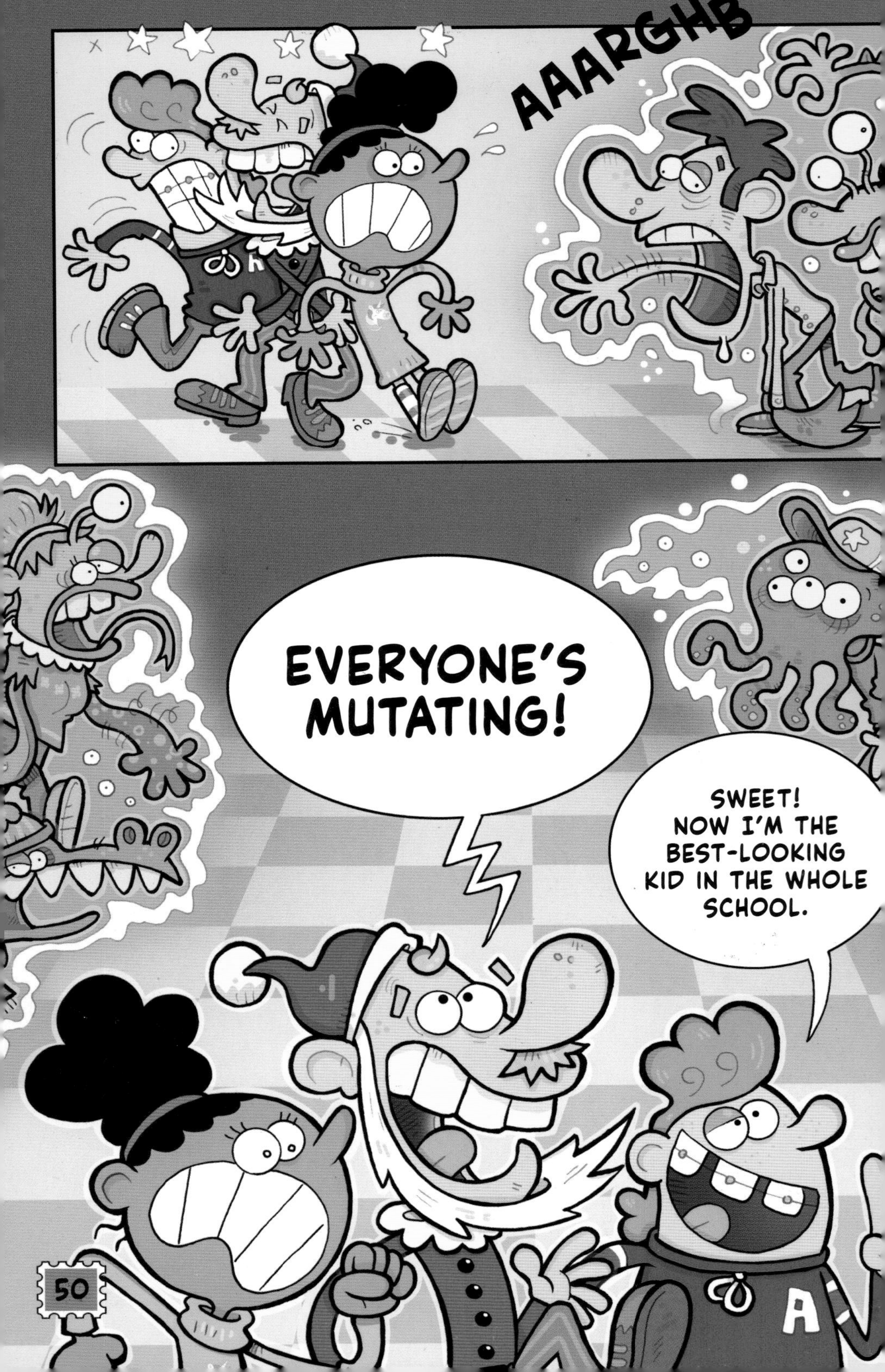
AAARGHB
EVERYONE'S MUTATING!
SWEET! NOW I'M THE BEST-LOOKING KID IN THE WHOLE SCHOOL.

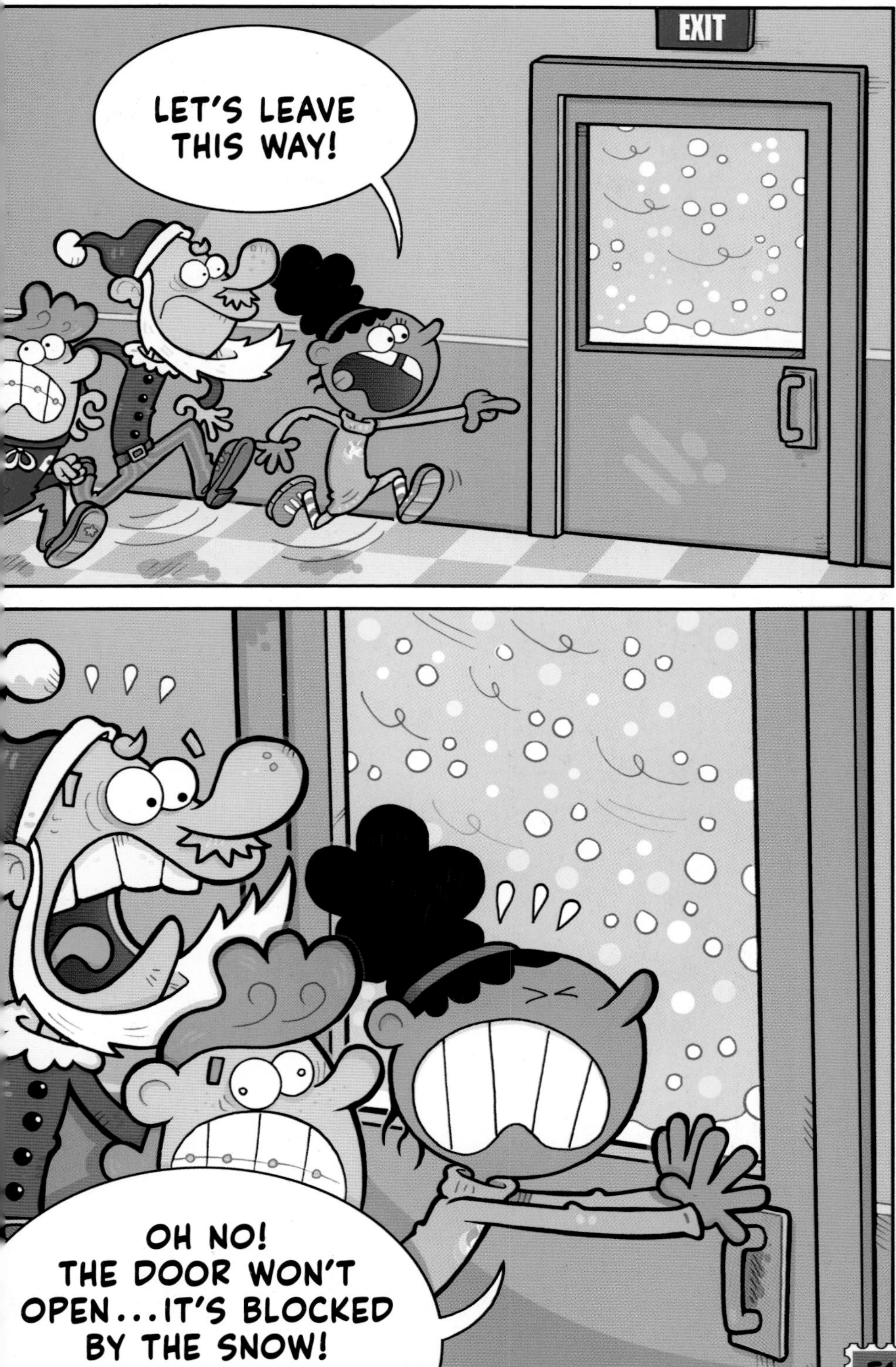
EXIT
LET'S LEAVE THIS WAY!
OH NO! THE DOOR WON'T OPEN...IT'S BLOCKED BY THE SNOW!

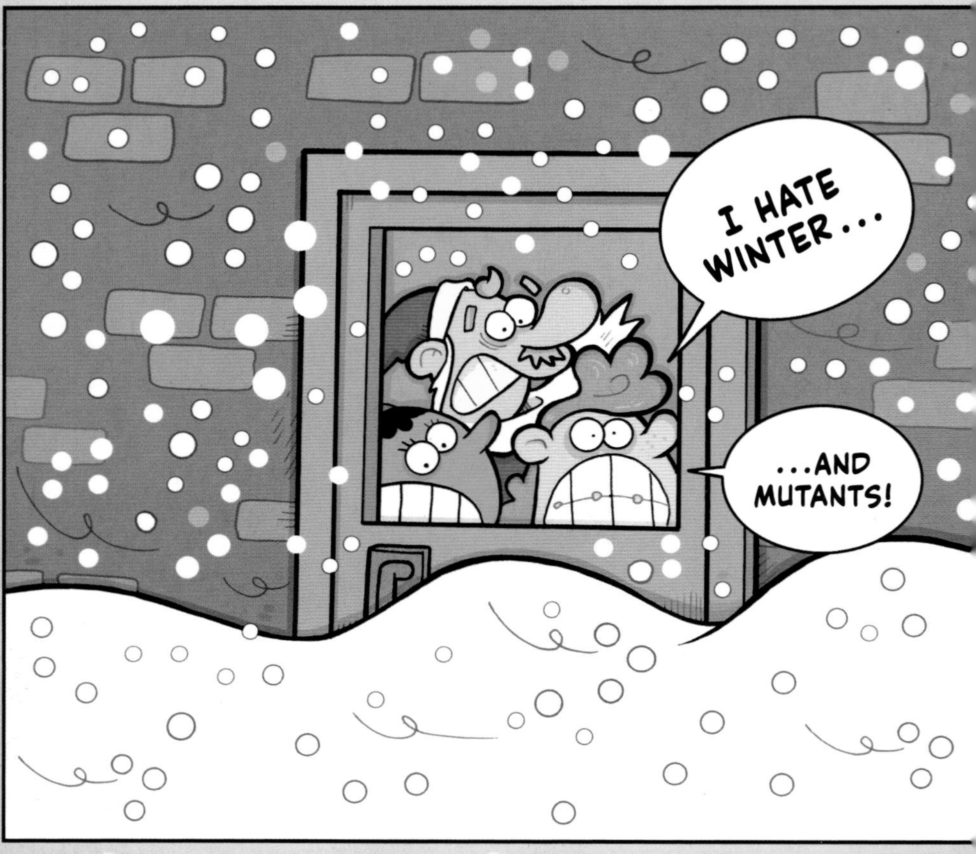
I HATE WINTER...
...AND MUTANTS!

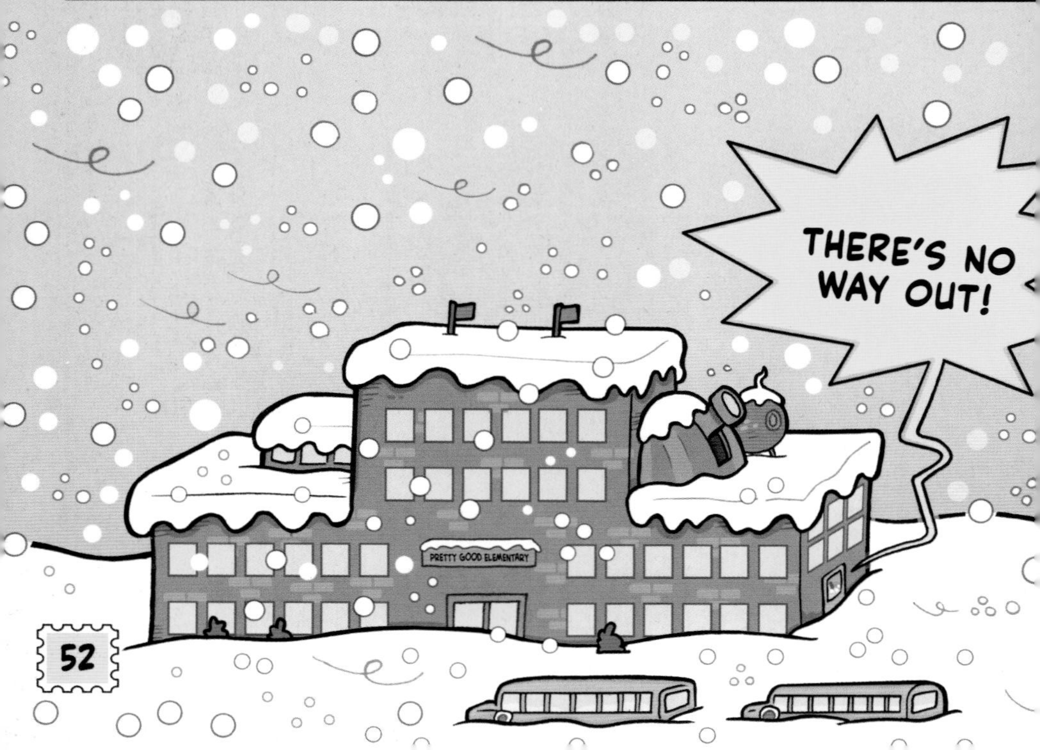
THERE'S NO WAY OUT!
PRETTY GOOD ELEMENTARY

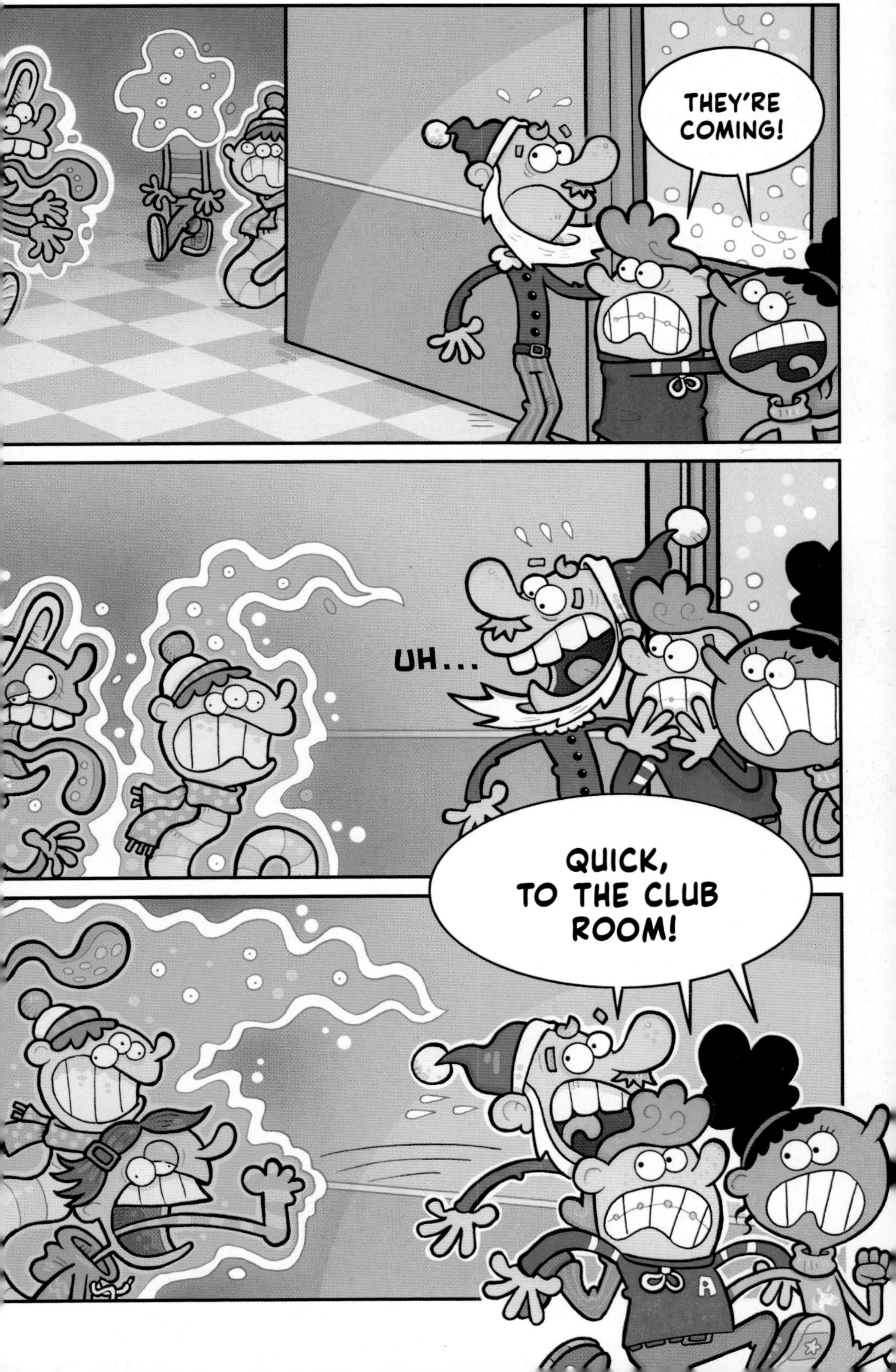
THEY'RE COMING!
UH...
QUICK, TO THE CLUB ROOM!

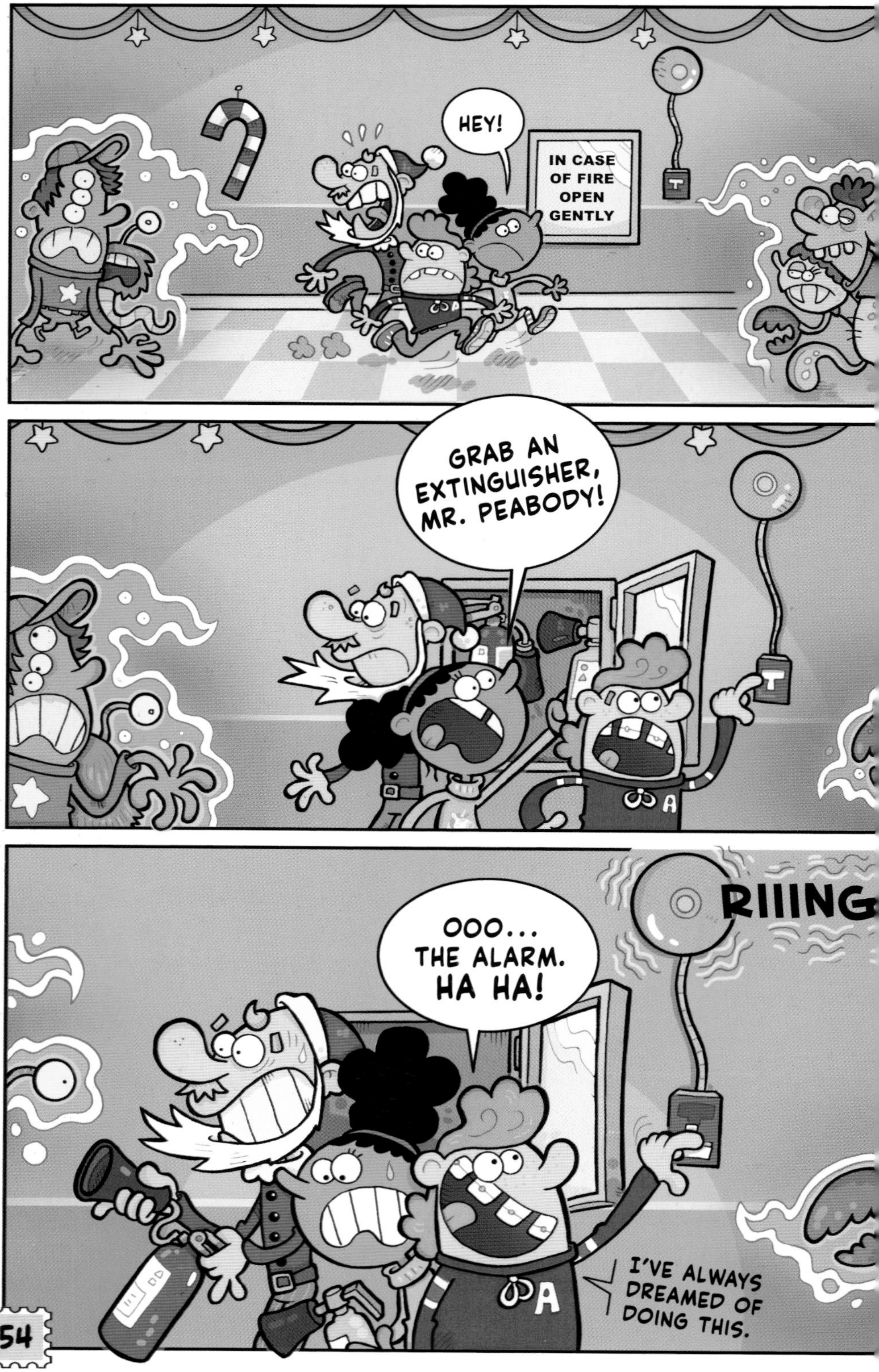
HEY!
IN CASE OF FIRE OPEN GENTLY
GRAB AN EXTINGUISHER, MR. PEABODY!
RIIING
OOO... THE ALARM. HA HA!
I'VE ALWAYS DREAMED OF DOING THIS.

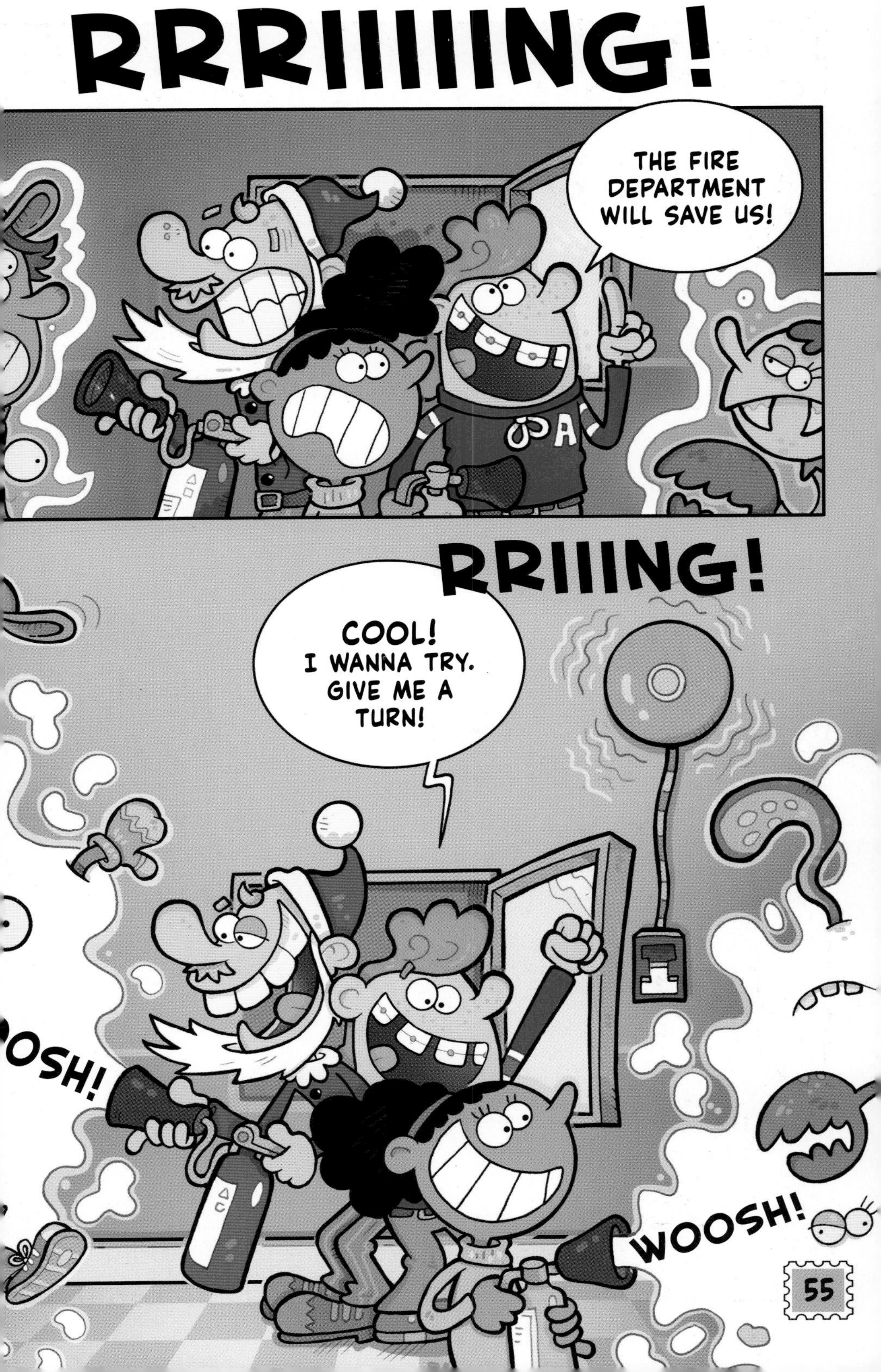
RRRIIIIING!
THE FIRE DEPARTMENT WILL SAVE US!
RRIIING!
COOL! I WANNA TRY. GIVE ME A TURN!
OSH!
WOOSH!

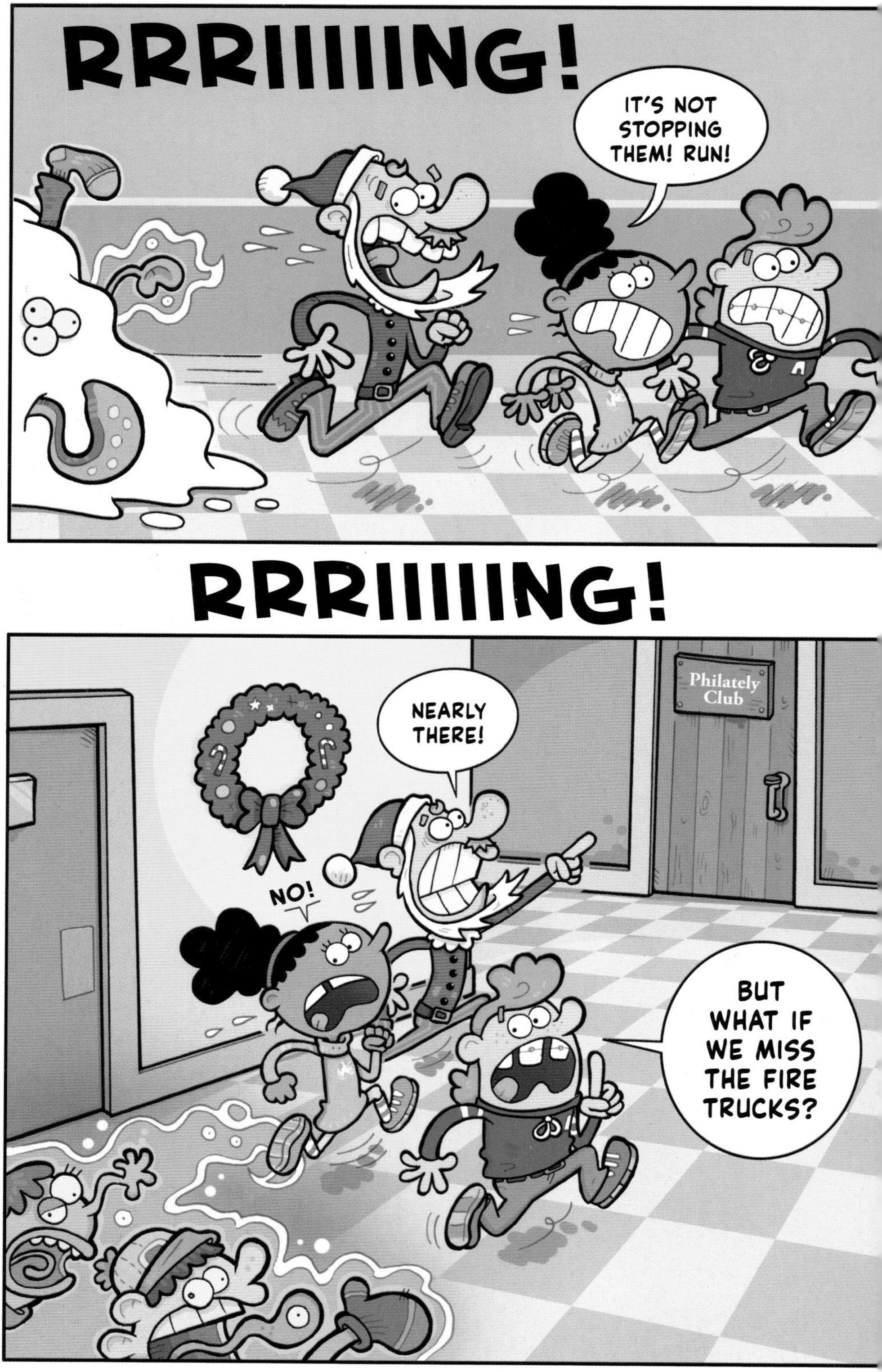
RRRIIIIING!
IT'S NOT STOPPING THEM! RUN!
RRRIIIIING!
NEARLY THERE!
NO!
Philately Club
BUT WHAT IF WE MISS THE FIRE TRUCKS?

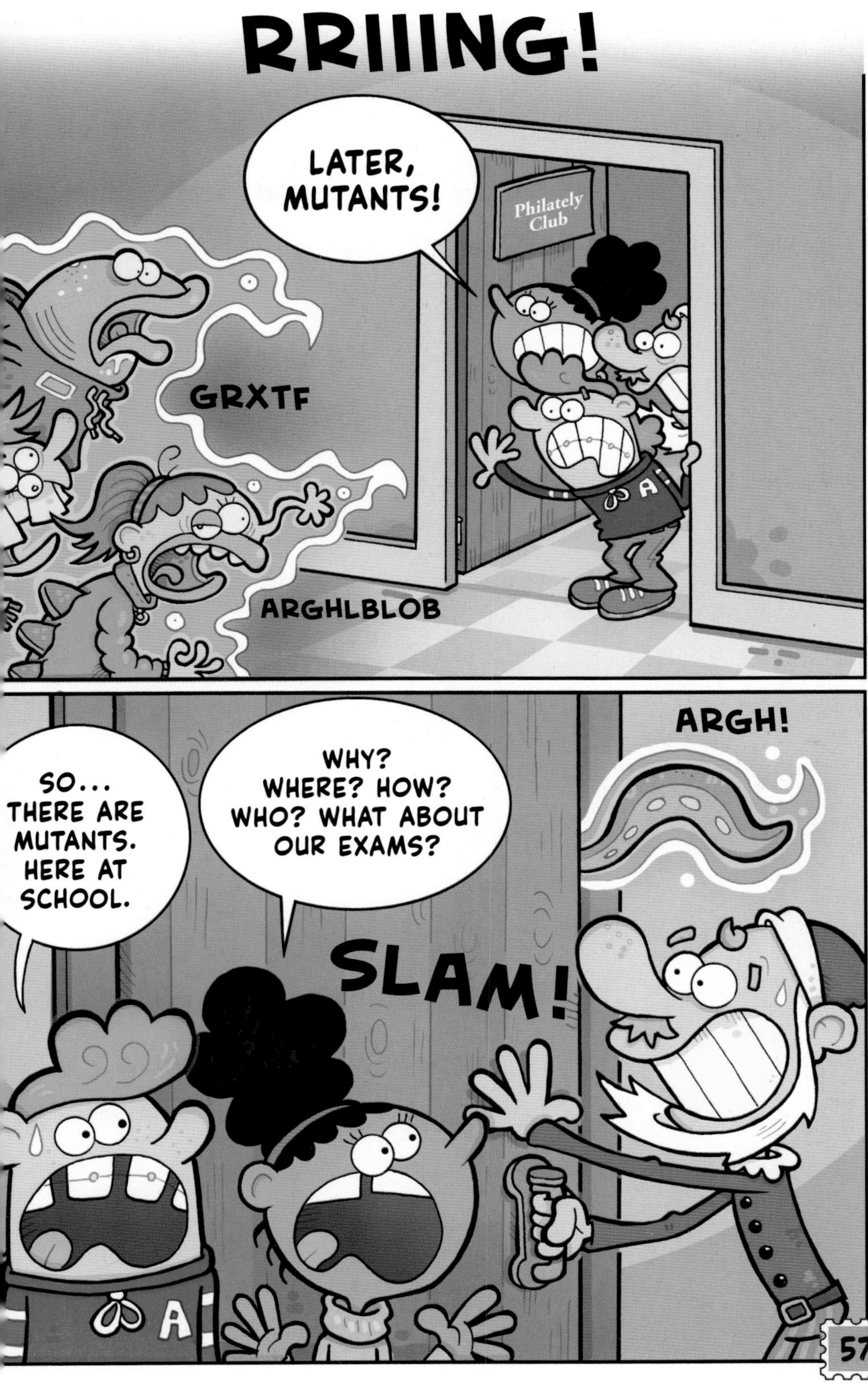
RRIIING!
LATER, MUTANTS!
Philately Club
GRXTF
ARGHLBLOB
ARGH!
SO... THERE ARE MUTANTS. HERE AT SCHOOL.
WHY? WHERE? HOW? WHO? WHAT ABOUT OUR EXAMS?
SLAM!

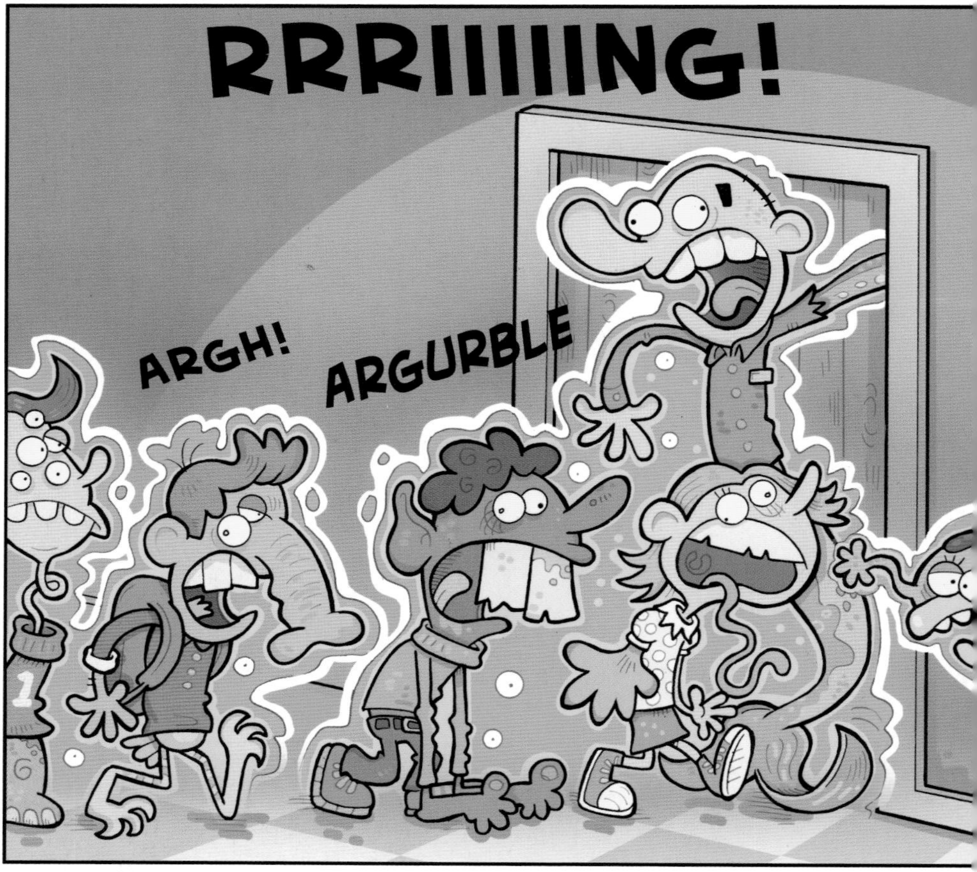
RRRIIIIIING!
ARGH!
ARGURBLE

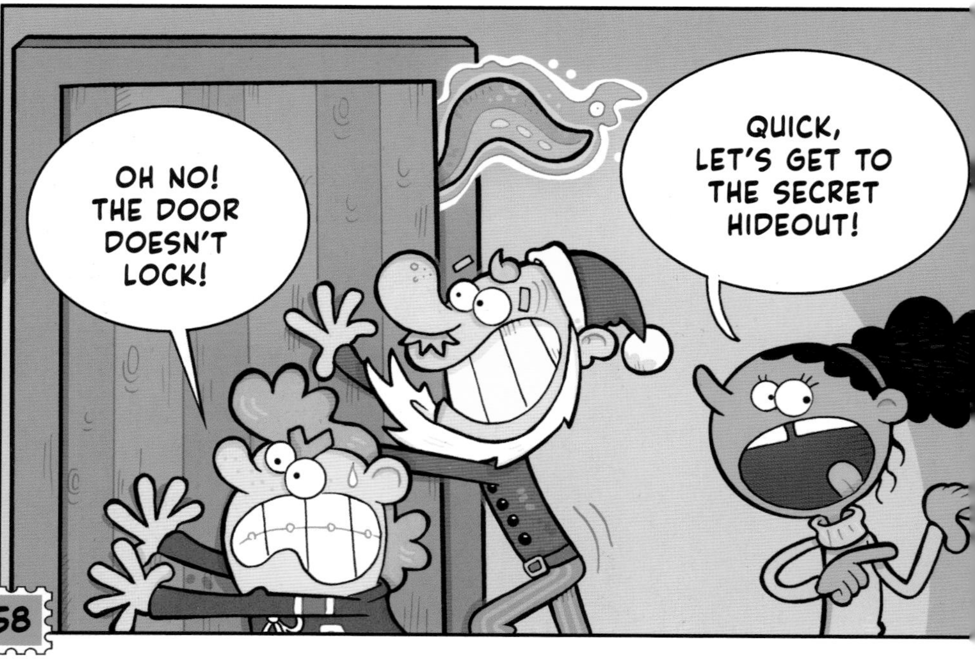
OH NO! THE DOOR DOESN'T LOCK!
QUICK, LET'S GET TO THE SECRET HIDEOUT!

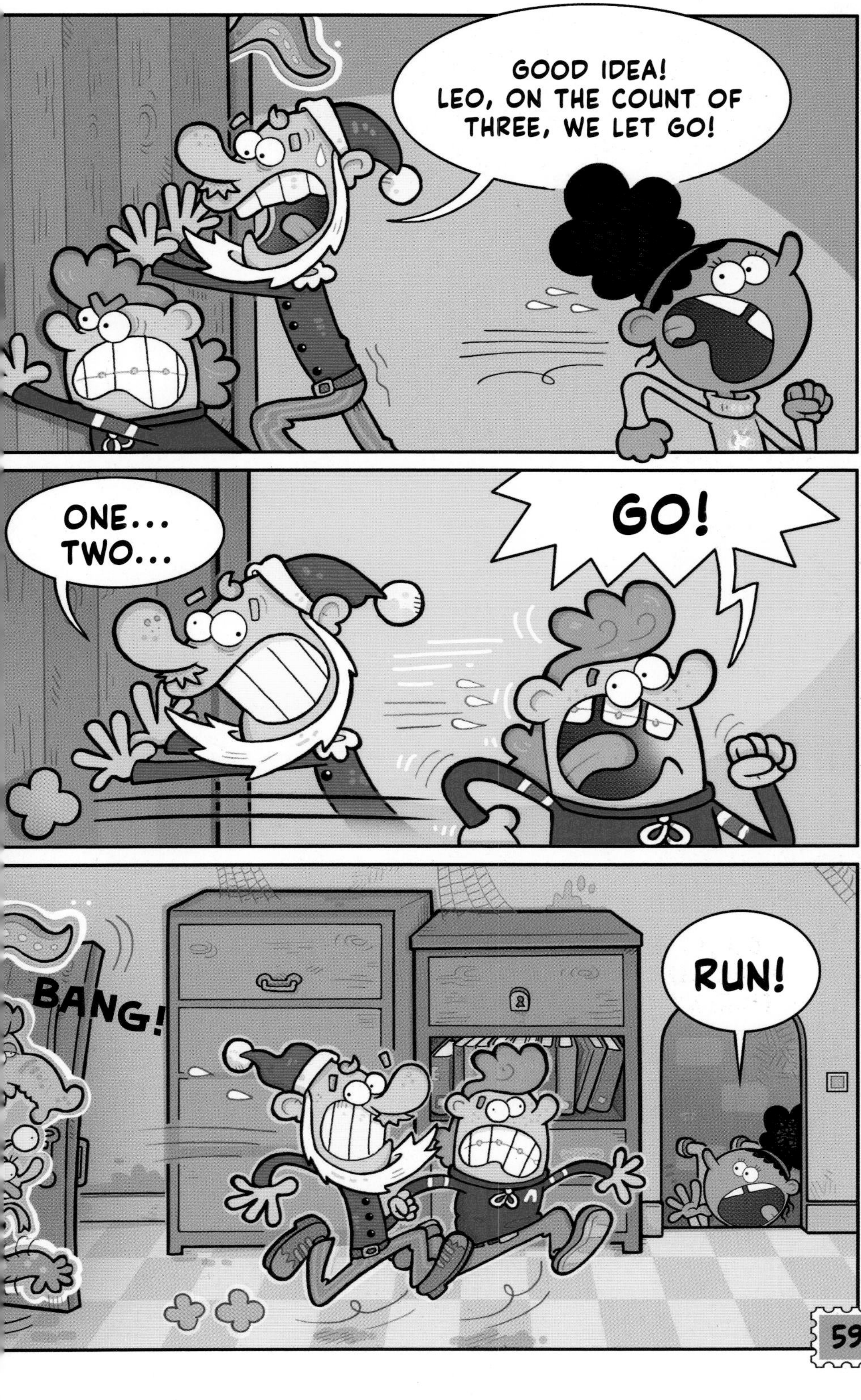
GOOD IDEA!
LEO, ON THE COUNT OF THREE, WE LET GO!
ONE... TWO...
GO!
BANG!
RUN!

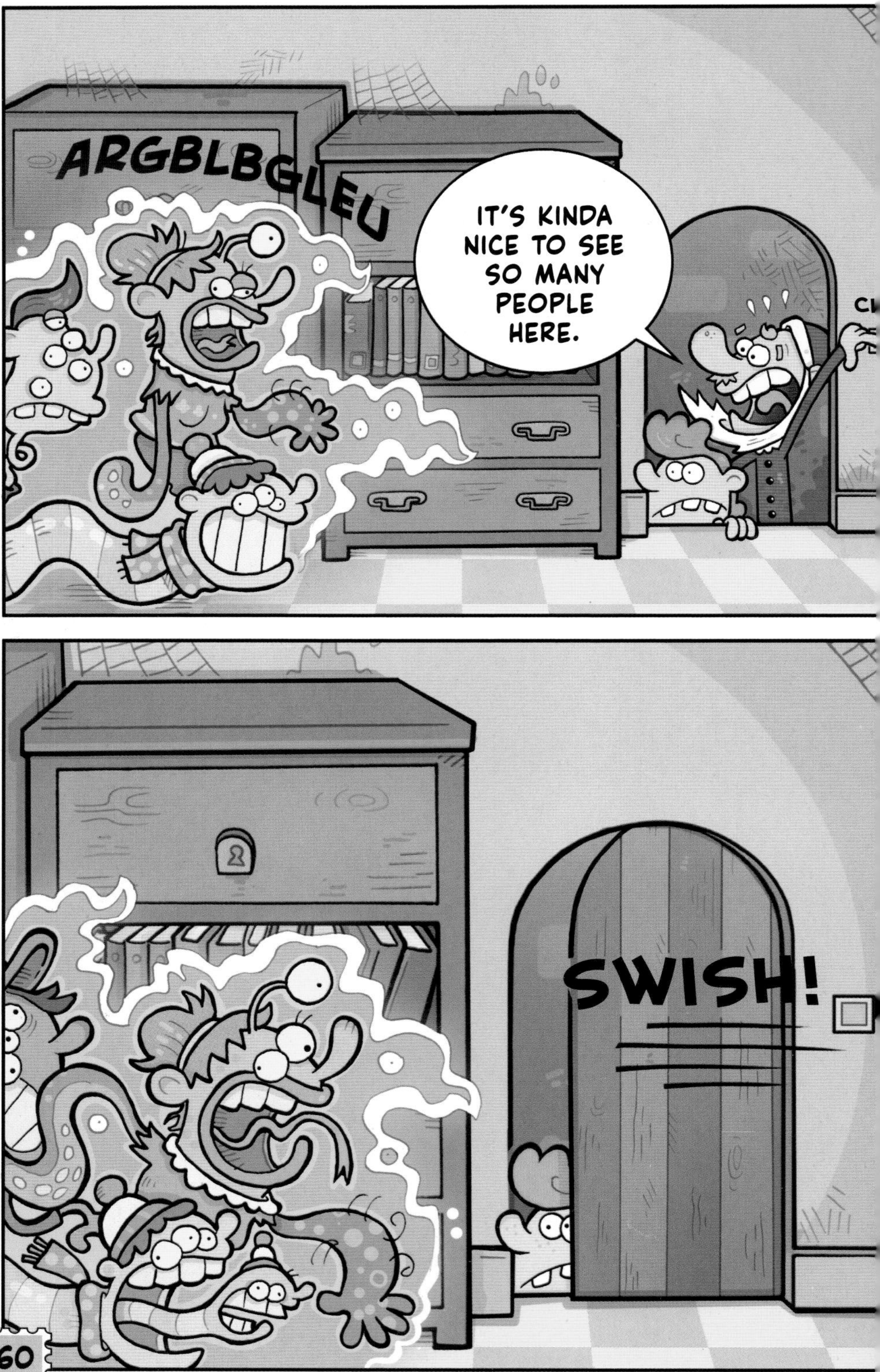
ARGBLBGLEU
IT'S KINDA NICE TO SEE SO MANY PEOPLE HERE.
SWISH!

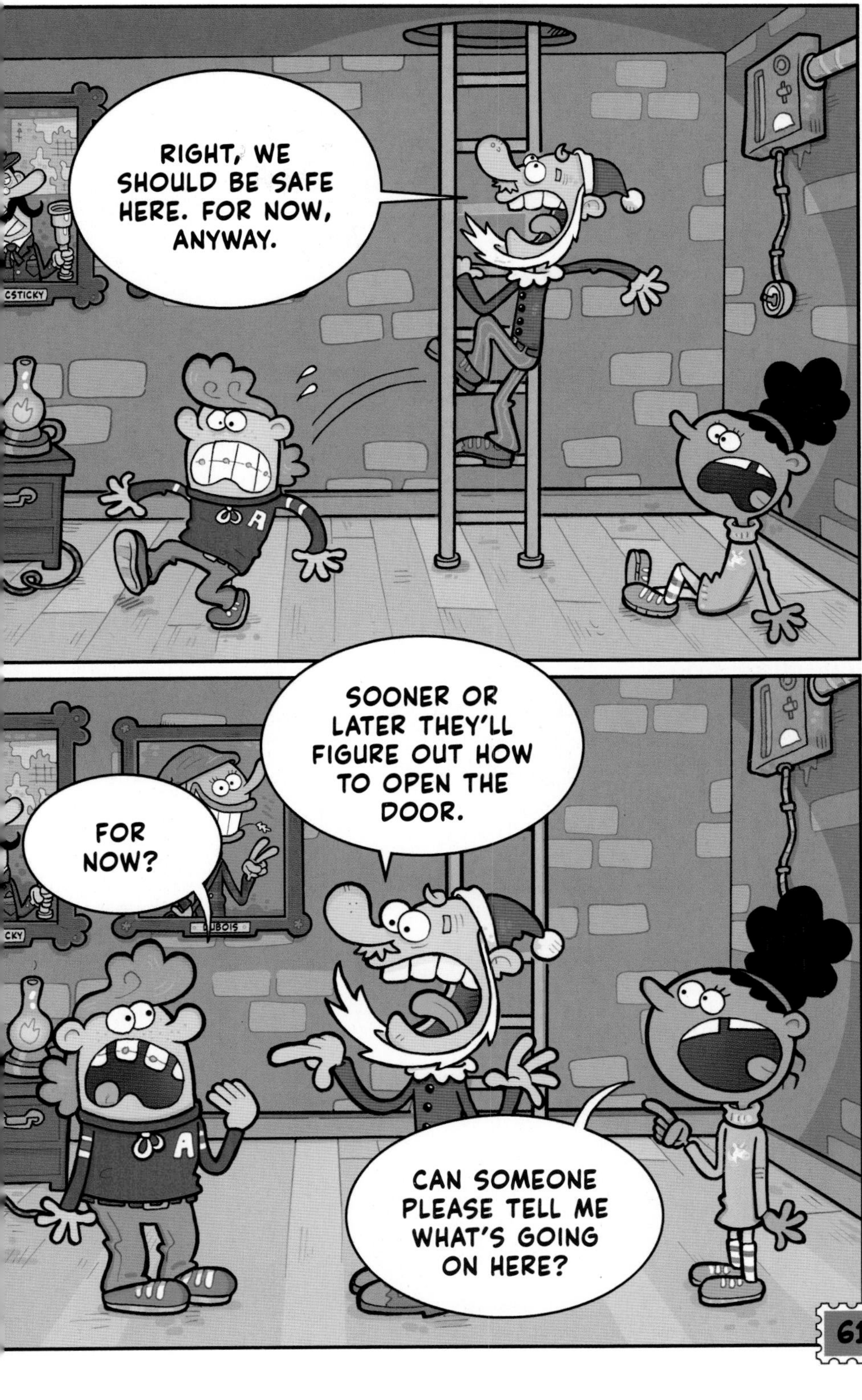
RIGHT, WE SHOULD BE SAFE HERE. FOR NOW, ANYWAY.
CSTICKY
FOR NOW?
SOONER OR LATER THEY'LL FIGURE OUT HOW TO OPEN THE DOOR.
CAN SOMEONE PLEASE TELL ME WHAT'S GOING ON HERE?

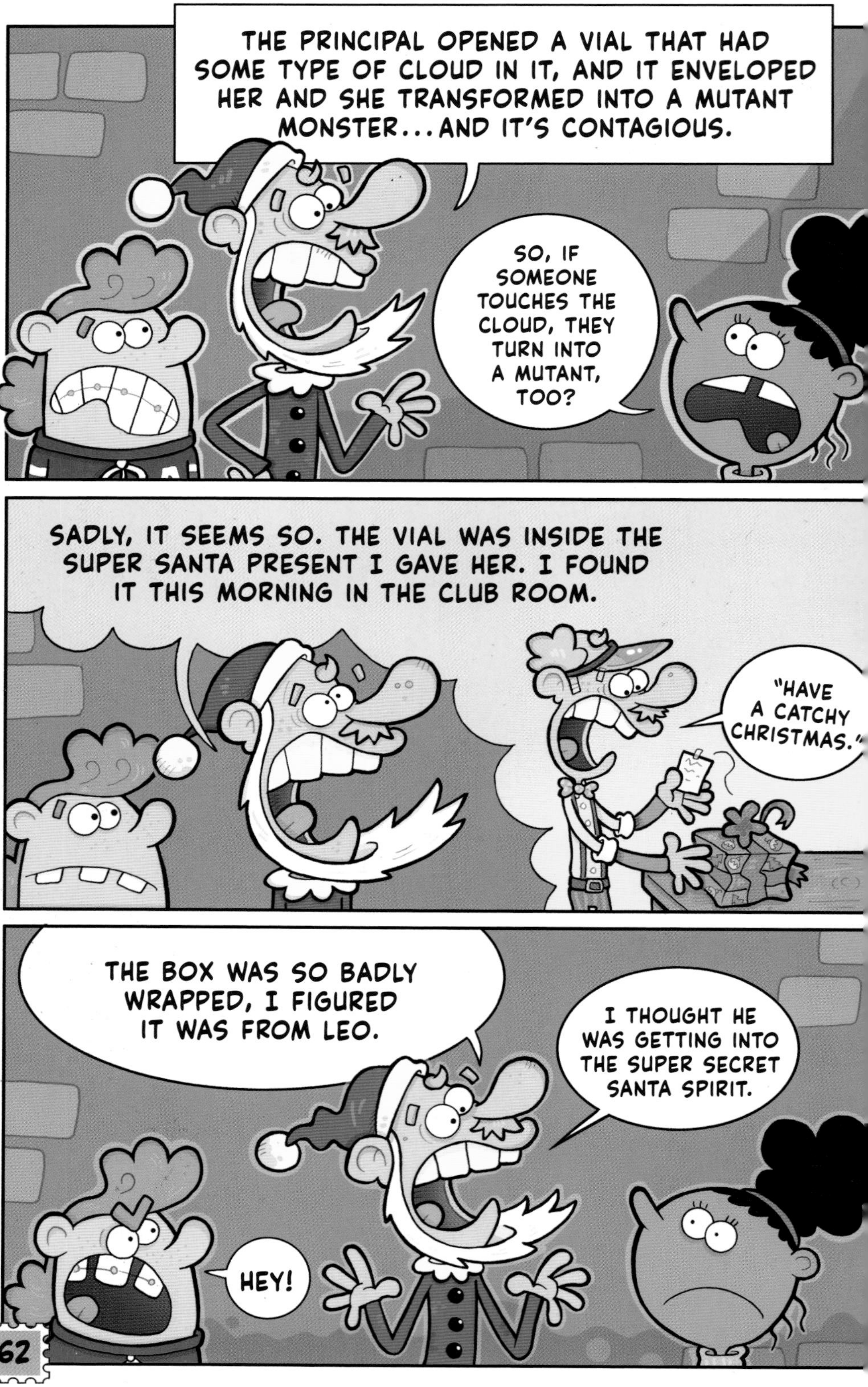
THE PRINCIPAL OPENED A VIAL THAT HAD SOME TYPE OF CLOUD IN IT, AND IT ENVELOPED HER AND SHE TRANSFORMED INTO A MUTANT MONSTER...AND IT'S CONTAGIOUS.
SO, IF SOMEONE TOUCHES THE CLOUD, THEY TURN INTO A MUTANT, TOO?
SADLY, IT SEEMS SO. THE VIAL WAS INSIDE THE SUPER SANTA PRESENT I GAVE HER. I FOUND IT THIS MORNING IN THE CLUB ROOM.
"HAVE A CATCHY CHRISTMAS."
THE BOX WAS SO BADLY WRAPPED, I FIGURED IT WAS FROM LEO.
I THOUGHT HE WAS GETTING INTO THE SUPER SECRET SANTA SPIRIT.
HEY!

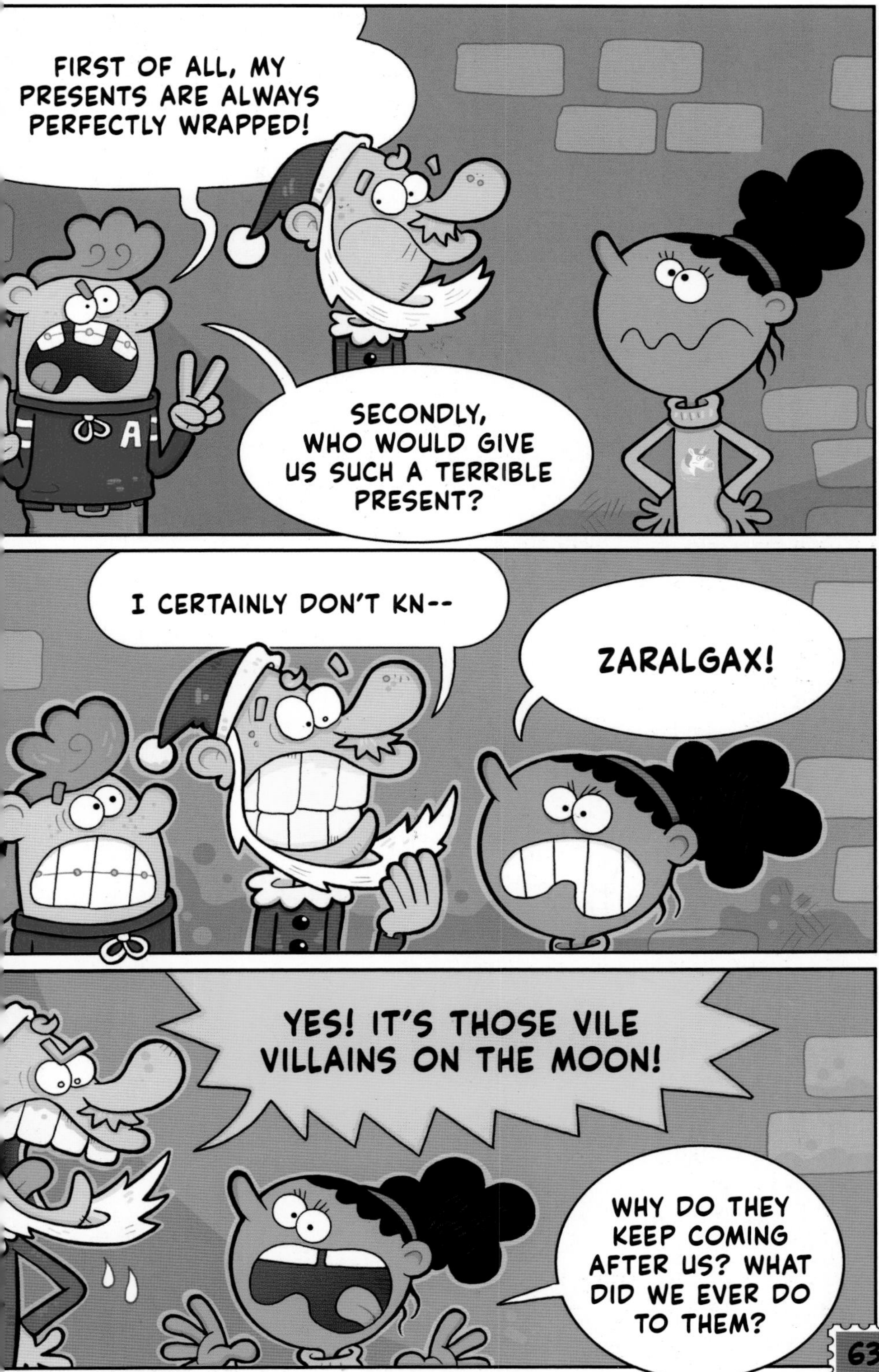
FIRST OF ALL, MY PRESENTS ARE ALWAYS PERFECTLY WRAPPED!
SECONDLY, WHO WOULD GIVE US SUCH A TERRIBLE PRESENT?
I CERTAINLY DON'T KN--
ZARALGAX!
YES! IT'S THOSE VILE VILLAINS ON THE MOON!
WHY DO THEY KEEP COMING AFTER US? WHAT DID WE EVER DO TO THEM?

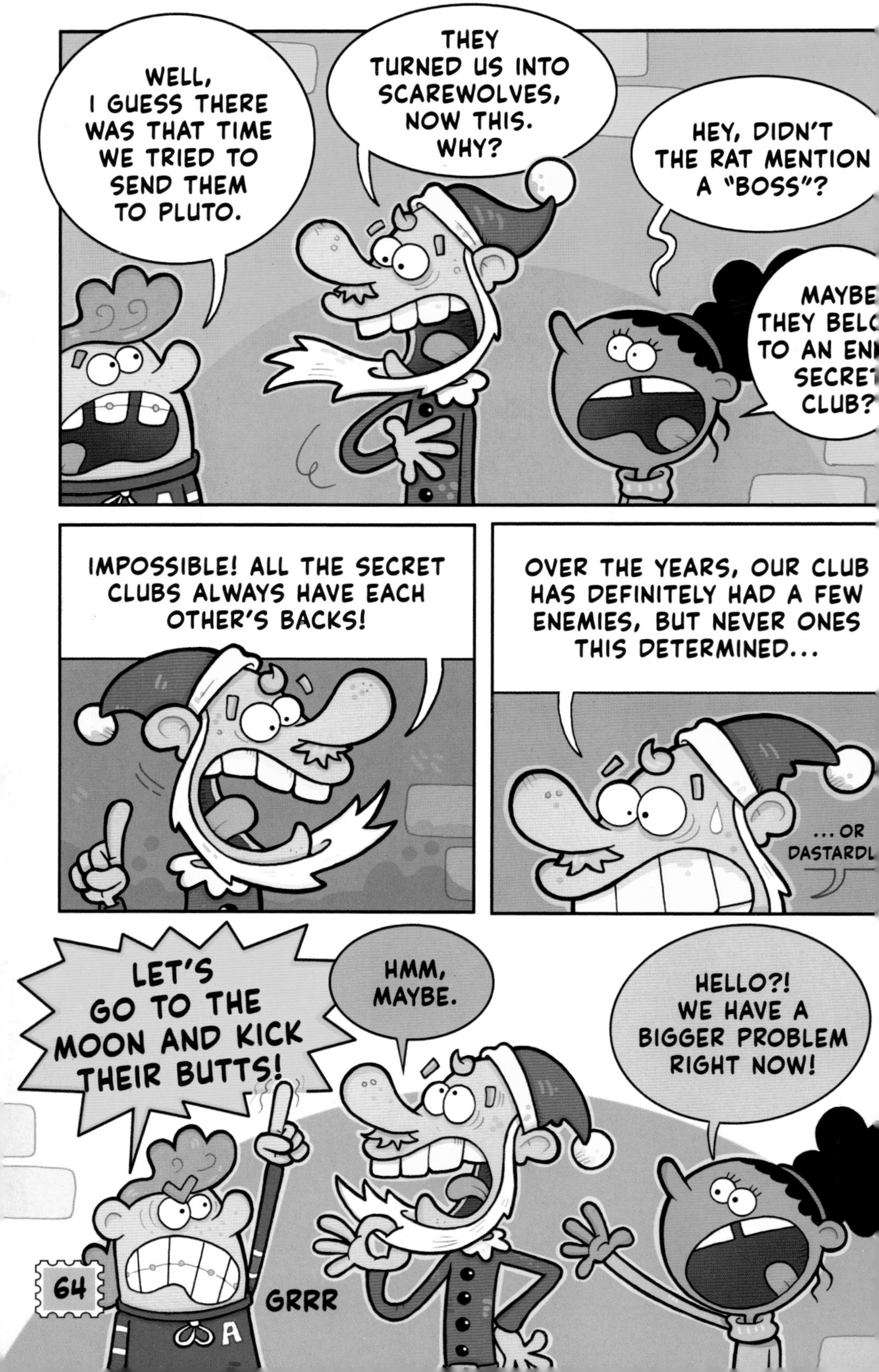

WELL, I GUESS THERE WAS THAT TIME WE TRIED TO SEND THEM TO PLUTO.
THEY TURNED US INTO SCAREWOLVES, NOW THIS. WHY?
HEY, DIDN'T THE RAT MENTION A "BOSS"?
MAYBE THEY BEL TO AN EN SECRE CLUB?
IMPOSSIBLE! ALL THE SECRET CLUBS ALWAYS HAVE EACH OTHER'S BACKS!
OVER THE YEARS, OUR CLUB HAS DEFINITELY HAD A FEW ENEMIES, BUT NEVER ONES THIS DETERMINED...
... OR DASTARDL
LET'S GO TO THE MOON AND KICK THEIR BUTTS!
HMM, MAYBE.
HELLO?! WE HAVE A BIGGER PROBLEM RIGHT NOW!
GRRR

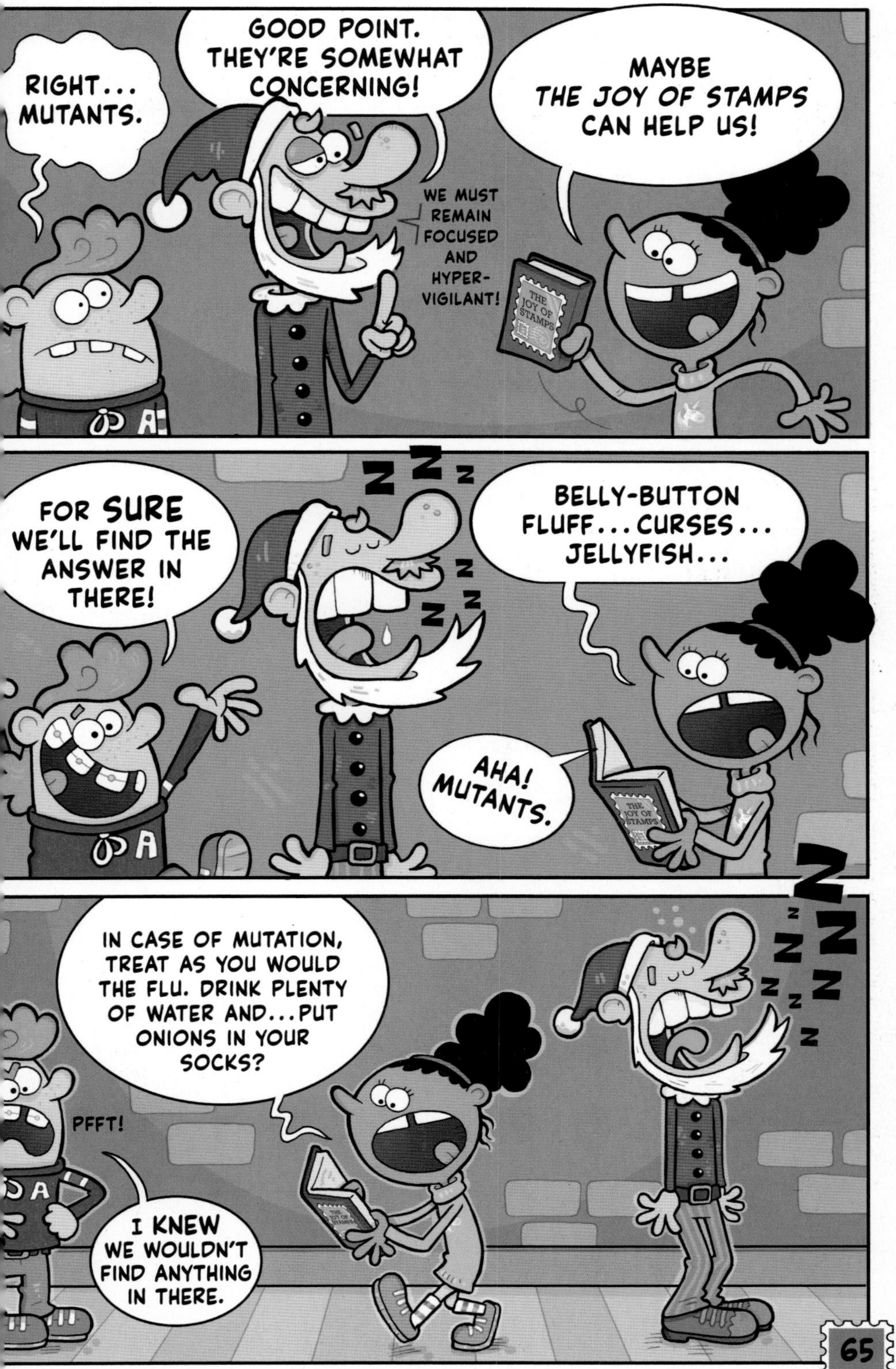
RIGHT... MUTANTS.
GOOD POINT. THEY'RE SOMEWHAT CONCERNING!
WE MUST REMAIN FOCUSED AND HYPER-VIGILANT!
MAYBE THE JOY OF STAMPS CAN HELP US!
THE JOY OF STAMPS
FOR SURE WE'LL FIND THE ANSWER IN THERE!
Z Z Z
BELLY-BUTTON FLUFF... CURSES... JELLYFISH...
AHA! MUTANTS.
IN CASE OF MUTATION, TREAT AS YOU WOULD THE FLU. DRINK PLENTY OF WATER AND...PUT ONIONS IN YOUR SOCKS?
PFFT!
I KNEW WE WOULDN'T FIND ANYTHING IN THERE.

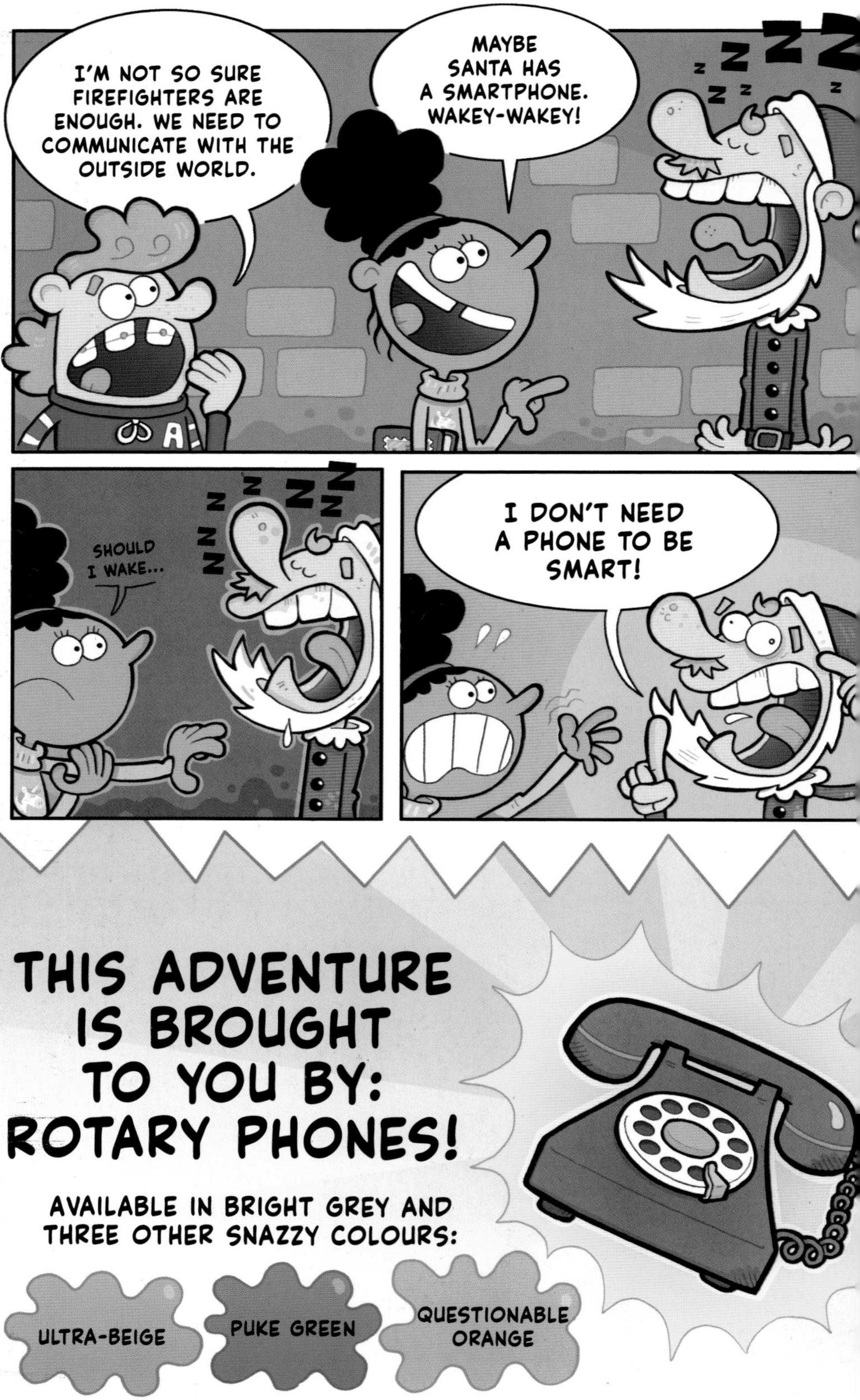

I'M NOT SO SURE FIREFIGHTERS ARE ENOUGH. WE NEED TO COMMUNICATE WITH THE OUTSIDE WORLD.
MAYBE SANTA HAS A SMARTPHONE. WAKEY-WAKEY!
SHOULD I WAKE...
I DON'T NEED A PHONE TO BE SMART!
THIS ADVENTURE IS BROUGHT TO YOU BY: ROTARY PHONES!
AVAILABLE IN BRIGHT GREY AND THREE OTHER SNAZZY COLOURS:
ULTRA-BEIGE
PUKE GREEN
QUESTIONABLE ORANGE

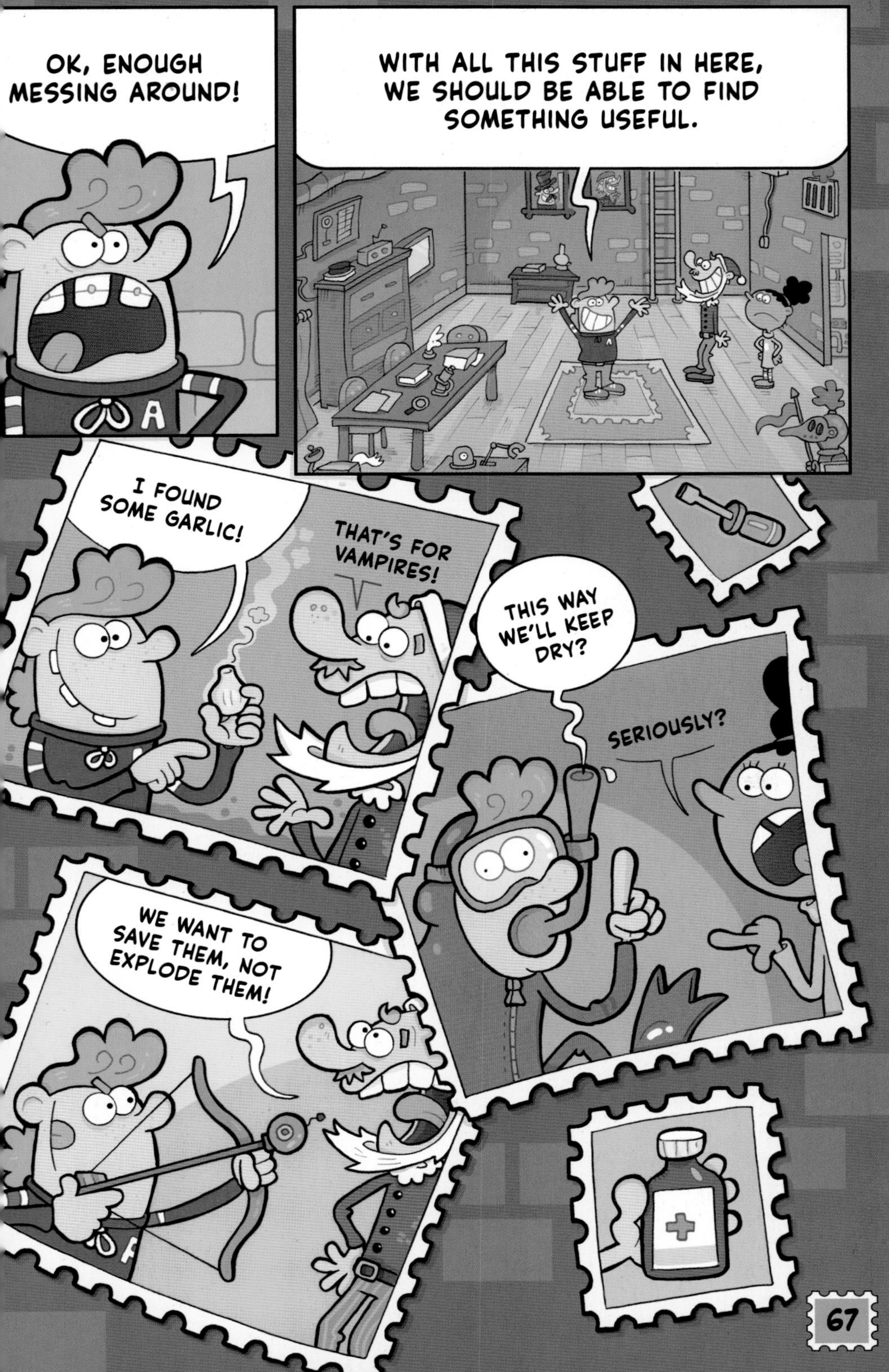
OK, ENOUGH MESSING AROUND!
WITH ALL THIS STUFF IN HERE, WE SHOULD BE ABLE TO FIND SOMETHING USEFUL.
I FOUND SOME GARLIC!
THAT'S FOR VAMPIRES!
THIS WAY WE'LL KEEP DRY?
SERIOUSLY?
WE WANT TO SAVE THEM, NOT EXPLODE THEM!

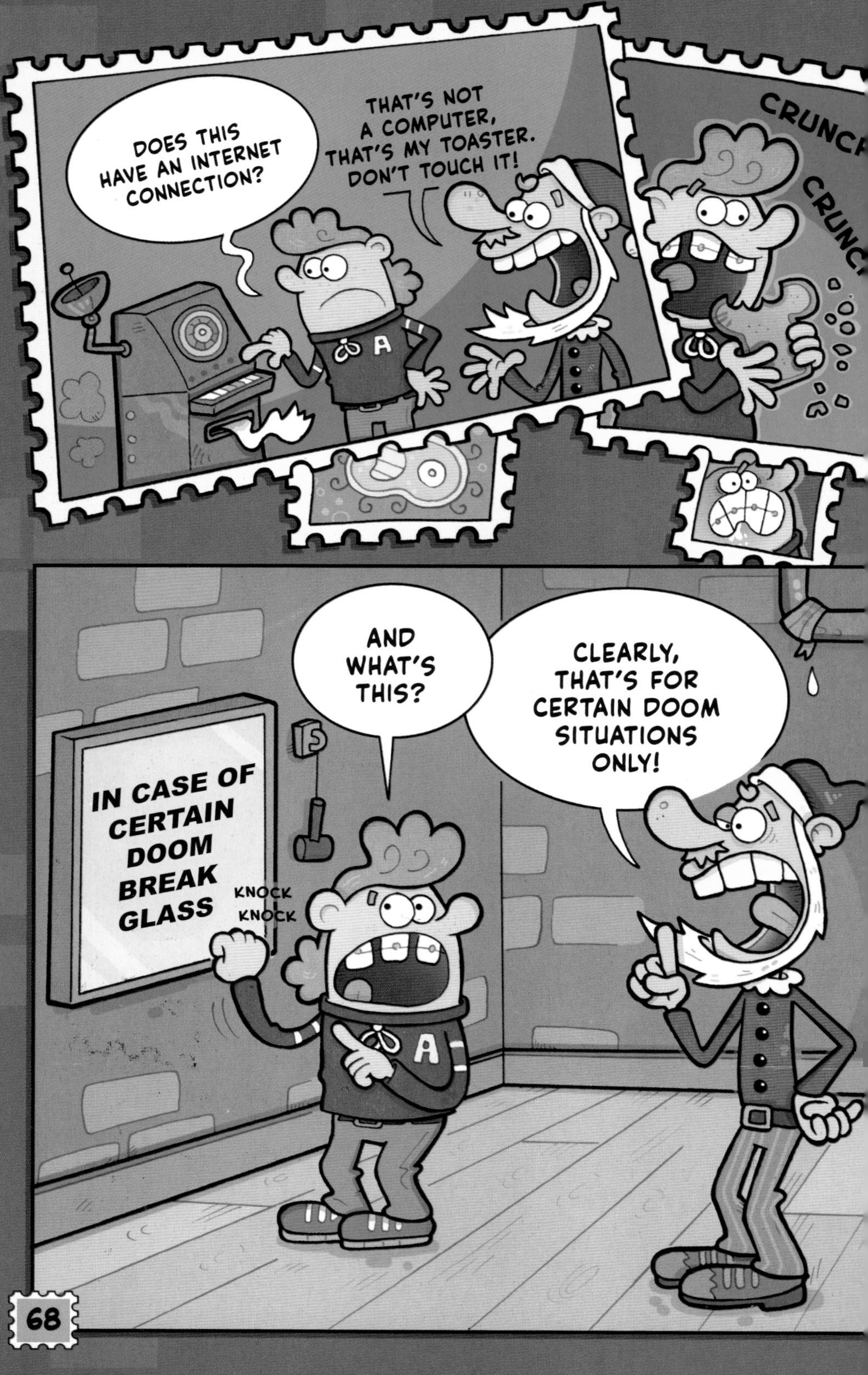

DOES THIS HAVE AN INTERNET CONNECTION?
THAT'S NOT A COMPUTER, THAT'S MY TOASTER. DON'T TOUCH IT!
CRUNCH
CRUNCH
AND WHAT'S THIS?
CLEARLY, THAT'S FOR CERTAIN DOOM SITUATIONS ONLY!
IN CASE OF CERTAIN DOOM BREAK GLASS
KNOCK KNOCK

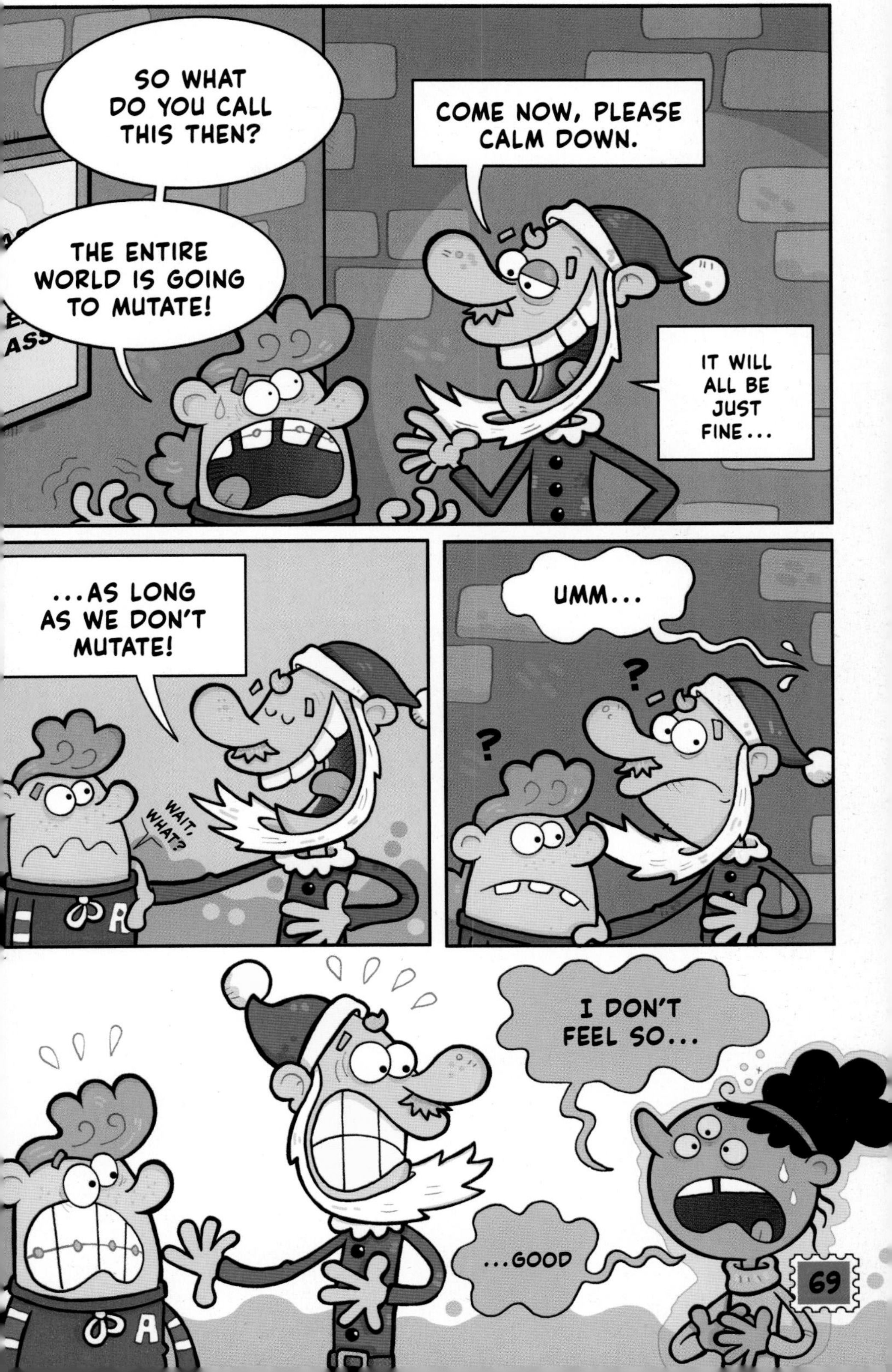
SO WHAT DO YOU CALL THIS THEN?
THE ENTIRE WORLD IS GOING TO MUTATE!
COME NOW, PLEASE CALM DOWN.
IT WILL ALL BE JUST FINE...
...AS LONG AS WE DON'T MUTATE!
WAIT, WHAT?
UMM...
?
?
I DON'T FEEL SO...
...GOOD

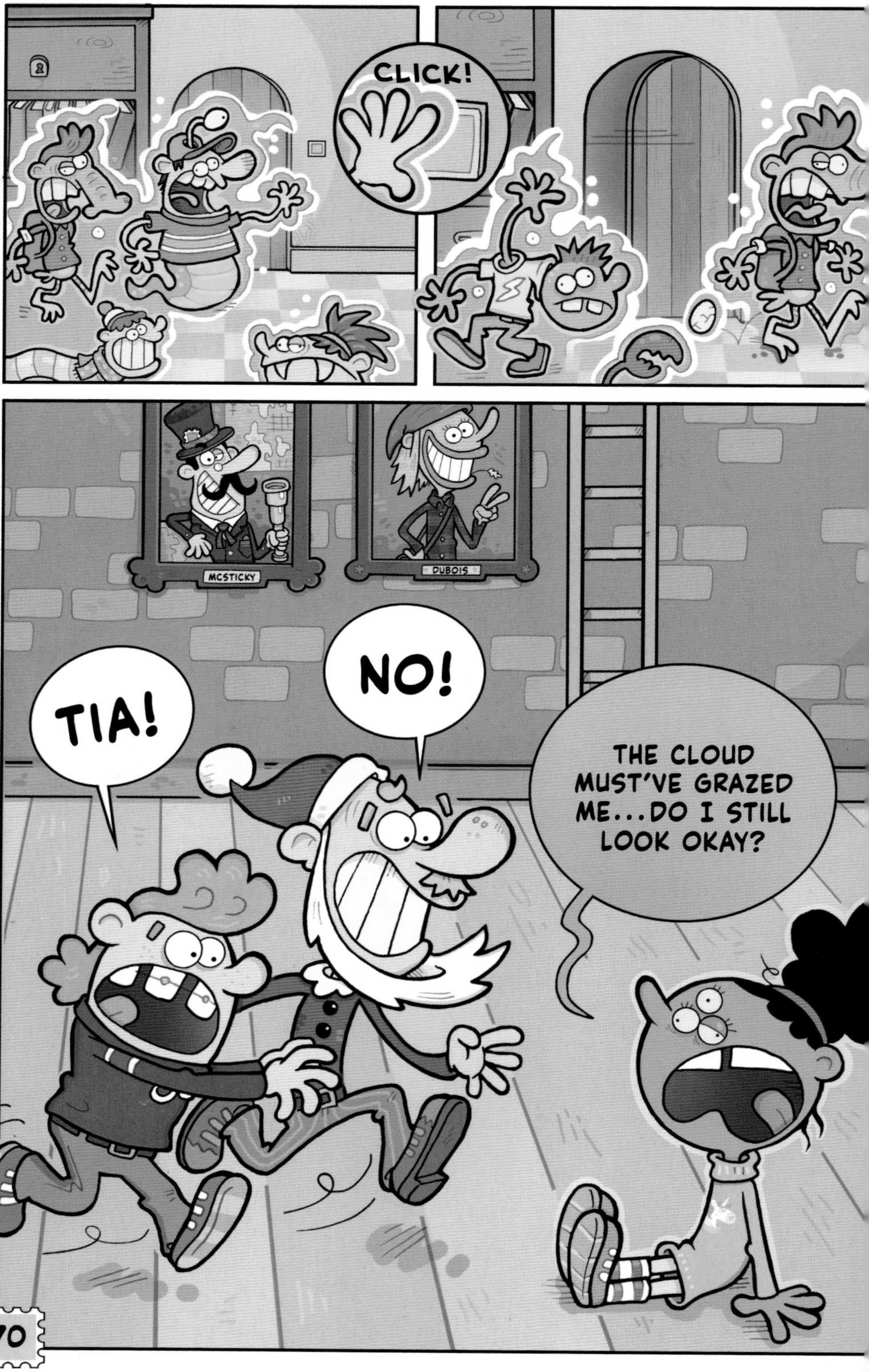
CLICK!
MCSTICKY
DUBOIS
TIA!
NO!
THE CLOUD MUST'VE GRAZED ME...DO I STILL LOOK OKAY?

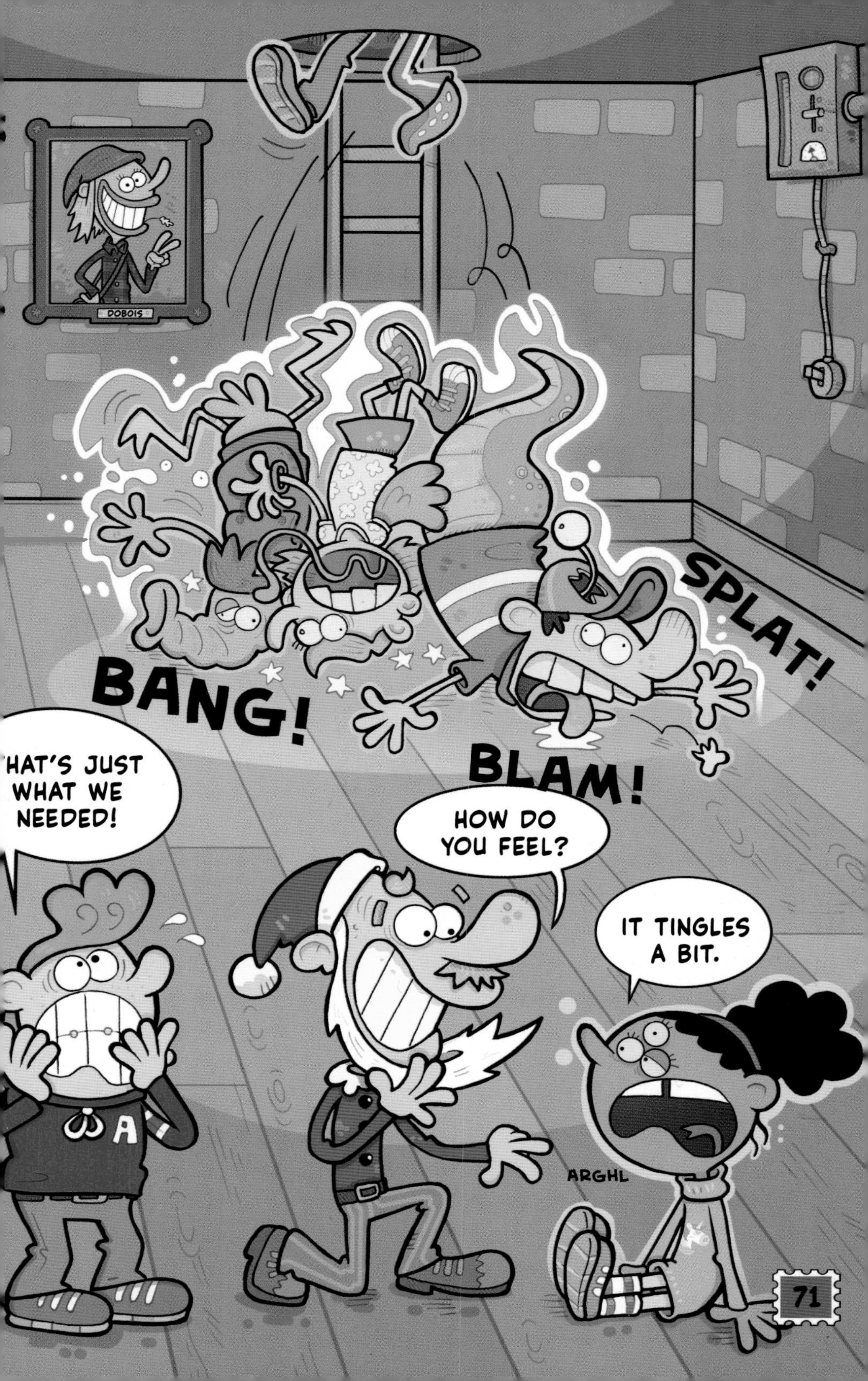
DOBOIS
SPLAT!
BANG!
BLAM!
HAT'S JUST WHAT WE NEEDED!
HOW DO YOU FEEL?
IT TINGLES A BIT.
ARGHL

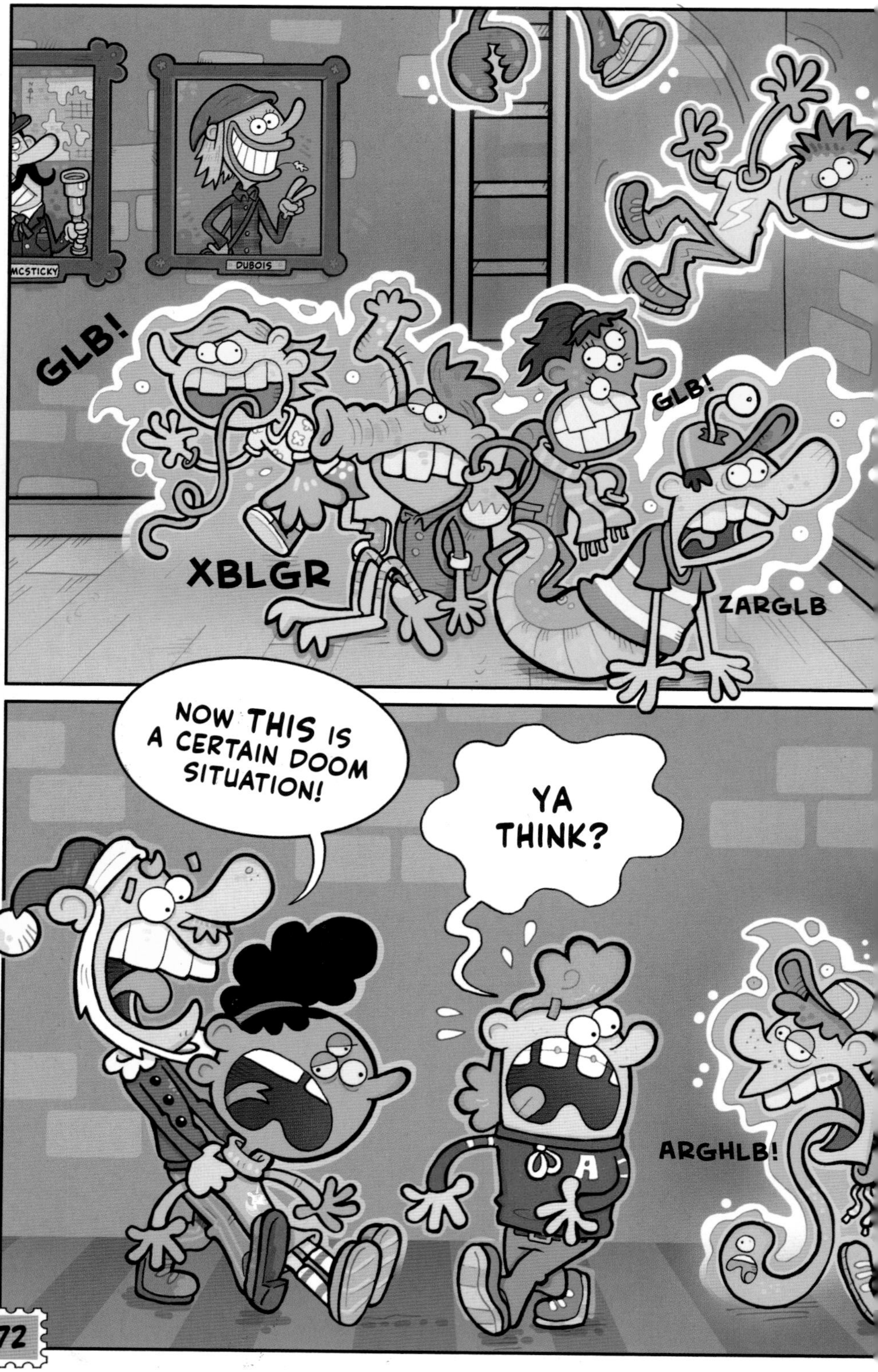
MCSTICKY
DUBOIS
GLB!
GLB!
XBLGR
ZARGLB
NOW THIS IS A CERTAIN DOOM SITUATION!
YA THINK?
ARGHLB!

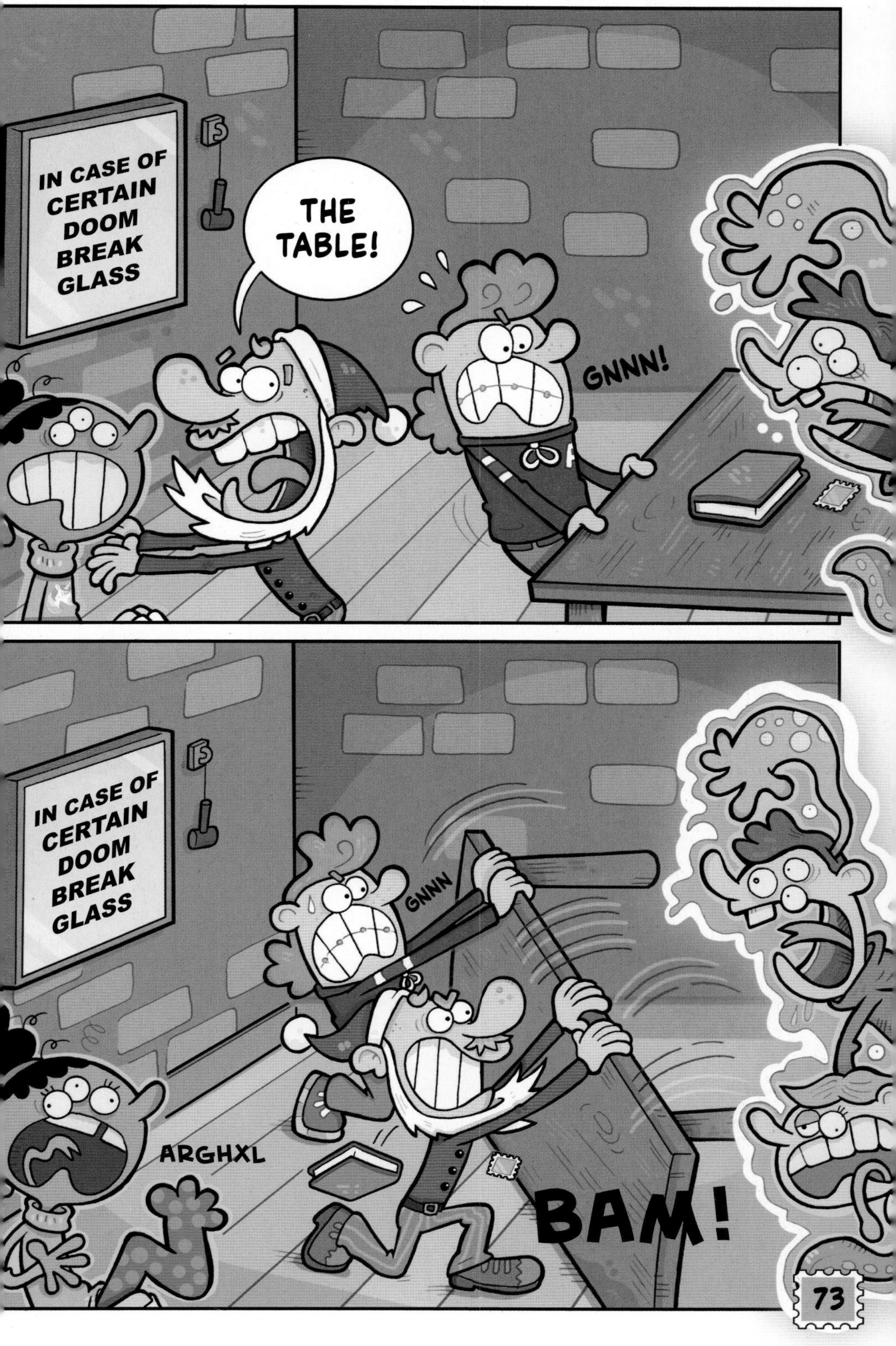
IN CASE OF CERTAIN DOOM BREAK GLASS
THE TABLE!
GNNN!
IN CASE OF CERTAIN DOOM BREAK GLASS
GNNN
ARGHXL
BAM!

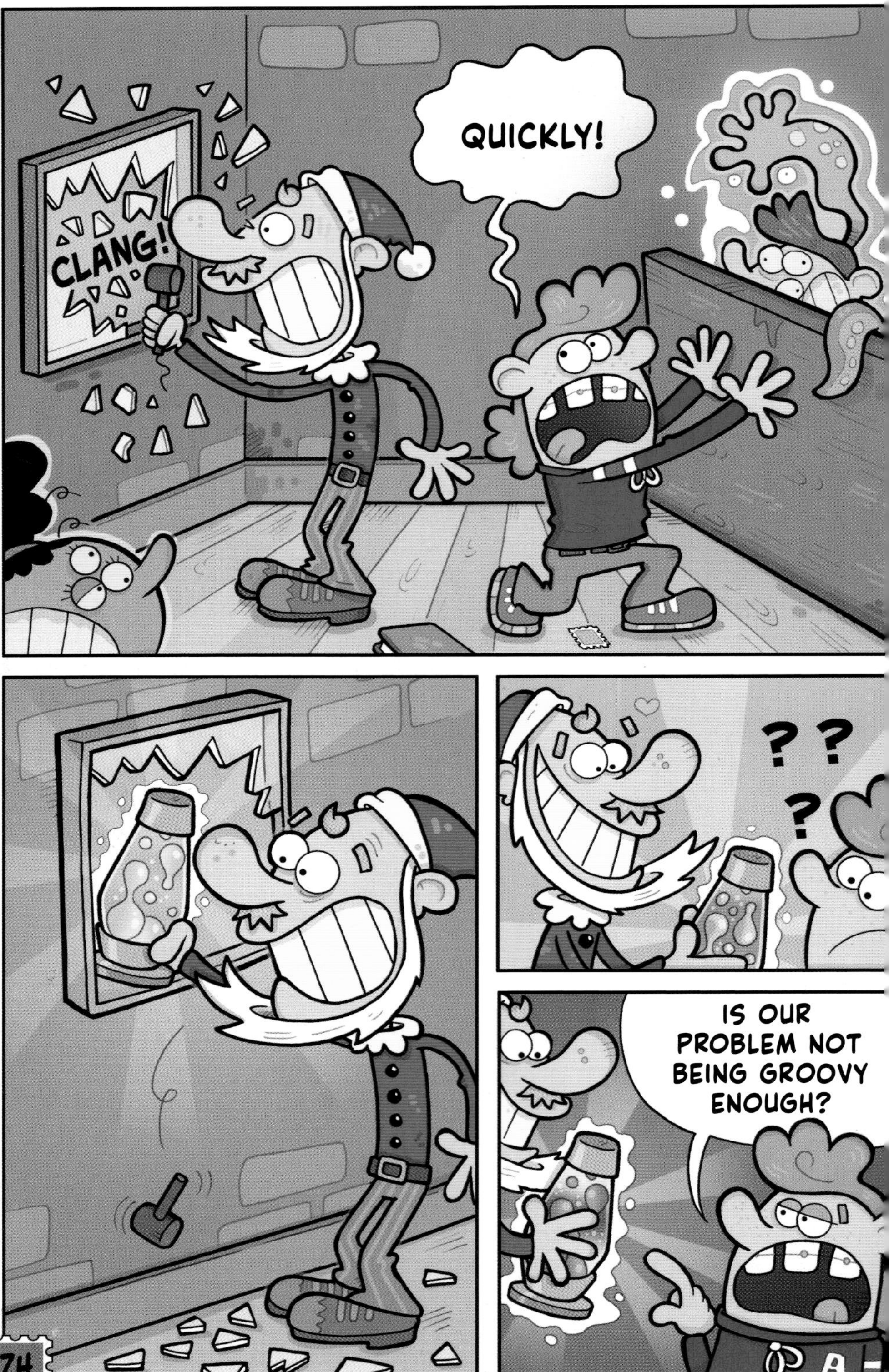
CLANG!
QUICKLY!
? ?
?
IS OUR PROBLEM NOT BEING GROOVY ENOUGH?

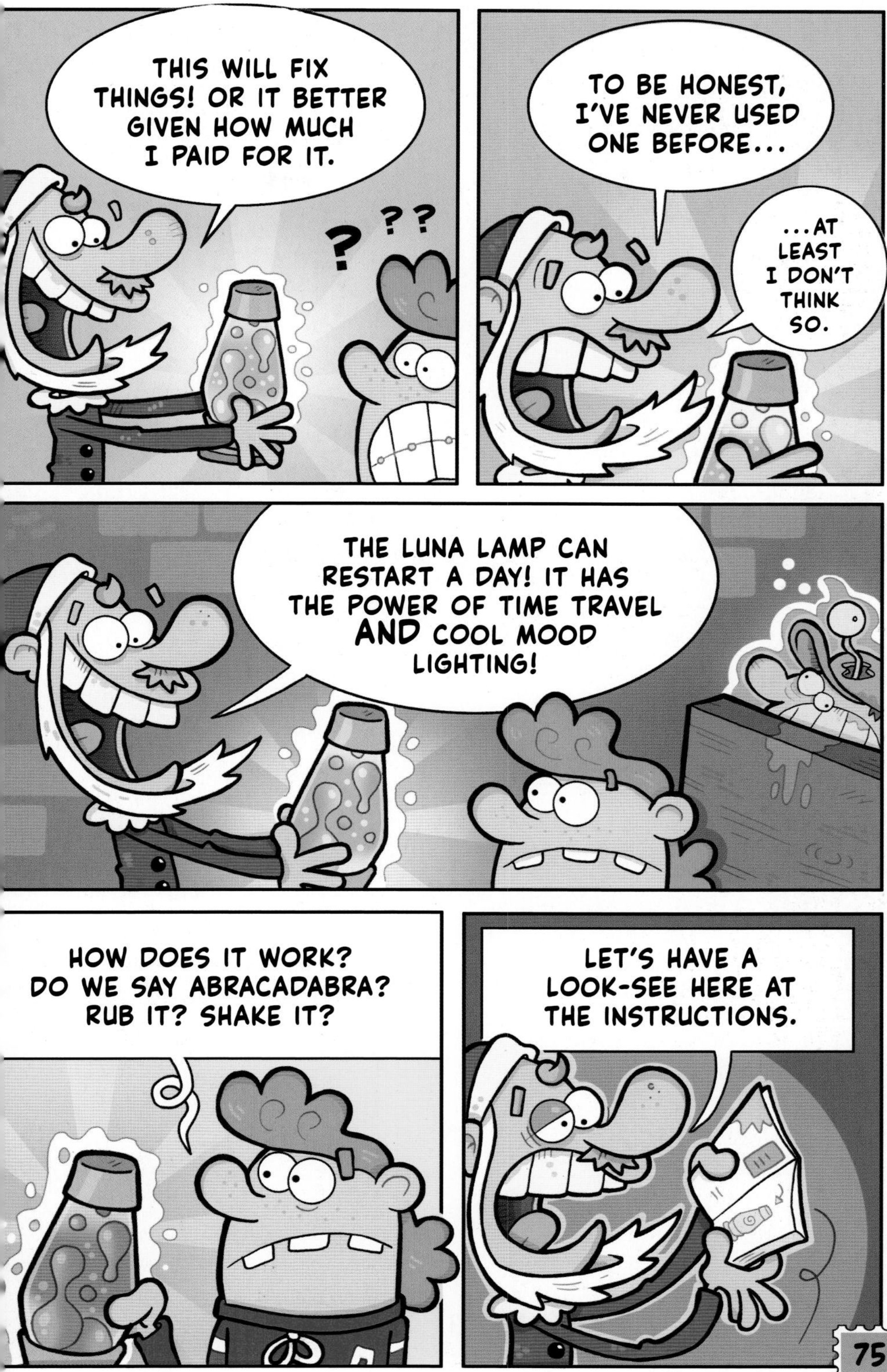
THIS WILL FIX THINGS! OR IT BETTER GIVEN HOW MUCH I PAID FOR IT.
? ? ?
TO BE HONEST, I'VE NEVER USED ONE BEFORE...
...AT LEAST I DON'T THINK SO.
THE LUNA LAMP CAN RESTART A DAY! IT HAS THE POWER OF TIME TRAVEL AND COOL MOOD LIGHTING!
HOW DOES IT WORK? DO WE SAY ABRACADABRA? RUB IT? SHAKE IT?
LET'S HAVE A LOOK-SEE HERE AT THE INSTRUCTIONS.

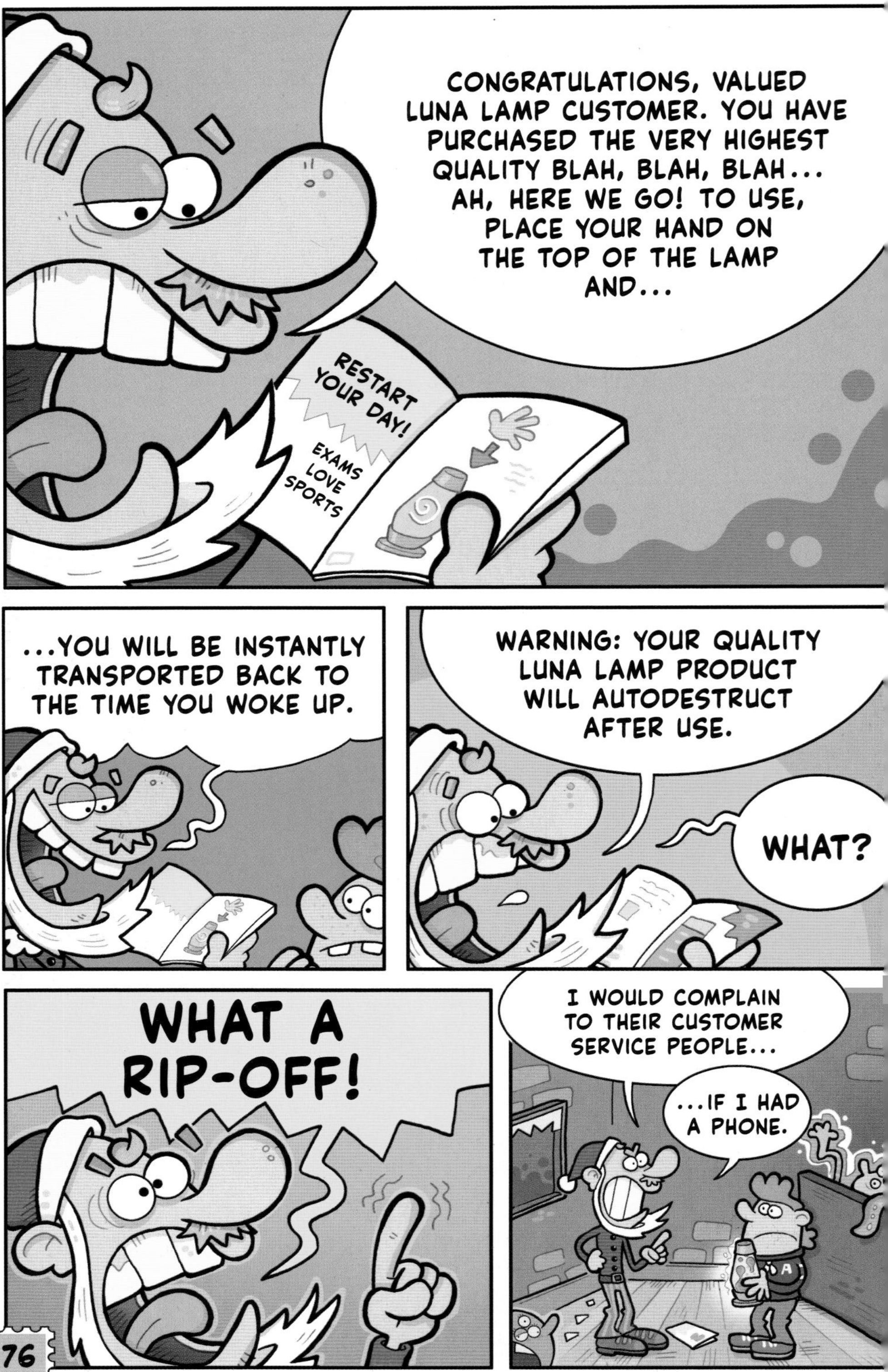
CONGRATULATIONS, VALUED LUNA LAMP CUSTOMER. YOU HAVE PURCHASED THE VERY HIGHEST QUALITY BLAH, BLAH, BLAH... AH, HERE WE GO! TO USE, PLACE YOUR HAND ON THE TOP OF THE LAMP AND...
RESTART YOUR DAY!
EXAMS
LOVE
SPORTS
...YOU WILL BE INSTANTLY TRANSPORTED BACK TO THE TIME YOU WOKE UP.
WARNING: YOUR QUALITY LUNA LAMP PRODUCT WILL AUTODESTRUCT AFTER USE.
WHAT?
WHAT A RIP-OFF!
I WOULD COMPLAIN TO THEIR CUSTOMER SERVICE PEOPLE...
...IF I HAD A PHONE.

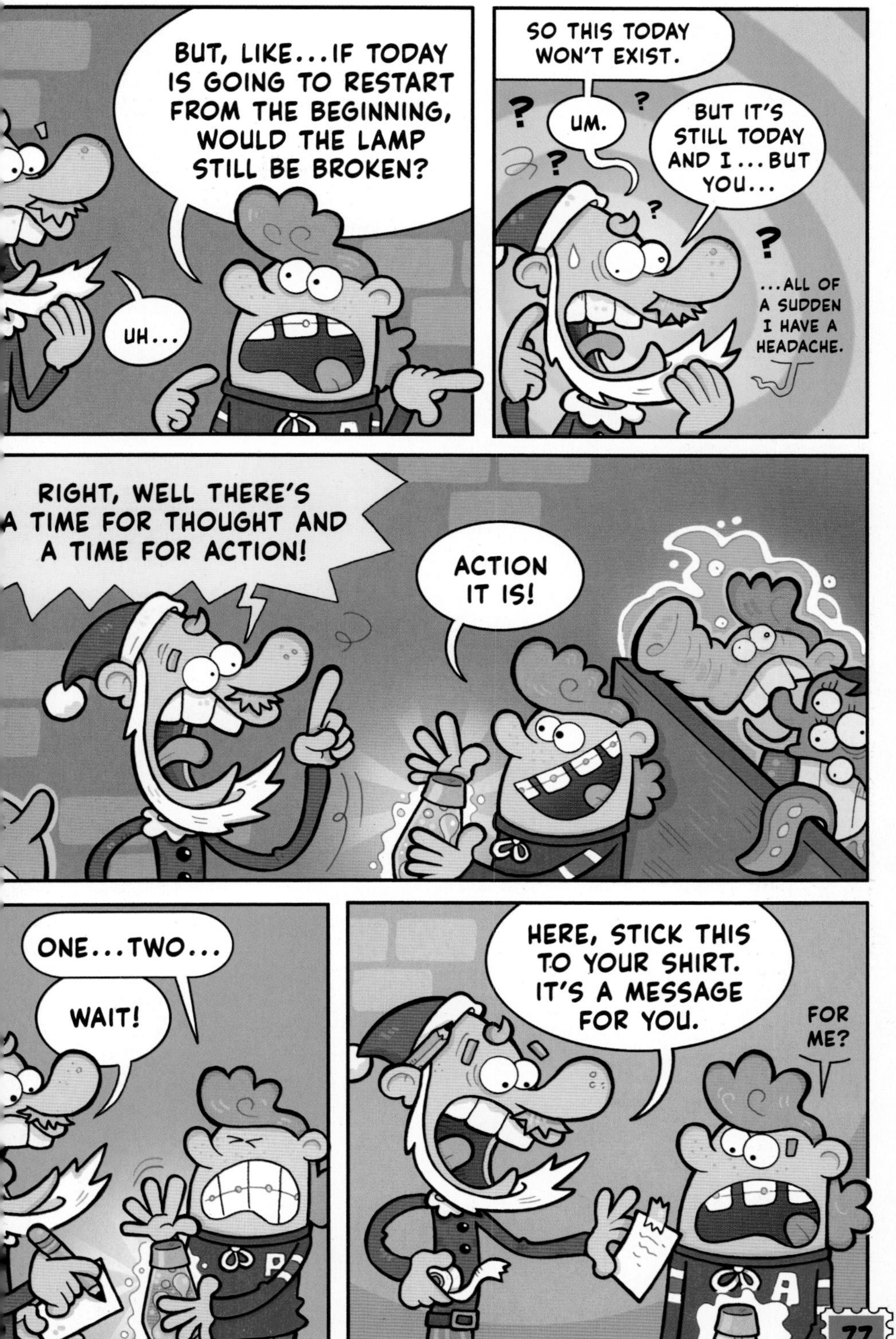
BUT, LIKE...IF TODAY IS GOING TO RESTART FROM THE BEGINNING, WOULD THE LAMP STILL BE BROKEN?
UH...
SO THIS TODAY WON'T EXIST.
UM.
BUT IT'S STILL TODAY AND I...BUT YOU...
...ALL OF A SUDDEN I HAVE A HEADACHE.
RIGHT, WELL THERE'S A TIME FOR THOUGHT AND A TIME FOR ACTION!
ACTION IT IS!
ONE...TWO...
WAIT!
HERE, STICK THIS TO YOUR SHIRT. IT'S A MESSAGE FOR YOU.
FOR ME?

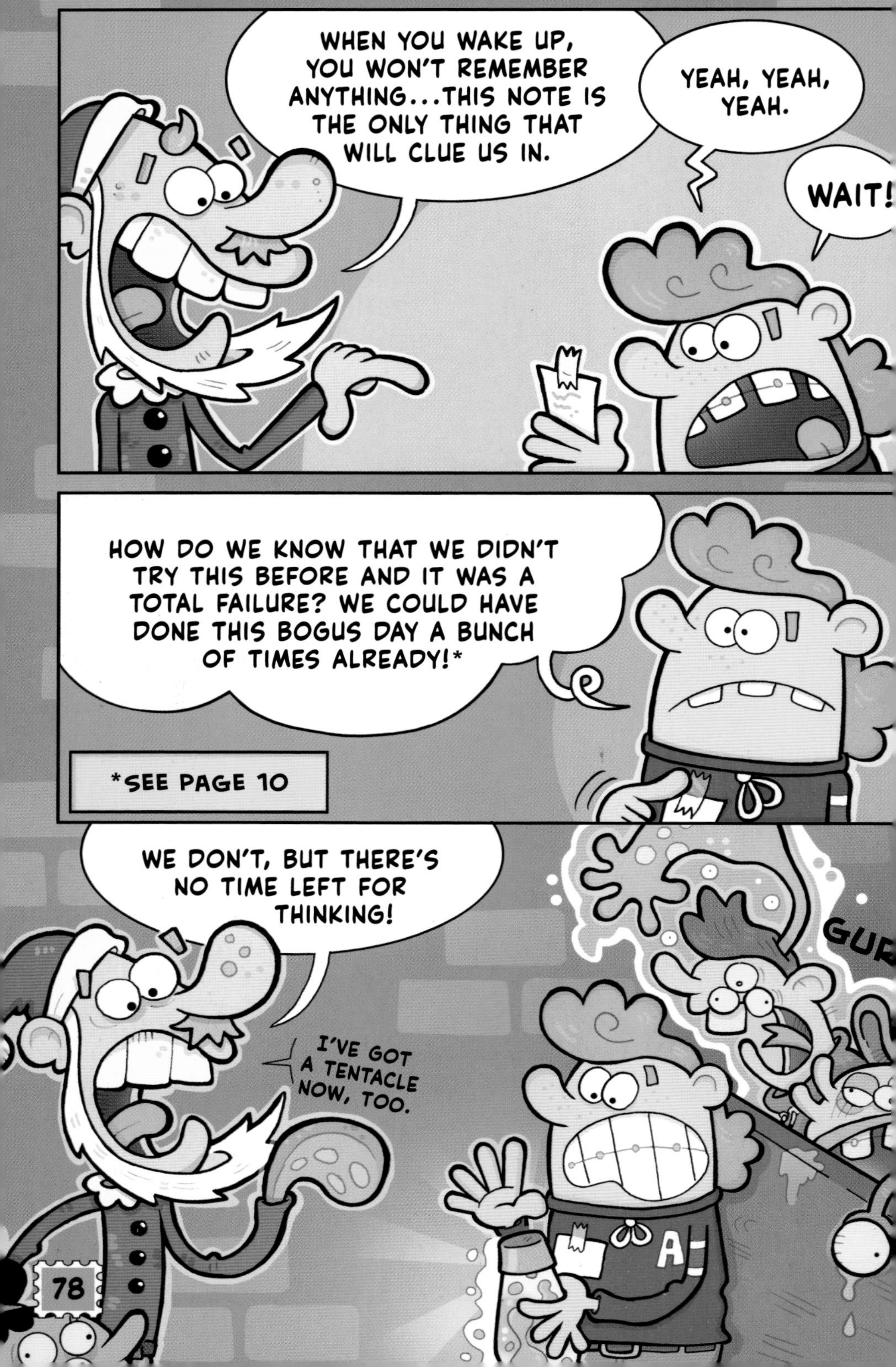
WHEN YOU WAKE UP, YOU WON'T REMEMBER ANYTHING...THIS NOTE IS THE ONLY THING THAT WILL CLUE US IN.
YEAH, YEAH, YEAH.
WAIT!
HOW DO WE KNOW THAT WE DIDN'T TRY THIS BEFORE AND IT WAS A TOTAL FAILURE? WE COULD HAVE DONE THIS BOGUS DAY A BUNCH OF TIMES ALREADY!*
*SEE PAGE 10
WE DON'T, BUT THERE'S NO TIME LEFT FOR THINKING!
I'VE GOT A TENTACLE NOW, TOO.
GUR

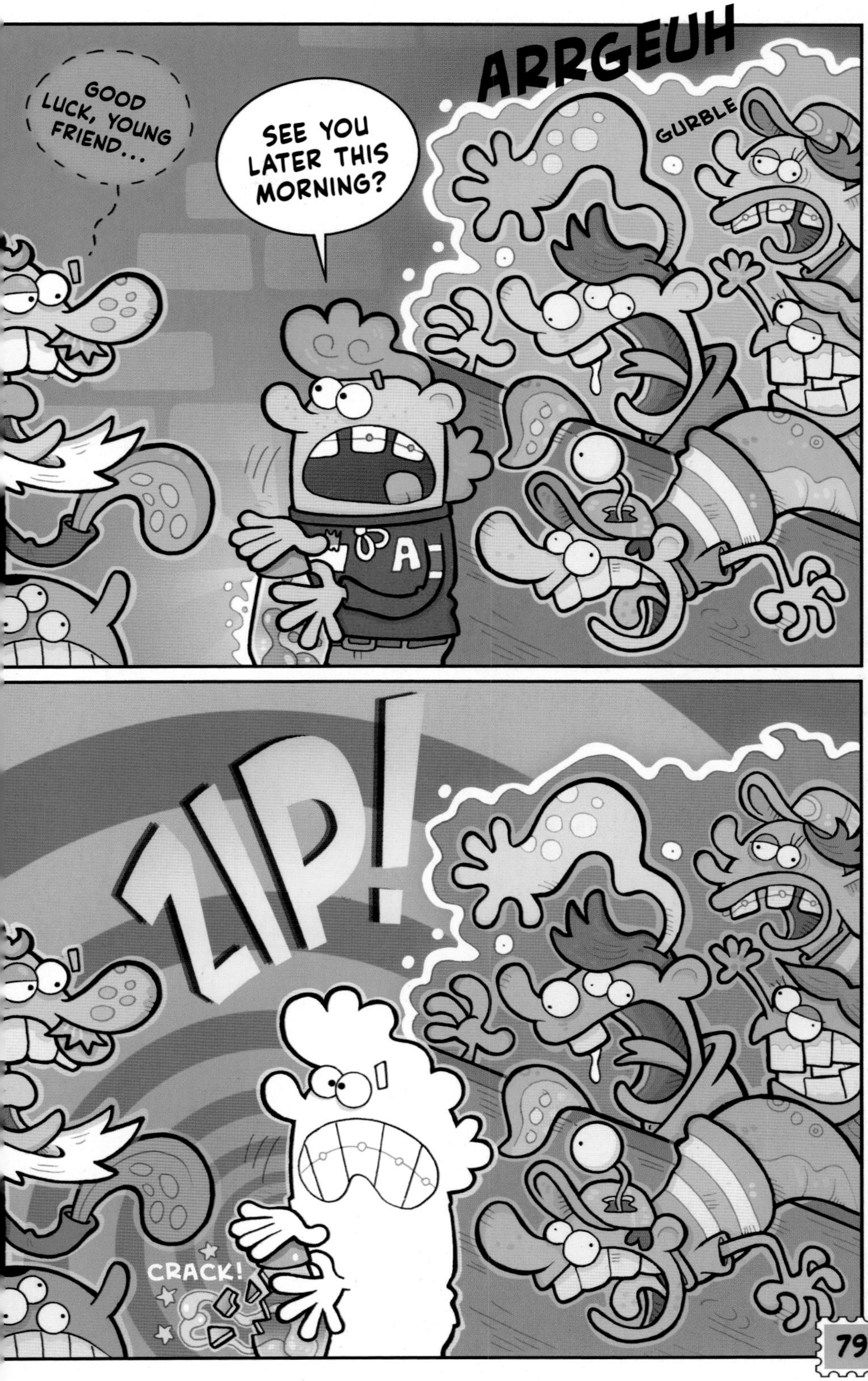
GOOD LUCK, YOUNG FRIEND...
SEE YOU LATER THIS MORNING?
ARRGEUH
GURBLE
ZIP!
CRACK!

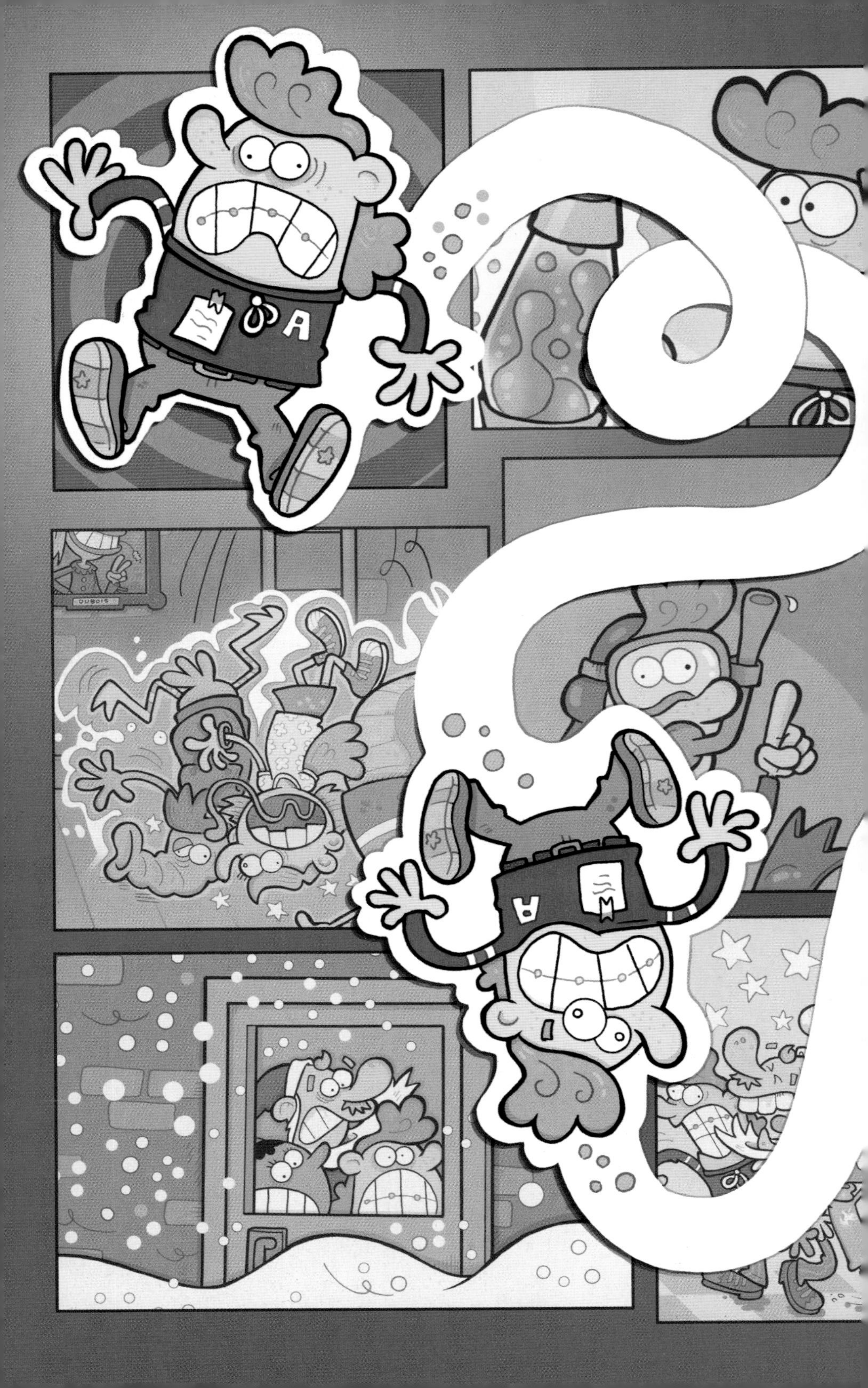
DUBOIS

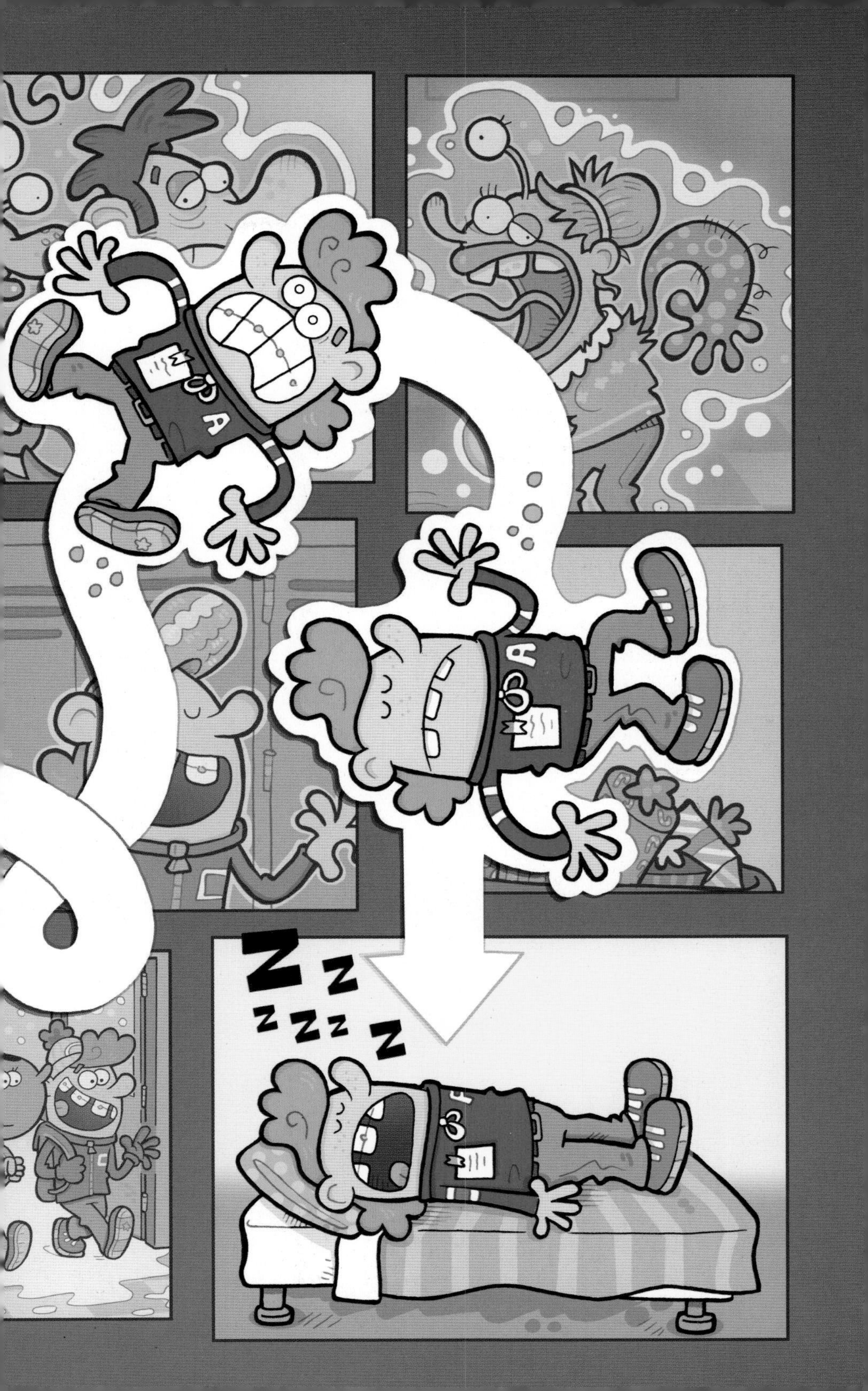
Z Z Z Z Z Z Z

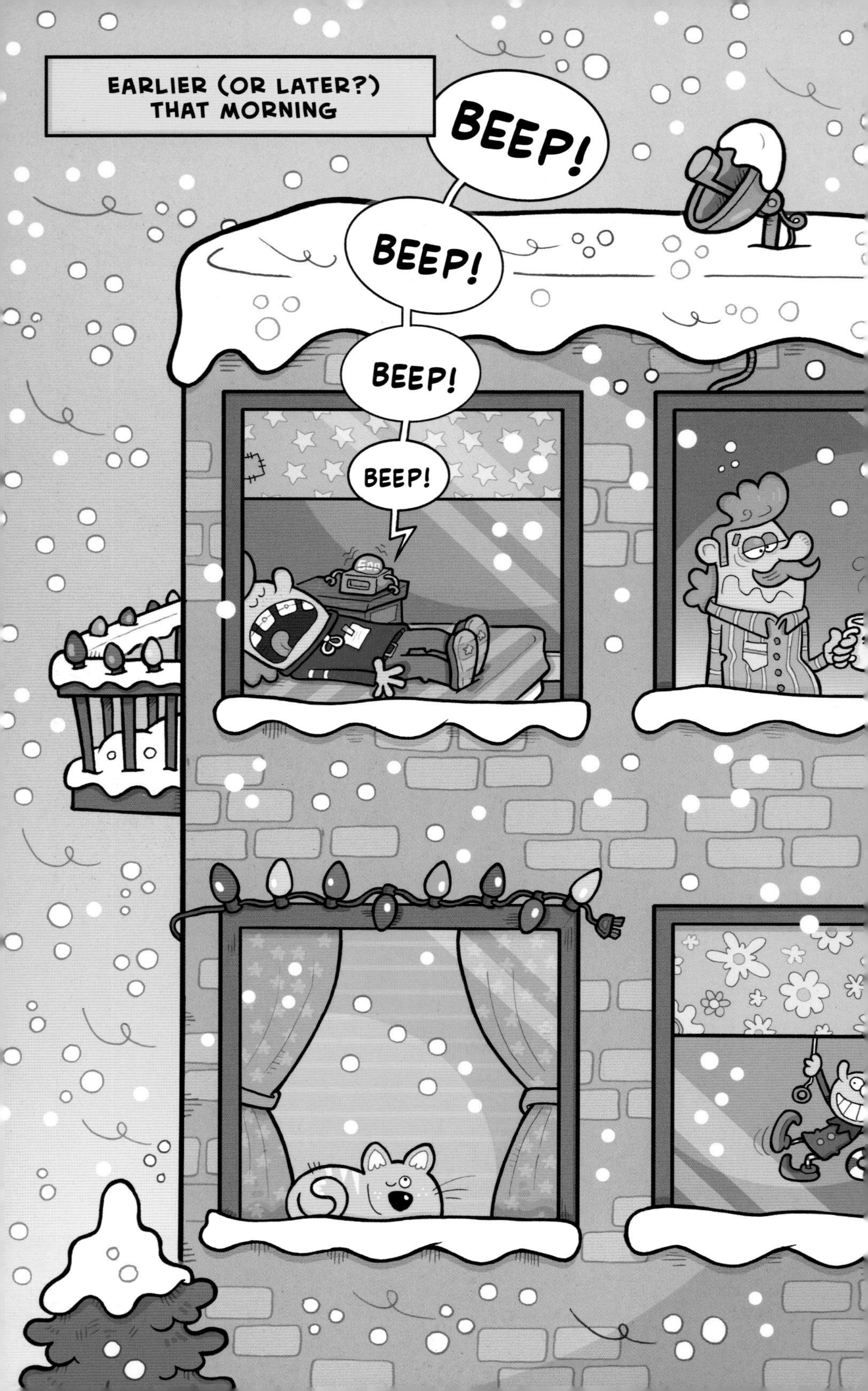
EARLIER (OR LATER?) THAT MORNING
BEEP!
BEEP!
BEEP!
BEEP!

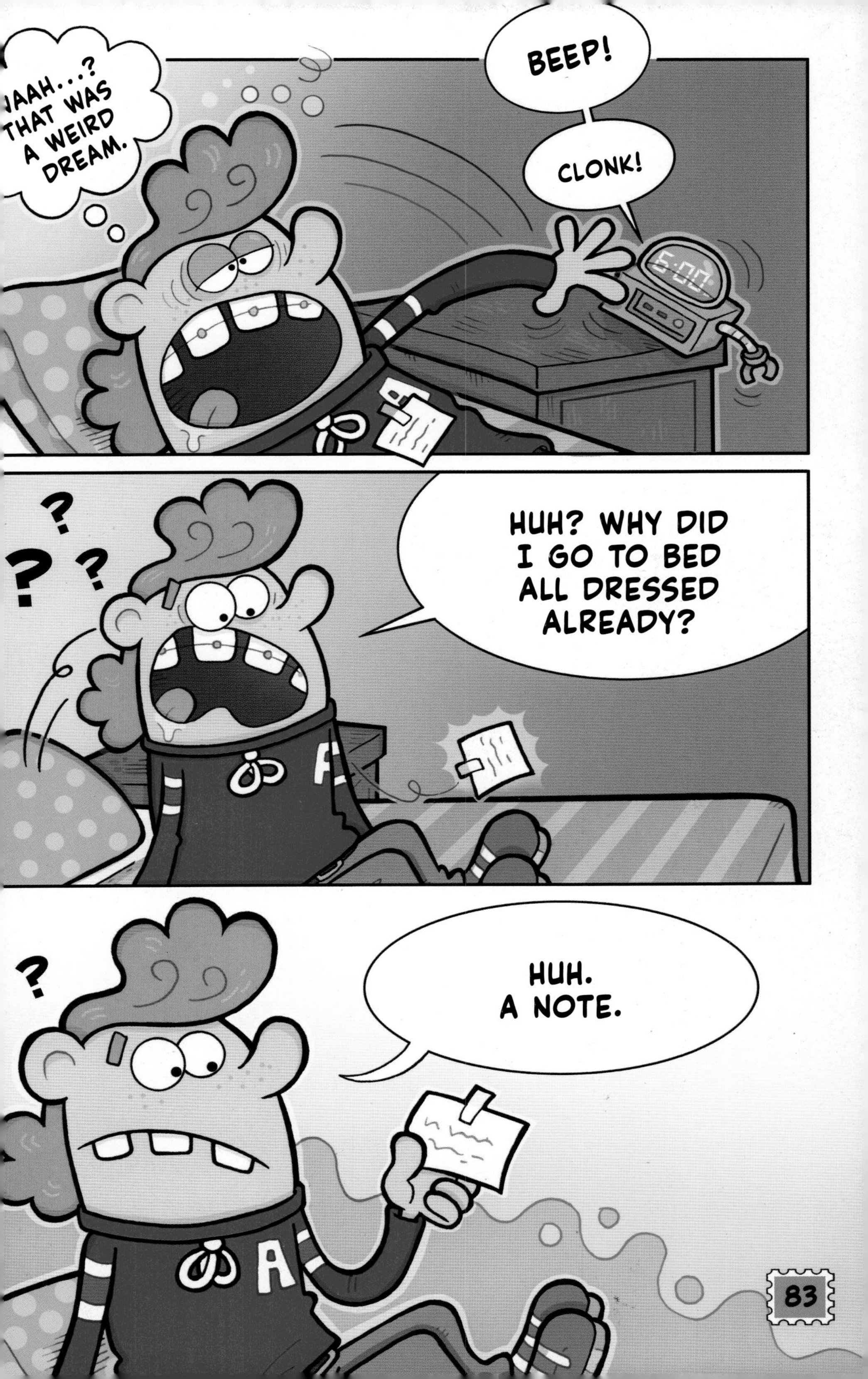

AAAH...? THAT WAS A WEIRD DREAM.
BEEP!
CLONK!
6:00
HUH? WHY DID I GO TO BED ALL DRESSED ALREADY?
HUH. A NOTE.

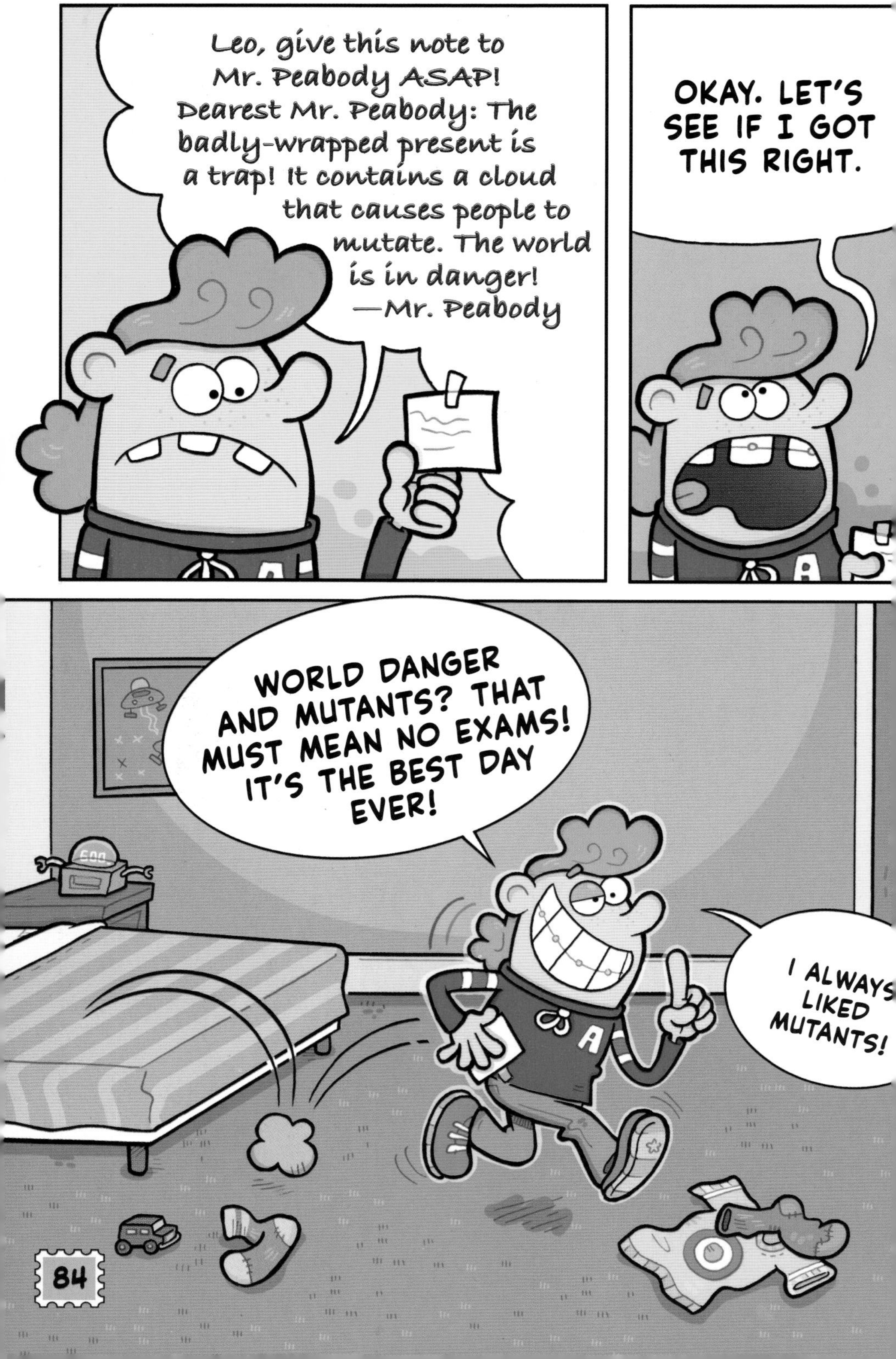
Leo, give this note to Mr. Peabody ASAP! Dearest Mr. Peabody: The badly-wrapped present is a trap! It contains a cloud that causes people to mutate. The world is in danger! —Mr. Peabody
OKAY. LET'S SEE IF I GOT THIS RIGHT.
WORLD DANGER AND MUTANTS? THAT MUST MEAN NO EXAMS! IT'S THE BEST DAY EVER!
I ALWAYS LIKED MUTANTS!

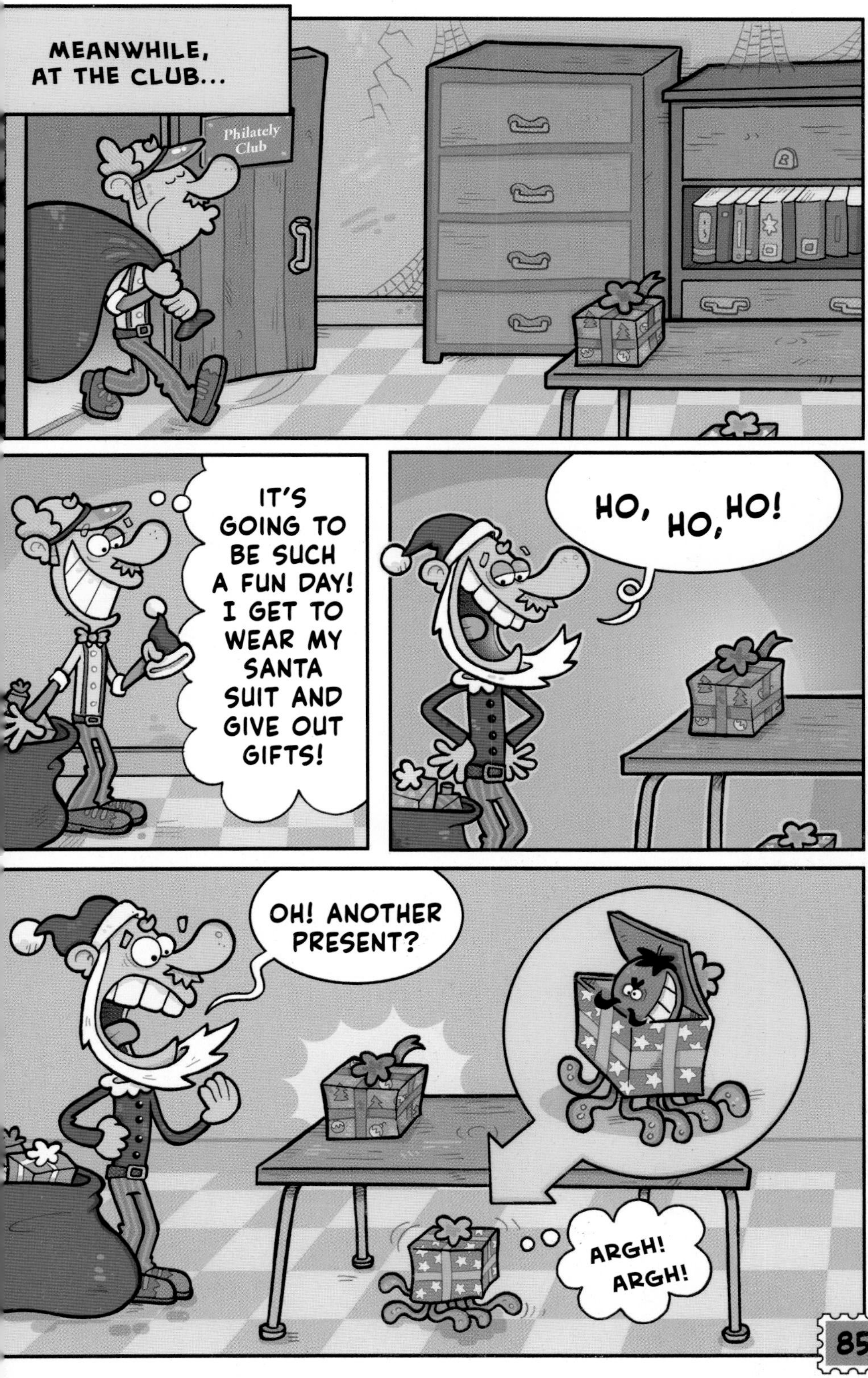
MEANWHILE, AT THE CLUB...
Philately Club
IT'S GOING TO BE SUCH A FUN DAY! I GET TO WEAR MY SANTA SUIT AND GIVE OUT GIFTS!
HO, HO, HO!
OH! ANOTHER PRESENT?
ARGH! ARGH!

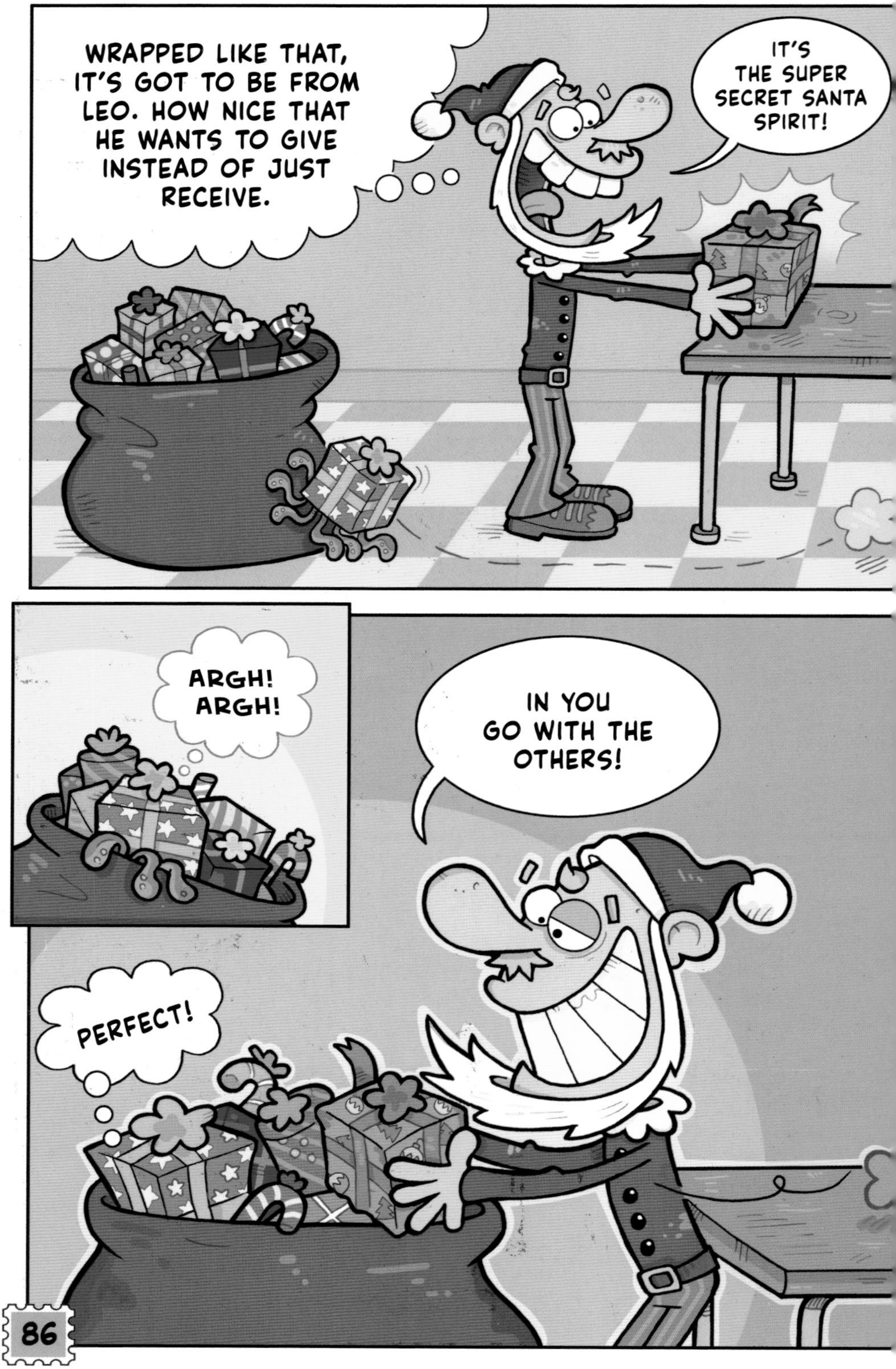
WRAPPED LIKE THAT, IT'S GOT TO BE FROM LEO. HOW NICE THAT HE WANTS TO GIVE INSTEAD OF JUST RECEIVE.
IT'S THE SUPER SECRET SANTA SPIRIT!
ARGH! ARGH!
IN YOU GO WITH THE OTHERS!
PERFECT!

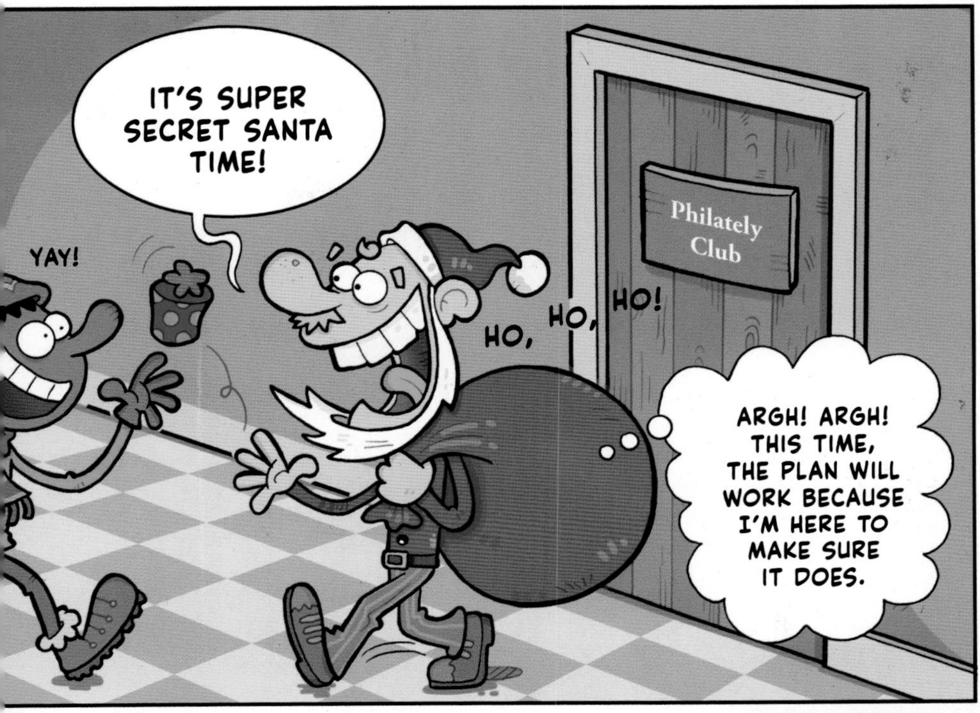
IT'S SUPER SECRET SANTA TIME!
YAY!
HO, HO, HO!
Philately Club
ARGH! ARGH! THIS TIME, THE PLAN WILL WORK BECAUSE I'M HERE TO MAKE SURE IT DOES.

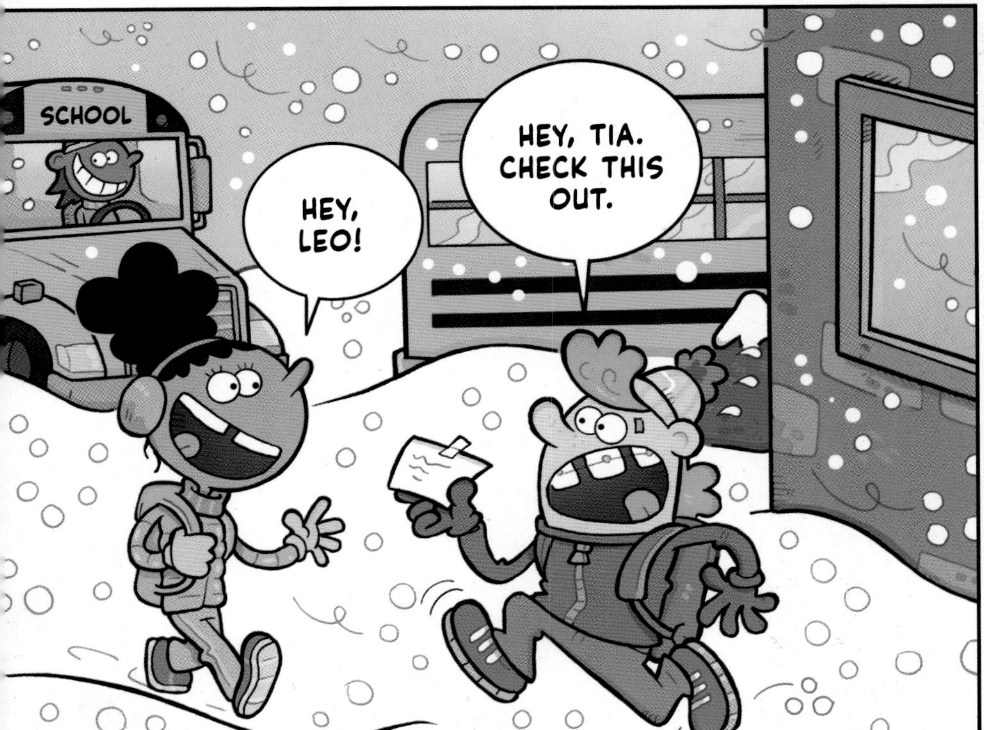
SCHOOL
HEY, LEO!
HEY, TIA. CHECK THIS OUT.

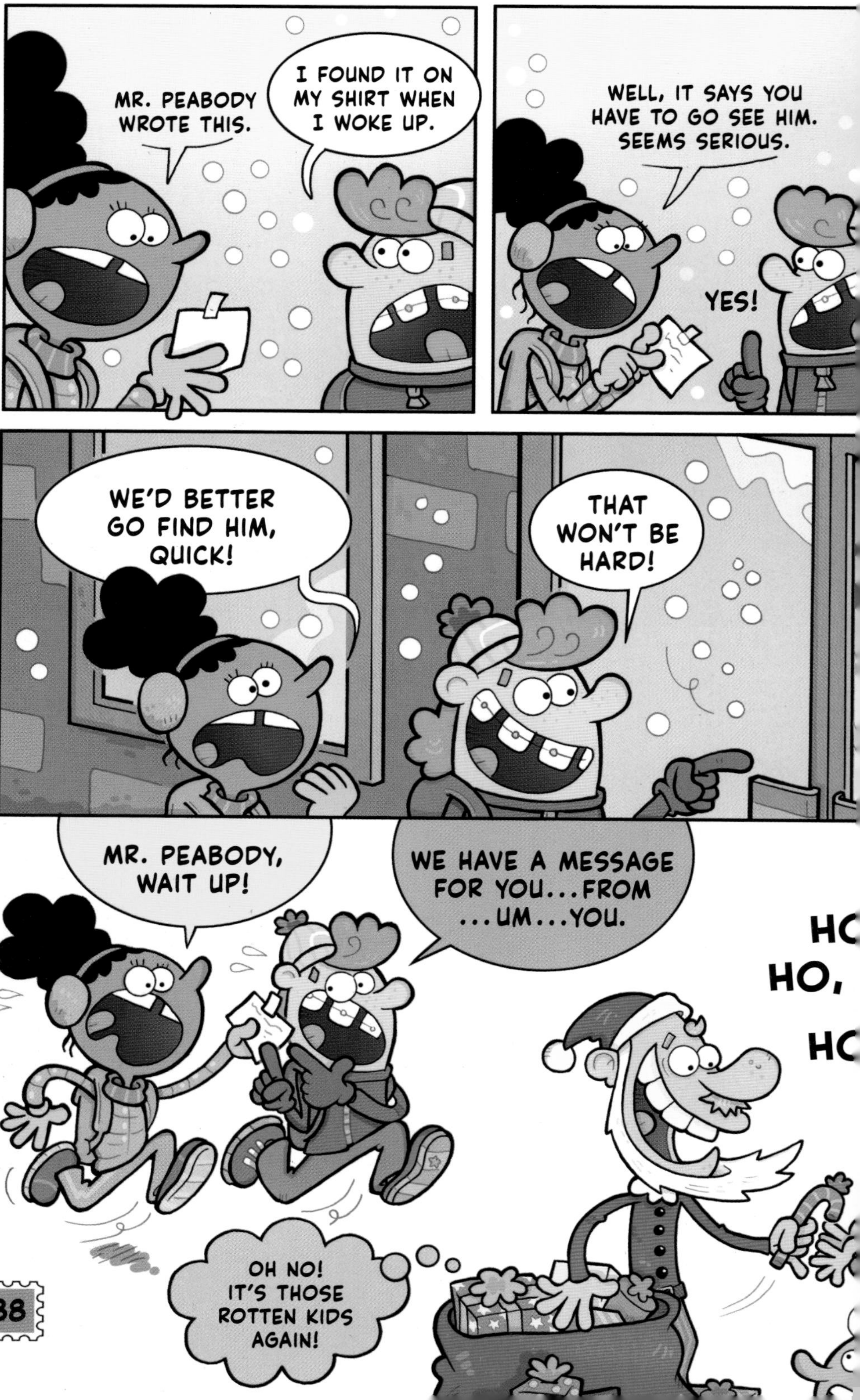
MR. PEABODY WROTE THIS.
I FOUND IT ON MY SHIRT WHEN I WOKE UP.
WELL, IT SAYS YOU HAVE TO GO SEE HIM. SEEMS SERIOUS.
YES!
WE'D BETTER GO FIND HIM, QUICK!
THAT WON'T BE HARD!
MR. PEABODY, WAIT UP!
WE HAVE A MESSAGE FOR YOU...FROM ...UM...YOU.
OH NO! IT'S THOSE ROTTEN KIDS AGAIN!

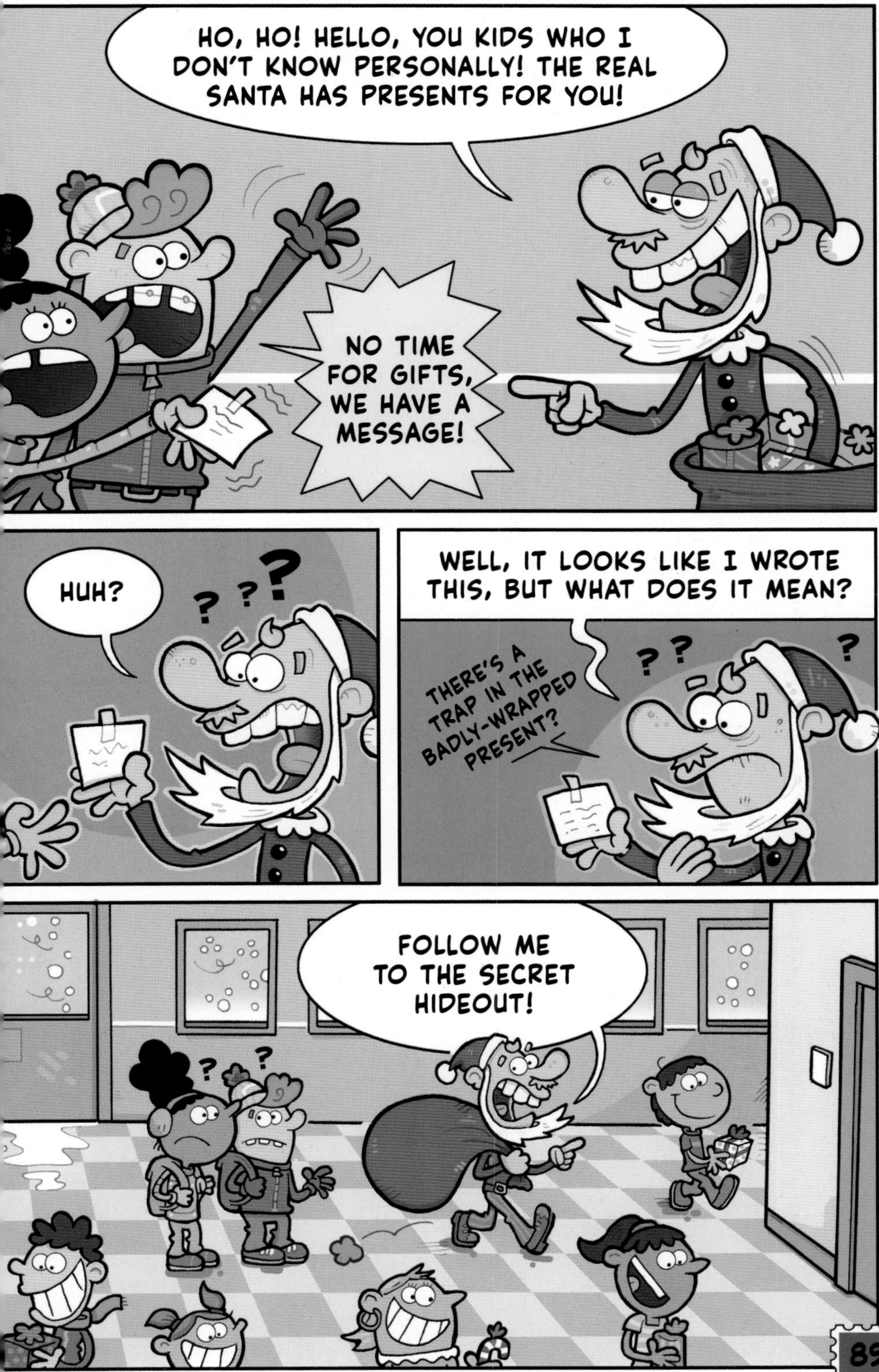
HO, HO! HELLO, YOU KIDS WHO I DON'T KNOW PERSONALLY! THE REAL SANTA HAS PRESENTS FOR YOU!
NO TIME FOR GIFTS, WE HAVE A MESSAGE!
HUH?
? ? ?
WELL, IT LOOKS LIKE I WROTE THIS, BUT WHAT DOES IT MEAN?
THERE'S A TRAP IN THE BADLY-WRAPPED PRESENT?
? ? ?
FOLLOW ME TO THE SECRET HIDEOUT!
? ?

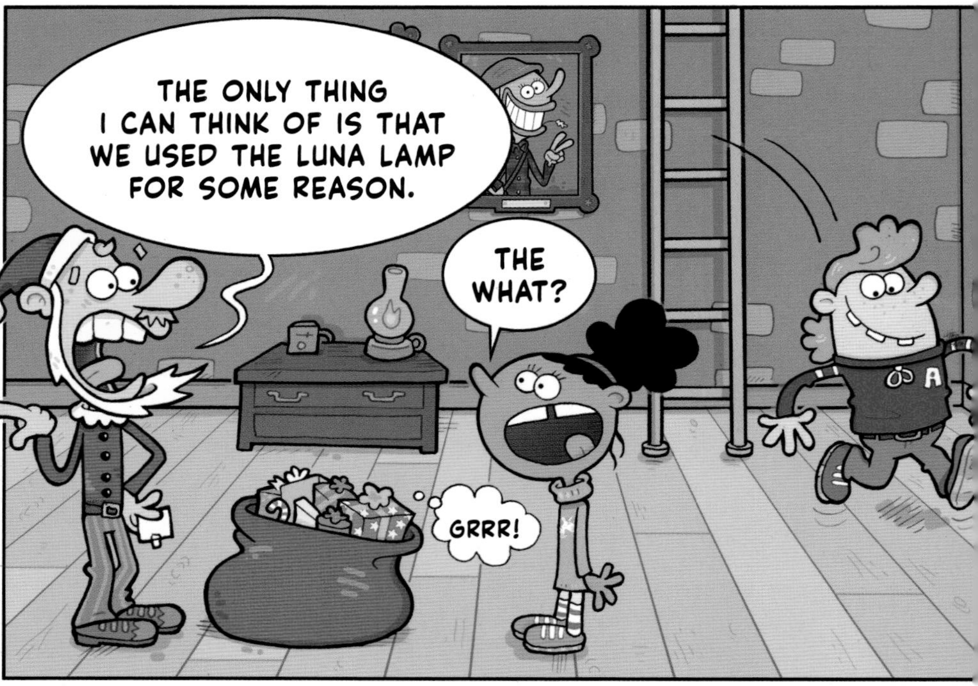
THE ONLY THING I CAN THINK OF IS THAT WE USED THE LUNA LAMP FOR SOME REASON.
THE WHAT?
GRRR!

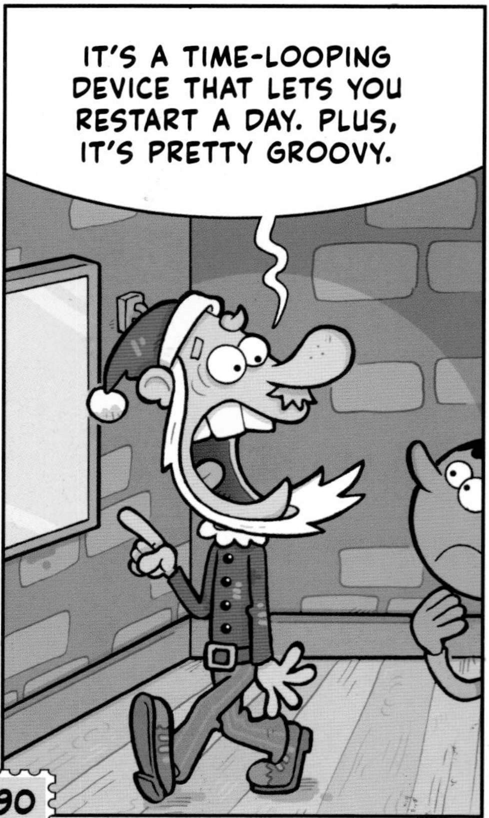
IT'S A TIME-LOOPING DEVICE THAT LETS YOU RESTART A DAY. PLUS, IT'S PRETTY GROOVY.

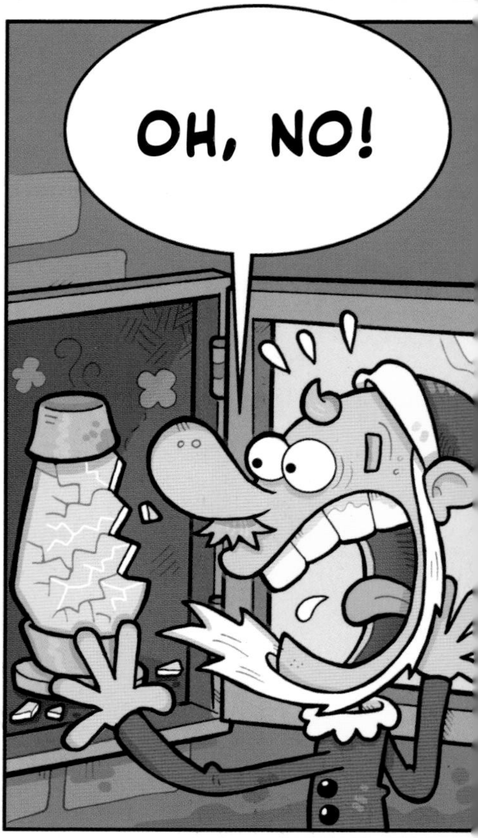
OH, NO!

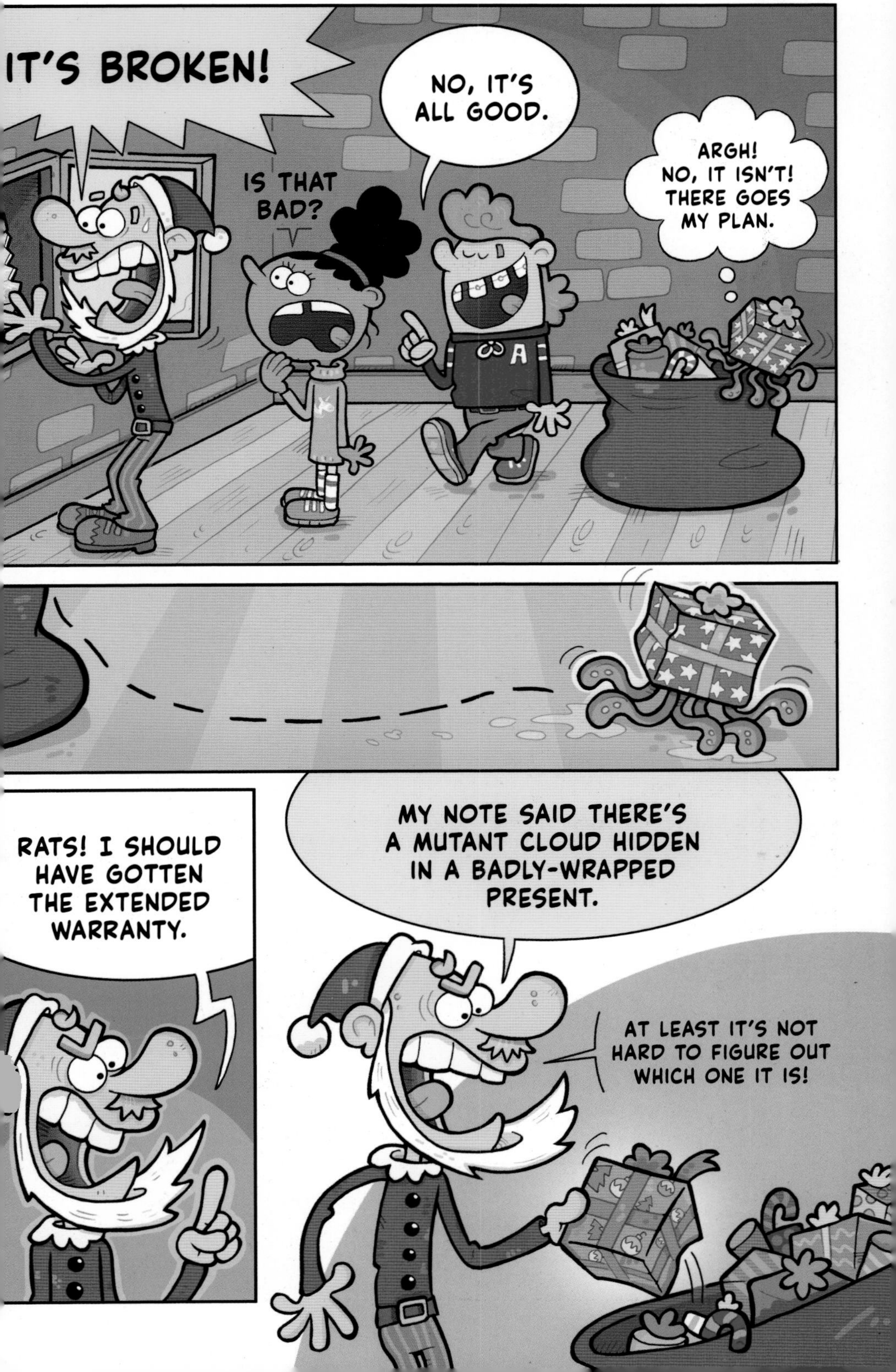
IT'S BROKEN!
IS THAT BAD?
NO, IT'S ALL GOOD.
ARGH! NO, IT ISN'T! THERE GOES MY PLAN.
RATS! I SHOULD HAVE GOTTEN THE EXTENDED WARRANTY.
MY NOTE SAID THERE'S A MUTANT CLOUD HIDDEN IN A BADLY-WRAPPED PRESENT.
AT LEAST IT'S NOT HARD TO FIGURE OUT WHICH ONE IT IS!

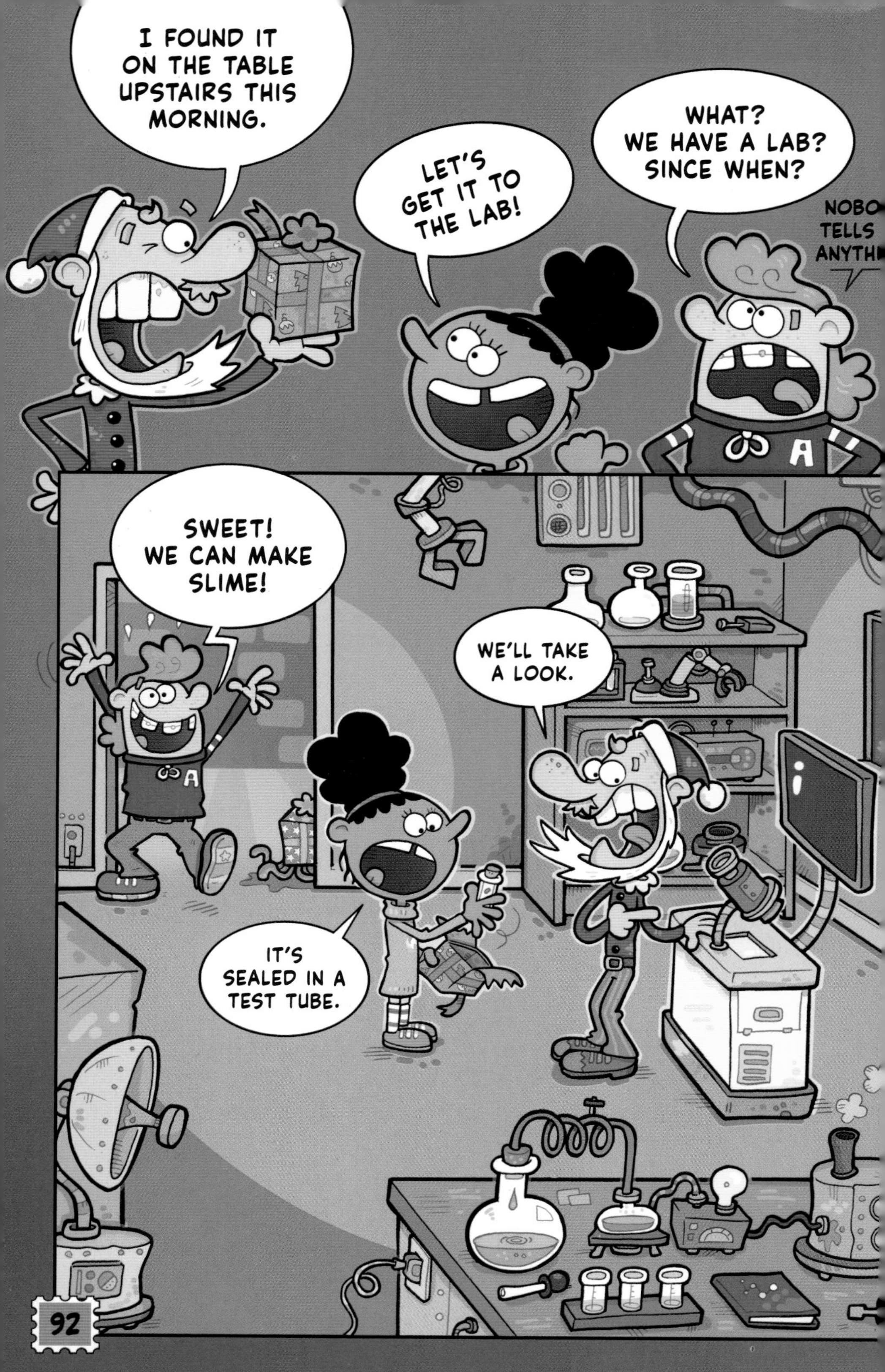
I FOUND IT ON THE TABLE UPSTAIRS THIS MORNING.
LET'S GET IT TO THE LAB!
WHAT? WE HAVE A LAB? SINCE WHEN?
NOBO TELLS ANYTHI
SWEET! WE CAN MAKE SLIME!
WE'LL TAKE A LOOK.
IT'S SEALED IN A TEST TUBE.

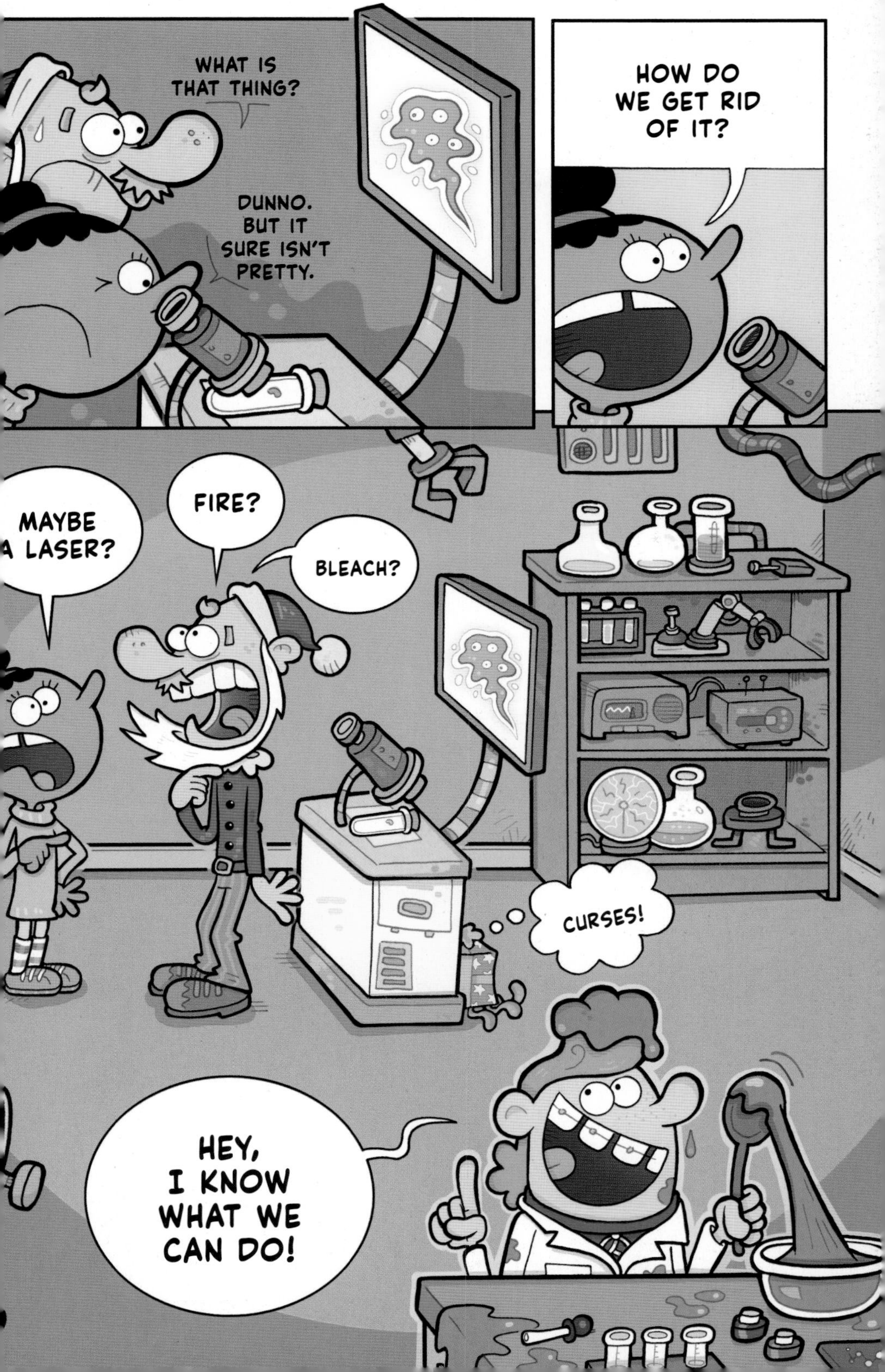
WHAT IS THAT THING?
DUNNO. BUT IT SURE ISN'T PRETTY.
HOW DO WE GET RID OF IT?
MAYBE A LASER?
FIRE?
BLEACH?
CURSES!
HEY, I KNOW WHAT WE CAN DO!

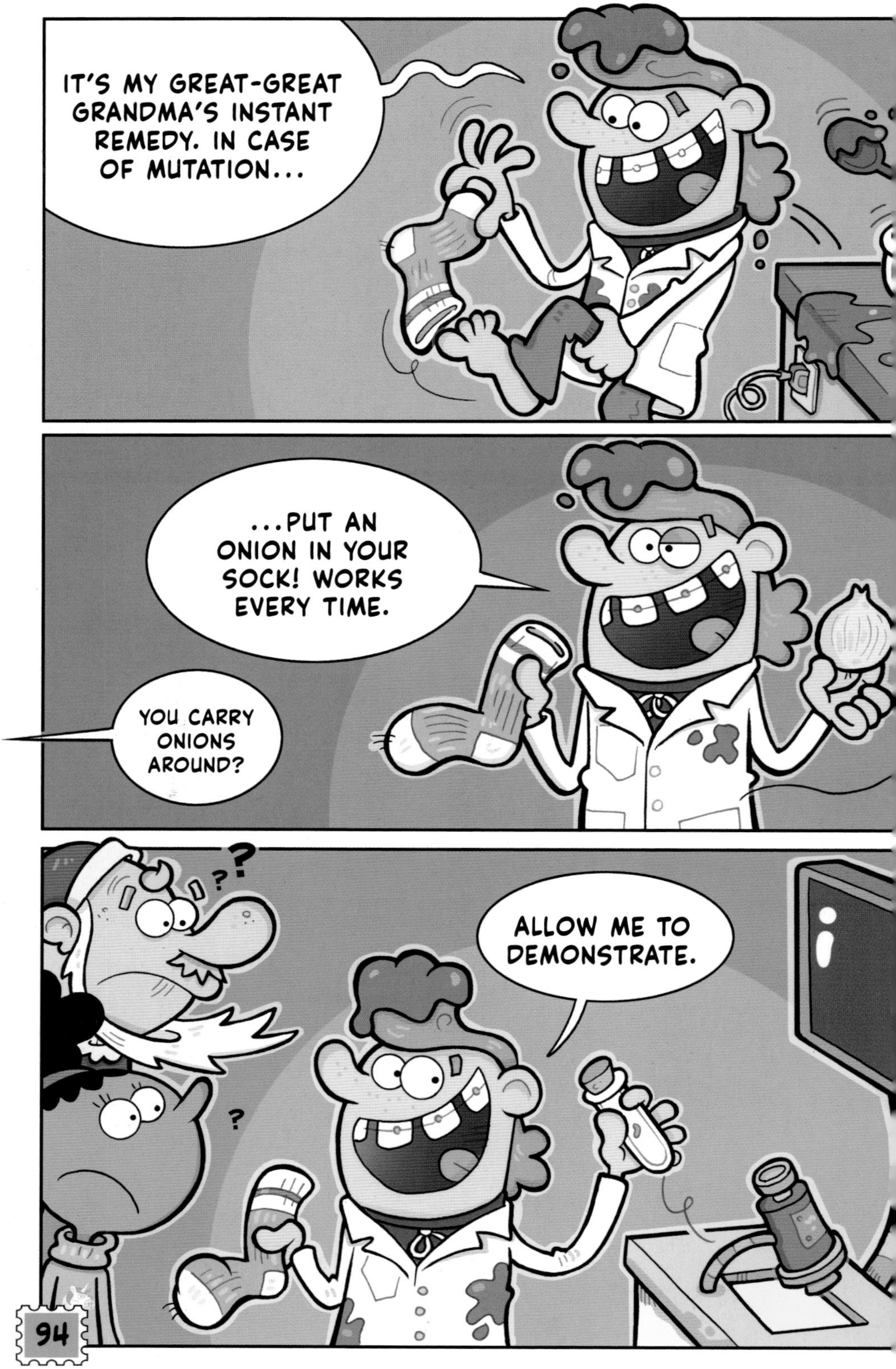
IT'S MY GREAT-GREAT GRANDMA'S INSTANT REMEDY. IN CASE OF MUTATION...
...PUT AN ONION IN YOUR SOCK! WORKS EVERY TIME.
YOU CARRY ONIONS AROUND?
ALLOW ME TO DEMONSTRATE.

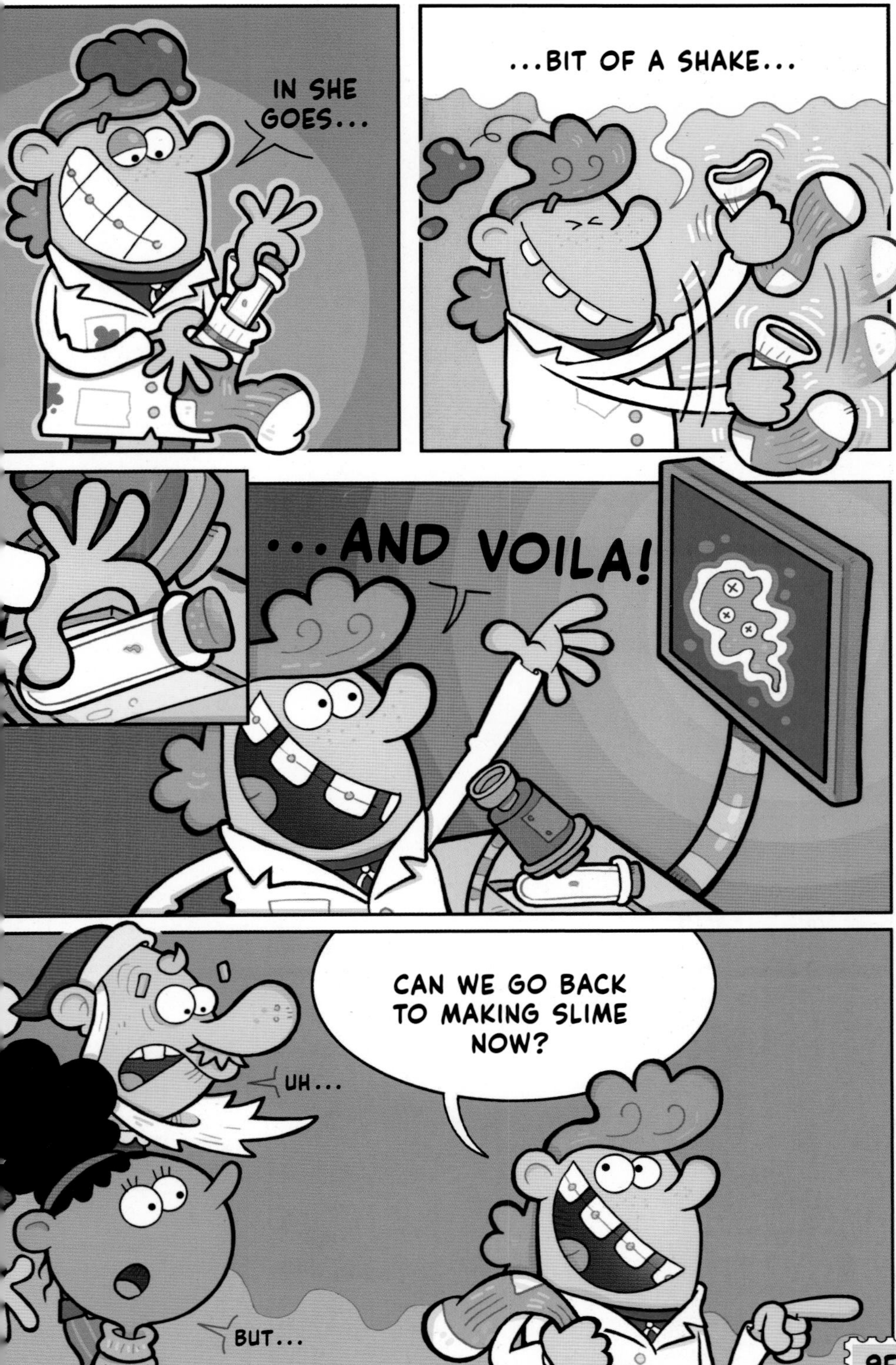
IN SHE GOES...
...BIT OF A SHAKE...
...AND VOILA!
CAN WE GO BACK TO MAKING SLIME NOW?
UH...
BUT...

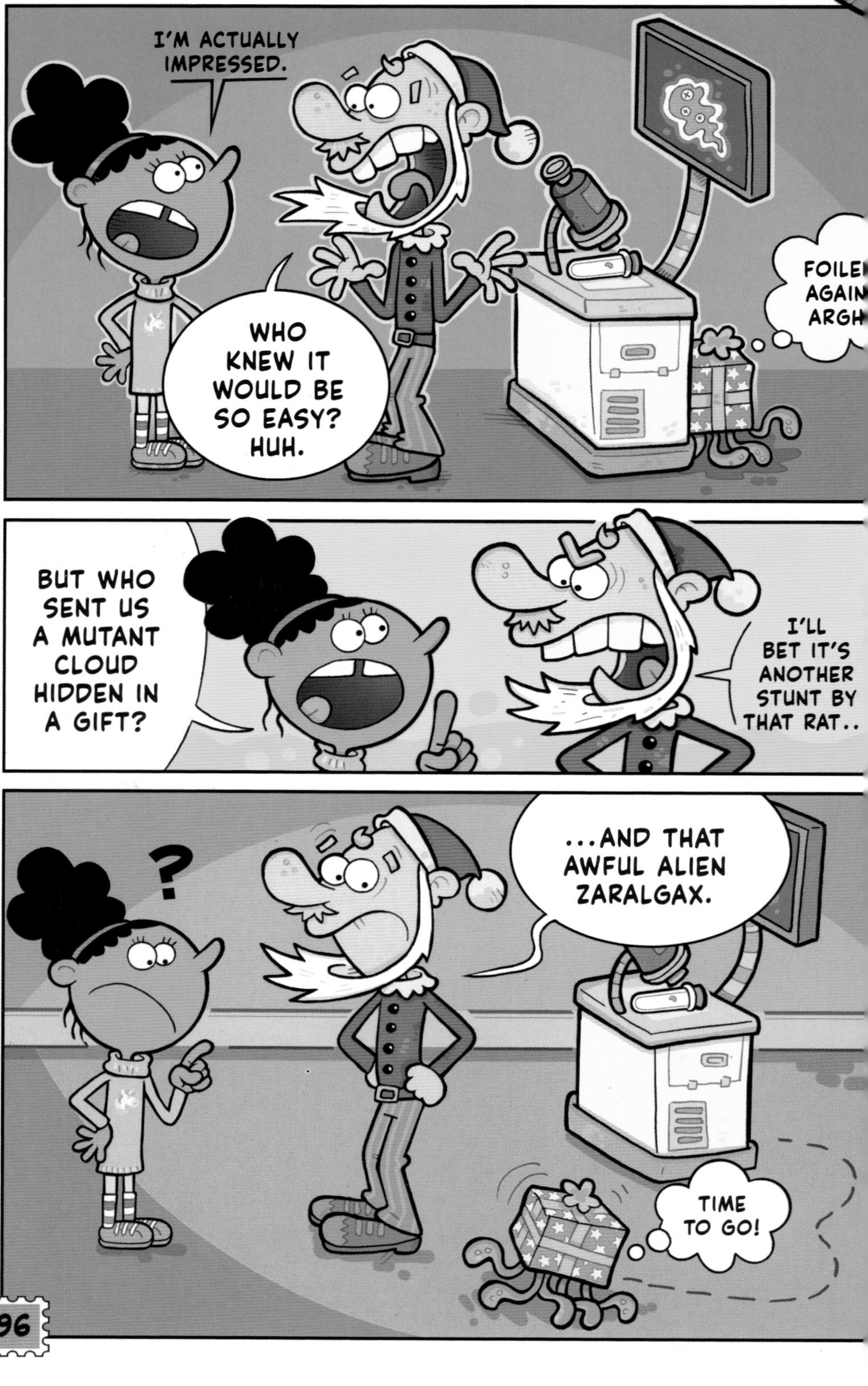
I'M ACTUALLY IMPRESSED.
WHO KNEW IT WOULD BE SO EASY? HUH.
FOILE AGAIN ARGH
BUT WHO SENT US A MUTANT CLOUD HIDDEN IN A GIFT?
I'LL BET IT'S ANOTHER STUNT BY THAT RAT...
?
...AND THAT AWFUL ALIEN ZARALGAX.
TIME TO GO!

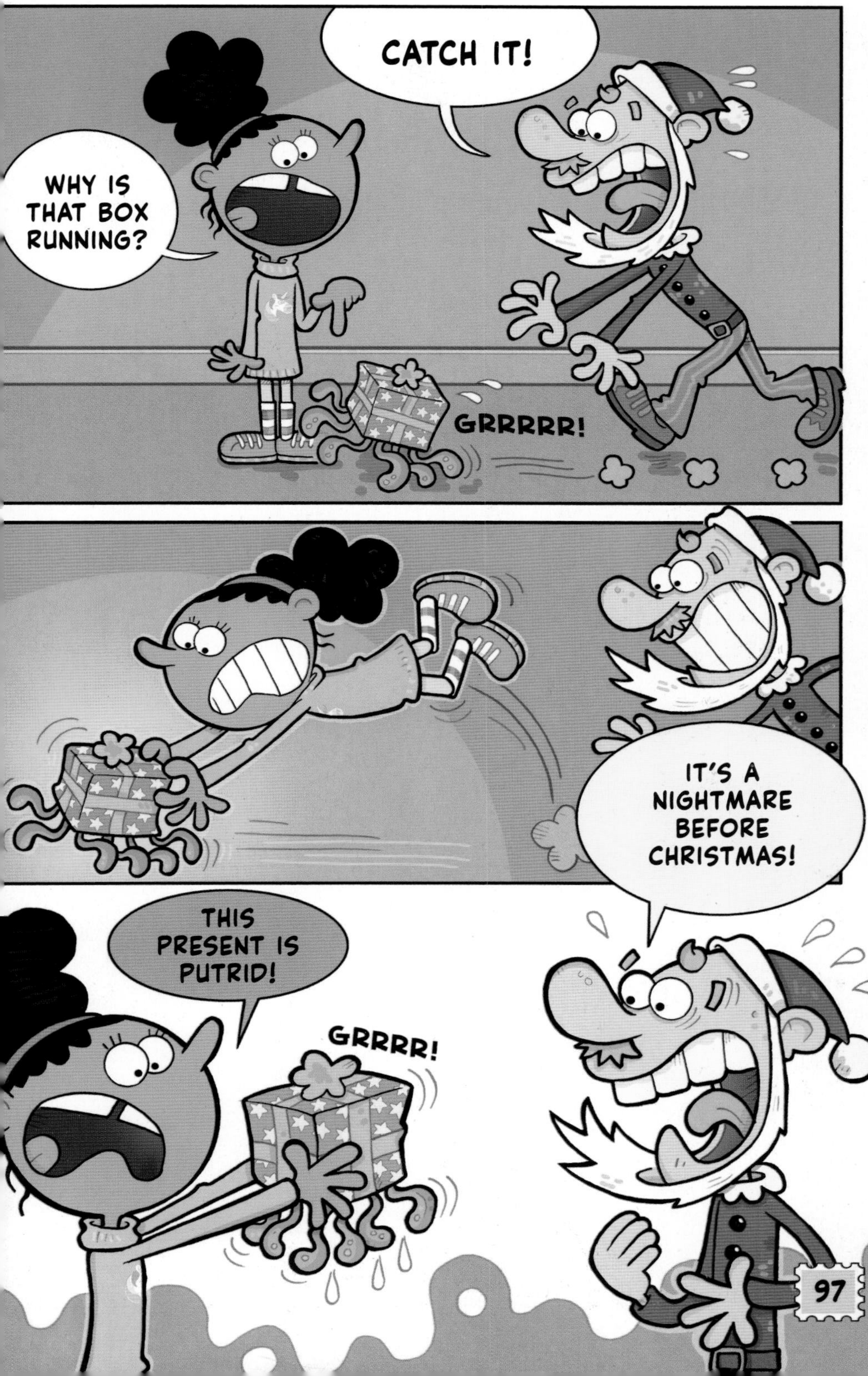
WHY IS THAT BOX RUNNING?
CATCH IT!
GRRRRR!
IT'S A NIGHTMARE BEFORE CHRISTMAS!
THIS PRESENT IS PUTRID!
GRRRR!

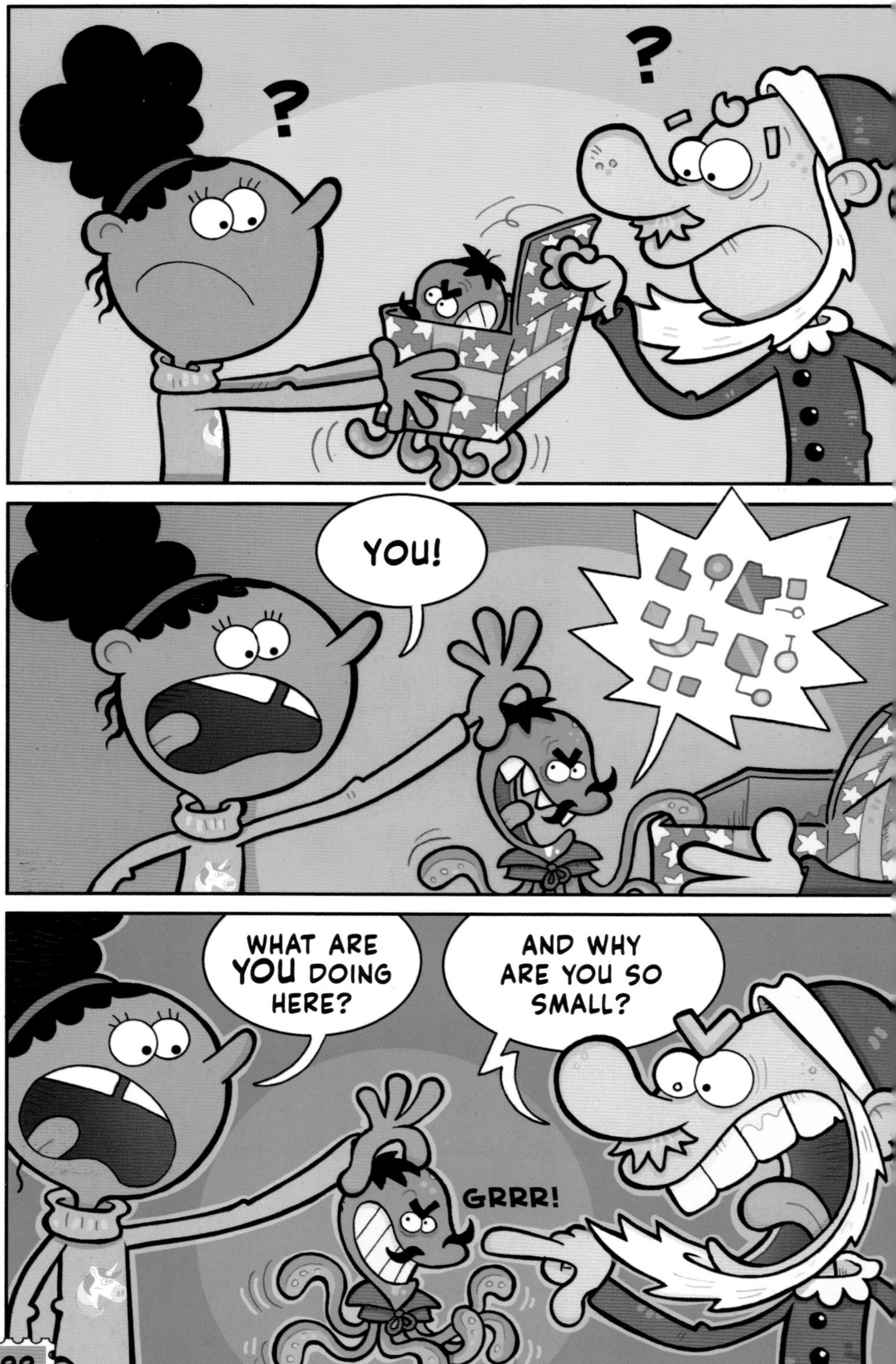
?
?
YOU!
WHAT ARE YOU DOING HERE?
AND WHY ARE YOU SO SMALL?
GRRR!

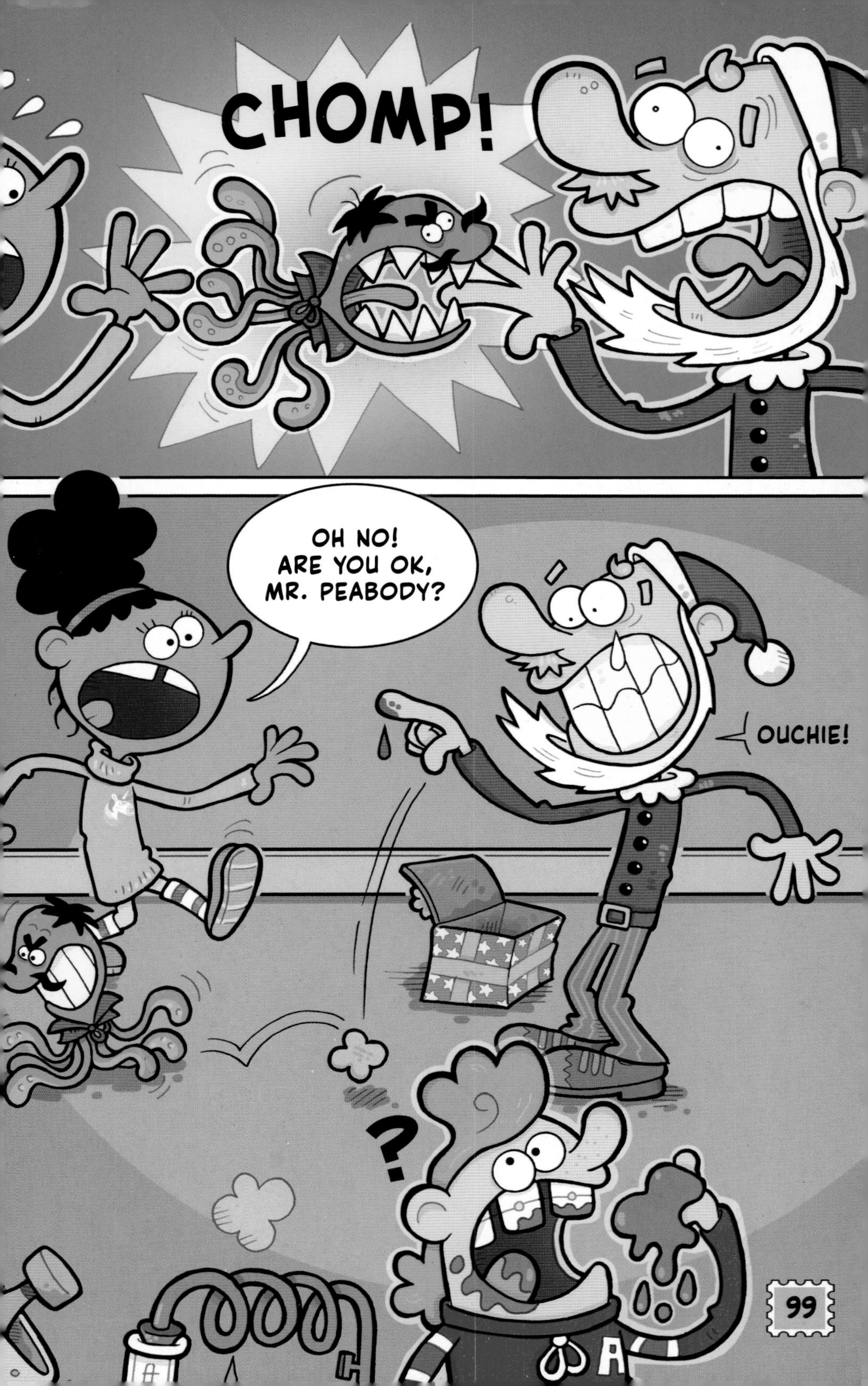
CHOMP!
OH NO! ARE YOU OK, MR. PEABODY?
OUCHIE!
?

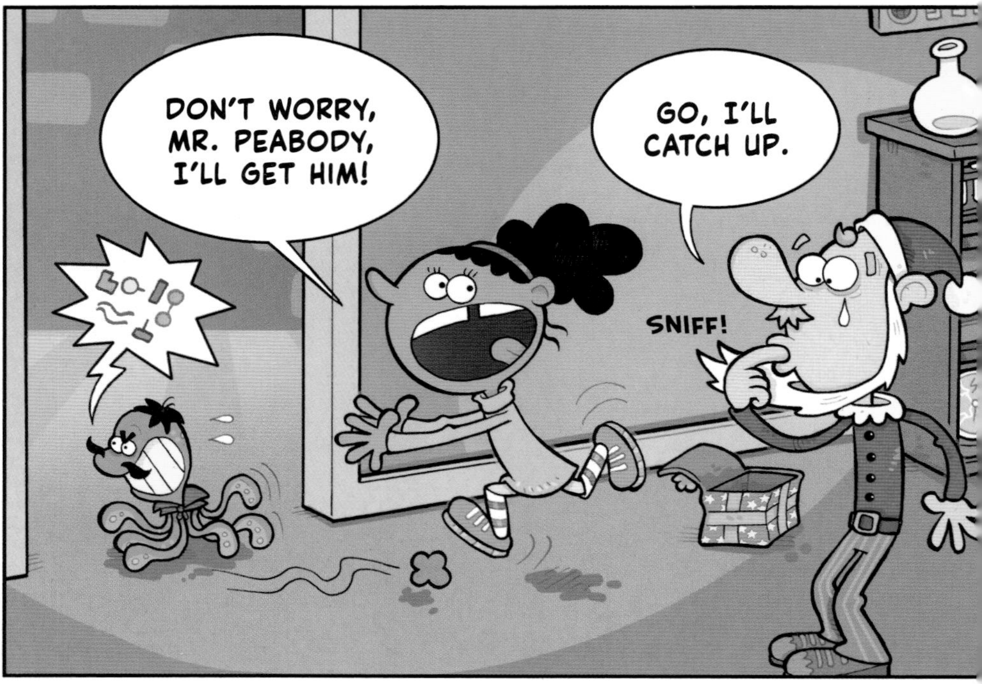
DON'T WORRY, MR. PEABODY, I'LL GET HIM!
GO, I'LL CATCH UP.
SNIFF!

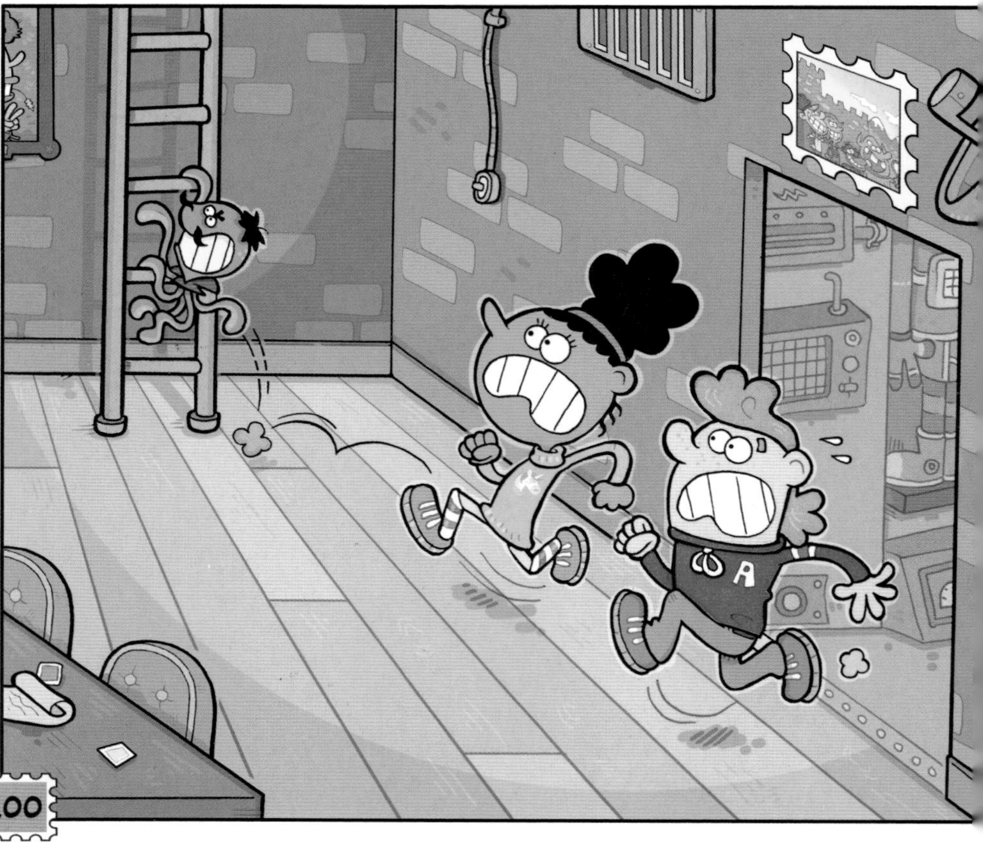

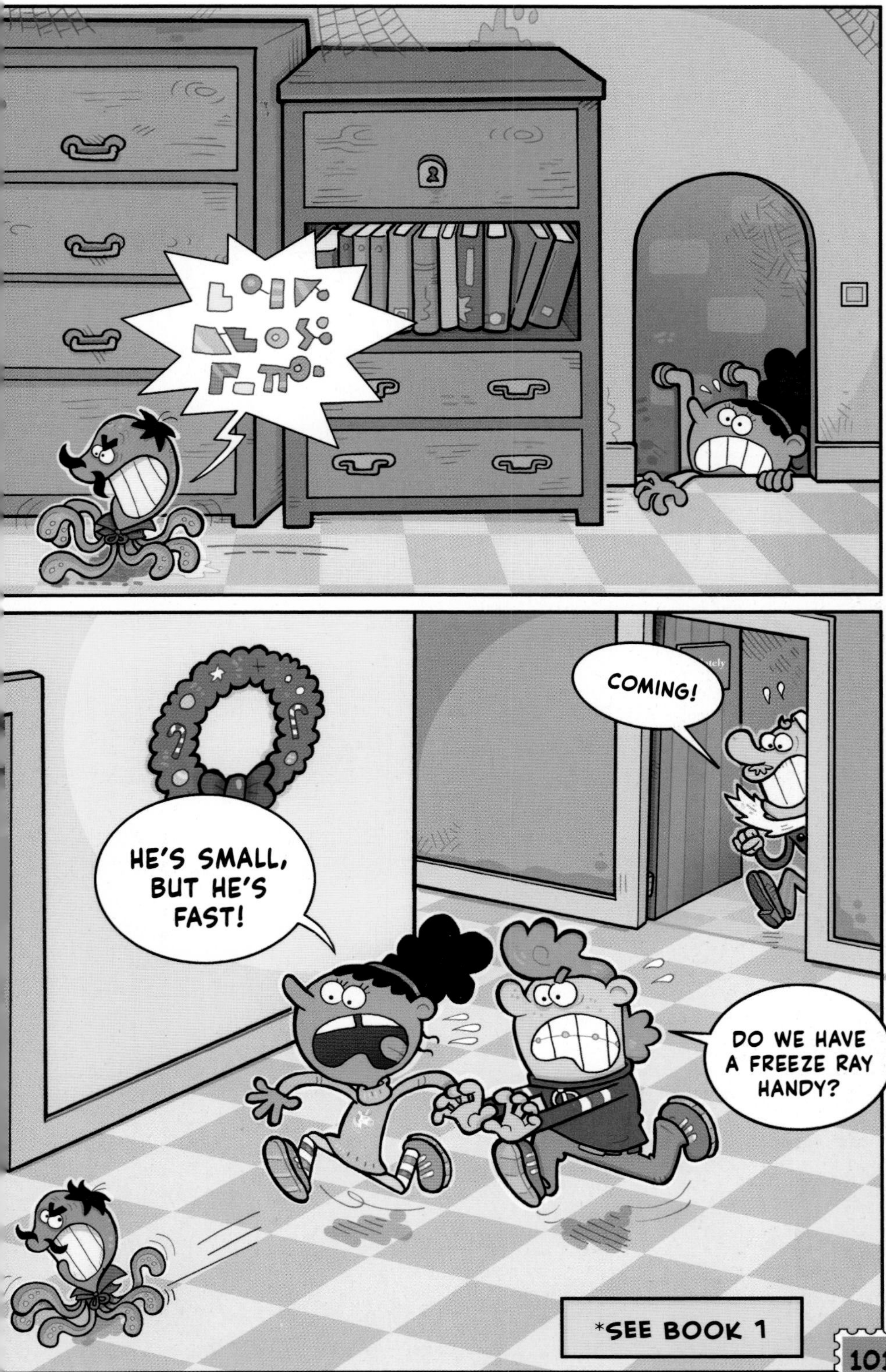
COMING!
HE'S SMALL, BUT HE'S FAST!
DO WE HAVE A FREEZE RAY HANDY?
*SEE BOOK 1

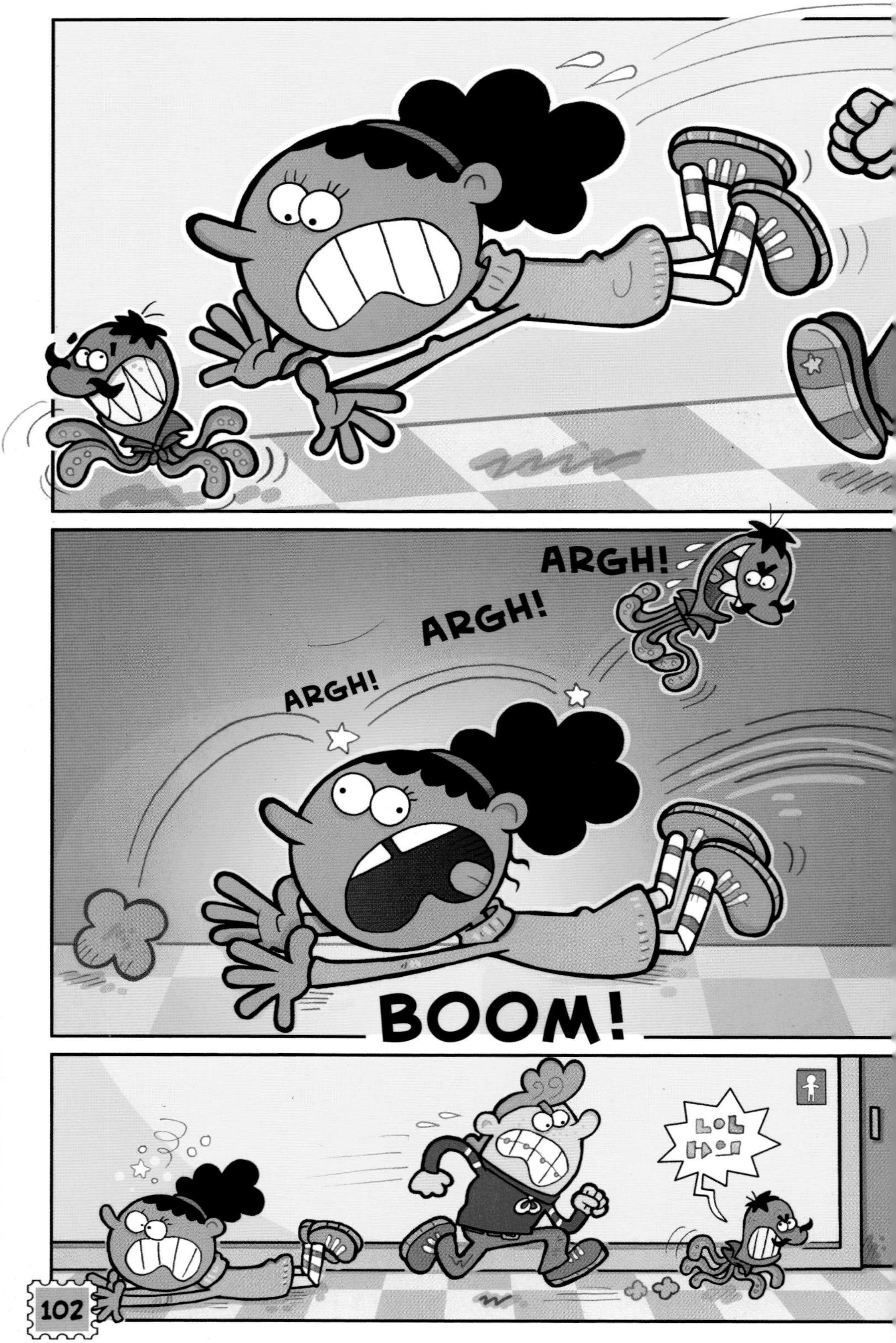
ARGH!
ARGH!
ARGH!
BOOM!

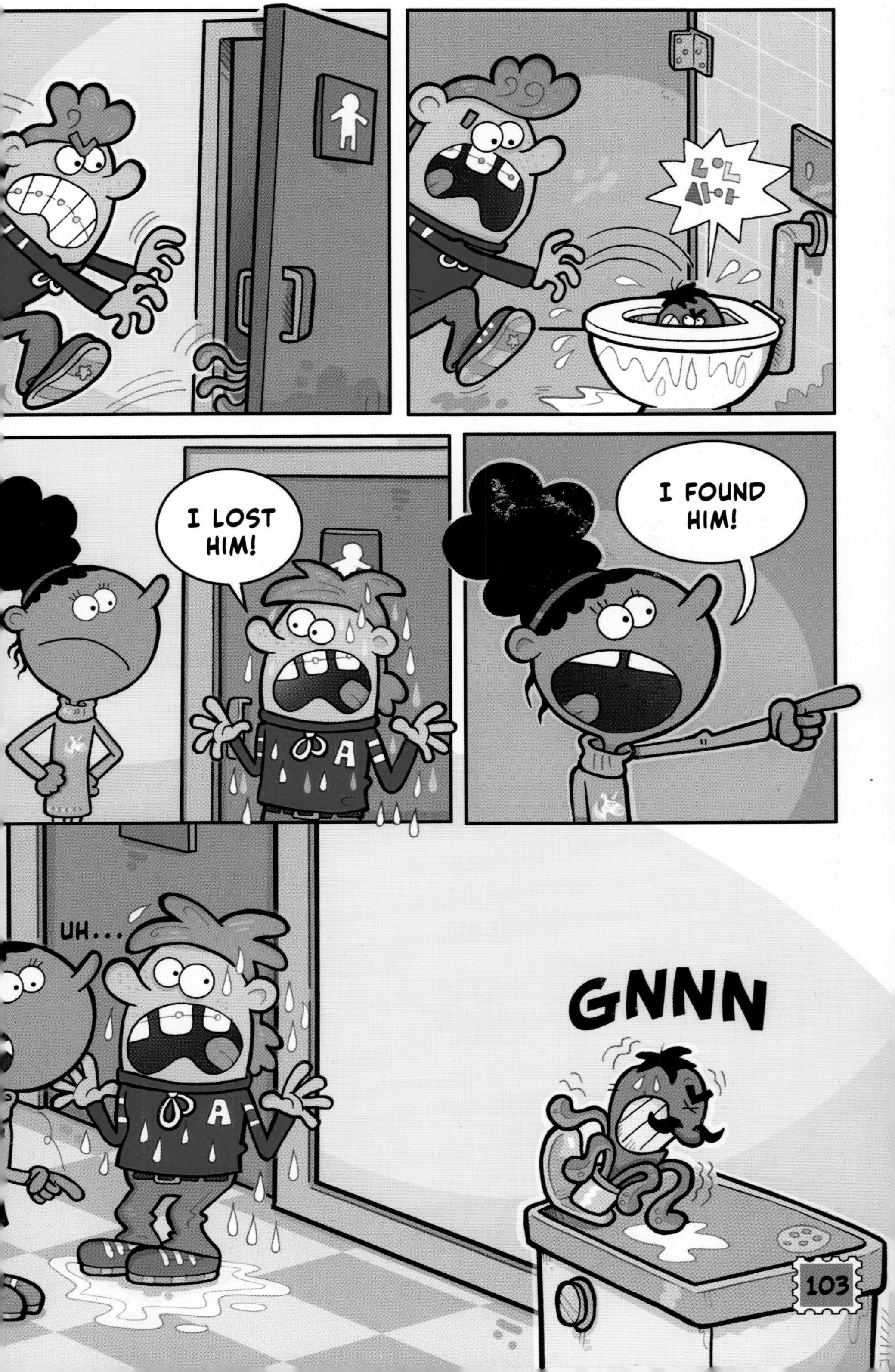

I LOST HIM!
I FOUND HIM!
UH...
GNNN

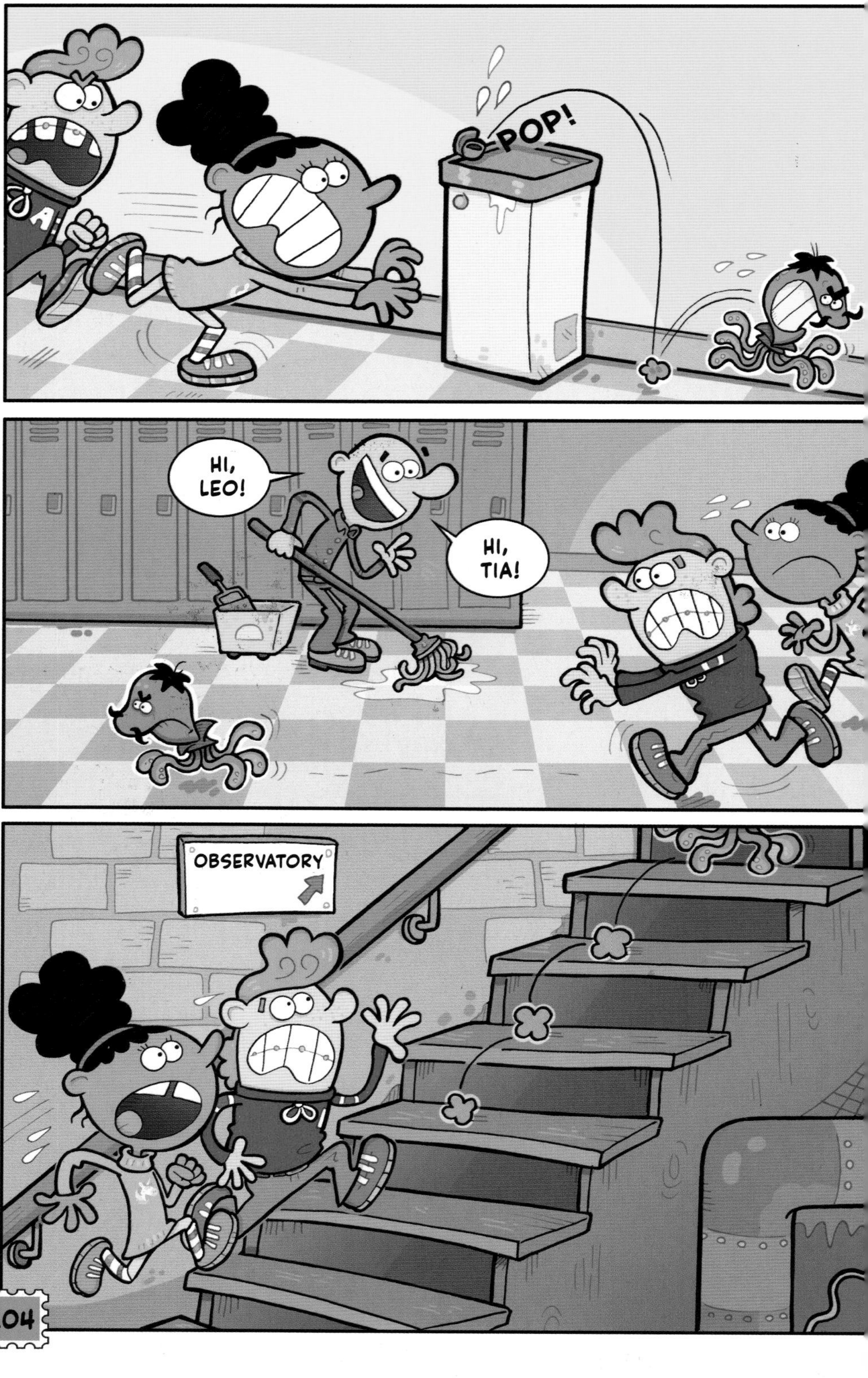
POP!
HI, LEO!
HI, TIA!
OBSERVATORY

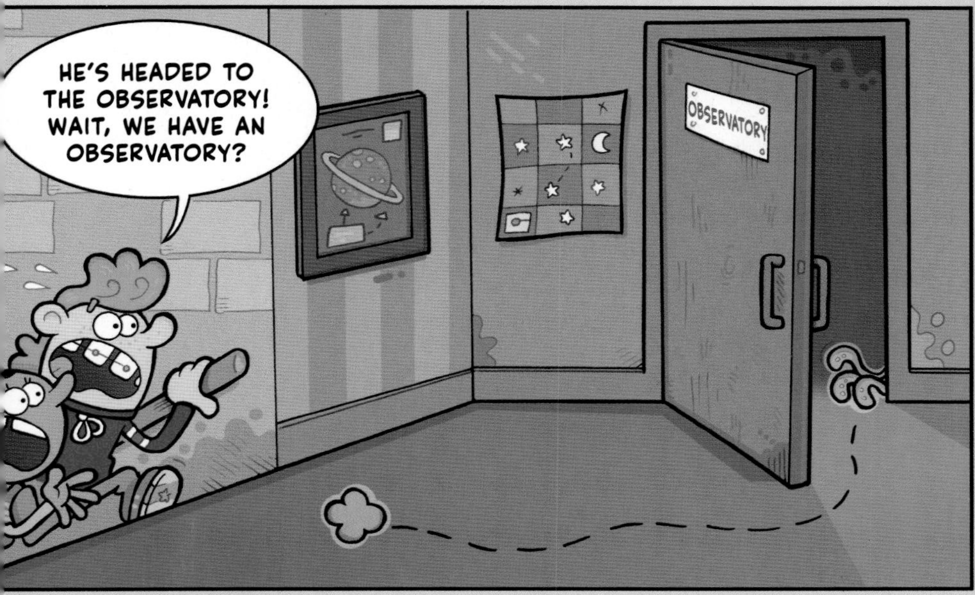
HE'S HEADED TO THE OBSERVATORY! WAIT, WE HAVE AN OBSERVATORY?
OBSERVATORY

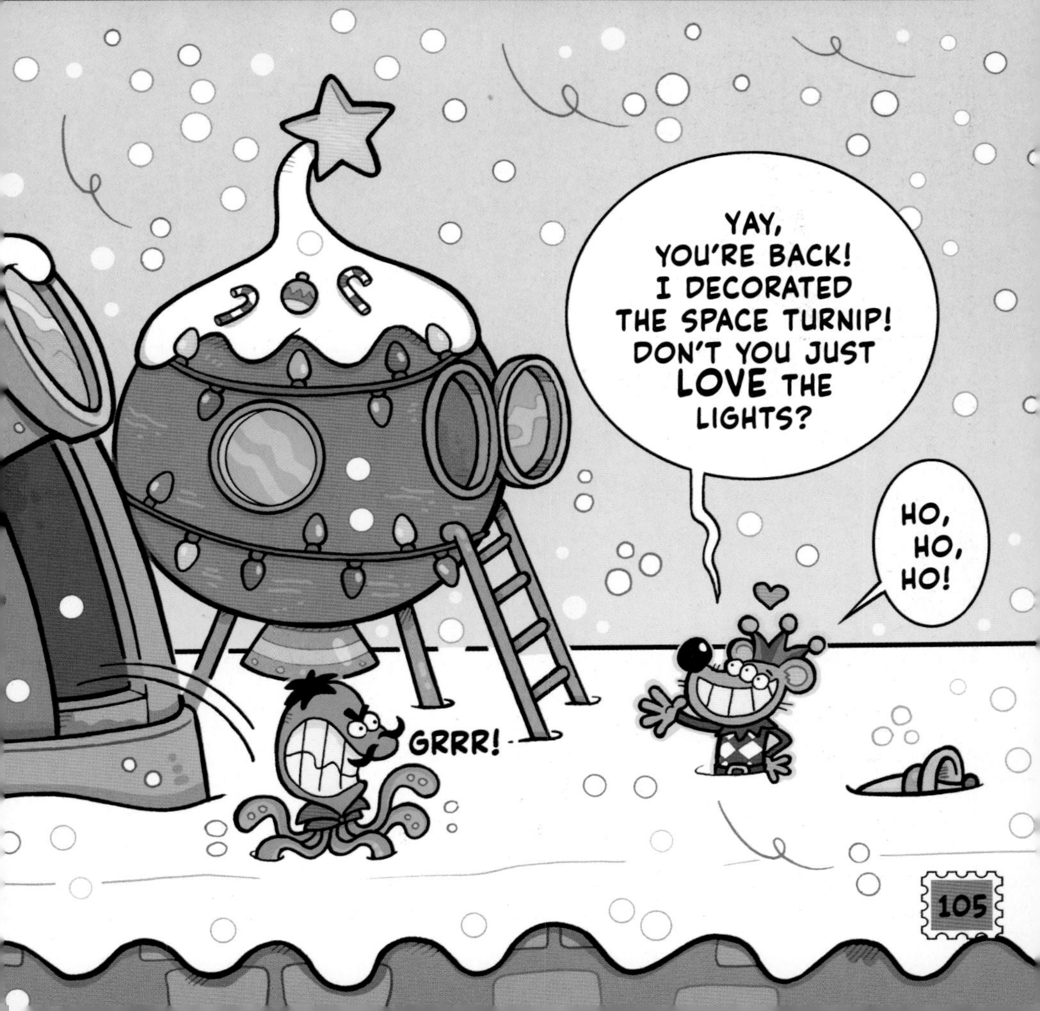
YAY, YOU'RE BACK! I DECORATED THE SPACE TURNIP! DON'T YOU JUST **LOVE** THE LIGHTS?
HO, HO, HO!
GRRR!

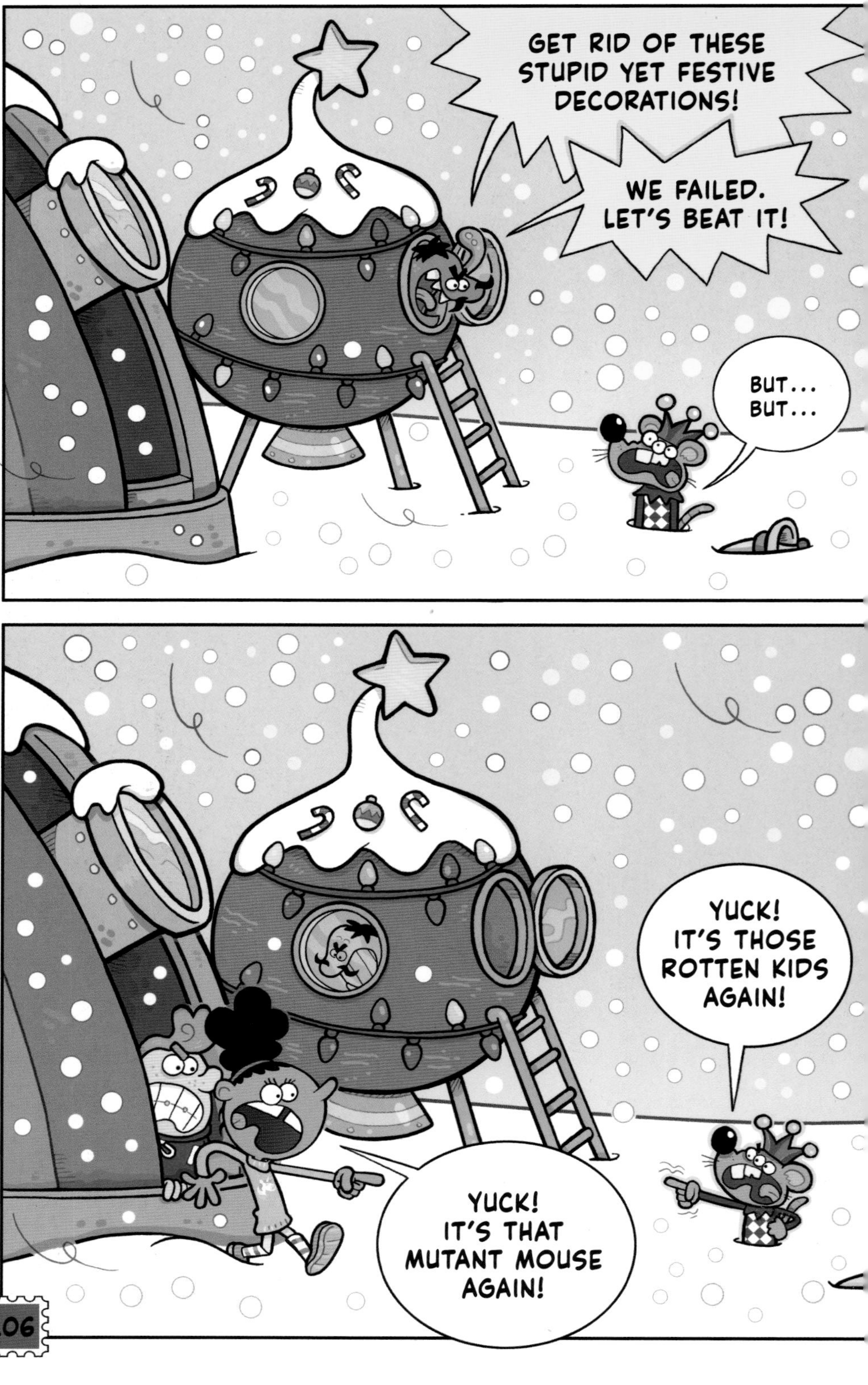
GET RID OF THESE STUPID YET FESTIVE DECORATIONS!
WE FAILED. LET'S BEAT IT!
BUT... BUT...
YUCK! IT'S THOSE ROTTEN KIDS AGAIN!
YUCK! IT'S THAT MUTANT MOUSE AGAIN!

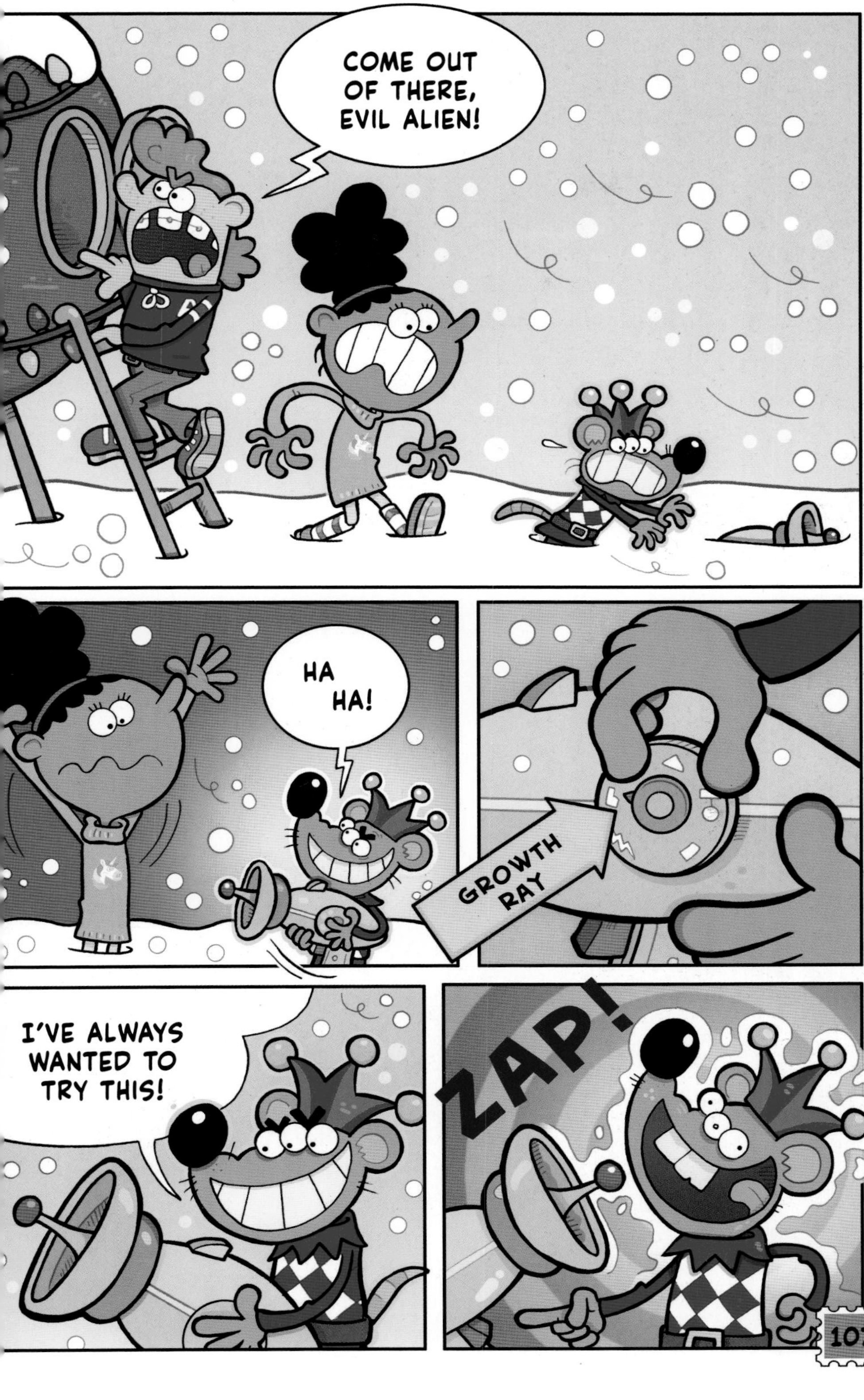
COME OUT OF THERE, EVIL ALIEN!
HA HA!
GROWTH RAY
I'VE ALWAYS WANTED TO TRY THIS!
ZAP!

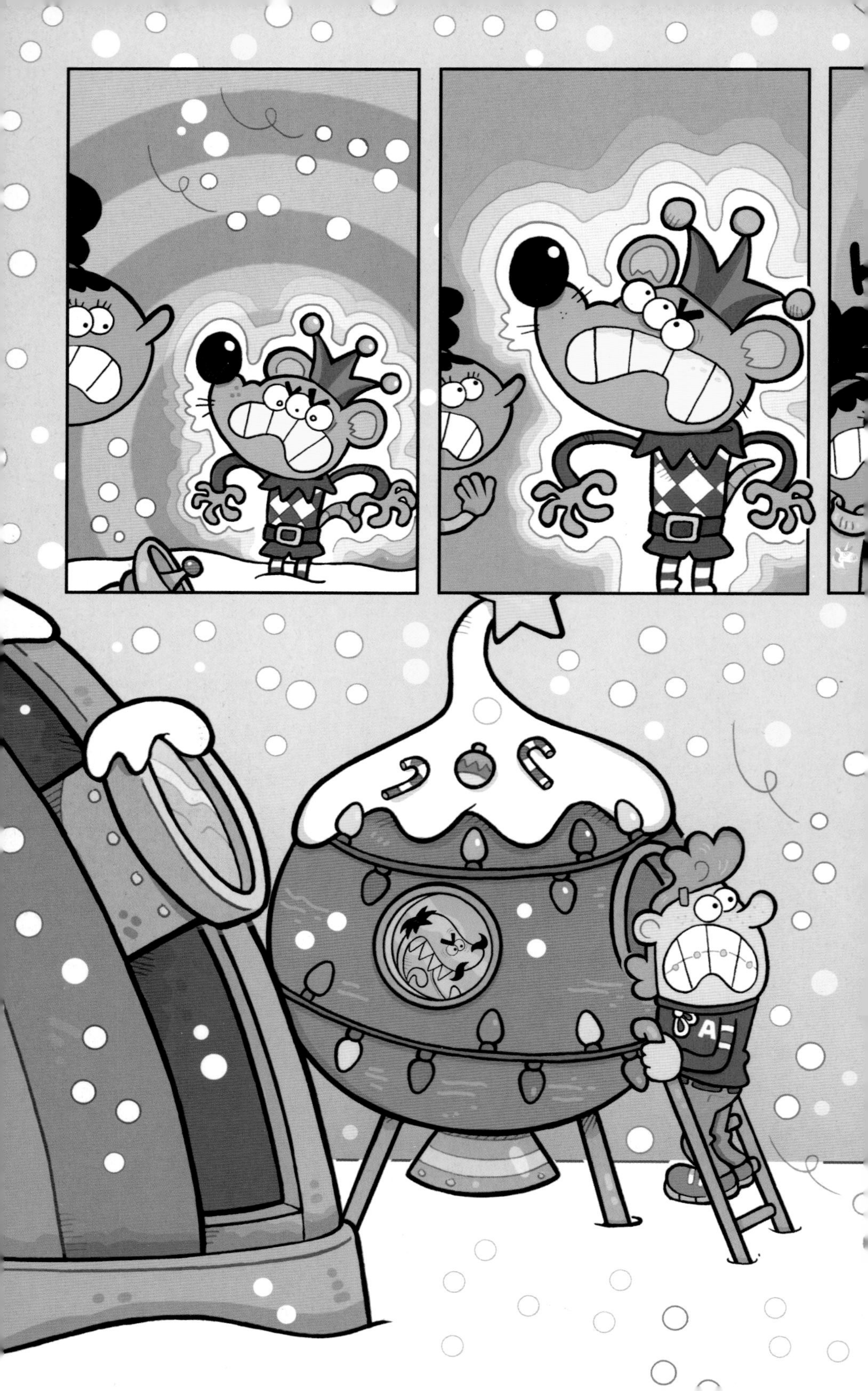

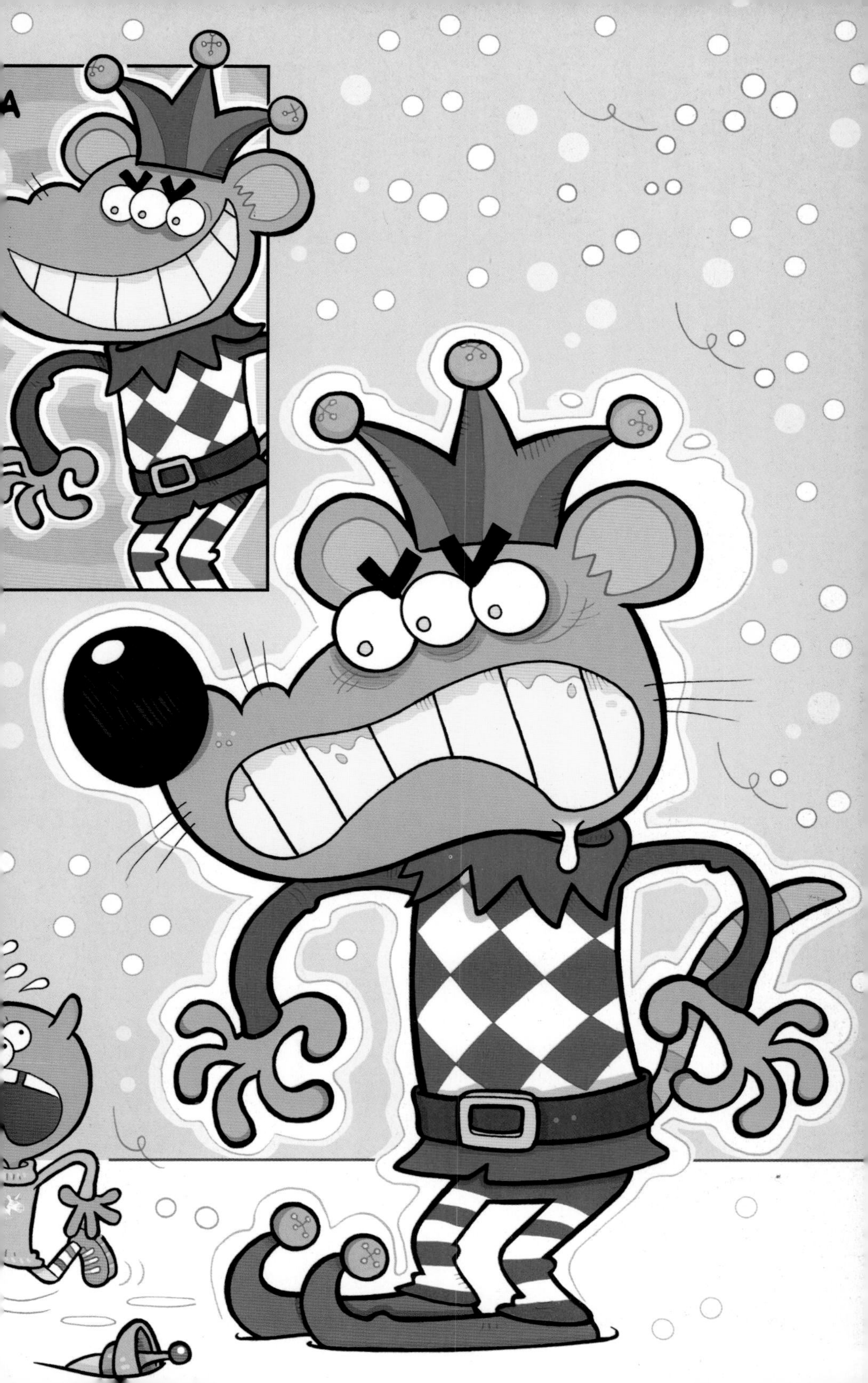

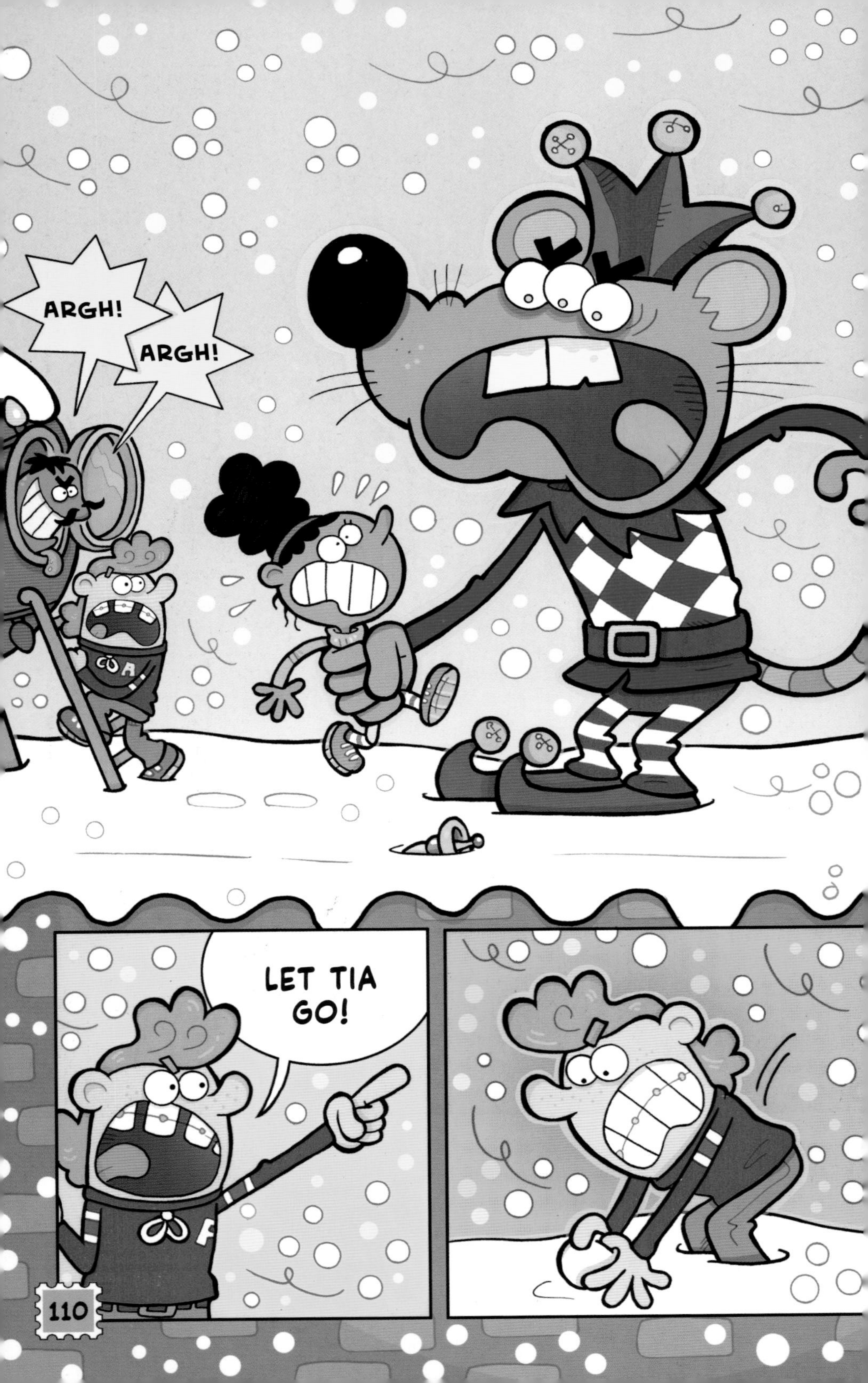
ARGH!
ARGH!
LET TIA GO!

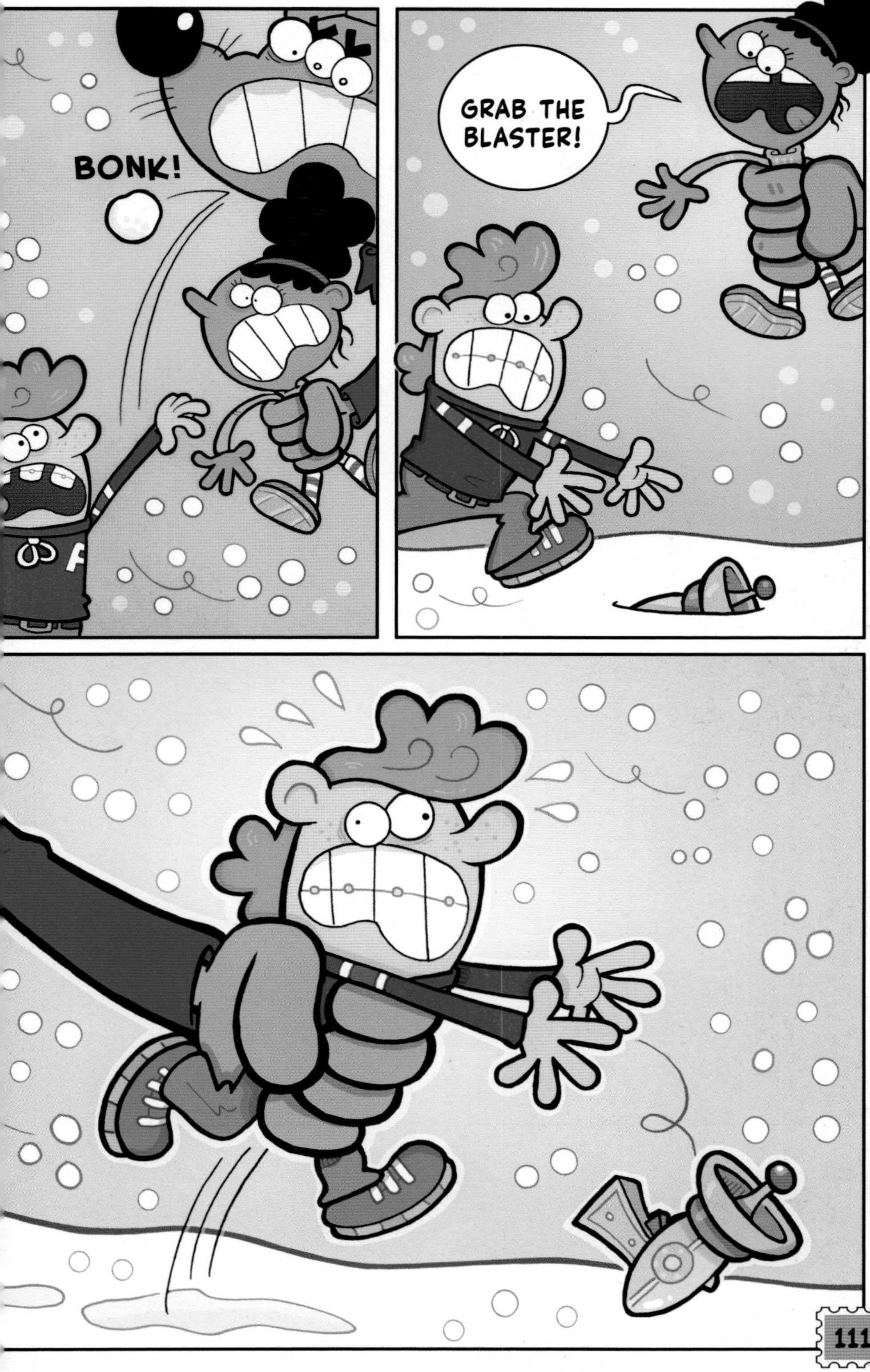
BONK!
GRAB THE BLASTER!

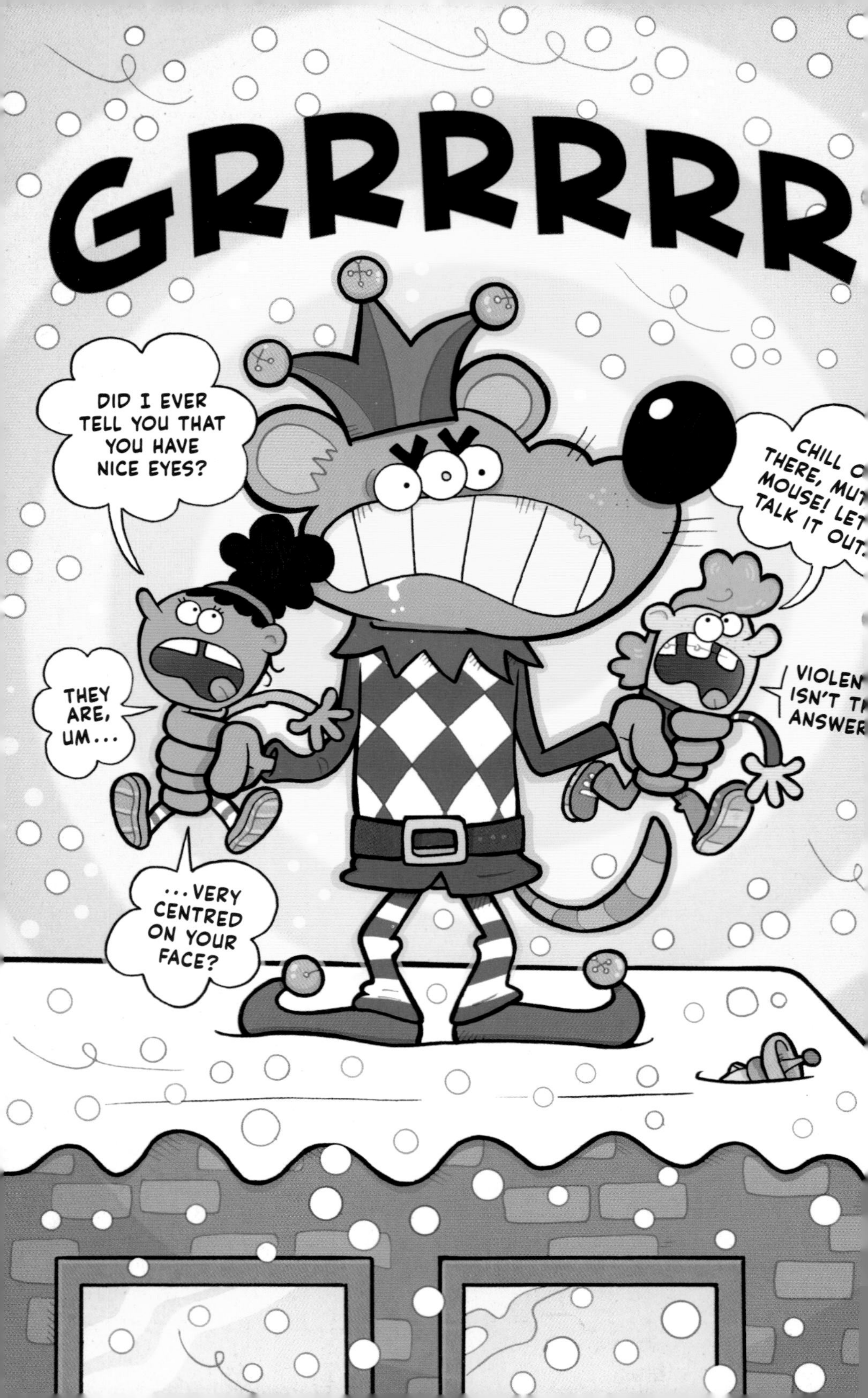
GRRRRRR
DID I EVER TELL YOU THAT YOU HAVE NICE EYES?
CHILL O THERE, MUT MOUSE! LET TALK IT OUT.
THEY ARE, UM...
VIOLEN ISN'T T ANSWER
...VERY CENTRED ON YOUR FACE?

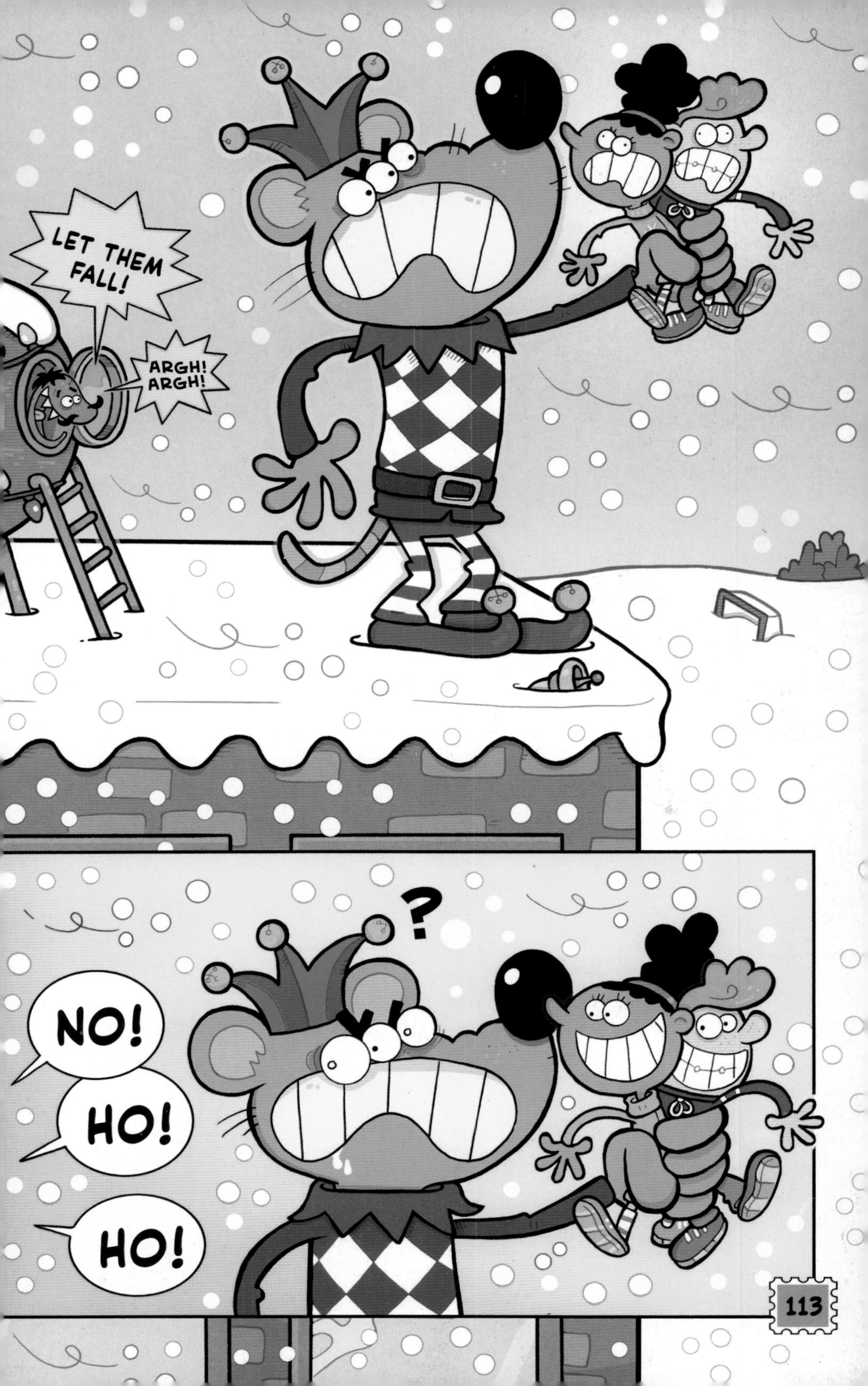
LET THEM FALL!
ARGH! ARGH!
?
NO!
HO!
HO!

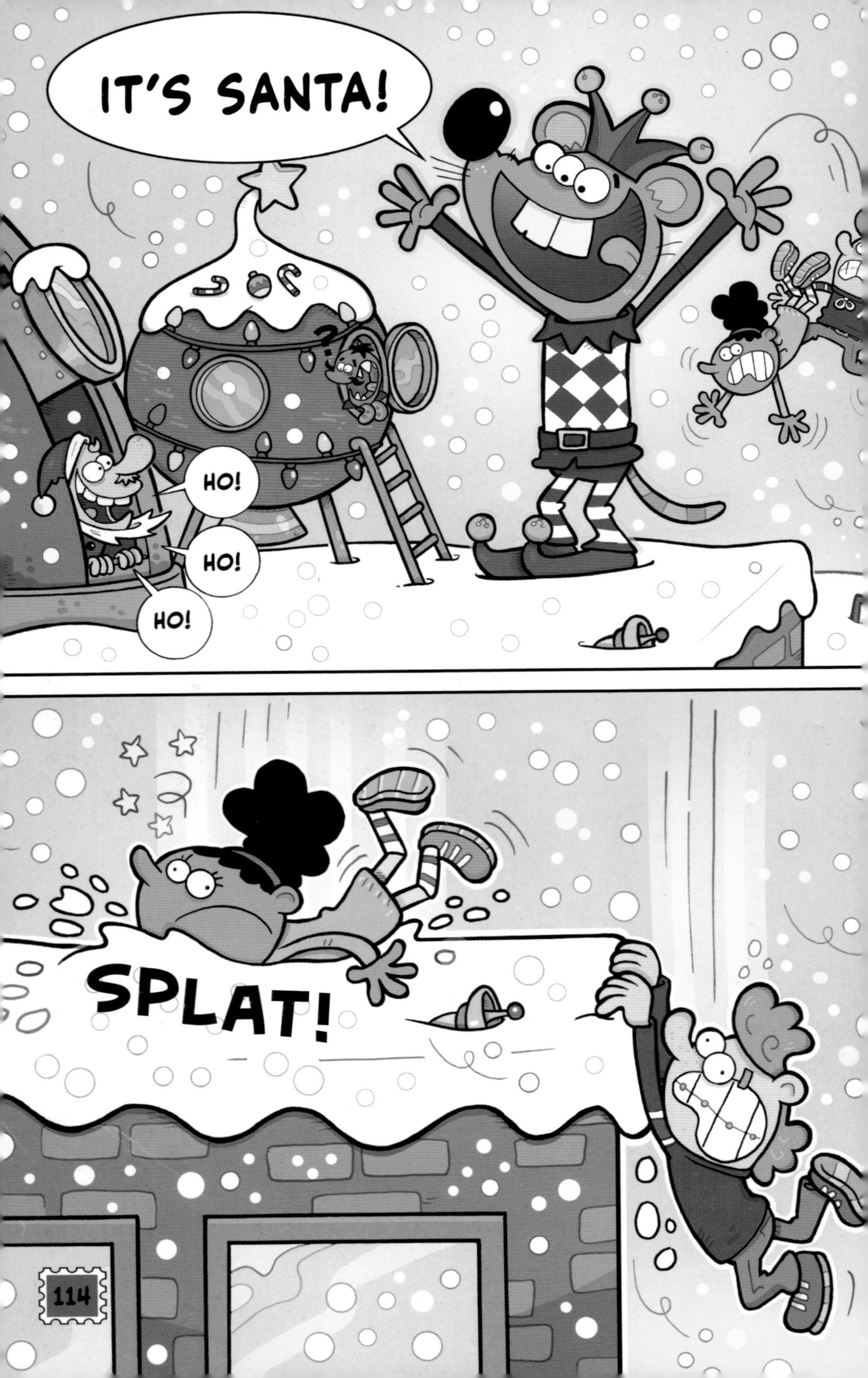
IT'S SANTA!
HO!
HO!
HO!
SPLAT!

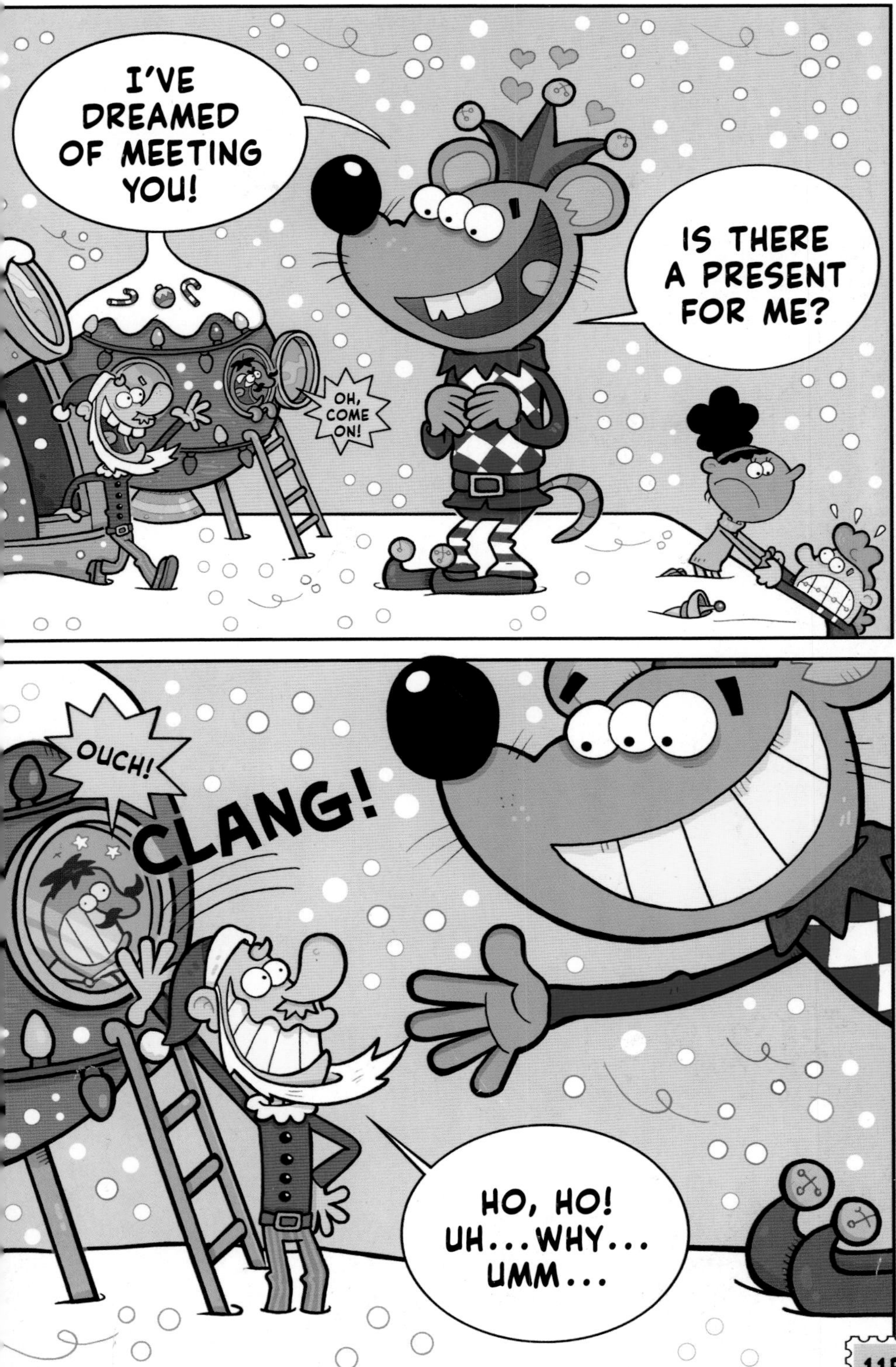
I'VE DREAMED OF MEETING YOU!
OH, COME ON!
IS THERE A PRESENT FOR ME?
OUCH!
CLANG!
HO, HO! UH...WHY... UMM...

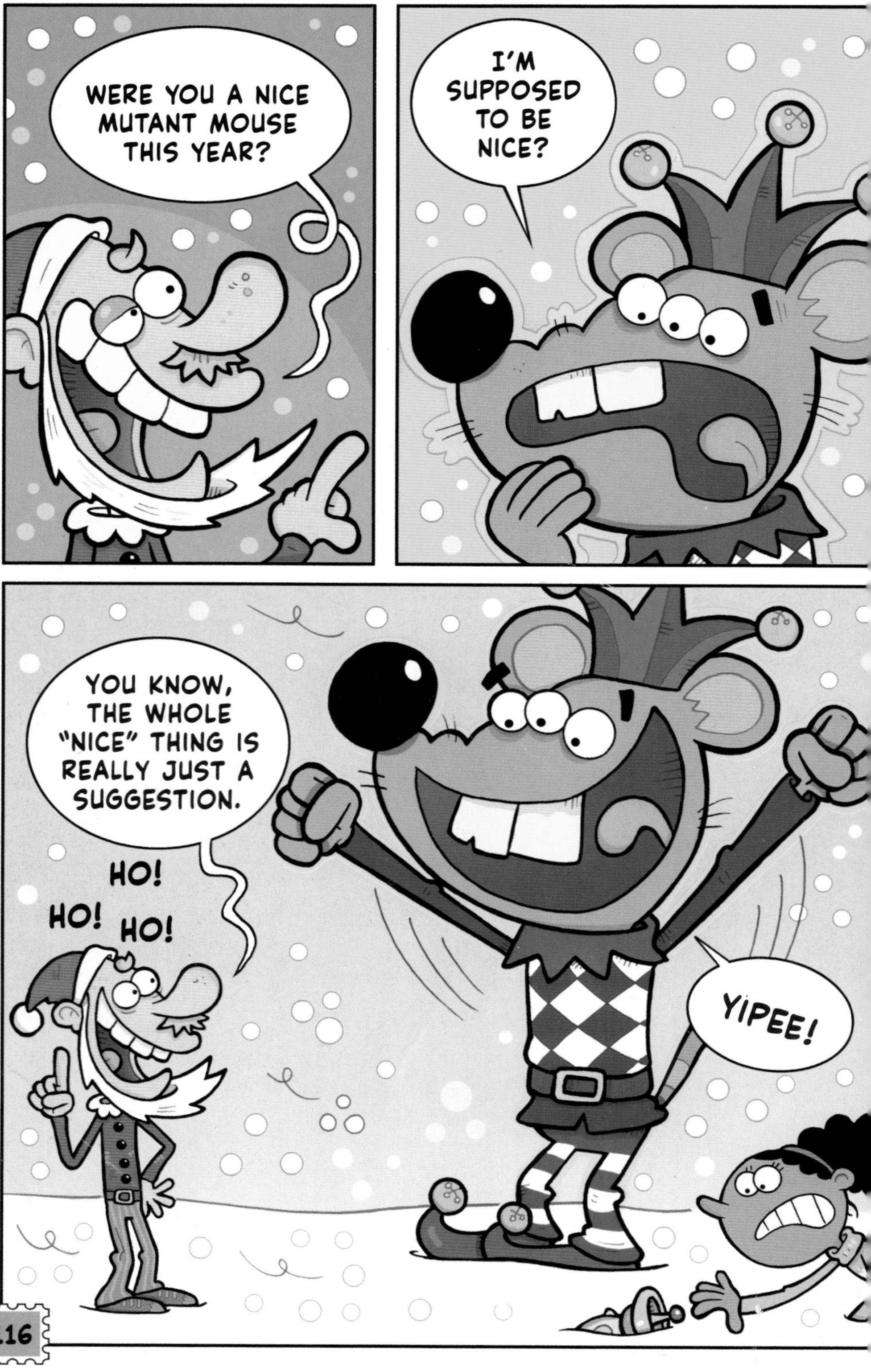
WERE YOU A NICE MUTANT MOUSE THIS YEAR?
I'M SUPPOSED TO BE NICE?
YOU KNOW, THE WHOLE "NICE" THING IS REALLY JUST A SUGGESTION.
HO! HO! HO!
YIPEE!

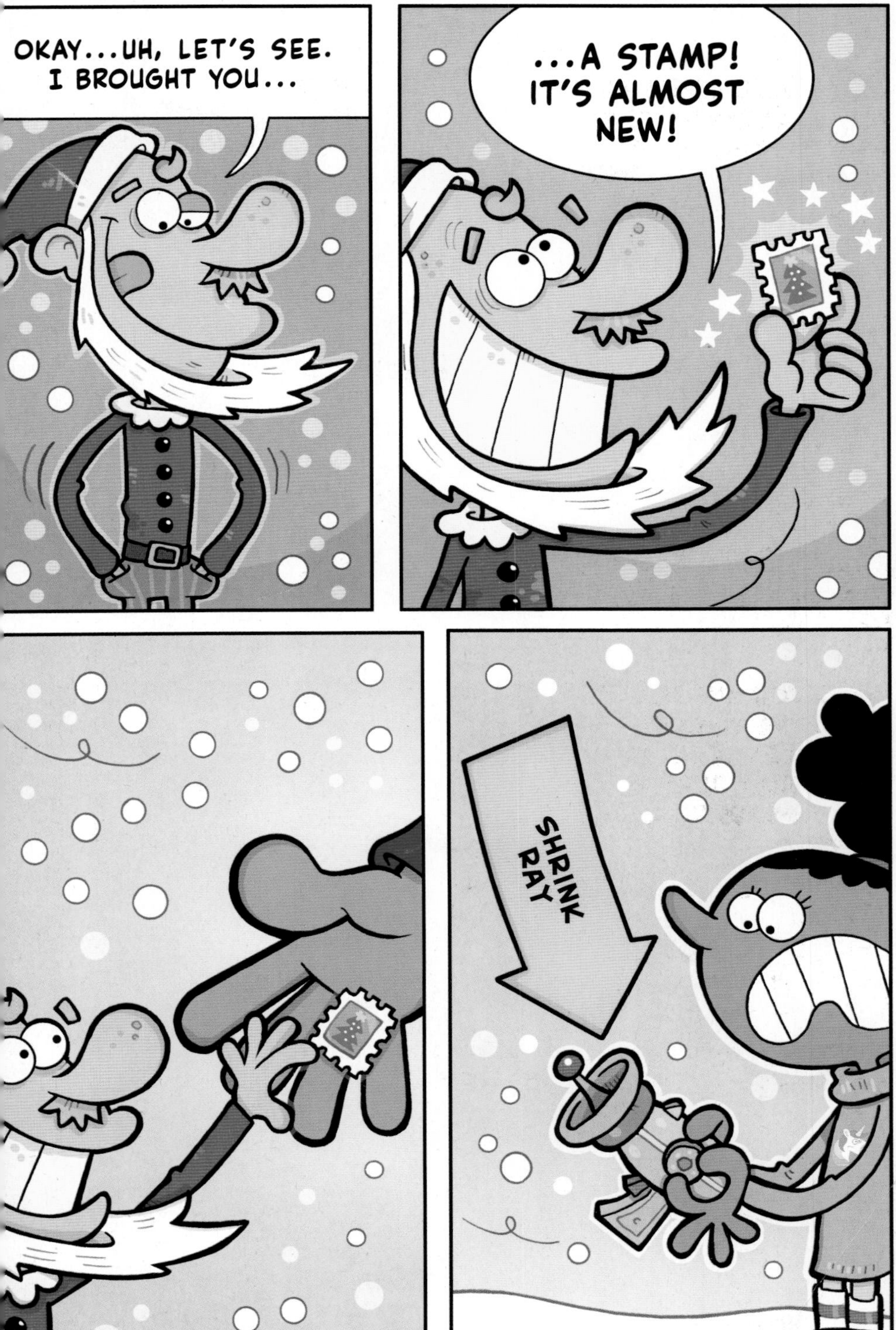
OKAY...UH, LET'S SEE. I BROUGHT YOU...
...A STAMP! IT'S ALMOST NEW!
SHRINK RAY

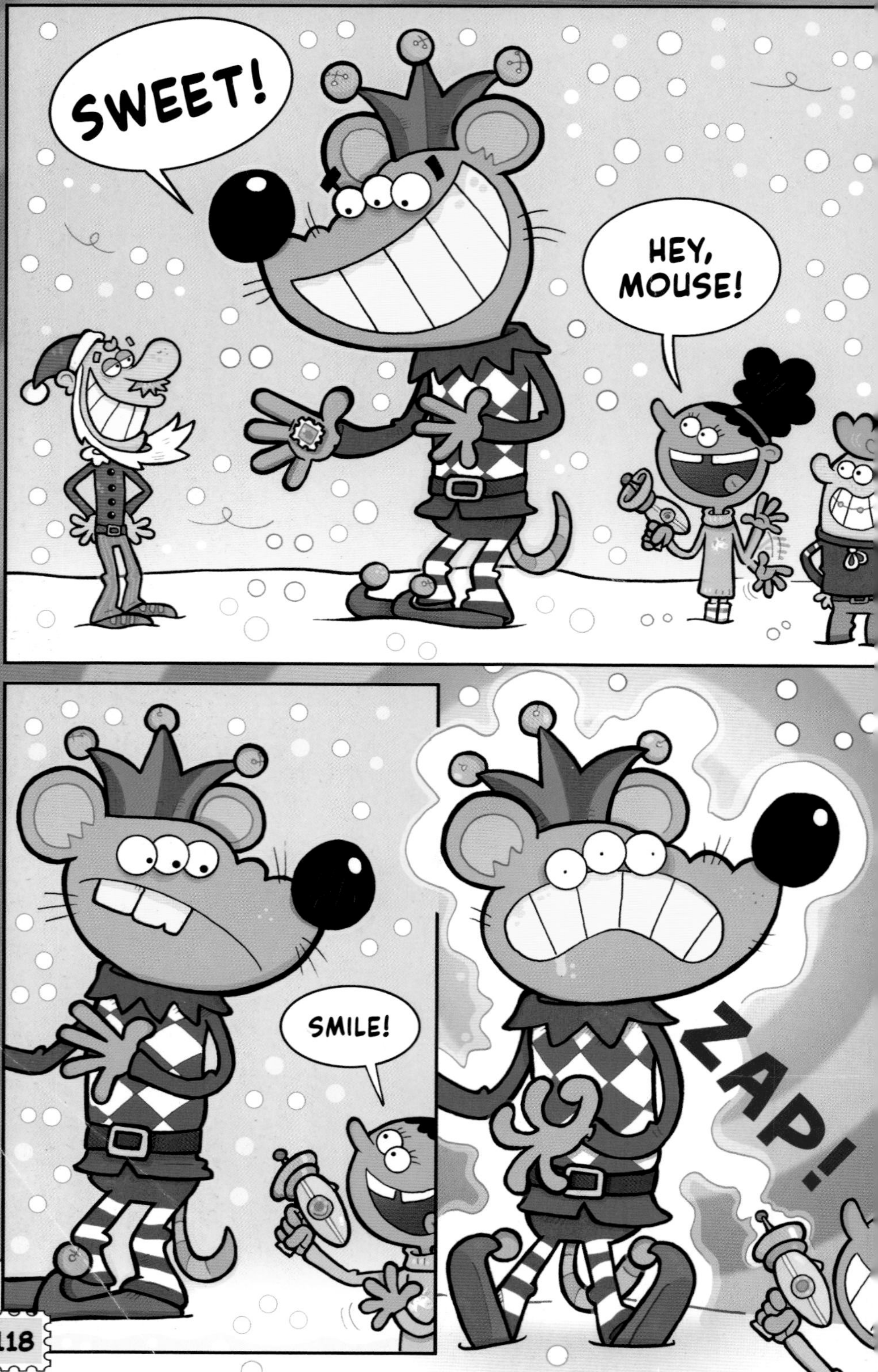

SWEET!
HEY, MOUSE!
SMILE!
ZAP!

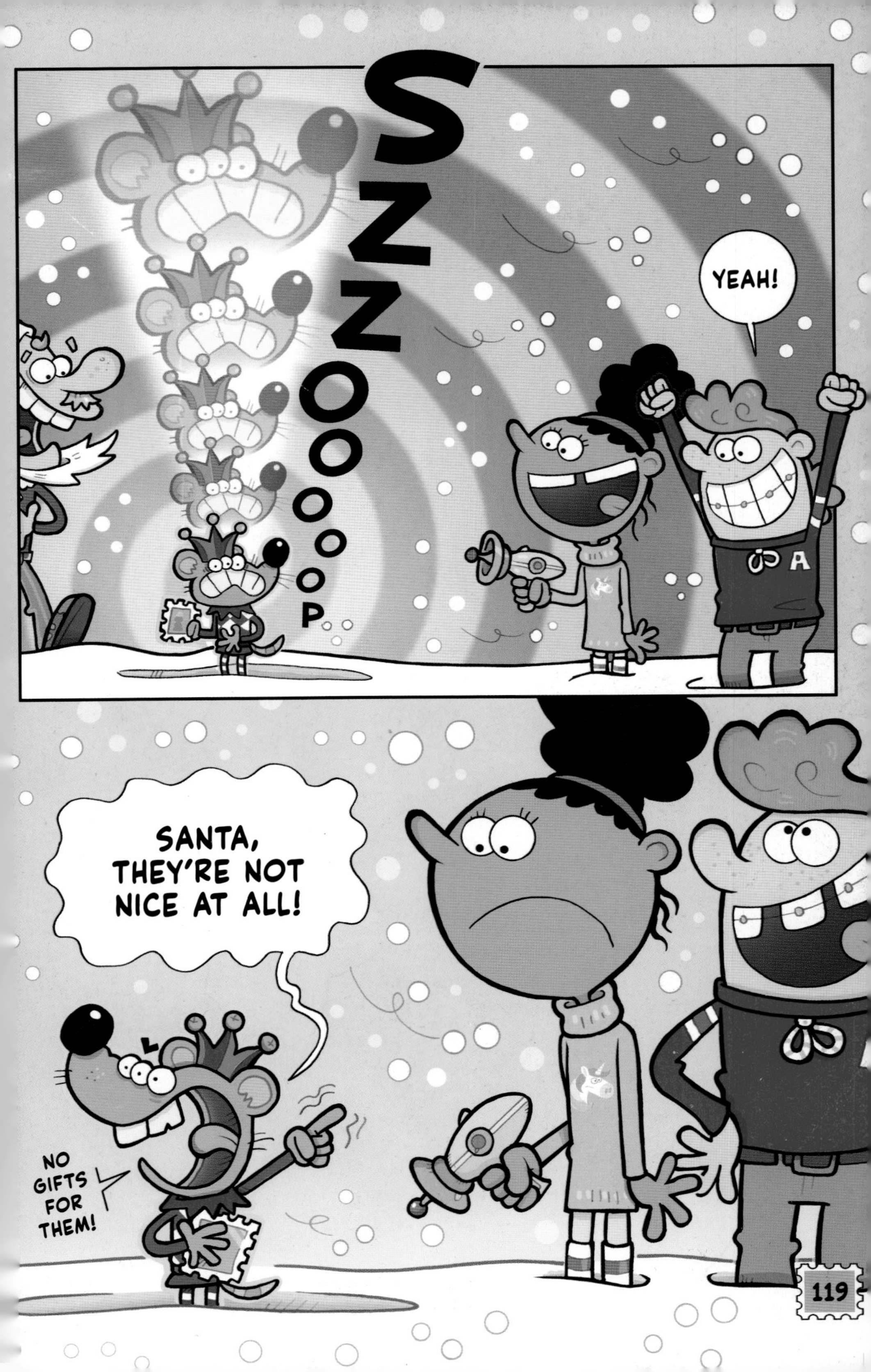
SZZOOOOOP
YEAH!
SANTA, THEY'RE NOT NICE AT ALL!
NO GIFTS FOR THEM!

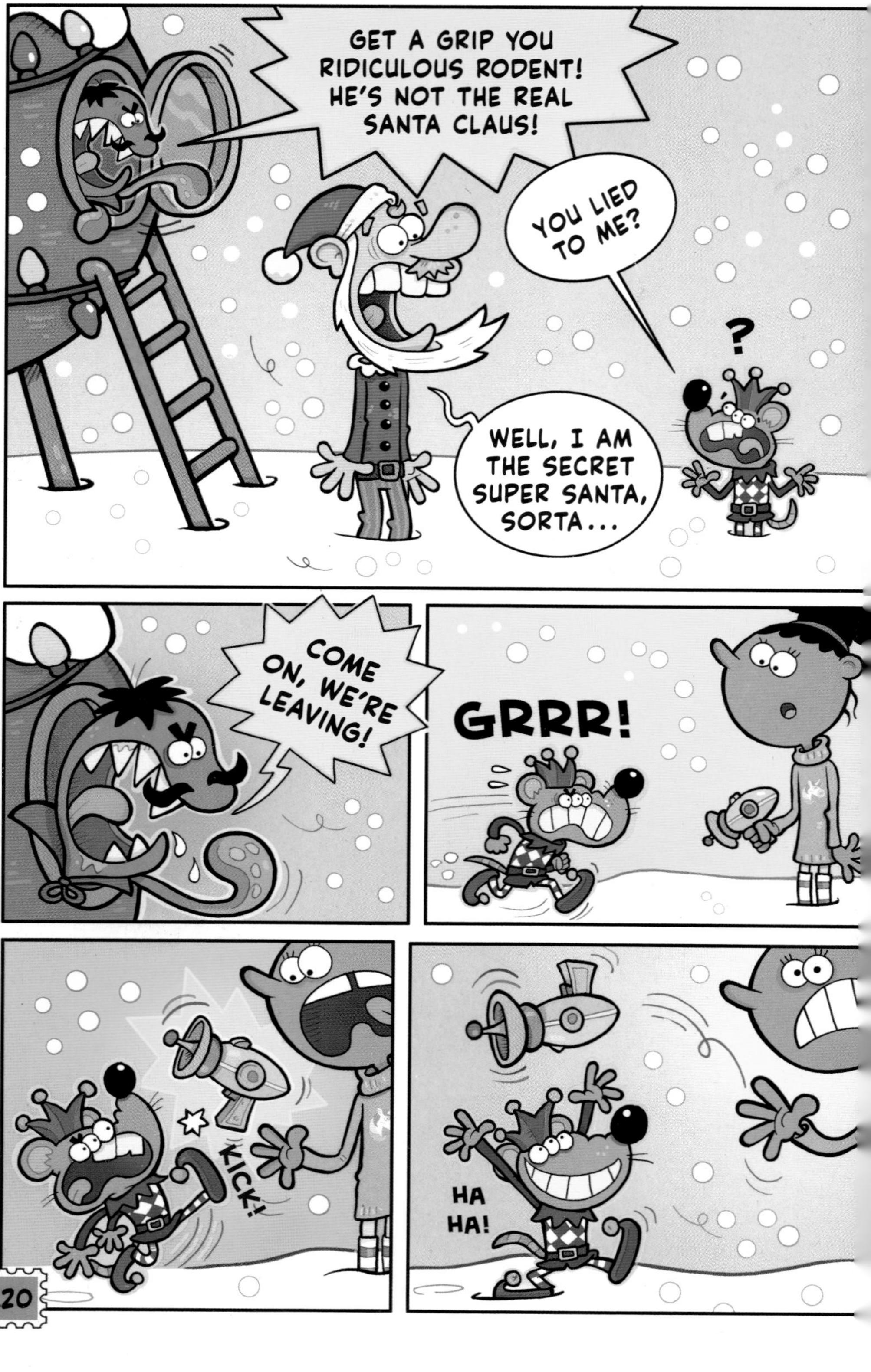
GET A GRIP YOU RIDICULOUS RODENT! HE'S NOT THE REAL SANTA CLAUS!
YOU LIED TO ME?
?
WELL, I AM THE SECRET SUPER SANTA, SORTA...
COME ON, WE'RE LEAVING!
GRRR!
KICK!
HA HA!

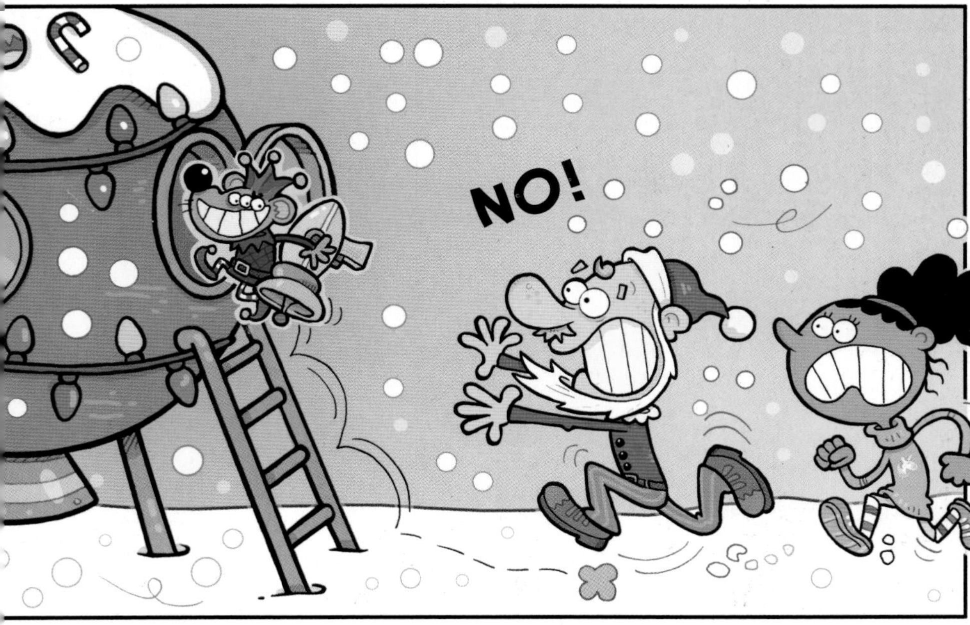
NO!

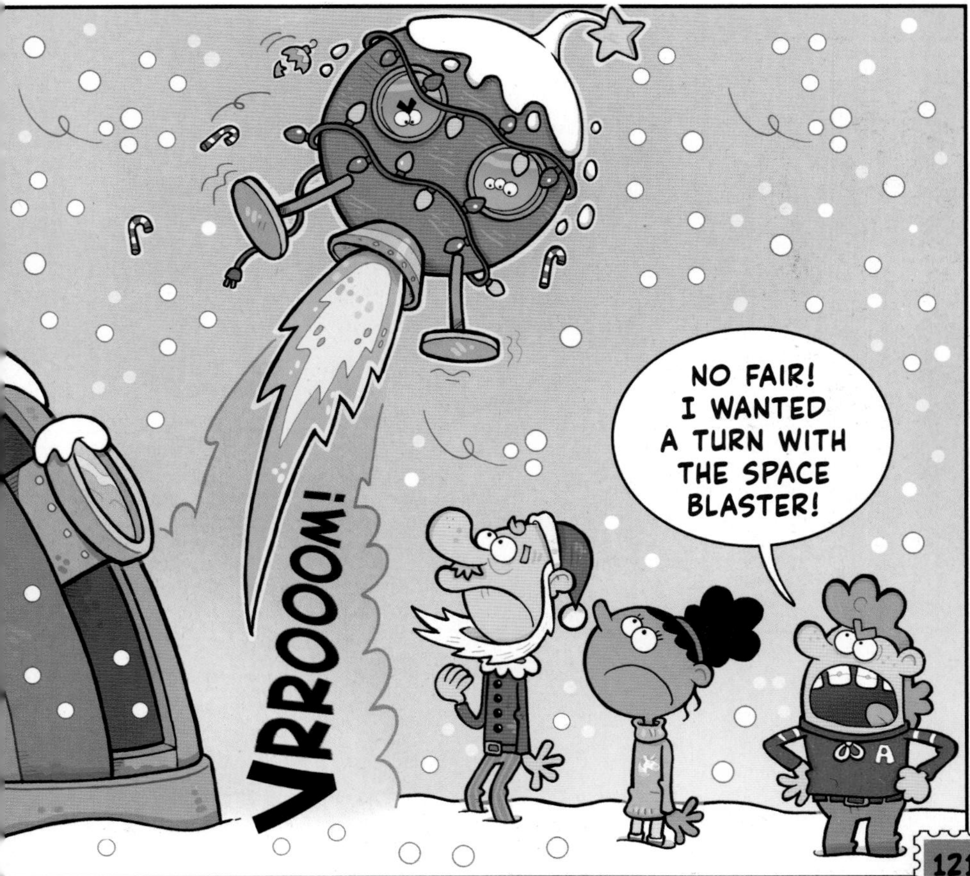
VRROOOM!
NO FAIR! I WANTED A TURN WITH THE SPACE BLASTER!

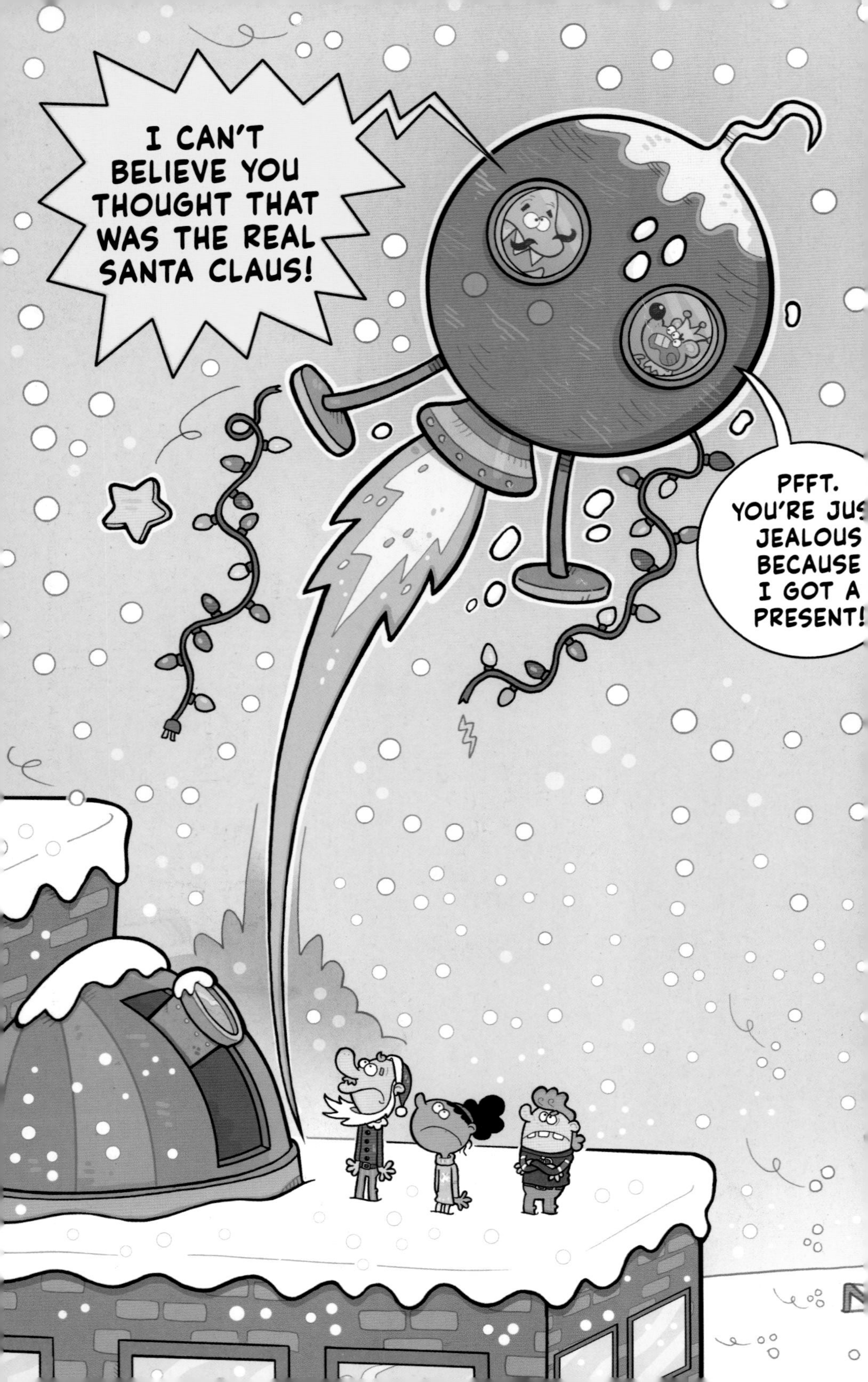
I CAN'T BELIEVE YOU THOUGHT THAT WAS THE REAL SANTA CLAUS!
PFFT. YOU'RE JUS JEALOUS BECAUSE I GOT A PRESENT!

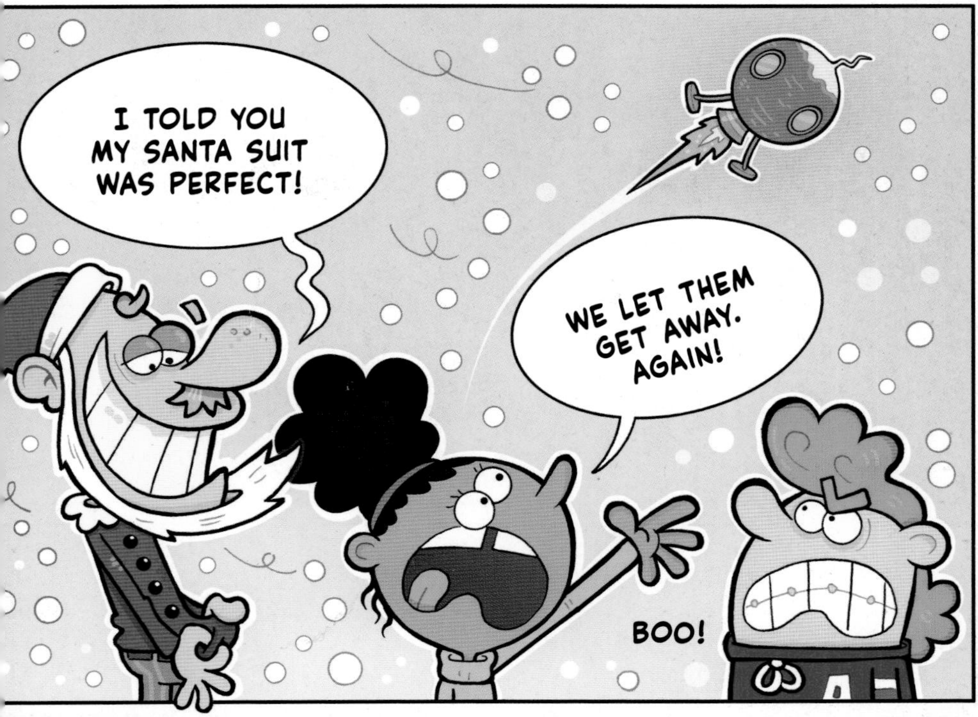
I TOLD YOU MY SANTA SUIT WAS PERFECT!
WE LET THEM GET AWAY. AGAIN!
BOO!

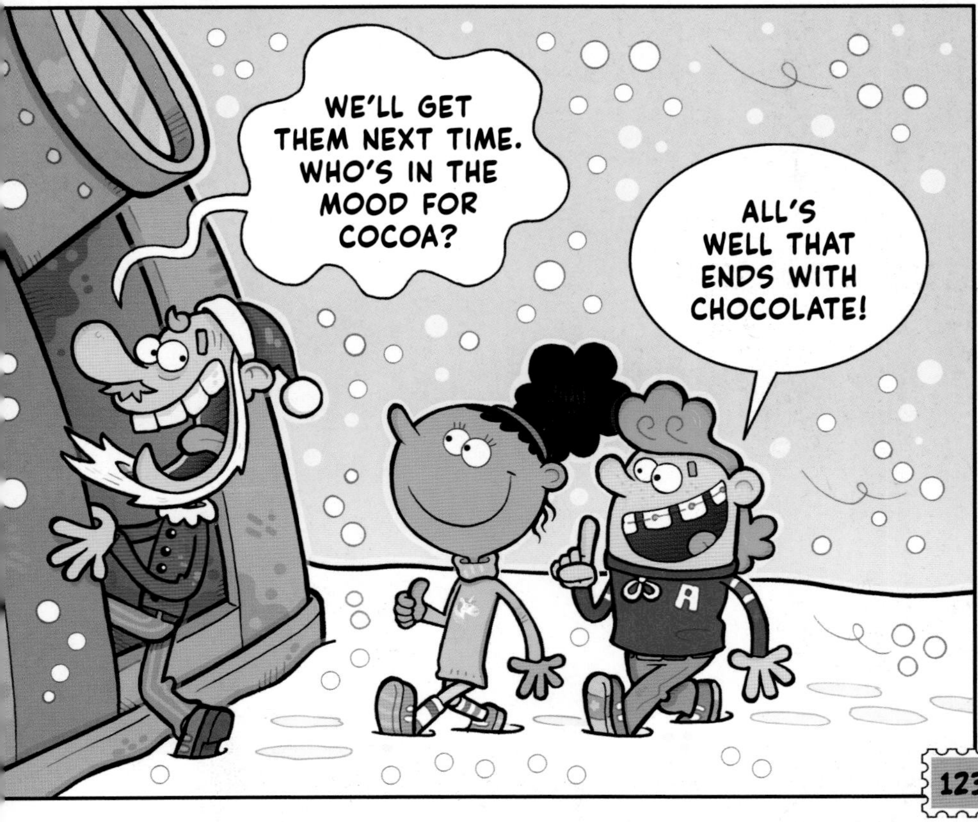
WE'LL GET THEM NEXT TIME. WHO'S IN THE MOOD FOR COCOA?
ALL'S WELL THAT ENDS WITH CHOCOLATE!

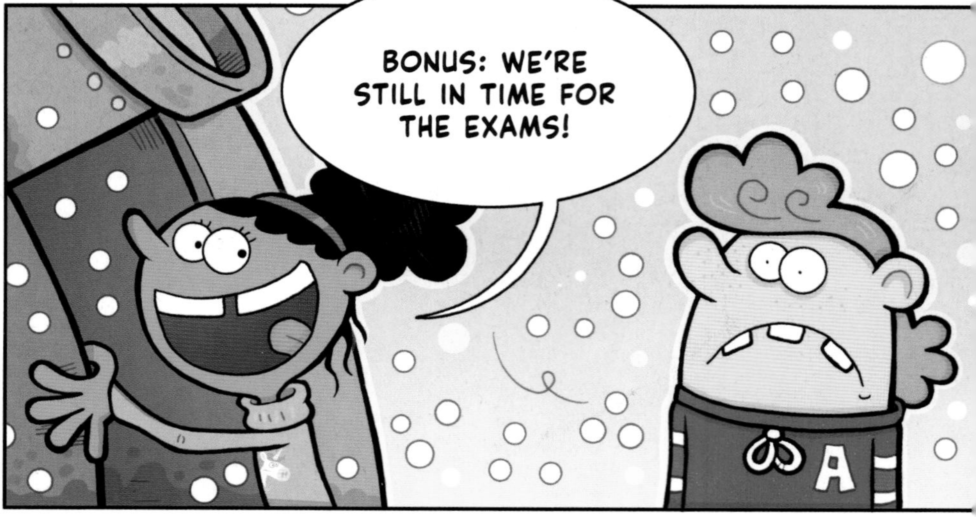
BONUS: WE'RE STILL IN TIME FOR THE EXAMS!

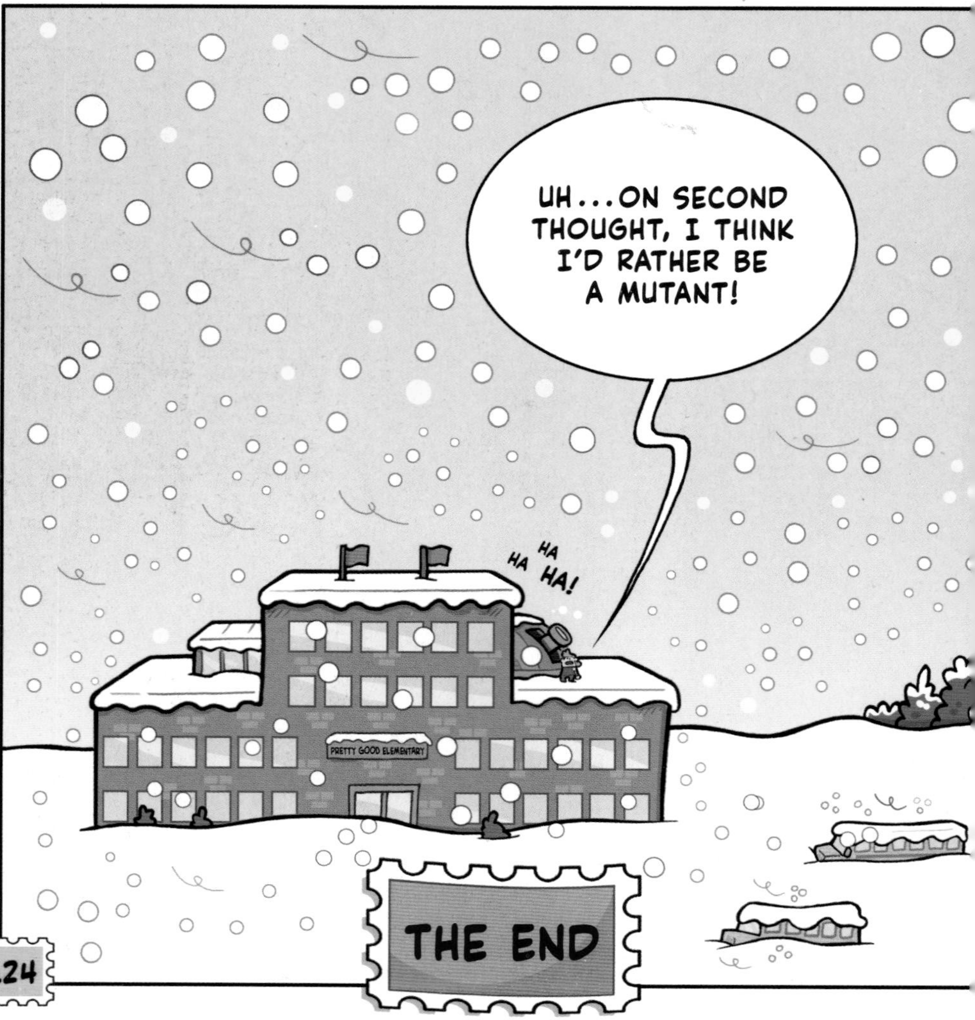
UH...ON SECOND THOUGHT, I THINK I'D RATHER BE A MUTANT!
HA HA HA!
PRETTY GOOD ELEMENTARY
THE END

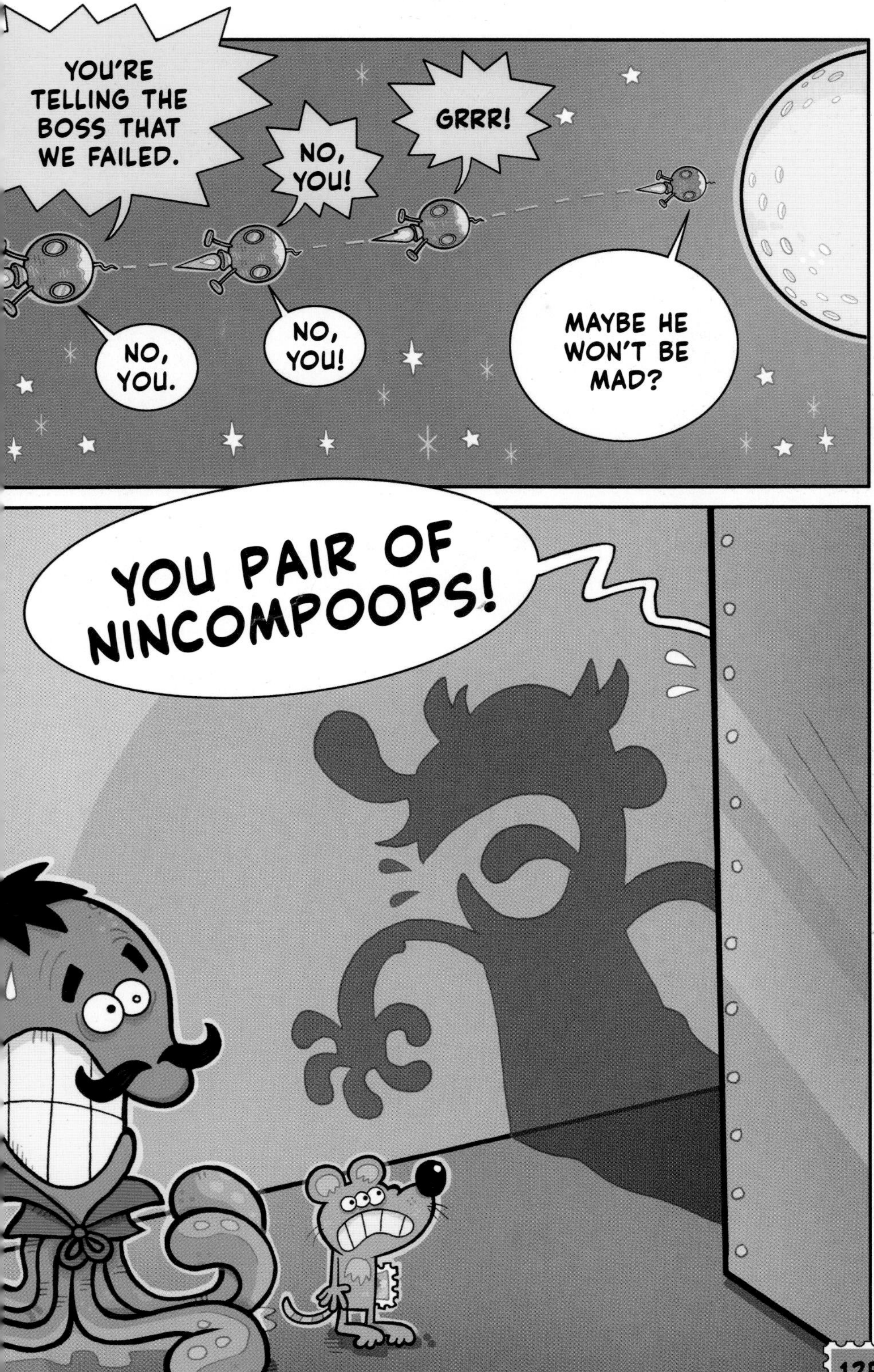
YOU'RE TELLING THE BOSS THAT WE FAILED.
NO, YOU!
GRRR!
NO, YOU.
NO, YOU!
MAYBE HE WON'T BE MAD?
YOU PAIR OF NINCOMPOOPS!

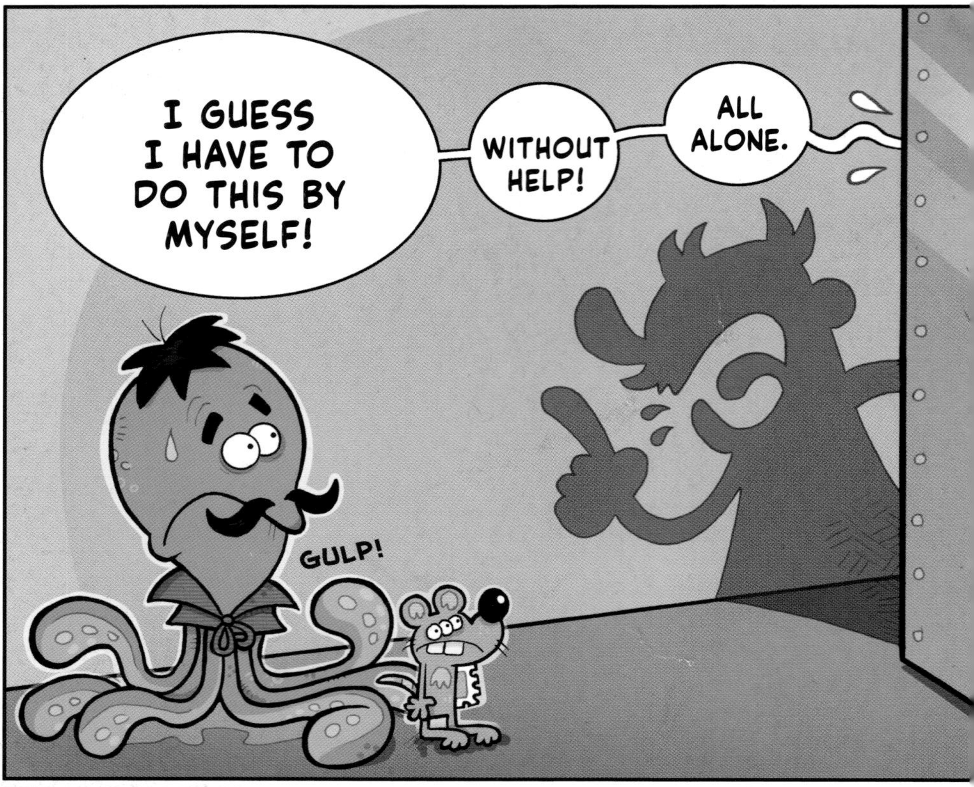
I GUESS I HAVE TO DO THIS BY MYSELF!
WITHOUT HELP!
ALL ALONE.
GULP!

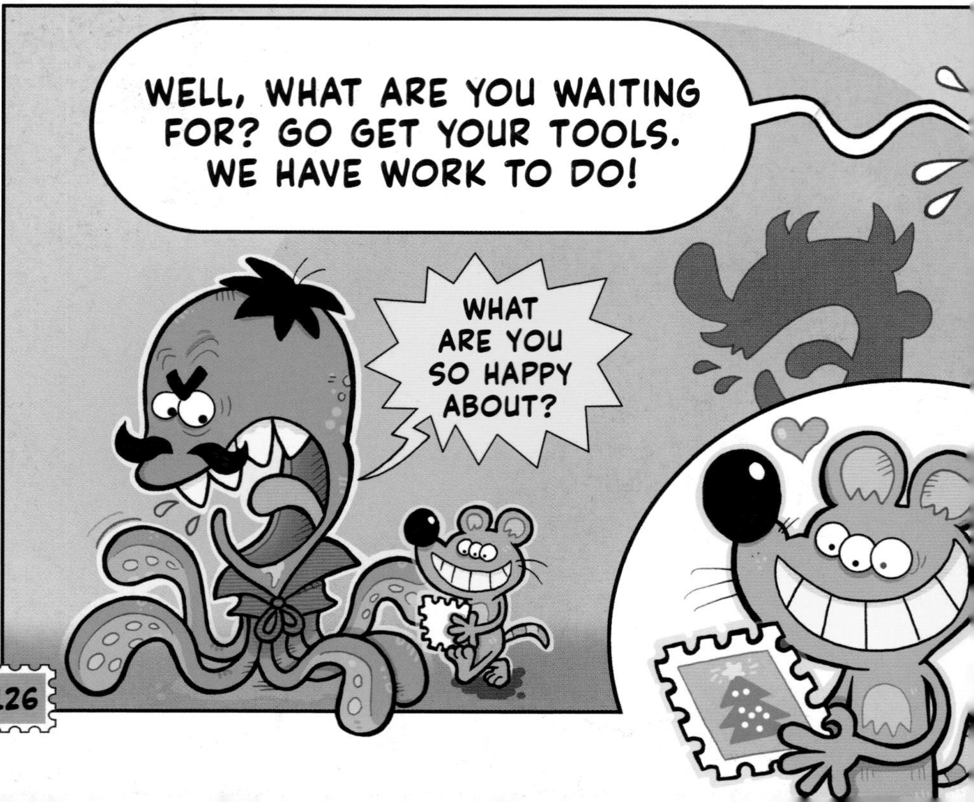
WELL, WHAT ARE YOU WAITING FOR? GO GET YOUR TOOLS. WE HAVE WORK TO DO!
WHAT ARE YOU SO HAPPY ABOUT?

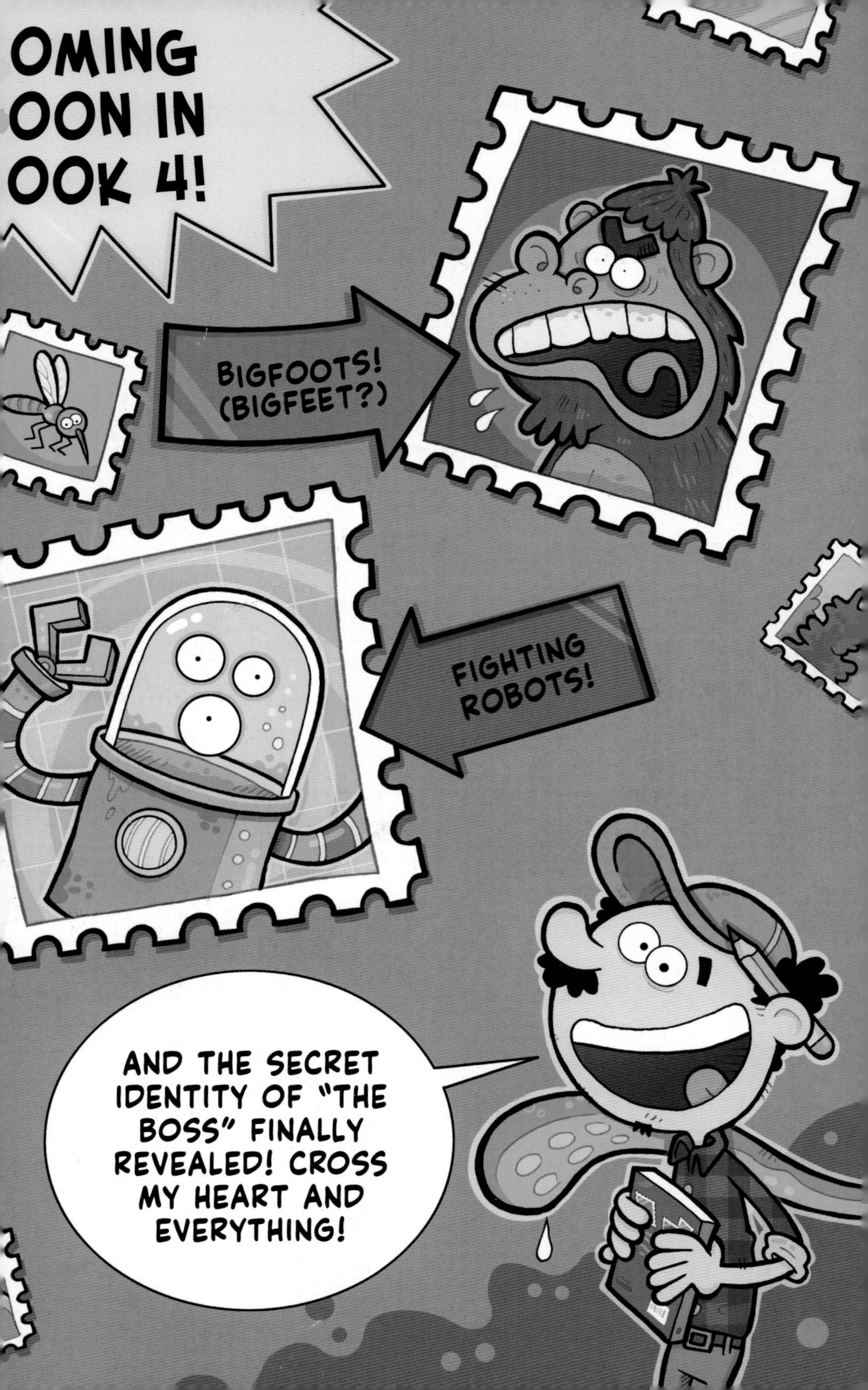
OMING
OON IN
OOK 4!
BIGFOOTS! (BIGFEET?)
FIGHTING ROBOTS!
AND THE SECRET IDENTITY OF "THE BOSS" FINALLY REVEALED! CROSS MY HEART AND EVERYTHING!

DOM PELLETIER

DOMINIQUE PELLETIER LIVES IN THE QUEBEC COUNTRYSIDE WITH HIS FAMILY. THEY HAVE THREE CHICKENS, TWO PONIES, A CAT AND A LAZY DOG, AND SOMETIMES MICE, BECAUSE THE CAT IS ALSO LAZY.

GROWING UP, DOMINIQUE WANTED TO BE EITHER A BASEBALL PLAYER OR A COMIC BOOK ARTIST, BUT SINCE HE DIDN'T UNDERSTAND THE RULES OF BASEBALL (AND STILL DOESN'T), HE DECIDED TO GO WITH DRAWING. DOMINIQUE HAS ILLUSTRATED MORE THAN ONE HUNDRED BOOKS. THE LUNCH CLUB SERIES IS THE FIRST THAT HE HAS ALSO WRITTEN.